Colorado Sunrise

Other Five Star Titles
by Tess Pendergrass:

Colorado Shadows
Colorado Twilight
Dangerous Moonlight

Colorado Sunrise

Book 3 of the Colorado Trilogy

Tess Pendergrass

Five Star • Waterville, Maine

This novel is a work of fiction. Names, characters, places and incidents are either the product of the author's imagination, or, if real, used fictitiously.

First Edition
First Printing: January 2003

Set in 11 pt. Plantin by Elena Picard.

Printed in the United States on permanent paper.

Library of Congress Cataloging-in-Publication Data

Pendergrass, Tess.
Colorado sunrise / Tess Pendergrass.
p. cm. Five Star first edition expressions series
ISBN 0-7862-4515-8 (hc : alk. paper)
1. Women ranchers—Fiction. 2. Colorado—Fiction.
3. Romantic suspense—Fiction. 4. Western stories.
I. Title. II. Series.
PS3566.E457C62 2002
813′.6—dc21 2002026774

This book would never have existed without all the support I received from my friends and family. Thank you for believing in me. Thanks especially to Mom and Dad for taking me to my first Colorado ghost town when I was four and to Dan for not asking, "When are you going to get a real job?"

I am particularly indebted to my editor, Hazel Rumney, for her unfailing encouragement and keen eye throughout the writing of my Colorado trilogy. Thank you for loving my characters as much as I do.

Prologue

Cheyenne, Wyoming Territory
September, 1878

She had been hell-bound for years, and now she was finally pulling into the station. Grand Central Hades. Just as she'd suspected, Satan's realm was not full of fire, brimstone, and engaging, if miserable, souls. Hell was flat, empty, cold and boring.

And it smelled like vomit and old sweat. At least, the section of it that included her train car did. As the train jerked and rattled into the station, Lissy shot an apprehensive look at the four restless, dirty children crowded against their parents on the bench across from her, but they seemed too excited about arriving somewhere to remember to retch again.

Lissy brought her cologne-scented handkerchief closer to her nose and fought the urge to throw herself screaming out the car's dusty window. Only a few more minutes, and she could step out into the fresh air of Cheyenne, a desperately appealing prospect, even if that air seemed to be howling down from the Arctic Circle at unprecedented speeds.

The train jolted again, wrenching Lissy's sore ribs so

hard she gasped out loud. Her back ached to breaking from the endless hours of sitting still, her feet in their trim black boots were so cold she could no longer feel them, and her eyes stung from coal smoke.

Her first journey west should have been spent relaxing in a Pullman car, all elegance and comfort, the monotony broken by leisurely meals in the Union Pacific's dining car, not being battered about in third class with nothing to eat but the bread she'd paid one of the homesteader's children to purchase for her at their last stop. Her stomach growled, the unladylike noise covered by the screeching of the train's brakes.

Lissy gritted her teeth. She could not afford self-pity any more than she could afford a first-class ticket.

Pampered, petted Miss Lissy might have taken luxury and genteel companions as her birthright, but older, wiser Mrs. Elizabeth Woodfin was going to have to learn to fend for herself.

Firmly in control, she turned back to the window. Cheyenne spread out beyond the station, a ramshackle railroad town grown into a bustling city. Though empty plains stretched away endlessly in all directions, sage and buffalo grass whipped by the wind, the town itself boasted fine hotels, cattle barons' mansions, and even an opera house.

Downtown hell apparently offered decent accommodations. Too bad Cheyenne wasn't her destination. She was headed for the wilds of hell. They couldn't be any more brutal than civilized Savannah.

The brakes screeched again as the train slowed to walking speed. Lissy tucked her handkerchief into her purse and was just about to reach under her bench for her bag when a flash of ruddy hair caught her eye. Thousands of men must have hair that particular shade of auburn. Dozens of them might live in Wyoming, with perfectly legitimate business in Cheyenne.

Yet Lissy's heart began to pound erratically as she scanned the crowd milling on the platform to catch another glimpse of that hair.

There. No hat to hide it. Thick, like the pelt of a fox, framing a narrow face with flat, animal eyes. Lissy's breath caught in disbelief as her fingers darted to the thin red slash along her hairline. Nerves and exhaustion had driven her mad. He couldn't be here. Couldn't have known she was coming here. She hadn't settled on the decision herself until she'd boarded the train.

But the apparition didn't disappear. The fox-like head darted from side-to-side, sly and vicious, predatory. Beside him lurked another thug, his long, dirty-blond hair mixing into his long, dirty-blond beard and mustache, the wiry hair unable to hide his prominent front teeth. He was more rat than fox, less cunning, perhaps, than the red-haired man, but no less dangerous.

If only she had a gun. This was the wild West, after all. Would anyone even turn a hair if a sweet, innocent young lady shot a couple of obvious lowlifes while defending her honor?

But she hadn't had the money for a gun, any more than she'd been able to afford a Pullman car. Her only defense was flight. Rabbits did sometimes escape the fox. Didn't they?

The two men were keeping pace with the train, two cars ahead of her. They exchanged a word, and then both turned to a third man she hadn't noticed before. Shorter than the other two, he was also broader, his plump face framed by short black hair, capped with a dapper bowler hat.

The spider.

Unlike with the two thugs, the beastly appellation wasn't her own invention. She actually knew his name. Blackstone Grant. Spider Grant. He'd been to her house, on errands for her husband and her brothers.

It didn't seem to bother him that his employers called him Spider. Given his squat, malevolent appearance and scuttling walk, even his friends probably called him Spider. If he had any friends.

He'd caused the nerves down her back to crawl, just standing on her doorstep with his bowler in his hand. Seeing him in the company of Fox and Rat, with no other possible purpose in Cheyenne except her capture, Lissy felt her skin go clammy from her scalp to her heels.

Rat glanced down the row of train cars, and Lissy jerked away from the window, shaking, though there was no way he could see her through the grimy glass.

There was also no way any of them could be here in Cheyenne looking for her. She hadn't told anyone her destination. Had been careful not to. Even if they'd followed her to Charleston . . .

The Reverend. If they had hurt the Reverend, it would be another sin on her head. But no. They wouldn't have had to hurt him. They'd only have had to tell him they were worried about her. She hadn't told him quite the whole truth about her return to South Carolina. He wouldn't know to keep her questions secret, not from Clay and Rafe.

She risked another look out the window, just in time to see Rat hop onto the moving train two cars down. Fox dropped back, taking the car behind that one, leaving Spider to lurk on the platform as the train rumbled past.

The first class cars.

Lissy almost laughed. If she'd had enough money to ride up front, they'd have been on her in a matter of seconds.

Despite her denials, they still thought she had Charm's money or that she knew enough to get some of it.

Good. Her eyes slitted as grimly as any hunted animal's. She would take any small chance she got. If they caught her again, if they dragged her back to Clay and Rafe, they wouldn't stop at a few bruises.

The memory of Fox's knife flashing sunbeams across her face caused her stomach to clench, and for a moment she was afraid she would be physically ill.

The train finally shuddered to a full stop, and the mass of passengers around her rose almost as one, jostling her as she hefted her one small bag.

Had Fox and Rat finished with the first class compartments yet? The dining car? The Pullmans? If they didn't find her there, they might think she had caught a later train. But she couldn't count on that.

Once she stepped out onto the platform, she would be exposed, with only the other passengers to hide her. She looked down at her dusky blue silk traveling dress. She would stand out from these cowboys and laborers and farmer's wives like a peacock in a hen house.

A coat. The mother of the brood across from her wore a shapeless black covering that blended naturally with the mass of passengers preparing to debark.

Lissy clenched her fist, feeling the tug of her diamond engagement ring against her tight kid glove. For a common wool coat? Her reluctance was purely practical. She had planned to pawn the ring when she had desperate need of funds. If she gave it up for a coat, she would have barely enough cash left for a couple of meals.

But if she didn't, she might not eat another meal.

She began tugging at the glove. "Ma'am? Pardon me."

The farmer's wife, struggling to get her youngest son

up from his fort under the bench, spared her a harassed glance.

"Please, ma'am, I need your help." The glove came off, and she gripped the ring. "I'm afraid I did not come prepared for this weather."

True enough. As the doors opened, the wind dropped the air temperature inside the compartment by fifteen degrees.

"I have a long journey still ahead of me and no time to buy myself suitable clothing. I hoped I could make you an offer."

The harried woman glanced at her equally weathered husband, and they both paused in corralling their herd to stare at her. Lissy decided to take that as interest.

"This is all I have with me," she said, raising the ring. Even in the dim light of the train car, the diamond glinted richly. Charm had an eye for jewels. "I am prepared to trade it for your coat."

The woman's eyebrows rose, and her mouth sagged at the corners. "What use'd I have for a ring?"

She grabbed her youngest's hand as the girl tried to follow her brother under the bench.

Lissy flashed the stone again. "It's worth a considerable amount of money. You could sell it, buy a new coat, and shoes for the children besides."

"My children have the shoes they need," the man spoke up roughly. He gestured toward the door, and pushed the older children ahead of him.

"Maybe someone else will take your ring," the woman said, her eyes not unkind. "We've got a long wagon ride ahead of us tonight. I'll need the coat myself."

Lissy's cheeks heated, but embarrassment was just one more thing she couldn't afford. She pushed in right behind the woman on her way to the door. The passengers were still her only camouflage.

"Show me the ring." The words came from the woman behind her. Even slenderer than Lissy, she looked like a girl playing dress-up with her mother's clothes. The hat on her thick, dark curls was the height of fashion—from ten years ago. Her coat was carefully tailored, but for a woman several sizes larger. Lace peeked from her collar and cuffs, but it had the yellow tinge of age and sweat. Even the girl's face had the look of being used and cast away.

A pickpocket, was Lissy's first thought, but there was no hunger in the girl's look, only a hint of curiosity. Keeping a tight grip on the ring, Lissy held it up for her inspection.

"Let me see it." The girl saw Lissy's expression and laughed. "I can't run while we're in the car."

She took the ring from Lissy's grasp and lifted it to her mouth. For a horrified second, Lissy thought she meant to swallow it, but she only bit the diamond and then examined it again.

"It isn't glass," she said approvingly.

"No," Lissy agreed.

The girl tilted her head, looking Lissy up and down. "I'll trade you, if you like. I don't got far to go. I don't expect I'll freeze."

Lissy hesitated. They had nearly reached the door. The farmer's family was tumbling out into the wind. Even if Spider Grant and his boys weren't looking for her, the coat's warmth would have been welcome. But giving up all she had for an old wool coat with a patch on one elbow . . .

The door connecting their train car to the next one down opened, and Lissy's heart almost stopped. Old man. Gray hair. Railroad company uniform.

She took a shuddering breath. "Yes. Trade."

"Your jacket, too?" the girl asked.

The impeccably tailored, striped silk jacket that would identify her as a southern belle once she threw the old wool coat on the nearest dung heap? "All right. If I can have your hat. Not to trade for mine. To keep."

She shrugged out of the jacket and put on the woman's coat, heartened to note it smelled only of warm sheep and nothing worse. Lissy took the offered hat with its grand, if bedraggled, feather. She'd probably get lice, but at least it had a swath of black netting that draped over her right eye. She tucked her own hat under the coat and settled her new one on her head.

The girl said nothing about Lissy's face. She put on Lissy's jacket, which enveloped her almost as fully as the coat had, the sleeves hanging nearly to her fingernails. She slipped the ring on her middle finger, and still it wobbled loosely. Without any apparent mockery, she lifted her hand and twisted her wrist in what she must have considered an aristocratic manner. She smiled, pleased with the effect.

"I'll sell it though," she confided to Lissy. "Or one of the other girls'll steal it."

Lissy hardly heard her. They had reached the door. Only the terror that Fox would come through the connecting door behind her could spur her to face the terror that Spider might wait on the platform ahead of her.

Ducking her head so the hat would hide her face, holding her new coat tight across her chest, she plunged out into the wind. Cold, was her first thought. Dry, was her second. A cold, dry wind that dug under your clothes and sucked the warmth from your body.

Summer still lingered in Savannah. If she were home this afternoon, she would be sipping lemonade out on the porch, hoping to escape the heat by catching the breath of a

breeze damp with the hint of the ocean.

She kept close to the other passengers, feeling like a flashing beacon despite her drab coat. She glanced furtively about her, but could see no sign of her pursuers. Her heart only beat harder. At least if she could see them, she would know where they were.

"I was in trouble myself, when I first got to Cheyenne." The dark-haired girl kept pace with her along the railway platform. "I'd've been bad off if a stranger hadn't helped me. Here, take your ring back. I'm doing okay for myself."

Lissy looked at her again, at the worn, but youthful face, the residue of makeup that only made her appear younger. The young woman's bright dark eyes held an innocence that wrenched at Lissy's heart even as she suddenly realized what the girl must be.

"No," she said impulsively, though she knew she needed every penny she could scrabble to hold. "You keep it. A bargain is a bargain." And the truth: "This coat could save my life."

The girl reached over to give Lissy's hand a squeeze. "I'm at the Lucky Horseshoe Club, two blocks down from the Opera House. Louella, she's the owner, she's always on the lookout for quality girls. She'll treat you fair and square, and she don't let the customers get rough."

A month before, Lissy would have withered the girl with a scathing retort. Hurrying along a train platform in Cheyenne with the wind chilling her to her bones, she knew she'd just received the most generous offer she'd had in weeks.

"I have to get to—" She cut herself off, shaken that she'd almost let her destination slip. "I'm traveling to San Francisco. I have a cousin there."

The girl nodded, neither believing nor disbelieving.

"Good luck, then. And if you come by the Lucky Horseshoe, I'll remember you."

Lissy watched for a moment as the girl walked away, rocked by a strange combination of pity and envy. The girl might make her home at a brothel, but it was close and it was warm, and she could count on a meal and a bed when she got there.

As the young woman reached the edge of the platform, a hand grabbed her shoulder, spinning her around. Her dark curls bounced as she turned, an instinctive knowing smile covering her consternation.

Lissy shuddered. No, she didn't envy the girl at all. But as she turned away, the image of the man who had grabbed the other woman connected with her brain. The round body, the black bowler, the white, white skin. She hadn't seen his face, but . . .

Unable to help herself, she risked a glance back. Spider Grant. Checking the young whore's face. Because she was a woman? Because she wore a fancy jacket? She wasn't even blond.

In the pounding of fear, Lissy chided herself that she hadn't thought of dying her hair. She had to get better at this game, or she was going to lose more than a diamond ring.

The spider's white hand still held the girl's arm as he waved a coin with his other. Asking about the young woman's fellow passengers? Her face expressionless and bored, the girl simply shook her head and shrugged. Lissy's heart squeezed with gratitude.

Forcing herself to move at a normal pace, brisk, to escape the wind, but not running, to bring down the hounds, she wove her path into the rapidly thinning crowd.

She risked asking directions to the Denver train, her

goal, safety. But it wasn't safe. What if Spider and his thugs knew she had a ticket to Denver? What if they weren't searching every westbound train coming into Cheyenne, but knew she had been on that particular train? It didn't matter that she didn't plan to take the train all the way to Denver. She still had to get on it, and it didn't leave for another hour. Plenty of time for the Beasts to search it thoroughly, running her to earth and tearing her to pieces.

Yet she could do nothing else besides board the Denver train. She didn't have enough money for another ticket. Fear made the fallen dove's offer tempting. Give up. Accept a strange sort of safety at any price. But no fear, no matter how great, could turn her from her path. She would never give up trying to reach the treasure at the end of her journey. Only death could stop her.

And death was an unacceptable option.

Her ears burned from the wind, but ached more from straining to hear footsteps behind her, the grunt of triumph that would signal her pursuers had her in their sights. She picked out a huge, red-bearded man in a poorly tanned leather jacket and became his shadow. Only a fool would grab that mountain man's wife. Only when he turned away toward the sound of a bar piano did she leave his side, darting behind a pile of crates to take a quick look around.

She caught a glimpse of the Fox, his ruddy hair a flash at the far end of the platform. His head turned, and she ducked behind her cover, her heart trying to pound through her chest. She couldn't stop.

Biting the inside of her cheek until the pain focused her, she strode out with her head held high to find the southbound platform.

If she had been forced to wait in the station, she might have collapsed from the terror, but the Denver train was waiting at its platform and loading passengers when she arrived. She found a free bench in one of the third-class cars and took the seat in the corner, keeping one eye on the window and the other on the passengers coming through the door.

A young man in a clerical collar took the seat across from her, his stubbly blond beard jerking as he nodded at her. A pair of even younger cowboys crowded in beside him. A round man in a threadbare suit and his considerably rounder wife sat beside her, the tantalizing smell of warm fried chicken wafting from a basket the woman carried.

After what seemed an eternity, the whistle shrilled, streaming behind the engine with the coal smoke, and the train jerked into motion.

Lissy huddled against the side of the car, her new wool coat not enough to protect her from the chill of her fear, and tried to find a prayer to say. She didn't feel safe. The beasts hunting her could be on the train even now, its departure from the station meaning only that she was trapped like a fly in Spider's web.

She had to remain vigilant. If they caught her, she would fight, though she knew these strangers crowding around her would not face down Fox's knife or Rat's fists for her.

Cold and fear and hunger dragged at her, like boots and petticoats on a drowning woman. She would not have guessed she could sleep under such conditions, but her eyelids drooped traitorously. If only she could drown, fall into sleep and never awaken. It would be so much easier that way.

But she'd spent enough of her life doing things the easy way.

Chapter 1

She looked like a dream.

Or a ghost.

Harriet Jackson looked at the woman in the mirror, the woman dressed in cream-colored satin that draped in folds over her hoops like the robes of a Greek sculpture, a stool for her pedestal. The woman whose ordinary, unruly dark brown hair gleamed like a marten's pelt under a backswept lacy veil. The woman whose blue eyes looked into hers with shock and only half recognition.

"Oh, Harry." Maggie Jackson's red head appeared beside her left shoulder in the mirror. "It's gorgeous. It fits you perfectly."

Henna Culbert's face popped up beside Harry's other shoulder, her amber eyes narrowed like a cat's as she examined Harry's reflection. "Could be taken in a little at the waist. The shoulders are all right. The hem's short, but we'll fix that by getting rid of those old hoops and adding a bustle in back. I never realized you'd grown taller than Jane, Harry. You've always been so slender."

The three heads, red, dark, and cinnamon brown, turned in unison toward the rolltop desk set against the eastern wall of the ranch house living room.

A picture in a silver frame hung just above the desk. The couple it portrayed stood stiff and still to avoid blurring the expensive photograph being taken. Yet even the rigid immobility of their features could not disguise the brightness in their eyes, the joy that hovered on their lips, the tenderness that showed in the clasping of their hands by the woman's waist.

The man wore a starched white shirt, black pants, and boots polished till they shone. A star made from a Mexican silver dollar, the symbol of the Texas Rangers, gleamed on his chest. Tall, blond, built big across the shoulders, he somehow managed to look almost boyish next to his young bride.

She wore the dress Harry now modeled, tailored perfectly for her strong form. Her dark hair, coiled beneath the veil, her eyes, wide and inquisitive, her mouth, just a touch too broad to be fashionable—Harry recognized them all with a shiver of shock, lifting a hand to her own mouth, half expecting her sister's image in the picture to do the same.

"You look just like her," Maggie breathed. "March has always said how much you look like your mother. I never noticed you looked like Jane."

"Me, either," Henna said, shooting another glance at Harry standing on the milking stool. "You look as beautiful as your sister did in that dress. We can only hope you'll be as happy wearing it."

Harry stared at the picture of Jane and Lucas. Happy. Yes, you could see it even in the colorless, flat lines of a photograph. It had lasted eight years, that happiness, through Lucas's absences with the Rangers, through flood and childbirth and starting this horse ranch tucked against the Colorado foothills. A dream.

A dream that had ended in nightmare when evil men had

murdered them and their young son right here in this very room . . .

Harry shuddered, tearing her gaze from the eyes in the photograph. The dress's high neck seemed to tighten about her throat. She looked once more at the girl in the mirror, eyes troubled with a past and a future her sister had never contemplated.

Still, she thought eight years filled with joy might be a fair trade for a long lifetime without it.

I've never noticed that marriage increased anyone's happiness. She shook the remembered words away. Maggie and Henna were proof enough that a woman could be happily married.

"Will a month be enough time to change the skirt?" Maggie asked. "I can help, if you need it, Henna."

"You can keep your hands away from that hem," Henna said, slapping Maggie's fingers. "A month will be plenty of time."

"If you're sure . . ."

Henna laughed at Maggie's obvious relief. "You can help Harry with her trousseau, if you've got so much extra time."

Maggie snorted. "I'll be happy to start embroidering handkerchiefs, just as soon as Harry starts changing diapers."

The thump of boots on the porch rescued Harry from having to reply. The front door opened to reveal her brother March, half-blinded by the bright fall sunlight outside.

"Everybody decent?"

"Not so's you'd notice," Maggie drawled. "Enter at your own risk."

March grinned at his wife. "That sounds like a challenge if I ever heard . . ."

His gaze caught on Harry, and the words drifted to a stop. He stared at her, hat half lifted toward the rack, a whole range of emotions playing across his face.

Harry stepped off the stool toward him, almost tumbling to the floor in the tangle of the skirt.

"It's too much, isn't it?" she said, shaken by the look in his eyes. "I can't wear it, wear Jane's dress. The memories. It's all right. I won't wear it, March."

He dropped his hat forgotten to the floor and strode to her, wrapping her in his arms, crushing her to him. She smelled the familiar March smells of horse and hay, and suddenly she missed him, so fiercely and desperately it hurt physically, in her heart. She missed him and Maggie and the ranch and the horses and the mountains and . . . and she hadn't even left yet.

When March's arms loosened, she looked up to see the hint of tears turning his blue eyes sea-green.

"You're beautiful," he said. A smile touched his lips. "I hardly recognize you."

The teasing didn't make her laugh. "It's all right. I can wear that blue satin Henna offered to—"

"Jane would be happy to know you're going to wear her dress, Harry. So proud that our baby sister's grown into such a remarkable young lady."

"Lady?" Harry asked skeptically, widening her eyes to dry her own threatening tears.

March laughed. "Well, you look like one, anyway." He kissed her forehead. "I promise not to tell Ash the truth until after the wedding."

"Can I get Harry back on the stool now?" Henna asked, shaking a box of pins. "The wedding's going to be here before you know it."

"And so is Ashton," March said, letting Harry go. "I

came in to let you know we're going to have visitors. Lemuel said he saw Ash and Mr. Brady in Oxtail, and they asked him to warn us of company. I was just up in the hayloft and saw a buggy on the road."

Maggie let loose an impolite word. "Doesn't anybody ask before they come calling anymore?"

"They asked Lemuel," March said mildly.

"Out!" Maggie pointed her husband toward the door. "Harry, take off that dress." Maggie's hands, so sure with a horse's tack, fumbled awkwardly at the tiny buttons down Harry's back. "We can't let Ash see you in this dress!"

"You'd rather have him see me naked?" Harry asked dryly as the dress began to sag off her shoulders.

"Get your smart mouth down to my bedroom," Maggie ordered, "along with the rest of you."

"I'll just go to mine."

"You are not going up those stairs in that dress! Careful of those buttons. And don't wake Sarah! Hurry up, young lady."

"Yes, Mother." Harry drawled, gathering her skirts and trudging down the hall to March and Maggie's room. Harry's mother had died when she was born, but Harry knew delicate, soft-spoken Sally Jackson had been nothing like her sister-in-law.

Besides, Maggie was only two and half years older than Harry, despite her three years of marriage and recent motherhood. At nineteen, Harry was more than old enough to be a wife and mother herself. She did not need Maggie treating her like a child, even in jest.

The worst part of it was, Harry thought as she opened the bedroom door and slipped quietly inside, that Maggie had the uncanny knack of acting like a mother just at the moment Harry was feeling most insecure and childlike.

Despite her caution closing the door, it knocked lightly against the frame. A noise emanated from the crib beside the bed, and Harry froze, not even daring to breathe. After a long moment of silence, she dared cross to the crib and peer inside.

Laid out on a brightly colored patchwork quilt, Sarah Jackson slept like an angel, her pudgy fingers curled tightly on her chest, tendrils of bright red hair curling softly on her nearly bare scalp. Even after a month, Harry could never quite believe this peaceful little creature was the same shrieking demon who kept the whole house awake until all hours of the night.

More amazing still was the way Maggie never lost her patience with the baby, no matter how shrill the screams. Her fire-tempered sister-in-law cooed and paced and sang until March made her go to bed and he cooed and paced and sang. Though March's singing was enough to make a grown person cry.

Harry stared down at the little bundle of joy—and, oh, what a joy she was, when she wasn't hollering—and a shiver curled itself in the pit of her stomach. Were she and Ash ready for that? How could anyone ever be ready for that?

Turning away from the crib, Harry fumbled with the rest of the buttons down her back. The yards of satin tangled around her in a jumbled mess. For an instant, she couldn't struggle free. She couldn't breathe. Fighting down the irrational panic, she managed to work her way out of the muddle of skirts without damaging the dress.

As she sat on the edge of the bed, catching her breath, the bedroom door eased open, and Maggie slipped in, a green-sprigged brown poplin dress draped over her shoulder.

"I brought this down from your room. I thought you

might want something to change into besides your blue jeans," she whispered, taking a quick look into the crib.

Harry glanced at the pants and the old flannel work shirt she'd thrown over the back of the new rocking chair Lemuel had made for Maggie. "They're clean."

"You wore them to muck stalls this morning."

Harry took the offered dress. "Oh, honestly. I can't believe you of all people want me to pretend to be something I'm not."

Maggie's eyes narrowed. "Something you're not?"

Harry held up the dress, irritated. "A lady. I have to wear a dress now that I'm engaged? If Ash won't think I'm acceptable in blue jeans, maybe he shouldn't marry me."

Maggie shook an old sheet out across the bed, then reached for the wedding dress, positioning it on the sheet. "You not a lady? You're one of the most perfect ladies I've ever met, Harriet Jackson, and trust me, I got shown up by plenty of them when I was growing up in Lexington. Just because you're also a halfway decent ranch hand doesn't mean you're pretending when you put on a dress for company."

She folded a sleeve of the wedding dress. "What's bothering you, Harry?"

"Nothing's bothering me," Harry lied, afraid Maggie's concern might drag the truth out of her—and whatever the truth was, Harry didn't think she wanted it dragged out. She slipped into her company dress, giving herself a minute to collect her thoughts—and her mood.

You shouldn't let anyone stifle your freedom. A stupid memory. What did freedom have to do with anything? She wore dresses most evenings, anyway.

The thin, dark thought spun through her mind that she didn't have that much freedom to lose. How free would she be spending her life as a spinster living on her brother's charity?

"There," she said brightly, spinning to flare her skirt. "Thanks, Maggie. The dress is much cooler than the jeans. It will be perfect for greeting visitors."

She gave Maggie an I'm-all-better-now smile, exercising the artificial social skills she'd learned in those miserable years at Mrs. Danforth's finishing school in Philadelphia. Apparently the years had been wasted. Maggie's green eyes darkened.

"Oh, Harry." She reached out to touch Harry's arm. "Everything's been so crazy around here lately. I didn't even think that trying on the wedding dress . . . It makes it all seem real, doesn't it? The wedding, marrying Ash, leaving home. It's all right to be scared."

"I'm not scared."

Maggie humphed. "Only a fool wouldn't be scared, and you're no fool. It's happened so fast. Maybe too fast. But sometimes you have to follow your heart. If you and Ash care about each other, you will make it work."

Harry didn't dare meet her friend's penetrating gaze. At the moment she couldn't even hear her heart, much less follow it. She was too busy trying to calm her spinning stomach.

Of course Ash cared about her. He wouldn't have asked her to marry him if he didn't. And she cared about him. Or she wouldn't have said yes. Everyone else she knew jumped into marriage without a thought.

Maggie was a fine one to talk. She and March had known each other all of three weeks before saying their vows. Three years later, they swore they loved each other more every day.

Henna's husband Jed Culbert had asked her to marry

him after one night in her arms at her former place of business. Sixteen years and four children later, they fit together like apples and cinnamon.

Just this past June, she'd attended the hasty wedding of their long-time family friend, Elijah Kelly, to his wife Jordan. It had made no difference to 'Lije that he'd known the woman barely a month, had never met her family, had almost nothing in common with her . . .

She lifted a hand to her forehead, pressing back the familiar litany.

"Harry? Are you all right?"

She shook her head, forcing a smile. "You were right. It's just hard for me to believe all of this is real . . . What on earth are you doing to that dress?"

Maggie's sharp eyes finally left Harry's face to return to the bed. "I'm wrapping it up so Henna can carry it home to make the alterations."

"It's not a horse blanket, Margaret." Harry nudged her sister-in-law aside with her hip. "Let me do that, or Henna will take it out of both our hides."

"Yes, Mother," Maggie mocked her tartly, but the threat of Henna's wrath backed her away from the dress, right into the baby's crib.

"Ehhh?"

Both women froze at the faint, innocent query from the depths of the crib. For a moment there was absolute silence. Harry breathed once. Twice.

"Ehhh? Aahhhhhh!"

"Now look what you've done," Maggie said helplessly. For a second she looked like a frightened child herself, bending over the crib. But as she lifted the wailing baby up into her arms, warmth crept into her eyes, and her voice lowered to a soft caress.

"Well, how are you this afternoon, Miss Sarah? Hungry, I bet. Didn't want to miss the company, did you? If I take you out to visit, will you promise to sleep tonight?"

Harry snorted.

Maggie snuggled the bundle of baby against her. "She'll learn. Eventually."

Unwilling to crush the faint, desperate hope in Maggie's voice, Harry set to wrapping up the dress while Maggie sat in the rocking chair to nurse the baby. In the fresh silence, they heard voices from the front of the house.

"That must be Ash and Mr. Brady," Maggie said, halting her rocking a second to listen. "I'm surprised they brought the buggy instead of riding. I hope Mr. Brady's back isn't bothering him."

Alexander Brady had taken a bullet in his chest in a gunfight three years earlier. Though his full recovery had amazed even Dr. Markham, his back still ached when he worked too hard, which, Harry reflected, happened about as frequently as you'd expect from someone as hard-headed as Brady.

"At least Ash isn't such a stubborn mule as his uncle."

Maggie laughed. "Just wait until after the wedding. Then you'll see his true colors." She shifted Sarah. "But you're right. He hasn't had to fight his way up from nothing like his father and Alexander. I'll be honest, Harry, I would have expected you to end up with someone less . . . proper. Then again, they say opposites attract."

Harry pursed her lips. "Like you and March."

"Exactly. Who would have thought that a marriage between someone as pig-headed and contrary as March Jackson and someone as good-natured and biddable as me would ever work out?"

"That's what I've always said about you, Maggie. You're biddable and good-natured."

Sarah shrieked for the twenty seconds it took Maggie to switch her from her left breast to her right.

"Sort of like your daughter. And she eats like you, too."

"At least when she's eating, she's not screaming," Maggie pointed out.

Harry finished folding the dress into the sheet and tied it up with twine. She managed to stretch the task out long enough to finish at the same time Maggie finished feeding Sarah.

"Hold her while I straighten up my dress." Maggie thrust the baby into Harry's arms.

Harry scrambled in the crib for a rag, just managing to drape it over her shoulder before Sarah burped up all over it.

"You do that on purpose," she accused her sister-in-law.

"What?" Maggie asked, all innocence. "No, you keep her. I'll get the dress. I want to see the expression on Ash's face when you walk in with a baby."

Harry managed to share Maggie's conspiratorial grin, but it felt shaky. The idea of having her own baby with Ash didn't seem real.

Nothing in Harry's life in the past two months had felt real to her, almost as though she were watching someone else live Harriet Jackson's life. But though Sarah had been born almost three weeks prematurely, at a month old she had a substance and solidity that was real enough.

"I think we can invite them to dinner," Maggie said, digging out a fresh rag for Harry and tossing the soiled one aside. No need for too much reality, Harry thought. "We can make extra cornbread to stretch the stew, and we've got those apple pies we baked this morning."

"Those are for the Culberts!"

"We'll make some more tomorrow. Henna won't mind."

No, she wouldn't. Harry followed Maggie out into the hall. And Harry could probably work it so she got to take the new pies down the road to the Culbert farm. And of course Henna wouldn't let her leave without sharing a big slice of pie and a glass of lemonade. And maybe a horse race with the older boys or a cuddle with Emily's kittens or a shoot-out in Tucker's fort.

Something to look forward to, if she survived this afternoon. One more thing she'd have to give up when she became Mrs. Harriet Brady and left Harry Jackson behind forever.

Hearty male laughter rang down the hall, but as she stepped into the front room, Harry realized it didn't belong to either Alexander or Ashton Brady.

"Harriet! Margaret! My dears!" A white-haired man sporting a dapper mustache and a carefully tailored pearl-gray suit greeted them with an irrepressible smile.

"Colonel Treadwell." Maggie set the dress package on the table by the sofa and took his hand. "It's so good to see you up and about."

"Bah! Doc Markham's got the whole county thinking I was on death's door. The bullet didn't even break the leg bone like he thought at first." He waved his silver-headed cane. "I only carry this to pacify the poor man."

"Besides," Maggie said slyly. "It's so dashing."

The Colonel laughed. "Mrs. P. said the same to me not a week ago over at Isling's General Store, and blast it if I didn't see that old goat Isling carrying one himself just this morning."

"Mr. Isling's sweet on Mrs. Pepperill," Maggie agreed. "She's not going to wait for you forever, Colonel."

"Margaret!" The Colonel's skin reddened up to the roots of his hair.

"Gunther Isling didn't take a bullet in the leg protecting Mrs. Pepperill from robbers," Harry reminded her sister-in-law.

"You haven't met my daughter, Colonel," March jumped in, rescuing the flustered man.

"That I haven't." Back on safe ground, the Colonel tucked his cane under his elbow and took the baby from Harry's arms. Harry and Maggie both opened their mouths to warn him Sarah didn't like to be held so straight and *definitely* did not like to have her cheeks pinched, but the babe only cooed and stared up at the Colonel's bushy face with fascination.

"You haven't lost your touch with the ladies, Colonel," March breathed.

Colonel Treadwell handed the baby back to Harry. "She's going to be charmer, just like her mother."

Sarah stared up at Harry for a moment, opened her tiny bow of a mouth . . . and blew back Harry's ears with her howl.

"Just like her mother," Harry agreed, handing her over to Maggie.

"So, Colonel," Maggie said, raising her voice over the noise emanating from the bundle in her arms. "What brings you out to see us? Did you finally take my advice and get rid of that ungainly beast you were renting out to people? March has a lovely little mare . . ."

Her voice slowed as the Colonel shook his head, and worry clouded her hazel green eyes. "A telegram? It's not trouble, is it?"

"No, no!" Colonel Treadwell held up a hand. "Nothing of the sort, my dear. Today I am just a guide for another visitor. She's . . . er . . . Henna . . ."

"Henna is showing her the facilities," March said blandly.

"Showing who the facilities?" Harry asked.

"The young lady's name is Elizabeth Woodfin," the Colonel said. "A lovely girl. A southern gentlewoman. I would like to see the South again, you know, under better circumstances—"

"The name isn't familiar," Maggie prompted.

"Ah, no." Colonel Treadwell scratched his mustache. "I brought her here because she asked me to. I'll let her tell you her story, but she is in some kind of trouble."

"A damsel in distress," Maggie said, with a wink at Harry. "We know you can't resist them, Colonel. Let's see, the last one you brought us, our horse threw her, your robbers kidnapped her, Harry almost got her killed, and our gunfighter married her. I'm surprised you'd entrust us with another one."

"Ah, Mrs. Braddock." The Colonel's face brightened, then sobered. "That is, Mrs. Kelly. I suppose if anyone can tame that devil, it's a woman like her."

Harry bit her lip, holding back her automatic defense of Elijah Kelly. If Jordan did tame him, it would only be a pity. But there was no sense opening herself to more worried looks from Maggie and March. They had fairly hovered over her after her return from Jordan and Elijah's wedding, as if her concern for her brother's oldest friend was unwarranted.

"Did you know Mrs. Kelly sent me a painting of Battlement Park, as a gift for my modest help with her travels?" the Colonel continued. "I have it hanging behind the counter at the hotel. Magnificent. As good as anything Albert Bierstadt did for the Earl of Dunraven."

"She sent us a painting, too," Maggie said, pointing to the fireplace. "Better than a landscape, any day."

Over the mantel hung a portrait of a little coffee-colored mare, her brown eyes sharp with intelligence, her delicate ears swiveling toward the sound of the painter's voice.

"Why, that's the little mare you sold her, isn't it?" Colonel Treadwell asked.

"Smoke," Maggie agreed proudly.

"Jordan Kelly is a clever woman," March said. "That painting is the only thing that reconciled my wife to losing such a fine mare."

"We didn't lose her, we sold her," Maggie reminded him. "We're in the business of selling horses."

"And it breaks your heart, every time."

Before Maggie could reply, the front door swung open and Henna entered, followed by a woman who could only be the Colonel's mysterious visitor.

She smiled tentatively at the group gathered by the sofa, her soft, coral lips appearing almost dark against the fairness of her smooth, clear skin. The dusky blue of her stylish traveling hat scooped low over the right side of her face, setting off the silver blond of her hair and adding a touch of color to her wide gray eyes.

She might have been an alabaster sculpture of an angel.

"Mrs. Woodfin," the Colonel greeted her, his usual effusiveness softened, as if he spoke to a horse that might spook. "Allow me to present Mrs. Margaret Jackson and Miss Harriet Jackson."

"Maggie and Harry," Maggie corrected, adjusting Sarah to shake the woman's hand. "And Sarah," she added, as Mrs. Woodfin edged aside the baby's blanket with one white-gloved finger.

"What a lovely child," she said, the slow warmth of

the South flavoring her words.

They were certainly the right words to say to Maggie. She beamed down at the bundle in her arms. "She is, isn't she? Even if I do say so myself. Won't you come have a seat, Mrs. Woodfin?"

"Elizabeth, please."

"Elizabeth." Maggie shooed the men to the chairs and sat on the sofa beside her guest. Henna sat in the rocker and Harry perched herself on the arm of the sofa beside Maggie.

"Colonel Treadwell said that we might be able to help you with a problem," Maggie said.

"Oh, I do hope so. I would never wish to impose on you, but . . ." A faint flush of pink warmed her porcelain cheeks. "I'm in such terrible trouble. I need help in locating my brother. I don't know where he is, but I must find him before it's too late."

Moisture glistened on her pale blond lashes.

Maggie gestured impatiently to March, who came up with a large white handkerchief, which Elizabeth took with a sniff of gratitude.

"Don't cry, my dear," the Colonel ordered. "The Jacksons will take care of it, just like I told you."

"I'm sorry," she said, with an attempt at that shy little smile. "I'm just so desperate. I have no one else to turn to."

"We'll help any way we can," Maggie said, patting the woman's shoulder.

"You think your brother's in Colorado?" March asked.

Elizabeth Woodfin nodded. "That is my hope. The last time we heard from him, he had stopped briefly here in Oxtail. If he's not in Colorado, I don't know what I'll do."

Harry had had just about enough of the woman's magnolia-soft histrionics. She could have given lessons to Mrs.

Danforth, Harry's draconian finishing school headmistress.

"I don't know what makes you think we can find him for you," Harry said flatly. "But it might help if you told us his name."

A faint laugh escaped their guest. "Of course. It's just that I've been frightened even to tell anyone *my* name. If I'm caught before I reach my brother . . ."

She shuddered, and there was nothing soft or fainting about her fear. She took a deep breath and brushed back a drifting lock of silver hair, setting her hat askew.

"He's the only one who can help me. If anyone can. I have been told he is a friend of yours. His name is Elijah Kelly."

As the woman looked up to see their reaction, Harry felt her stomach clench. At the name, yes. And at what Elizabeth Woodfin's dislodged hat had revealed.

There was color in her alabaster face, after all. A heavy application of powder could not mute the shocking green-black bruise that spread across her cheek under her right eye. Or the razor-thin slash along the hairline at her temple. It might have been made by a razor. It did not look accidental.

Mrs. Woodfin, Harry thought, might be in just as much trouble as she claimed to be.

Chapter 2

"I didn't know 'Lije had a sister," March said, pulling them all back from staring at Elizabeth Woodfin's bruise.

"Oh, I'm not surprised." She shrugged prettily. "The boys were older, and they didn't care much about having a baby sister. Besides, after Mama died, Papa sent me to live with his sister in Savannah. I only saw Elijah and Malachi once or twice a year.

"Then, when I got married, they didn't approve. I was angry. We lost touch. They thought Charm was nothing but trouble." Her eyes returned from the past with their first flicker of fire. "It turns out they were right."

Slowly, she lifted her hat and set it aside on the arm of the sofa. When she turned her face back to Maggie, Harry saw Maggie's free hand rise unconsciously to where her own thin, white scar ran from her right temple almost to her jaw.

Elizabeth Woodfin's delicate features had sharpened. "I came to you because Papa said Elijah often visits you here in Oxtail. When I met Colonel Treadwell at the Grand Hotel in town and asked him where you lived . . . he was so kind." She turned her shy smile on the Colonel, whose mustache danced. "I told him everything. He said you might have good news for me."

"I didn't want to get her hopes up if Kelly's moved on," the Colonel said gruffly. "A leopard can't change his spots—no offense, my dear Mrs. Woodfin—and I've always thought Kelly a leopard, through and through."

"Even an old leopard might learn to appreciate a warm spot by the fire," March said mildly. "He seems to have taken to mountain guiding, though I have to confess, I have a hard time picturing it."

Harry did, too, though the one time she'd seen Elijah since his marriage, when he'd brought his son, Wolf, home to Henna, he had seemed content with his new life. He had not been living it long, but Harry had to admit, in the darkest part of her heart, that she had never seen his keen face so relaxed, his hazel cat eyes so warmly gold. It had cut her. Deep.

Maybe she had never known him as well as she thought she had. Yet, if 'Lije could adapt to a settled life, surely she could, too. Surely she could be happy keeping Ash's house in South Park, even if it meant she had to give up some of her ranch work and riding.

"Elijah *is* in Colorado, then?" Elizabeth asked, leaning toward March. "How close? How soon can I get there?"

"He's in Battlement Park," March told her. "And so is Malachi, last I heard."

"Mal's here, too?" She seemed to need a minute to process that information. Harry could hardly blame her. Malachi was . . . difficult. "Where is Battlement Park?"

"A hard day's ride through the pass between here and there," March said. "But you can take the train from Oxtail to Longmont, and there's a coach that will take you to Battlement Park's resort hotel from there. You could reach 'Lije by Thursday night."

Elizabeth was shaking her head. "Not the train. I can't take the train again."

"It isn't far," Maggie assured her. "And it's mostly flat prairie from here to Longmont. Nothing dangerous."

"You don't understand." Their guest took a deep breath to steady herself. "The man who did this to my face, he is still hunting me. He was in Cheyenne. He searched my train. If he catches me, I doubt that this time he will stop with his fists."

"Your husband?" March asked grimly.

Elizabeth Woodfin's gray eyes shifted away. "No." Her fists tightened around March's crumpled handkerchief. "He has done work for my husband. Charm helps to run an import and export company out of Savannah. It has brought him in contact with some unsavory characters."

Harry couldn't decipher whether the woman's discomfort came from fear that they wouldn't help a woman running from an abusive husband—he had every legal right to demand her return. Or whether her evasiveness indicated that her husband's business dealings were not entirely legitimate. Perhaps both.

Either way, Elizabeth Woodfin's troubles could cause complications for anyone offering her aid. And Harry had the niggling feeling the woman might not be telling them the worst of it.

"I will pay you," Elizabeth said, her chin tilting up with a flash of pride. "I don't expect charity. If you will guide me to this Battlement Park, I will repay you generously."

Misinterpreting the protest in March's expression, she added, "It's my own money, not my husband's."

"We can outfit you with a horse and saddle," Maggie said. "For the same fair price we would ask of anyone. Do you have riding experience?"

The woman's chin tilted just a bit higher. "Of course."

"You would be better off taking the train," Henna said

bluntly, leaning back in the rocker. "The trail from here to Battlement Park is no better than a deer track. It's hard riding, and the mountains can be treacherous, especially at this time of year."

"I'm willing to take the risk," Elizabeth said, just as bluntly.

"Perhaps March is not," Henna retorted, her amber eyes flashing with protective fire.

"It's not that," March said, the peacemaker as always. "The weather looks dry for the moment, and despite that taste of fall yesterday, it hasn't turned cold yet. But I have to take a shipment of colts to Denver day after tomorrow. I won't be back until late next week. If the weather is still fair then, I could arrange to guide you, if you still want to ride."

All the softness had planed away from Elizabeth's face, leaving her pale skin tight across her cheekbones. "I can't wait that long."

March's mouth twisted ruefully. "I can't change these plans."

"You could take the same train March will take with the colts day after tomorrow, Mrs. Woodfin," Henna suggested. "He would make sure you arrived safely in Longmont."

Glancing at her thoughtful, unassuming brother, Harry guessed there were those who might mistakenly doubt his ability to handle a large-fisted bully. But Elizabeth Woodfin's refusal was too fast to stem from anything but desperation.

"No." Steel laced the word. "Do you have a hand you could spare for two days?" The sweet smile looked forced this time. "I hate to cause such inconvenience. If you can't help me, perhaps Colonel Treadwell could suggest someone in Oxtail."

"No," Maggie said, as steely as Elizabeth. She tucked

Sarah a little more firmly against her chest. "That could well be worse than what you've already been through." Though she now had good friends in Oxtail, Maggie's initial experience in the town had left her distrustful of drifters and cowboys.

Slowly, her expression brightened. "Harry can take you."

"Harry?" said Harry and Elizabeth at the same time, with almost the same amount of surprise.

"I can't do it," Harry said. "I don't have time."

Maggie was too delighted with her plan to acknowledge Harry's protest.

"Rover's ready to return to Elijah," she said. The gunfighter's horse had spent the spring and summer recovering from a bout of pneumonia he'd contracted the winter before. "You could take him with you."

"The wedding's only a month away," Henna reminded her, coming to Harry's aid.

"It will be good for Harry to take her mind off the wedding for a few days."

The Colonel's mustache twitched his disapproval. "Miss Harriet is a fine horsewoman, Margaret, but this is hardly the sort of expedition for a young lady. I would guide Mrs. Woodfin myself, if my leg would cooperate, but it's too dangerous of an undertaking for two young women alone."

Harry bit back her reply to that. She had Maggie to defend her, whether she wanted it or not.

"Harry knows the way. She's taken that path to Battlement Park already this past summer. She knows the mountains. She knows how to use a rifle. And it's only a day's ride. Even Harry shouldn't be able to get into too much trouble."

"I don't see why she can't just take the train," Harry said.

"My opinion exactly," Henna agreed.

"There must be someone in town—" Elizabeth began, but further argument was cut off by the sound of a hearty bellow from the ranch yard.

"Hello, the house!"

March crossed to open the front door, eyes squinting into the bright midday light. "Hello, yourself, Mr. Brady. Ash. Lemuel warned us you were coming."

"And you didn't all run out to hide in the barn?" Alexander Brady asked. Harry heard him knocking his boots against the steps. "I see you've already got company. Is this a bad time?"

Harry could see Henna's and Maggie's heads nodding in time with her own, but March could not.

"No, of course not. Come on in, the both of you. You'll be part of the family soon. It's time you started being inconvenient."

Alexander Brady's hearty laugh preceded him into the house. The cattle baron's stocky shape filled the lower two-thirds of the doorway for a moment, his balding head catching a stray glint of sunlight. Anyone who didn't know Brady might think him a harmless, rather comical figure with his stout frame and broad face, a jaunty bowler tucked under his arm. Anyone who failed to notice the perfectly tailored cut of his pinstriped suit, the resolute set of his chin beneath his meticulously trimmed beard, and the shark's intensity of his clear, dark eyes.

Brady was one of the richest men in Colorado, and he'd never shied away from his reputation as a ruthless businessman. But to Harry he would always be the brave man who had almost lost his life helping to save her brother's ranch from a vicious outlaw.

Despite the uncomfortable swoop of her stomach at the

arrival of the new visitors, she put on a welcoming smile and rose to greet him.

"Harriet, dear!" Brady took her hands in his. "You're always a balm for a dreary day. I was just telling my nephew what a lucky man he is. Almost as lucky as I was, winning my Emmeline."

His nephew entered on cue behind him.

"Hello, Harriet." Ashton Brady had a wry smile that was enough to make a saint's heart skip, and Harry was no saint. "It's a good thing Uncle Alexander's in love with my aunt. I'd hate to face that competition."

"Ha! It would be no competition at all. I'd never have given you a second look, Ash." Harry gave Alexander Brady a peck on the cheek that brought a broad smile to his face.

"That girl is a prize filly," Brady said approvingly. "High spirits, like my own girls. You'll be a fine addition to the family, my dear."

Harry's voice stretched a little high. "A prize filly?"

Ash laughed. "You're lucky. He rarely makes comparisons to anything but cows."

"At least he had the sense not to mention brood mares," Henna muttered dryly, rising from her seat with Harry's wrapped dress in her arms. "I'll have your saddle blanket ready in no time, Harriet. If you all will excuse me, I've got six hungry mouths waiting back home."

"You're welcome to stay to dinner with us," Maggie said.

"I promised Wolf I'd rescue him from Tuck and Emily so he could go fishing. No one else would catch anything this time of day, but I expect Wolf will bring home enough for supper."

No one else might have caught the concern in Henna's amber eyes, but Harry could almost complete her thought.

Wolf needed to get away, have some time to himself. Henna's foster son had turned thirteen that past May, and though he worked as hard as any of Henna and Jed's own boys, it was becoming more and more clear to everyone, except perhaps to Wolf himself, that he would never be content settling down as a farmer.

Maggie and March had arranged to hire the boy to take Harry's place on their ranch after her marriage. Harry knew Henna hoped the excitement of training horses would keep Wolf close to home, away from the life his gunfighter father had recently lived.

Harry walked Henna to the door, half wishing she could dash out after her. Maybe more than half. The sun beat hotly on the ranch yard outside, the grass burned yellow by the late summer sun and now mellowing to gold with the coming of fall, but the breeze in the mountains would be fresh with pine, the streams cold on her bare feet.

Henna hooked her arm and took her the few steps out onto the porch, bending only a moment toward Harry's ear.

"I'm glad you've sense enough to stay home," she whispered flatly. "That Woodfin woman is trouble with a capital 'T'."

Ash's arrival had stirred up the confusion of Harry's own problems, briefly driving Elizabeth Woodfin's from her mind.

"Not that all the Kellys aren't trouble." Henna glanced back over her shoulder, her amber eyes troubled. "But there's something about her story that doesn't ring true. I'm not going to mention her to Wolf."

Harry met Henna's gaze. Normally, she'd have stood up for her young friend's right to meet his aunt, but it seemed the world had tilted and all her responses were foreign to her that day.

"I won't say a word," she promised. "With any luck, she'll have left Oxtail by morning."

Henna nodded, eyes sharp, the protective tigress never far beneath the surface of her calm demeanor. "If she's still in Battlement Park the next time Wolf goes to visit his father, well enough. If not . . ."

She puffed the worry out her nostrils and patted the package she carried. "The wedding will be beautiful, Harry, and so will you. Don't worry."

She smiled at Harry then, with a warmth that made Harry glad she was one of the cubs under Henna's protection—though two months ago she would have chafed under any such maternal regard.

Harry returned to the living room, the sudden change of light nudging the outlines of objects slightly off-kilter, increasing her sense of dislocation. Maybe she was in a dream, after all.

The new guests had apparently been introduced to the old. Even Alexander Brady looked to have succumbed to the white knight syndrome surrounding the fair, tragic Mrs. Woodfin. He had his billfold out and was pressing a ten dollar bill into her hand.

At least Elizabeth had the grace to act chagrined, shaking her head vehemently. "Oh, I couldn't, Mr. Brady. It's too much. You don't even know me."

"For good luck," Brady insisted gruffly. "I certainly won't miss it."

Harry's gaze slid to where Ash stood leaning on the back of Henna's vacated chair. His slight smile showed nearly as much amusement at his uncle as appreciation for Elizabeth's charms.

Harry wrestled down the tiny worms of jealousy that she'd never known lived in her heart until the previous fall when she'd first met Jordan Braddock.

"Mr. Brady, you and Ash will stay to dinner with us, won't you?" Maggie offered, rising to jog the squalling Sarah in her arms. "I've already insisted the Colonel and Mrs. Woodfin stay."

"No, no, my dear." Brady pulled a heavy gold watch from his pocket. "The invitation is very kind, but we haven't the time. We just dropped by so Ash could deliver a bit of news to his Harriet."

Taking the hint, Ash walked over to offer Harry his arm. "Why don't we go for a walk outside?"

Harry felt a surge of reluctance to leave the safety of her family. Shame at the unexpected cowardice propelled her out the door. Ash led her down the porch steps and turned her toward the small apple orchard to the west side of the house.

The muscles of her fiancé's arm—*her fiancé?*—were strong beneath her hand. Despite the expensive tailoring of his jacket and the careful trim of his nails, there was no mistaking that his hands and his body were used to hard ranch work. It was that, perhaps, that had appealed to her when she had first seen him attending church with his uncle's family that second Sunday in July.

No. She glanced up. Honestly, it had been his fine, chiseled features that had attracted her, the gray-blond hair that brushed his ears, the hazel eyes that always seemed to find something amusing in every situation. His physical toughness, his appreciation of an honest day's work was what had made her look twice.

And then, she wasn't quite sure now how it had happened, she had found herself sharing the Sunday picnic with him. He had asked permission to visit the ranch. She had gone riding with him and his cousins, Brady's daughters. Had dined at the Brady ranch. Had said yes when Ash proposed . . .

Her throat constricted, and she felt for an instant as she had when she couldn't get out of Jane's wedding dress. Trapped by his arm, by his closeness, by what she had promised. She barely knew this man, this tall boy only a year older than she.

You shouldn't let anyone stifle your freedom. Damn Malachi Kelly, anyway, him and his unwanted advice. It was his fault she couldn't breathe, not Ash's, Mal's bitterness and cynicism—and it was only bitterness and cynicism, for all the concern in his voice when he'd said the words. He didn't understand love.

Harry pushed back the thought that maybe they had that in common.

Ash led Harry into the shade of the trees, stopping at the edge of the orchard where the view opened up to the foothills, forested with Ponderosa pine, with the grandeur of the Rocky Mountains rising behind them.

"You can't stay for dinner?" Harry asked finally, Ash's silence unnerving her.

"No, I'm sorry."

At the guilty melancholy in his voice, her heart thudded queerly. She met his gaze, catching a glimpse of something that might have been apprehension. For a second she wondered if his thoughts had been paralleling her own. He had realized how rash this was. He meant to tell her he could not go through with the wedding.

Something dark twisted in her heart. Dear Harry. Wild, spoiled Harry. Good sport Harry. Everybody's sister, friend, niece. Everybody's pal. Good old Harry, always there until somebody better came along. Had he met a woman more like Jordan Kelly or Elizabeth Woodfin? A proper lady. What on earth could she have been thinking to believe that someone like Ashton Brady would find her beautiful, interesting, desirable?

Yet mixed with the bitter disappointment, like the liquor of patent medicine, was the faintest taste of honey . . .

"I'll just say it, Harriet. I've got to go home to South Park. I've had a telegram that my brother had a run-in with a steer and ended up the worse for it. My father needs my help with the ranch."

"Of course." Harry kept her face clear of everything except concern. "Is your brother going to be all right?"

"Lionel? He's got a broken leg, but he'll be fine. He's already survived two broken arms, a broken collarbone and a split skull. He'll survive this." Ash's smile faded. "Unless I kill him myself."

"He can't help it. Working with cattle is hard business."

"Lionel's always had bad timing. The wedding's only a month away. But he was supposed to do some business for Father in Denver, and he won't be traveling anywhere for a while."

Harry shook her head, looking away, knowing her face was turning white and red by turns. "We can postpone the wedding."

"No." Ash turned her to him, that small smile playing around his mouth again. "Why don't you come with me? Forget the wedding."

"What?" Harry stumbled, though she was standing still.

"We'll get married by a justice of the peace on the way."

For a second, all she could hear was the wild beating of her heart. The flutter of a falcon trapped in a canary's cage.

"No! I mean, no, I can't . . ." She couldn't leave March and Maggie and the baby. Couldn't leave Oxtail. Couldn't leave her home and the hills and mountains she loved, that were as much a part of her as her own hands and feet.

The very things she would have to leave, after the wedding, whether tomorrow or a month away.

"C'mon, Harriet," he wheedled, his eyes sparkling, for all the world like a little boy begging her to skip school for an afternoon at the swimming hole. She almost caught the feeling. Crazy, impulsive. A Harry adventure, if there ever was one. If he asked if she was chicken, she'd be on the next train to Den—

"There's so little time before the wedding, anyway. This way I wouldn't have to come all the way back here to fetch you. My father won't want me to waste the time when there's so much to be done on the ranch."

A cold ball formed in Harry's stomach. They weren't children anymore. She had better remember that. Ash's responsibilities on his father's ranch would become hers soon enough.

"I have responsibilities here, too," she said. "I can't desert March and Maggie a month early. They need the help."

"They're taking on that Culbert boy next week, aren't they? The quiet one."

"Wolf." Had she never told him Wolf wasn't a Culbert, but a Kelly? What else had she forgotten to mention? What had they talked about on those afternoon rides? "He'll be a good hand for them, but I'll need time to show him—"

"I don't think it will take him that long to catch on to the work you've been doing around here. The boy's been raised on a farm."

Which was true enough. "But with March leaving for Denver—"

"Good lord, Harriet, it's about time March hired another man. Expecting a girl to muck out stalls and rope horses. My father wouldn't have stood for it. Besides, the boy'll have the muscles for the work. He'll get twice as much done in half the time."

Harry could only stare mutely as Ash reached out a hand to brush her dark curls back from her face. He smiled gently.

"I know it's sudden, but you don't have to be scared."

"Maggie wants me to guide Elizabeth Woodfin to Battlement Park tomorrow. To take her to Elijah." Where had that come from?

Something flashed in Ash's eyes. "That's ridiculous! Two women alone? At this time of year? You could freeze to death. And I don't care if Elijah Kelly is a friend of your family, I don't want my wife spending time with a two-bit outlaw."

The lump in Harry's stomach expanded, freezing her tongue to the roof of her mouth.

Ash smiled then, a sudden gentleness in his eyes. "I was right, wasn't I? You are scared. I know you're not foolish enough to ride out on Maggie's whim. You're not wild like she is."

Harry saw suddenly the picture she made in her sweet green-sprigged dress, slender, even delicate, as her sister Jane had always thought her, her skin fair as any town belle, though hers was more often covered with a broad-brimmed hat and heavy work gloves than bonnet and kid leather.

Had Ash not once seen beneath that surface appearance these past two months? Had she been so frightened of what he might think if he did?

"It's all right. I understand." Ash's smile turned crooked. "Uncle Alex said you wouldn't elope with me. He said no woman could resist a party in her honor. And you deserve it. You are so beautiful."

He leaned toward her then, and Harry tilted her face to meet him, eyes shut tight against tears, pressing her lips to his. She reached her hands to his neck, tangling her fingers in his hair, pulling him closer, willing the kiss to burn away the memory of his words, the fear that kicked in her chest like a mule.

"Hey. Hey, there." He squeezed her shoulders as he leaned back from the kiss. "I'm having a hard enough time leaving you already."

He smiled down at her, hazel eyes catching the September light like copper leaves swirling downstream. Harry struggled to breathe. He was so beautiful. And he didn't even know he didn't know her.

"I'll be back. I promise. Just one month." He dropped a kiss on the tip of her nose. "And not a day longer. You've had fair warning!"

He slipped his arm through hers and turned her once more toward the house. "There now, don't look so upset. I know what you're really thinking. You've learned that you've got me wrapped around that little pinky finger of yours. Well, I don't care who knows it!"

Harry dredged up a smile from somewhere, though her voice remained out of reach. Probably just as well, she thought. For she had learned something in the past ten minutes. Several things.

One: She didn't recognize this Harriet who wasn't "wild like Maggie," who didn't speak her mind, who didn't *know* her mind.

Two: She had only a month to figure this strange woman out, to find out who the real Harriet Jackson was before she ceased to exist altogether and became Harriet Brady.

Three: She had changed her mind about guiding Elizabeth Woodfin to Battlement Park.

Chapter 3

"Do you take this man, to have and to hold . . ."

Yes. The word stuck hard and hot in her throat. Not a sound escaped to betray her.

"I do."

No. *No!* She could shout until the word rang from the rafters of the huge room, until it burned like the sun reflecting off the mountains through the extravagantly tall windows at the north end of the hall.

Nothing she said would change anything. Not how she felt, not the outcome of the dream. Even buried in sleep, she knew the blade had fallen and there was no turning back. No rescue. No last-minute reprieve.

Where was the cavalry when you needed them? Working for the enemy, apparently.

She watched numbly as former Seventh Cavalry Captain Malachi Kelly closed his little book, his expression almost as shuttered as her own.

"By the power invested in me, as a Justice of the Peace for the State of Colorado, I now pronounce you man and wife. God help you both."

Harry pasted on a smile, just a twist of irony at the edges to show she didn't take herself too seriously, as the handful of family, friends, and hotel guests pushed forward to congratulate the happy couple. None of them noticed the agony that wrenched her heart, any more than they noticed the smile that hid it. No one saw anything but the glow of joy suffusing the bride's face, the heart-wrenching happiness in her new husband's smile, his dangerous eyes softened by love.

"Almost enough to make you sick."

The voice beside her only firmed her smile.

"Why, Malachi Kelly, don't tell me this joyous occasion doesn't warm your heart. Here I had you picked as an irrepressible romantic."

Mal Kelly's deep green eyes had nothing of his brother's panther-like flatness. His posture, arms crossed over his chest, held none of his brother's catlike grace as he watched Elijah and Jordan Kelly share their first moments of married life. He stood only a few inches taller than Harry, with a compact build, though his intensity filled the space around him.

"I wish 'Lije and Jordan all the happiness in the world," Malachi said. His southern drawl had faded during his years in the West, as Elijah's had not, replaced with a blunt edge of honest cynicism. "I've never noticed that marriage increased anyone's happiness."

Harry felt a kick of guilt in her gut. She did *not* want 'Lije and Jordan to be unhappy. Maybe that would have been easier, to hate them, to hate Jordan and pity Elijah. But there was something between them, something that in her dream had become almost tangible, a shimmering in the air of the Fox and Hound's grand entrance room. Something that made her heart ache with emptiness.

"My brother, March, and his wife are happy," she said. "And Wolf's guardians, the Culberts."

"I'll have to take your word for it until I finally meet them," Malachi said skeptically. "Myself, I don't plan to marry." For a second his green eyes flashed at her. "You should be glad you're not married yet, either. You shouldn't let anyone stifle your freedom."

She opened her mouth to object that her marrying Ash was none of his business, stifling or not, but then she remembered that she hadn't met Ash yet. Let the dream take its course as it followed her memory. It always did.

A hand clapped on her shoulder, another on Malachi's.

"Splendid day for a wedding, eh? Jolly good ceremony, Mal. You looked positively sepulchral."

They both turned their heads to meet Tony Wayne's enthusiastic smile. He looked even more handsome than usual, his blond hair freshly trimmed, his muscular frame perfectly filling out the blue dress uniform of an English major.

" 'This is my beloved, and this is my friend,' as Elijah might say."

"Do you have to be so damn cheerful?" Malachi growled.

" 'Almost enough to make you sick,' as Mal might say," Harry put in.

"Especially on an empty stomach."

The hotel proprietor patted their shoulders. "What could be better than to see two dear friends happy? The triumph of true love and all that. Though the supply of single girls in this county is dwindling at an alarming rate."

Tony slipped his hand down Harry's arm to take her elbow. "Allow me to escort you to the fabulous nuptial supper my Norwegian chef has prepared. Do you have a Norwegian chef, Mal?"

Malachi made a rude noise. "No, thank the Lord. If I

never taste herring again—"

"Capital." Tony guided Harry toward the dining room, following the bride and groom and their well-wishers. "I still have a leg up on the competition. Now, what were you two talking about that was so revoltingly serious?"

Harry fluttered her eyelashes helplessly. In the banter with her companions, she could almost forget her heart was breaking. "I do believe Malachi just asked me not to marry him."

"Good God!" Tony exclaimed, his warm brown eyes widening in alarm. "A lovely, intelligent, charming, dare I say refined young lady like you—"

Malachi snorted.

"—with a vulgar, obnoxious scoundrel like Mal? Terrifying thought. I'm certainly glad you're sensible enough to accept his anti-proposal."

Malachi raised one sardonic eyebrow. "She hasn't yet." Those green eyes might not have had Elijah's calculated flatness, but they could be just as baffling, Harry thought as they studied her. Then humor flashed as he winked. "I think she likes me."

"Miss Jackson? Harriet? *Harry!*"

Harry opened her eyes to the pale gray light of dawn, just enough dampness clinging in the air to prove that there had been no frost overnight, however much she felt as though she were freezing.

Elizabeth Woodfin's pale face hovered ghostlike over hers. "Are you all right? You were making noises in your sleep."

"Nightmare," Harry mumbled, trying to push herself up to a sitting position without letting her blanket slide from her shoulders.

"A nightmare?" Elizabeth hunkered back on her heels,

gray eyes skeptical. "You were laughing."

"Sometimes my nightmare monsters say things to amuse me."

Harry blinked away the last of her sleep as she tried to wiggle her frozen fingers and toes, fighting down chagrin that the city girl, Elizabeth, was not only awake and alert, but she'd already done her hair in an elaborate chignon behind her hat. Her bedroll was stowed—somewhat haphazardly—behind her ridiculous sidesaddle, which was settled—somewhat more expertly—on her palomino mare's back. She was ready to leave, and Harry was still wrapped in blankets, shivering with cold and the memory of dark green eyes.

At least there was a reasonable explanation for the cold. The fire pit Harry had built so carefully the night before was not even smoldering.

"You let the fire go out."

"I put it out. It was smoking."

Harry blinked again. They were huddled in a copse of pines, only a thick blanket of needles between their bedrolls and the cold, hard ground, halfway to the sky—or at least halfway up a mountain halfway to the sky—in September, and this, this *southern belle* had put out their fire.

"Do you want to freeze to death?" Her voice sounded surprisingly calm to her own ears. "Have you ever heard of hypothermia? Does it never get *cold* in Georgia?"

Elizabeth stood. "Of course it gets cold. This isn't even freezing." She dropped her arms as if she hadn't just been hugging her old wool coat to her chest. Her lips looked blue.

Harry struggled to her feet, unabashedly clutching her blankets around her. It was bad enough that her charge's insistence on riding sidesaddle had slowed them to a crawl climbing the mountain, bad enough that Elizabeth's ridiculous heels had broken off her boots, leaving her barely able to negotiate the rocks in the spots where they had to lead the horses, bad enough that Elizabeth's utter unpreparedness for mountain travel had forced them to spend a night out in the cold; she didn't have to make the night even colder because she couldn't tolerate a little pine smoke.

"It doesn't have to be freezing for you to die from exposure," Harry said. "And it very well could have frozen overnight. We're in the Rockies now. No more magnolias and pralines."

Not to mention no hot coffee—it would take too long to restart the fire. Harry's voice finally rose in annoyance. "If you don't respect the dangers out here, you're dead."

Elizabeth tilted up her chin. "No coral snakes, no cottonmouths, no alligators. And the only chance we've got of dying this morning seems to be sitting around talking ourselves to death."

Harry did not like this sugar-coated, steel-eyed damsel in distress. She reminded herself of that as her mouth bent in a reluctant smile.

"In the mountains, bad weather can be as sudden as Judgment Day," she explained, a little less gruffly. "And in bad weather, fire can mean the difference between life and death. A little smoke in your eyes won't hurt you."

Elizabeth glanced down the ravine they'd struggled up the afternoon before. "It wasn't my eyes I was worried about." She looked back at Harry, and those gray eyes were clear and cold as ice. "My nightmare monsters don't tell amusing stories."

Harry shuddered, but not from the cold. Elizabeth's voice left Harry no doubt that for all her careful gentility, the other woman was no silly fool jumping at shadows.

Whatever she was afraid of, it was worse than the cold. Maybe worse than freezing to death.

"The going is easier from here," Harry said, shaking off her blankets so she could roll them up. "We should be in Battlement Park before noon. We'll have to make do with jerky this morning and no coffee, but we'll get a hot meal there."

Elizabeth nodded, her stance relaxing a little. "I am indebted to you, for guiding me there."

Harry shrugged, uncomfortable with the knowledge that she wasn't tramping about on a cold mountainside out of kindness for the other woman. She still wasn't at all sure why she was tramping about on a cold mountainside. She only knew she could fill her lungs easily for the first time in two months, despite the keen air.

In fact, the cold mountain, with its bone-jarring rocks, slashing tree limbs, touchy bears, blood-chilling streams, and treacherous terrain felt more like home than home had felt all summer. If only she could stay where she was, not having to face Ash back at the ranch or Elijah at Battlement Park, she might manage to figure out where she'd lost the joy she had so recently felt in her life.

She felt a stab of envy for trappers and prospectors and all the hairy, scarred, inarticulate mountain men she'd ever seen trading skins or meat or pitiful pouches of gold dust for supplies at Isling's General Store. They would never know freedom from want or fear or loneliness. They had traded those for something they prized more. Freedom from other people's expectations.

Harry glanced at Elizabeth, enmeshed by propriety into corset and hose, sidesaddle and civility. She'd been contemptuous of the woman the day before, when the civilized trappings had added an overnight camp to their trip. This morning, flouting fashion and good breeding in her own blue jeans, flannel shirt and riding boots, hair flying loose waiting for her broad-brimmed hat, Harry suddenly realized she might be equally ensnared.

Elizabeth walked over to hold Portia's bridle while Harry lifted her sensible, battered, Mexican-style saddle on the horse's back. The chocolate-colored mare, normally balky around strangers, took this as a courtesy. Harry decided to do the same. "Thanks."

"I'm sorry about the coffee."

This time Harry couldn't fight down the smile. "You'll be sorrier when we get to the Fox and Hound. Tony Wayne's a tea man."

Malachi Kelly hated tea.

No, hate was too weak a word. He despised tea. He loathed it. He detested the delicate, sophisticated fragrance of it, the mild flavor with its gentle boost of energy. He abhorred it plain, with milk, with sugar, with lemon and honey.

If he had to swallow one more drop of the insipid, odious, *civilized* swill . . .

"Just a little more, Mal?" Jordan Kelly asked, the spout of her flowered china teapot hovering over his cup.

"Please."

Even after three months, Mal couldn't tell whether his sister-in-law's smile came from delight because she believed he enjoyed her tea or delight that because he pretended to enjoy it, she could force more on him.

He had never believed in slighting honesty for social grace, and his experiences in the army had left him with even less patience for politeness. He despised simpering pleasantries even more than he loathed tea.

But he'd discovered that this one white lie was worth seeing that sparkle in Jordan's sapphire eyes. Besides, he paid ample penance for it by having to drink the stuff.

"Nothing like a spot of tea to make a perfect afternoon even better," Tony Wayne observed, his smile purely malicious joy at Mal's struggle to down the liquid in his cup.

Tony slouched back in his rough wooden chair and lifted his feet to the porch rail in front of him. The last time Mal had tried to match the long-legged Englishman's leisure pose, he'd ended up on his butt on the porch.

"And this is certainly a perfect afternoon," Tony added with a sigh of contentment.

"The afternoon could not get better," Mal agreed. Unless he could think of some way of spilling his tea without being offered more.

Indeed, the morning, which had started fresh and cold, had mellowed into one of those golden fall days that made apple cider, falling leaves and growing old seem equal pleasures in God's world.

The sun streamed low over the lip of the high mountain valley, warming his right shoulder even as the glacier breath of the peaks whispered down his neck. The dancing, carefree aspen were just putting on their fine golden glories, chimes and laughter against the somber green of spruce and pine and fir.

His brother and sister-in-law's new cabin looked east, giving a sweeping view of the lower end of Battlement Park, including the crenellated ridge to the left that gave the Park its name and, down to the right, a glimpse of Tony's resort hotel, the Fox and Hound.

He could think of nowhere he would rather be than sitting comfortably with friends on the porch of a cabin he had helped to build, in such a setting, pleasantly tired from a hard ride in the mountains hunting a stolen horse . . .

Perhaps that hunt accounted for his nagging sense of disquiet, for the restlessness that dragged his thoughts in directions he would rather not follow. The feral animosity in the eyes of the horse thief he and Elijah had caught that afternoon lingered in his mind. The smell of violence and fear. They reminded him of the life he'd left. Reminded him of screaming women, dying children, men begging him to kill them, put them out of their agony.

He was *not* going to remember. For one day, one afternoon, one hour, he was going to pretend he deserved this peace, these friends, this respite from himself.

"The afternoon could not get better," he repeated, gulping the dregs of his tea.

"Which logically implies it can only get worse," his brother drawled. Elijah leaned his hip on the porch railing where it met the cabin's edge, his gaze scanning the scene in front of them, hand resting on his thigh as though he held a rifle there. Mal doubted Elijah would ever lose that look, the cat keeping one eye open for an unwary mouse, but the eyes glinted warmly as he glanced back at Mal. "I am personally hoping it does get better. I thought I smelled venison stew when Jordan brought out the tea."

"You have a point. That could improve the day. If there were enough for three, and I didn't have to eat the swill Tony's cook is undoubtedly brewing down at the lodge . . ." Mal raised an eyebrow at Jordan seated beside him.

"My Norwegian chef," Tony said sternly, "makes a very fine venison stew. Though his apple pie doesn't quite live up to our dear Mrs. Kelly's," he added hopefully.

"Venial self-gratification wins out over crass commercial interests," Mal noted. "A beautiful moment."

"She's my wife," Elijah said placidly. "It's my stew. And my pie."

"It's *my* stew and *my* pie," Jordan said, equally placid. "And if the three of you want any, you'll go finish roofing my painting studio before supper's ready to be served."

"You mean that horse shed over there?" Mal asked, pointing to the sturdy little building they'd put up earlier that week.

Elijah's boots hit the porch with a thud, narrowly missing the silver and white wolf-dog lounging beside him. "Don't joke," he warned. "She's not bluffing about the food."

"Loki would be happy to share with me," Jordan agreed.

The wolf looked over at her with hope bright in his silver eyes, his tail thumping happily.

Tony laughed, bouncing to his feet. "That's the one thing that makes your afternoon better than ours, 'Lije. A wife."

He grabbed Jordan's hand, kissing it gallantly. "Almost makes you believe in love, don't it, Mal? Maybe we should give marriage a chance."

Mal shook his head. Tony adored women. And they adored being adored by the handsome British major. But Tony never lost his head over them. Mal suspected this was at least partially because Tony had no wish to return to the society the ladies who visited his hotel craved.

And as for himself . . . Any capacity he had for love had shriveled and died long ago, bled away by slaughter and lies and betrayal. If his life held a taste of emptiness his brother's did not, well, he was used to it. It suited him.

"Give over, Mal." Tony thumped him hard on the shoulder. "Don't be such a sourpuss. Jordan, you and I are going to have to take this poor chap in hand and—"

"Quiet a minute," Elijah's voice stilled them all. "Someone's coming."

On a shift of the afternoon breeze, Mal heard the jangle of bridles, a snatch of a conversation. He joined Elijah looking down over the porch toward the path from the lodge.

A flash of color glinted in the trees. A golden horse broke into the clearing below them, its fine white mane no match for the silver-blond hair under its rider's twilight blue hat. Several paces behind the first horse a fine-boned brown mare pranced, annoyed with the restraining hand of the jeans-clad figure on her back. They led a third horse, a coffee-colored bay with a sure step.

Beside Mal, Loki's heavy, arched tail began to thump.

The second woman's hat hung down her back, bouncing against her tangled brown hair in rhythm with the mare's gait. Mal's mouth curved in a smile. He'd have to be sure to tell her how young she looked like that. Battlement Park hadn't been quite the same with Harriet Jackson's temper gone.

His smile faded. Harry was supposed to be in Oxtail, preparing to be married.

Mal had hoped, hearing the news of Harry's betrothal, that she had recovered from the infatuation with his brother that had been so painfully obvious to him at Elijah and Jordan's wedding. Yet here she was, riding up to 'Lije's cabin, looking flustered and ragged—were those pine needles in her hair?—with no sign of a fiancé in her wake.

If the man had hurt her . . . He wrestled down his anger in favor of a more accustomed cynicism. A rat of a fiancé would be easier to deal with than Harry returning to beg Elijah to leave his wife and run away with her.

Unexpectedly, that image brought the anger back. As he

glared down at the approaching women, unnoticed details began to catch his eye. The woman in front—Jordan's cousin Nicky? No, too silver blond. Besides, Nicky had returned to Denver with her husband and new baby just a week before. The woman in front was forging up the hill with ramrod determination while Harry hung behind, not even raising her eyes to the group on the porch. Her mouth, always too wide to make the pert bow she'd envied in Nicky, was set in a grim line that suggested she'd rather be riding to her own execution.

She didn't want to see Elijah at all. Maybe her heart was still broken, but that hadn't squashed her pride.

Mal's smile returned. Harriet Jackson was back in Battlement Park. That ought to liven the place up. She would scandalize the handful of European guests squeezing the last warm days out of September at the Fox and Hound. She'd put Tony in his place. Maybe she'd even give Mal the opportunity to win back the silver dollar he'd lost in that sharpshooting contest.

Perhaps he'd been wrong. Apple pie and a contest of wits with Harry. The perfect afternoon was looking up after all.

"Harry's brought Rover," Elijah said. His eyes narrowed. "And that's Honey."

"An old girlfriend?" Tony asked with a wicked grin.

"The horse," Elijah growled. "The palomino. One of March and Maggie's horses. I don't know the woman." He paused. "I don't *think* I know her. There's something about her, though."

Elijah's troubled tone turned Mal's attention from Harry back to the other woman. Riding sidesaddle up the Rocky Mountains. He shook his head. Nice clothes, undoubtedly the latest fashion. But a little the worse for wear. It occurred to him that both she and Harry had apparently slept in their current attire the night before, and not in a feather bed, either.

Blond hair, fair skin. He couldn't see much more under that swooping hat, but . . . Elijah's unease was catching. There was something about her that raised Mal's hackles.

Tiring of her battle with her impatient mare, Harry finally let the horse prance up beside the other visitor as the two women trotted up to the cabin.

"Harry!" Jordan exclaimed. "What a wonderful surprise!"

Mal heard genuine warmth in her voice. Jordan was not the type to hold an adolescent crush on her husband against the young woman who had helped to save her life.

Jordan checked her tea pot. "Tony, bring out two more chairs for the ladies. They look like they could use a seat and some refreshment. Mal, hold those horses for them."

At this, of course, Harry swung herself down from her own horse with a flash of challenging blue eyes. But the other woman let him take her reins as he reached the bottom of the porch steps.

"Malachi," she said, her soft voice barely audible, even in the quiet mountain afternoon. "Don't you recognize me?"

A shiver worked its way up Mal's spine as he tilted his head back to look up into her face, its pale, porcelain beauty framed by the stylish hat. Bruises. A nasty slash made by a knife, or a razor. Unfamiliar tension in the jaw, unfamiliar sharpness along the cheekbones.

But those gray eyes, the darkest, most expressive features in that lovely face, those eyes were most definitely familiar.

"Lissy?" He'd felt this same shocked terror the time as a kid he'd grabbed a garter snake to scare the girls at school and discovered he held a baby cottonmouth in his hand.

"Hell." He should have been content with the afternoon he'd been living. This new one he suddenly found himself in boded nothing but trouble. "Hell and damnation. It's Lissy Wilmer."

Chapter 4

Lissy lowered her lashes to hide her dismay at the greeting. She should not have expected anything else from Malachi. It was his brother she had come to beg from. She imagined both Kelly brothers would enjoy the sight of Lissy Wilmer groveling, but at least Elijah would be too polite to show it.

But she didn't have time for self-pity, anger, or shame. She would stand her ground against them all. Or rather, she would once she got down from her horse.

"Malachi Kelly," she said, offering him her hand and her sweetest smile. "I do declare, you are as charming as ever."

As he helped her off the mare, she tilted her head up toward the group on the porch. Yes, Elijah was there, a taller, leaner version of Malachi, standing beside a well-dressed blond man and a tall, dark-haired woman. Elijah's expression, always more hooded than Mal's, did not even show surprise at her sudden arrival on his doorstep.

"Elizabeth," he said. Not cool. Neutral. "Woodfin now, isn't it?"

"Where are your brothers?" Mal demanded. "I hope you haven't brought them with you. I don't have my vermin traps handy."

"You should be careful how you talk about her relatives," Harry said beside her, her cool blue eyes lingering on Lissy. "She told us you and Elijah were her brothers."

Lissy's stomach twisted at the disappointment in her voice. Perhaps she should have tried to explain the lie to Harry during their ride that morning, when it seemed the young woman might be warming to her. But Harry's good will didn't matter. Only Elijah's did. And she had to re-ignite any he'd ever felt for her immediately.

She would never pull this off if she faltered at a little lying and manipulating. Her name might be Woodfin now, but she was still a Wilmer.

"Brothers in affection only," she said, fluttering her lashes to make the most of the all-too-real blush suffusing her cheeks. She decided to ignore Malachi's snort. "I'm so very sorry for the deceit and the abuse of your kindness, Harry, but I didn't know any other way to find Elijah and Malachi. They are truly my only hope."

She risked a glance at Elijah, but his golden eyes were flat as ever. This could take more luck and cunning than escaping Spider Grant and his thugs.

"Don't leave the ladies standing there," the tall woman on the porch broke into the uncomfortable silence. When she moved to the stairs, Lissy saw that her skirt, striped with purple and blue flowers, was split for riding over baggy bloomers, her mud-spattered boots belying the cool elegance of her face. "Come up here and sit before you tell your tale—Elizabeth, is it? You look like you could use some tea. You, too, Harry. Mal will take care of the horses."

Lissy picked her way up the porch stairs behind Harry, clinging gingerly to the axe-hewn handrail, her broken boots awkward on the rough planks. She hoped someone at the hotel down the high mountain valley—or the Park, as

Harry had called it—would be able to nail the heels back on. She couldn't afford new shoes, any more than she could afford satisfaction at Malachi's dour expression as he led the two horses behind the cabin.

The woman on the porch gave Harry a warm hug, which Harry took with an odd look of embarrassment. The woman was older than Harry, Lissy noticed, perhaps a year or two older than herself, with hints of lines at the corners of her eyelids and a depth to the sapphire blue of her eyes that came only from surviving sorrow. The eyes smiled though, as she reached a hand to take Lissy's.

"Welcome," she said. "I'm Jordan Kelly."

"Kelly? Mal's *married?*" Lissy asked, instantly cursing herself for the rudeness, but the shock—

"She's Elijah's wife," Harry's voice had no echo of Jordan Kelly's warmth in it. "I'm sorry I can't introduce her, Jordan. I don't even know her real name."

"Elizabeth Woodfin *is* my real name," Lissy said, keeping tight control of her own temper. "Naming Elijah and Malachi my brothers was the only liberty I took with the truth."

God apparently decided not to strike her dead for that blatant falsehood. Which was a considerable relief, since she didn't intend it to be her last. These people were not her friends or family—just as well, considering that all she'd gotten from her family and friends was betrayal.

These strangers had no reason to help her other than self-interest, so that was what she had to awaken, whatever it took—with a little sweet southern honey to help it along.

"Elizabeth Woodfin was still little Lissy Wilmer when I left home," Elijah said. "Our families were practically neighbors in Charleston."

Jordan's brow furrowed as she looked at her husband.

"Wilmer? Isn't that the name of those boys—" She glanced at Lissy. "No. Your brothers aren't *the* Wilmer brothers."

"The very same," Elijah said, the smile on his lips never reaching his eyes.

"Who are the Wilmer brothers?" Harry asked, with the forced good humor of someone who's been left out of the joke.

"The bane of my childhood," Elijah drawled carelessly, though Lissy thought she saw the calm in his eyes flicker. " 'They gaped upon me with their mouths as a ravening and a roaring lion.' Clayton Wilmer was two years older than I, and twice as big. Rafe was younger, but grew faster. They taught me how to run and to watch my back. I owe much of the success of my gunfighting career to the Wilmer boys."

"They were bullies," Malachi growled from behind Lissy. She had hoped he'd be longer taking care of the horses. "They were rotten, ugly bullies when they were boys. And they're rotten, ugly thugs now they're grown. I suppose it's too much to hope for that they finally bullied the wrong man and got a rope around their necks."

"Must you, Mal?" the blond man beside Elijah broke in with resigned frustration. He smiled at Lissy. "Forgive his manners. He hasn't any."

English accent, Lissy noticed, upper class. But not stuffy. His wheat-colored hair fell carelessly around his face like a mussed boy's, and his brown eyes were brightened by a gold glint of humor. It was the eyes that gave character to his clean, even features, as his clothes made the most of his lean, muscled frame.

Too handsome for her own good. Perhaps at one time in her life, she would have been dazzled by such a smile. But she had learned the hard way that good looks meant nothing without good character beneath them. This Englishman would not find her easy to charm.

"Elizabeth, may I introduce Major Anthony Wayne." Elijah proved his manners were a cut above his brother's. "Tony, Mrs. Elizabeth Woodfin."

"A pleasure to meet you, Mrs. Woodfin." He took her hand and raised it to his lips, a gesture that should have been laughably pretentious, but which his exuberant good humor turned engaging. He kept her hand in his a fraction of a second longer, the warmth sending a shiver up Lissy's arm.

She rescued her hand. If the devil danced behind those warm brown eyes, well, she had been trained to waltz with the best of them.

"Major Wayne. The pleasure is all mine."

"Tony, please."

Her smile was cool. *Not a chance, Major.*

"There, Mal, is that so hard?" Tony asked.

"Manners are no excuse for avoiding the truth," Malachi said. Lissy remembered that stubborn set to his mouth. Even Clay and Rafe had never managed to pound it out of him. "The Wilmer brothers are brutal criminals. They would have hanged on general principle long ago if their father wasn't a judge."

Tony gave Lissy an apologetic smile. "They *are* the lady's brothers."

"Mal is welcome to waste his breath on my brothers," Lissy said, knowing too well that circumstances forced her to share Malachi's focus on grim reality. "But Clay and Rafe are back in Savannah. He might put his energy to better use setting out those traps he talked about. Another set of vermin aren't far behind me, and they have very sharp teeth."

The fire in the heavy iron stove filled the cabin with cozy

warmth, but Lissy could feel the breath of fall whispering to her from the corners of the room. As Harry had repeatedly warned her during their ride the day before, temperatures dropped fast in the mountains when the sun went down. Lissy suppressed a shiver, along with the roiling in her stomach.

Jordan had insisted Lissy's story wait until everyone had been properly fed, but it wasn't the rich venison stew, complete with fluffy dumplings and a helping of steaming apple pie, that twisted her insides. This tale she was about to tell was her last chance. She had to tell it right.

Elijah and Malachi had pushed the narrow dining table against one rough-hewn wall of the cabin's main room after supper, but six people and one enormous, big-toothed wolf crowded the living space. Jordan and Elijah had sat on one of the table benches with Loki curled on their feet and had insisted that Lissy take the gold and black upholstered settee. No one had joined her. The blond Englishman lounged in the armchair beside the settee, Harry sat straight-backed as a judge in a slatted chair beneath the window, and Malachi brooded darkly by the door.

Lissy grimly took advantage of her outcast state. She held court in the center of the settee, arranging her travel-stained blue dress so it shimmered with quicksilver highlights in the flickering lamplight. The stage had been set, and she planned to deliver the best performance of her life.

Her life depended on it. But that was a small matter compared to the stakes she played for.

"The Beasts work for my husband. Or at least Spider Grant does." She kept her voice soft, despite the fear and anger edging it, drawing her audience in as they strained to listen. "Spider probably hired the others. Off the docks or out of the sewers. Wherever beasts usually come from.

"I learned soon after my marriage that Charm, my husband, was not the man I'd thought. But I had sworn an oath for better or for worse." Her voice faded away. The silence could tell them all they needed to know of betrayal and lost love.

"I did make the best of it," she continued, unable to hide the hint of hard pride. "For almost eleven years."

"Eleven years?" Jordan echoed. "You must have married very young."

"Seventeen."

Against her will, Lissy's gaze flicked toward Malachi, searching for the accusation in his eyes. His uncharacteristic silence unnerved her.

She broke her gaze away. "I made the best of it," she repeated. Even the disappointment, the hurt, the slow knowledge that the man she had chosen to be her husband had neither love nor strength of character for her to lean on, all of that had still been better than what she had left at home, her father's violent temper, her mother's acquiescence to it.

"I tried to be a good wife. But money caused us trouble from the beginning." That statement was true enough. She had to make the rest equally convincing. "I had received a considerable inheritance from my grandfather in the form of a trust. Charm was furious that he couldn't touch the principal, so he expected me to run the household on the income.

"My other grandfather, my mother's father, lost everything during the war, and since he died, my grandmother has scarcely been able to afford food for the table. She refused to ask my father for money—not that he'd have helped her if she had." Lissy clenched her teeth against the familiar anger. "She is only a Cally, not a Wilmer. My mother and I did what we could. She was too proud to move in with me and Charm, even if she wasn't a Wilmer."

"Sometimes all a woman has of her own is pride," Jordan said.

For a moment, the compassion in the woman's voice tempted Lissy to tell the whole truth, to believe that kindness and justice could bring her audience to her cause. She raised a hand to her temple. Perhaps she was losing her mind. Had she learned nothing from Charm?

She leaned forward, pushing on with her tale. "I couldn't let my grandmother starve. I sent her what I could save out of my household expenses each week, and I sold some jewelry, too. Charm liked to show me off wearing a new bauble at every occasion. I thought he'd never miss a few of the smaller pieces."

"He didn't like you selling his jewels behind his back," Elijah concluded dryly. He sat on the bench beside his wife, his legs stretched out in front of him, his thick dark hair carelessly ruffled. He looked relaxed, almost lazy. But Lissy read the skepticism in the tautness of his mouth.

"Charm gave me that jewelry. I didn't steal it." Lissy's voice flared, before she caught it. "When he found out I'd sold it, he went wild. He sold the rest of the jewelry. He convinced my father to force the bank to turn my inheritance over to him, and he told me that if I didn't pay him back every cent I'd given my grandmother, he'd sell me, too, down on the docks like a common whore."

She stopped, her breathing hard in her fury, cheeks flaming in shame. She hadn't meant to say that. Even if the threat had been made.

"You had to know he'd be angry," Harry said. "Or you would have told him what you were doing."

"I knew it." Lissy agreed. And Charm certainly would have been furious about her selling the jewelry for her grandmother. If he'd had a chance to find out about it. "Maybe I even guessed what he was capable of, but I did it anyway. What wouldn't you risk for the one person you love most in the world?"

In the flash of Harry's eyes, Lissy saw the answer she expected from the young woman. Harry would risk whatever it took. Just as Lissy was doing.

"I had to leave," Lissy continued. "Charm knew I couldn't pay him back. He didn't want me to pay him back. He wanted to hurt me. I was so desperate I went to my father's house." She still could not believe she had asked her father for help. What a fool she had been. "He told me I'd made my own bed and I'd better lie in it. There was no one in Savannah to help me. I waited until Charm left on a business trip, and then I went back to Charleston to my grandmother's house. That's where the Beasts found me."

She brushed an impatient hand across the bruises on her face. "The Rat, the one with the teeth, hit me. He said he didn't mean to leave a mark on my face, but I fought back when he punched me in the ribs. The Fox, the red-headed man, he's the one who cut me. He said if I didn't meet my obligations, he'd make it so no one ever wanted to look at my face again."

"Any man who strikes a woman is a coward," Tony Wayne said, his voice tight. "A man who would hire other men to hit his wife is a bloody cur."

Lissy pushed on, though the truth was harder to tell, the words dry and hot in her throat. "Rat and Fox stole everything of value left in my grandmother's house. They said if I couldn't find more, they would be back for me. I believed them."

"They didn't catch you, though," Jordan said, reaching out across the lounging wolf-dog to squeeze Lissy's wrist.

Lissy looked down at Jordan's hand, and the first tear stained her cheek.

"Mrs. Woodfin." Tony offered her a fawn-colored handkerchief, and she pressed it to her eyes, struggling for control.

"I ran." She cleared her throat, tried again. "My grandmother didn't want me to leave, but I couldn't bring danger to her. Charm won't let me go. I knew the Beasts would have orders to bring me home. I was right. I saw them in Cheyenne, looking for me. Fox and Rat and Spider Grant. I have nothing left. If they catch me, they won't stop at a beating."

She clenched Tony's kerchief until her knuckles turned white. "I don't intend to let them catch me."

"Why did you come looking for me and Malachi?" Elijah asked. "I can't imagine the name Kelly is fondly spoken in Charleston, even now."

"I was desperate." She could not keep the wryness from her voice. "No one else in Charleston or Savannah would dare to help me, not if my father and brothers would not. And your father always helped those in trouble."

"If they could survive the trouble he was always in," Elijah said. "And the sermon that went with it. 'Blessed are you, when men shall revile you, and persecute you, and shall say all manner of evil against you falsely, for my sake.' "

A smile pulled at the corners of her mouth. He sounded just like the Reverend. She could imagine it had not been easy for Reverend Kelly's young, motherless sons to live with the man's righteous convictions, but he had seemed the model of a good man to her, perhaps partly because her father hated him, but also because he had always taken time to listen to her troubles, even when they must have seemed terribly trivial compared to his own.

"It's not much of a secret anymore that your father helped slaves disappear before the war," she said. "Reverend Kelly was never afraid to seek justice for those who could not seek it for themselves."

"Even if true justice runs counter to the letter of the law," Elijah acknowledged with the faintest of smiles.

As it would in the case of a woman running from her lawful husband. Lissy nodded.

"I thought . . . I don't know what I thought, but when he told me you were in Colorado, it seemed I was being given a chance where I'd had none. I remembered how chivalrous you were to me as a little girl, despite my brothers.

"Perhaps it was a foolish notion, but I was at wit's end. All I could think of was finding you and begging for your help." Lissy's mouth twisted bitterly. "And I *am* begging."

"What help are you begging for?" Elijah asked, his eyes flat and unreadable in the lantern light.

"You're quite safe here in Battlement Park, Mrs. Woodfin," Tony assured her grimly. "If those blighters look for you here, we'll give them a capital send-off, I promise you."

"We?" Elijah drawled, a panther's purr. "I assume 'we' are also going to provide free room and board for her at the Fox and Hound."

"As long as necessary," Tony agreed.

She met the Englishman's eyes directly, searching for his motive. He didn't even know her. What did he expect in return?

Jordan squeezed her wrist again and let her go. The woman's smile could be almost as dangerous as Elijah's. "I don't think Elijah will have any trouble taking care of a couple of bullying thugs."

"They'd have to get past me before Elijah got a crack at them," Tony said, with a bland smile that did not hide the simmering anger in his eyes.

"And what about the next pack of rats?" Lissy demanded, fighting exhaustion and surrender. It would be so easy to quit now. To rest in the care of these strangers until they tired of her and threw her out. But her own safety meant nothing if she didn't complete her task. "The sewers of Savannah have more than their share of vermin. These won't be the last. I can't hide here forever. And I won't live on charity."

"What are you asking for then?" Elijah asked.

Lissy gathered her resolve. "I want you to come with me when I face Charm."

"Face him?" Jordan repeated. "He's threatened your life."

"He's taken my life," Lissy corrected, feeling the fire once more. "And I intend to take it back from him."

"Beard the lion in his den." Tony considered that. "I do see the appeal. A few minutes with our Preacher Kelly would undoubtedly put the old boy in a more godly frame of mind."

"My brother may be many things, but he is not a thug for hire," Malachi said, his first words that evening all the more dangerous for their quiet tone.

"I don't want violence," Lissy said. Maybe she did, but it would be counterproductive. "All I want is for Charm to call off his Beasts and return the money he stole from me. I need help asking."

But Elijah was already shaking his head. "I am the town marshal here in Battlement Park," he said. "And I've agreed to guide a group to the top of Battlement Peak before the snow starts. I am sorry for your trouble, Lissy, but I cannot leave my responsibilities. We can keep you safe if you wish to stay here, but that is all I can promise."

"No. Please." Lissy leaned forward, clutching Tony's handkerchief like a talisman. "Hear me out. The money Charm stole from me is considerable. I need very little for myself. Just enough to live on and to help my grandmother. It would not take much of your time, and I would pay you as much as you make as town marshal in a year. In two years."

"You married Charm. Legally it's his money," Malachi said. "I wouldn't be so generous with it if I were you."

"It is *not* Charm's money," Lissy said hotly, almost forgetting she had invented it. "My grandfather put it in a trust. It was to go to our children." Her voice broke on the word, but she pushed on. "And if we had no children, it was to go to my brothers. If I get it back from Charm, they won't challenge me for it."

At the moment, she would have said anything to convince them. But what came out was the simple truth. "I have no one else to turn to."

Jordan turned troubled eyes to her husband. "Elijah?"

To Lissy's surprise, she saw the hardness in his expression soften.

"There must be something," his wife said.

"I can't leave my responsibilities," he said. He sighed and looked at his brother. "Malachi, would you—"

"No!" The word burst from her. "Please, Elijah. It wouldn't take long."

"With our outlaw population dwindling, and the hotel business dying down for the winter," Tony said speculatively, "neither Malachi nor I are particularly busy at the moment."

Lissy shook her head. Even if she were desperate enough

to ask, Malachi would never agree to help her. "Not Malachi."

She could not help a glance at him, in the shadows by the door. She was surprised to catch the faintest flicker of disquiet cross his grim face.

Tony coughed. "Mal may be a bit . . . difficult, but he knows which end of a gun to point at the villains. We don't have the same fierce mien as 'Lije, but—"

"Oh, honestly!" Harry's voice silenced the room. "This is ridiculous. None of you can go running off to Savannah to threaten anyone. First of all, you'd probably get arrested. Second, you don't have any proof she's even telling you the truth. Third—"

"Harriet, please," Tony said, but Malachi interrupted brusquely.

"Harry's right. No one is going to Georgia on Lissy Wilmer's wild goose chase. I'd cut off my own foot before I'd set it down in Savannah again."

Lissy caught her breath to compose herself, though she could feel her arms shaking with tension. "Charm's not in Savannah. Didn't I tell you he was away on business?"

There was no help for it now. She was desperate enough, after all. She turned the full force of her plea on Malachi. "I did not travel here from Savannah on a whim to ask for help. When your father said Elijah was in Colorado, it seemed almost divine providence. At least worth the chance.

"If you come with me to find Charm, you won't be away from home for more than a couple of days. He's right here in Colorado. Charm is in Denver."

Lissy shut the outhouse door behind her and took a deep breath to settle her stomach. Even the air in Colorado tasted foreign. The humid atmosphere of Savannah carried a rich tapestry of scents, heavy floral sweetness woven with human activity and animal waste and a hint of sea salt. This thin mountain air whispered only of pines and snow and emptiness.

The very stars seemed strange above her. Smaller, sharper, strewn with outrageous largesse across the infinite sky.

Charm had refused to hunt with her brothers. He hated the dense, close, Georgia woods, the ancient, moss-hung trees. He said they felt haunted. Lissy thought so, too, but that had never bothered her. Despite the snakes and bugs and beasts, she had felt wrapped in a cloak of sympathetic spirits.

Here, there was nothing to stand between her and the inhuman wilderness. Nothing to stand between her and God. Not a pleasant feeling, given the current state of her soul.

Still, if God could hear the pounding of her heart as clearly as she could, perhaps he would hear a prayer. *Let them help, Lord. I have no one else to turn to.* She couldn't ask it for herself. But she could ask it for those she loved.

At least they had not refused her yet. Tony had promised she would have an answer the next morning. She couldn't quench the fear that by morning he would have recovered from the bout of chivalry he had suffered from all evening. But he was the only one who could convince Malachi to aid her, and if she couldn't have Elijah's deadly poise, she needed Malachi's blunt tenacity.

She shifted the lantern in her hand and began picking her way back toward Elijah and Jordan's cabin, a slow process in her broken boots.

As she came around the side of the building, she heard

Malachi's voice from the porch. He'd pitched it low, but the frustration carried.

"Hell and damnation, Tony, Lissy Wilmer is trouble. She was trouble when she was five, and she's trouble now. All you're seeing is a pretty face."

Lissy paused, shuttering her lantern. Compared to her recent actions, eavesdropping was a minor sin.

"I see a lady in distress," Tony's voice replied calmly. "Who has nowhere else to go."

"And would you still be playing her knight errant if she didn't have silver hair and a sweet smile? I was afraid you were going to start drooling in there."

Lissy could almost hear Malachi's teeth grinding. She edged forward toward the edge of the porch, hoping to see the two men.

"Have you ever known me to be discourteous to a woman regardless of her attractiveness?"

"I've certainly never known a woman who could resist your courteousness," Malachi growled. He grunted. "Except maybe Harry."

"Harry adores me!"

"Harry humors you. But that's not the point. Elizabeth Woodfin is not one of your widowed countesses or sophisticated baronesses, Tony. She's a married woman with a load of trouble on her trail. She's not someone you can romance for a week and send back home."

The front of Lissy's slick boot sole came down on a rock and slipped out from under her. She skidded forward, the lantern clattering like the pots in a restaurant kitchen as she desperately tried to regain her balance.

She managed to gather her feet under her and collect her dignity for the short walk forward to where Malachi and Tony stood at the base of the porch stairs.

She tilted her head for a humorless smile at Malachi. "I declare, I wouldn't have expected such a defense from you. I thank you for trying to protect my good name, but I'm afraid you're a little late. I've already run away from my husband and been disowned by my father. I have very little reputation left."

"I'm not concerned for your reputation in the slightest." Malachi's eyes were black as the night. "I don't give a damn what other people think of you. I know what I think. And Tony's the one I intend to protect."

He turned to his friend. "The man who gets involved with a Wilmer is sledding for trouble down an avalanche. I don't want you to be that man."

With a last dark glance at Lissy, he stalked away into the night, with neither moon nor lantern to guide him.

If she'd had a better week, Lissy might have cried. But at this point, Malachi's contempt barely rated a headache.

"Was he always like this?" Tony wryly broke the awkward silence.

Lissy dredged up a smile. "The Reverend told me once that Malachi interrupted him in the middle of an Easter morning service to tell him he'd gotten the order of a baptism wrong. Mal was four years old at the time. I don't remember him ever being afraid to speak his mind."

But she didn't remembered this hostility. She remembered a boy who had given her half his stick of candy when Rafe knocked her down and skinned her knee. She remembered a young man who had burned his hands pulling her bumbling, drunken uncle out of the fire he'd helped her brothers start while trying to burn down Malachi's father's church.

Malachi Kelly had his reasons for distrusting her. For his bitterness toward her. But nothing she had ever done explained his anger and bitterness toward the world.

"You must be tired," Tony said. "You've said your goodnights to the Kellys. Why don't you let me escort you down to the Fox and Hound. I promise you won't find a room with a prettier view in all of Colorado."

"Why, that sounds lovely, Major Wayne."

"Tony, please." He took her lantern and offered her his free arm with a smile that dazzled the eyes. Given a choice between taking the arm of a charming devil or sliding on her rear end down the hill, she gave in to temptation.

Perhaps Malachi was right about women being unable to resist Tony's courtesy, or perhaps the wildness of their surroundings had infected her, but her own smile felt incorrigibly wicked. She tilted a glance up at him as they started down the path. "Anthony Wayne. Tell me, are you as mad as your namesake?"

"It's rather hard to have people assume one is mad before they have a chance to know one and discover it's true." Tony's tone was rueful, but the soft lantern light caught the impish glint in his eye. "My father called me Anthony after my maternal grandfather. It was a great disappointment to him to discover he had inadvertently associated his second son with a rebel American general. And I have continued to be a great disappointment to him ever since."

The lantern illuminated only a few feet of the path in front of them, throwing startling shadows of tree limbs through the surrounding forest. The contrast with Tony's cultured voice and polished manners was only sharpened by her observation that he wore a gun belt beneath his military style overcoat. She could see the butt of the revolver when the coat swung with his stride.

"What brings a man like you to a wilderness like this?" she asked. "Why do you run a hotel in Battlement Park?"

Tony grimaced. "The hotel is my father's idea. He didn't appreciate having a son earning his living as a hunting guide, so he built this resort and installed me here. Exiled, but still under his thumb. I've disappointed him yet again by making a success of the place."

"Exile?"

Tony's gaze met hers, briefly stripped of superficial pleasantry. For a second his genial, urbane facade slipped, leaving him looking younger. Vulnerable.

Lissy sternly subdued the sympathetic jolt in her heart.

"It's an unpleasant story." He guided her around a protruding root. "A young lady of my parents' acquaintance got herself into trouble and decided I would make a better catch than the gentleman she had been seeing. My father said I could either do the honorable thing or resign my commission and leave the country, never to return.

"Since I had not impugned the lady's honor in any way, I did not think it honorable to perpetuate her deception. My definition of honor was not the same as my father's." His smile held only enough humor to cut the edge of his words. "Mal was not precisely telling you the truth when he said he was not concerned for your reputation."

Meeting his sober gaze, Lissy felt an insane impulse to smooth the furrows from his forehead, as she had comforted another troubled brow not so long ago, though it felt like a lifetime. Fortunately, her boot hit a slick patch of needles, and she had to clutch his arm to keep her feet.

"Are you all right? Jolly good." He helped her down a washed out portion of the path. She could see the lights of the hotel lodge not far ahead. "My honor is important to me, despite those who believe I haven't got any. I hope you will accept my word on it that yours is safe with me."

Malachi had as much as said that Tony was a lady's

man. His own story did not dispel the idea. Yet there was something in his self-deprecating honesty that tempted her to believe him. Even to trust him.

A rush of near terror poured through her veins. She was not going to make that mistake again.

"I thank you," she said quietly, politely noncommittal, though her pulse fluttered in her throat. She was going to have to watch herself around this Englishman.

He was a very dangerous devil indeed.

Chapter 5

Harry sat on a rock a hundred yards from the cabin, Loki's head heavy and warm on her lap. The lights in the cabin above had gone out half an hour before, and the night air had chilled her despite the thick wool coat she'd thrown over the lilac-striped muslin dress she'd changed into for supper. But the thought of turning in for the night in the tiny spare room next to the bedroom where Elijah and Jordan slept kept her sitting in the cold.

The moon showed only a sliver of silver, but its soft light kissed the dark trees and meadows below her. The stars burned cold and bright, shimmering on the meandering creek, shaming the mountaintops in their shabby, patched coats of snow. Winter would cloak them in ermine finery soon enough, but for now the sky and the water had stolen their glory.

Harry pulled in a lungful of frosty air, but it couldn't cool the ache in her heart. Tony's convincing Elijah, and even Malachi, to consider Lissy's plea for help had infuriated her. The woman was a liar and a confidence artist. At best. Frustration still simmered in Harry's gut.

But sitting alone with only Loki and her dark thoughts for company, a small, quiet voice in her heart had begun to whisper that maybe Lissy Woodfin was not the source of her discontent.

She shook her head to silence it.

Loki puffed a heavy breath from his nostrils and raised his head, ears twitching. He turned his nose toward the trail to the Fox and Hound, the lodge's rectangular bulk lost in the distant dark of the trees.

Harry kept her fingers buried in the fur on Loki's neck, alert for a growl, her own ears straining for the sound that had alerted the wolf.

She had thought the night quiet just a moment before. Now, the sigh of a breeze in the trees, the rustle of a mouse in the grass, the song of the creek suddenly filled her ears.

But she was used to filtering the sounds of the night for the groan of a mare in labor, the cough of a mountain lion, the breathing of her brother camped beside her. She heard the faint scrape of boots on pebbles as a shadow detached from the trees below, making its way up the hill toward her.

Loki snuffed again, then settled his head back on Harry's thigh. Tony's fair hair would have caught the moonlight, so . . .

"Malachi?"

"That's a great place for you to sit. Exposed like a marmot on a mountaintop. If I had been one of Lissy's Beasts, I could have caught you before you got halfway to the cabin."

"You could not."

His eyes flashed for a second as he took a switchback in the trail. "Before you got a quarter of the way. You probably wouldn't make it a hundred feet running uphill in that dress."

"I wouldn't have to run," Harry said primly. "Loki would have your throat out before you even got close."

Malachi reached her rock and looked down at the wolf beside her. Loki's silver eyes flickered at him briefly, then closed with a sigh.

"I'm shaking in my boots."

"Careful," Harry warned, her irritation reawakening Loki's eyes. "He likes me better than he likes you."

Malachi snorted. "Doesn't everyone?"

He rested a hip against her rock and reached into his coat. Metal flashed moonlight from his hand. He unscrewed the cap and took a swig.

She could smell the whiskey then, a faint sourness on his breath. She had never liked the scent of liquor. It reminded her of her father, a sad, empty smell. Yet there was something about the warmth of it from Malachi's mouth on the cold night air that made her skin prickle.

"What are you doing?" she demanded.

"Forgetting." The blandness of his tone irritated her.

"That's not going to help you. My father drank himself into a stupor every night and never once forgot to wish he was with our dead mother instead of us."

Her tone warned him against sympathy, and she was glad he knew her well enough not to offer it. "What happened?"

"After ten years of being drunk, he got his wish."

Malachi nodded. "That's a bit more trouble than these memories are worth." He offered her the flask. "Want some? You're right; it's not doing me any good."

"I can just picture Mrs. Danforth's face at the thought of one of her pupils drinking malt whiskey from a flask."

"Mrs. Danforth?"

"The headmistress at Danforth's Finishing School for Young Ladies in Philadelphia. Jane and March sent me there after I broke my arm trying to rope my brother's herd stallion. They thought I was too delicate for ranch work."

"Delicate?" Malachi's free fingers closed briefly around the muscle of her upper arm. He grunted. "And did Mrs. Danforth finish you?"

"As a young lady," Harry answered. She took the flask he offered to distract herself from the strangely unsettling warmth of his touch. She tilted the narrow opening to her lips, misjudging the fullness of the flask. More liquid splashed down her chin than down her throat.

"Gack." She choked, fire burning into her lungs and up her nose. Coughing and snorting, she thrust the flask back at Malachi.

"Very ladylike," he commented.

"You *drink* that? It tastes like turpentine."

"You've drunk turpentine?"

Harry tried to give him a quelling look, but it still hurt to breathe. "Now I have."

He shook his head. "Taos Lightning."

Her eyes narrowed. "Tony doesn't serve Taos Lightning at the Fox and Hound."

Despite the dark, she could see his amusement. "That's why I like it." Yet he twisted the cap back on his flask and stuck it back into his coat pocket.

Loki sighed, and silence settled around them. Though it wasn't settled, Harry thought. The atmosphere of the night had changed. Perhaps it was the whiskey burning her stomach that warmed the breath of the wind, that sharpened the rustlings in the grass.

Loki must have felt the sudden charging of the air, for he raised his head, his gray-fringed ears swiveling as his nose tested the breeze. Once more, Harry put a hand on his neck, but this time he didn't relax. Instead, he flowed to his feet, suddenly huge beside her, his eyes gleaming briefly, savagely red.

His stance relaxed briefly as he turned to swipe his tongue across Harry's ear. Then he was gone, his leap from the rock almost soundless, though she could feel the impact as his lean ninety pounds hit the ground six feet away. The wolf didn't glance back, his nose turned into the wind as he slipped like a shadow into the trees.

The wind shifted, and Harry smelled whiskey again, whiskey and the faint hint of sweat and soap and horse from the silent man lurking beside her. He sat staring down the mountain, so still and intent on his thoughts that she wondered if he had forgotten she was there.

Not a mistake she would make. Even in his stillness he radiated energy into the night. Suddenly aware of the depth of the darkness around them, Harry's heart thumped harder.

Silly goose. She wasn't afraid of the dark. Not as long as she could see the stars and breathe clean air. The root cellar was a different story, but she was not afraid of the night.

And she certainly wasn't afraid of Malachi Kelly. She'd spent an entire week that past June riding with him, tracking Lucifer Jones's outlaw gang, a right she'd won by besting Malachi in a sharpshooting contest. She could shoot rings around him with a rifle. She could ride as well as he could, saddle a horse just as fast, rope better and skin a rabbit cleaner. He was a better tracker, but she was learning.

An entire week. Was that really all the time they'd spent on that hunt? It seemed like longer, the time spent in easy camaraderie with Malachi, Tony, Wolf, and Elijah, the friendship with Jordan and Nicky, a feeling that would stay with her for the rest of her life.

Ash had never heard of the Harry who had ridden as a member of Malachi's posse. The ache in her heart expanded as she realized she would never tell him about that Harry. There was no point. That Harry was dead, a memory.

She glanced toward Malachi. He had barely acknowledged her at all that evening. She had felt like a ghost, watching the others listen to Lissy's story. Like the ghost she'd seen in Jane's wedding dress.

Now, suddenly, she felt real again, much too real, flesh and blood disturbingly aware of Malachi's presence beside her.

He was not as tall as his brother, hardly taller than Jordan. But even leaning against the rock, his legs stretched out in front of him, he was taller than Harry. She hadn't noticed before how broad his shoulders were or how his upper arms filled out the sleeves of his coat. How strong his thighs looked, tensed against the slope of the hill.

She wished he would break the silence. Mrs. Danforth had repeatedly assured her pupils that gentlemen liked nothing better than to talk about themselves, but Harry didn't quite dare to ask Malachi about his father, his brother, or what had happened to him during his time in the Seventh Cavalry. Though she suddenly wanted to know. She wondered if his past would explain the lack of grace in his manner, the darkness that sometimes haunted his eyes, the tension she suddenly felt in his presence.

She shivered.

"You're cold."

"No." It unsettled her that he had been as closely aware of her as she had been of him.

He turned to look at her. She couldn't see his expression

clearly, only the gleam of his eyes. "Why did you come out here?"

"I knew I couldn't sleep. I needed some peace and quiet."

"No." He ran a hand through his thick, dark hair, his tone uncharacteristically uncertain. "I mean here in Battlement Park. Why did you come back?"

"I thought it would be bad for my soul to let Elizabeth Woodfin get lost in the mountains and die an agonizing, lonely death. Perhaps I was wrong."

"Where's your fiancé?" he asked. "He didn't mind you traipsing off into the wilderness right before your wedding?"

"He doesn't—" Harry caught herself. "He doesn't mind."

One dark eyebrow crept up Malachi's face. "He doesn't know, you mean."

"He does so." *Great comeback, Harry.* She took a breath to cool her flustered nerves. "Not that it's any of your damn business."

Malachi shrugged, reaching into his coat for the whiskey flask. "Does he know you swear?"

"Only at you."

He didn't acknowledge her glare. "Obviously he doesn't know you well enough not to let you out of his sight. Does he know you can hit a running jackrabbit between the ears with a .22, but can't hit the side of a barn with a pistol? Does he know you taught Wolf how to spit? Does he know you're not afraid of snakes, but the idea of crawling into a cave gives you hives?"

He untwisted the flask cap and took a swig. "What about you? Do you know what he expects of a wife? He's not going to make you ride sidesaddle like Lissy, is he?"

Harry shook her head, though a sliver of apprehension

pierced her heart. *You're not wild like Maggie is.* "I'm not a child, Malachi Kelly. I know what I'm doing."

"Do you?" He took another swig of whiskey. "Do you know what you want? Or are you just marrying this Brady fellow because you can't have my brother?"

For a moment the very air froze still around them. Then Malachi muttered a curse. "I'm sorry. That was the whiskey."

Something more than anger, deeper than humiliation burned her throat. But she couldn't find words to answer him.

"I consider you a friend, Harry. I think we've been friends. I can't pretend I don't see you hurting. How well do you know yourself? Do you even know what you want?"

"I know Ash will be a good husband." She bit out the words.

"That's what Lissy Wilmer thought. She ended up married to Charm Woodfin. You can see how well that turned out."

"I'm not seventeen." She found that Lissy's story had reawakened her sympathy, despite her skepticism about Lissy's motives. "She wanted to get out of the house where her father and brothers lived. You said yourself they're unpleasant."

She had been young, her head turned by a handsome, eligible man. Maybe marriage to anyone looked good. Anything to get on with her life.

Harry bit her lip against the comparisons. Ash was not a violent man. She knew that. As well as he knew her?

Malachi looked down at the flask in his hand. "You're right, this does taste like turpentine."

"Maybe Lissy didn't think she had any other choice."

"Of course she had another choice." His laughter

sounded more like whiskey than mirth.

"And what was that?" Harry demanded. "Be an old maid in her father's house? Never live her own life?"

Malachi drew back his arm and heaved the flask out toward the sky. It spun for a moment in the starlight before thunking against a rock somewhere below them.

"She could have married me."

Harry pushed open the door to the guest room, silently cursing the creak of the new hinges. Elijah, Malachi, and Tony might be pretty proud of themselves as jacks of all trades, but they couldn't hang a door properly.

She slipped out of her soft muslin dress, unlacing the corset she could never bring herself to tighten far enough. Lissy Woodfin obviously had no trouble. Not that her figure needed any help.

Mrs. Danforth had drilled into her young ladies that such things were exactly what a man looked for in a bride. A pretty dress, a good figure, a soft voice. He didn't want blunt speech or callused hands or too much intelligence. He would never propose to a girl who was too forward, who used coarse language, who knew how to mount a horse all by herself.

Men wanted women like Lissy Woodfin and Jordan Kelly. Was it Jordan's soft voice and prim clothes that had caused Elijah not to give Harry a second glance after Jordan arrived? The truth was, Elijah had never given her a first glance. Not in that way.

But Ash Brady had. Even without Lissy's silver-gold hair or Jordan's easy grace with strangers, Harry had turned his head. His mother had shopped him around Denver society, introducing him to all the lovely misses in her circle of friends. Yet he'd chosen Harry.

Harry sat on the chest at the end of the bed to unlace her boots.

Ashton Brady. Younger and more handsome than either of the Kelly brothers. Heir to one of the largest cattle ranching enterprises in the state. A man who could cut steers, brand calves, dance a waltz, and sing a hymn like an angel.

And he'd chosen her.

She slipped her night shift over her head and folded her dress carefully across the chest. The cold air curled around her bare legs, and she hugged the cotton shift around her.

Ash loved her.

As she lifted the bedcovers and slipped beneath, another thought slithered after that one.

Ash loved the Harry who wore sweet dresses, blushed at a kiss, and had forgotten how to speak her mind.

Does he know you swear? Does he know you can hit a running jackrabbit between the ears with a .22, but can't hit the side of a barn with a pistol?

Harry buried her head in the thick feather pillow, but that didn't drown out the words.

She didn't care what Malachi Kelly said. He didn't know anything about marriage. He'd never been married. Because Lissy Woodfin had broken his heart?

She could have married me.

Harry pressed her pillow tight against the unaccountable tears that stung her eyes.

The pounding on Malachi's door broke through the pounding in his head. He opened his eyes to sharp needles of sunlight and the knowledge that the day was only going to go downhill from there.

The knocking on the door continued unabated as he

struggled to free himself from the tangle of linen sheets and fine wool blankets the Fox and Hound provided for its guests. He managed to throw his legs over the edge of the bed, but his stomach heaved, forcing his head down between his knees as he struggled for breath. He noticed he hadn't changed out of yesterday's blue jeans.

"Hell and damnation," he muttered. "I didn't drink that much."

His head didn't believe him. It throbbed in rhythm to the noise at his door. His gut didn't believe him, either. And he had the unfortunate feeling that its queasiness didn't arise so much from the alcohol he'd consumed as from the suspicion he'd made a complete idiot of himself while consuming it.

That wouldn't surprise him. He'd made more than his share of idiotic decisions in his life. Like responding to the lunatic pounding at his bedroom door.

"Go away!" The command was more of a moan, but the pounding stopped.

"Jolly good! Glad to hear you're alive, old man!" an impossibly cheery voice boomed through the varnished pine boards. "I've been knocking you up for a quarter hour."

Mal groaned and let himself fall back onto the bed. "Go away!" he repeated with more force. "I would rather be dead."

Instead, he heard the sound of a key in the door's lock, and Tony Wayne burst into the room, his crisp white shirt and crisp white teeth as painfully bright as the sunshine streaming through Mal's window. "It's nearly nine o'clock. We expected you hours ago."

Mal closed his eyes, but he could still feel Tony appraising the sight he made sprawled in agony on the feather bed.

"You're drunk."

Mal snorted. It hurt. "Not anymore."

The bed jolted beneath him as Tony plunked himself down on the edge of it. "You look like hell."

"Thank you."

"Whiskey?"

"Turpentine." Mal's stomach clutched again. Harry. He'd made a fool of himself in front of Harry. He couldn't quite remember how. He didn't want to remember.

"That's what you get for drinking alone. What got into you?" Tony's voice managed to combine sympathy, impatience and amusement. "It's Elizabeth Woodfin, isn't it?"

Lissy. "Oh, hell." He'd told Harry about his proposal to Lissy Wilmer. He'd never even told his father or brother about that. Especially not his father or brother. He certainly wasn't going to enlighten Tony.

"Listening to that outlandish story would drive anyone to drink," he grumbled.

"I've heard your stories about the Wilmer brothers," Tony said. "I can't say I blame you for holding a bit of a grudge. But the girl can't be blamed for their boyhood pranks."

"Clay and Rafe Wilmer and their uncle twice tried to set my father's church on fire. Once while the entire congregation—small as it was—was in it." Mal opened his eyes just far enough to glare at his friend. "That's not a prank."

"You still cannot hold that against Mrs. Woodfin."

"I don't." Mal pulled the feather pillow over his head, shutting out the sunlight. "Lissy Woodfin is a liar, a schemer, and cares about nothing but her own skin. That's what I hold against her."

The bed moved again as Tony rose to his feet. Mal knew the man rocked it on purpose. "I'm accustomed to you being a pain in the ass, Mal. I've never known you to be unfair. What has she done to you—besides ask your brother for help instead of you?"

For a supposed gentleman, Mal noted, Tony often aimed his blows a little low.

"Elijah's the gunfighter," he mumbled through the pillow. "Of course she'd ask him. I'm just glad he had sense enough to refuse to run off on her wild goose chase. He promised Jordan he was out of that life for good."

It must have tempted him, though. Elijah had relished his life honing his skills on the razor edge of danger. Mal suspected the secret of his longevity at his hazardous profession stemmed from the paradoxical fact that his own life hadn't held enough value to him to be a distraction. Until he'd met Jordan.

The thought of his brother strapping his guns back on and putting his and Jordan's new life at risk set Mal's stomach rolling again, upsetting him much more than Lissy's preferring his brother's help to his own.

"If Lissy thinks she's going to bring her trouble down on our heads and endanger innocent people, she's going to have to think again."

"Ha." Tony kicked the bedpost. "You and I are not exactly innocents. Who else is she endangering?"

Mal ripped the pillow from his face. "Besides everyone in Battlement Park? What about Harry, for one?"

"Harry can take care of herself."

"Harry's a nineteen-year-old girl who's supposed to be safely at home getting married." Mal heaved himself back into a sitting position, ignoring the spinning in his head. "She's supposed to be worrying about flowers and dresses and whatever fluff goes along with weddings, not wandering around the wilderness being hunted by vicious thugs."

"She'll be going home today."

"Alone." Mal fumbled for the blue shirt hanging across the chair by his bed. "What if those thugs follow Lissy's trail to the Jacksons' ranch? What will happen then? What if something happens to Harry—or to her brother and sister-in-law? Their baby? Will I be allowed to hold that against Lissy Woodfin?"

He was surprised to feel his teeth grinding in anger. He could barely get his arms into his shirtsleeves. "Hell, Tony, what about your staff? What about your guests?"

"You're right," Tony agreed.

Mal's head snapped up. Tony never agreed with him.

"I *am* right."

"You are." Tony reached down to pick an imperceptible speck of lint off his carefully creased navy trousers, making a great show of considering Mal's words. "You are. Innocents have been put in danger. There's only one thing to do."

Somehow Mal did not think Tony meant sending Lissy straight back home. Even Mal might have to agree she shouldn't be returned to danger. Savannah was out. Alaska, on the other hand . . .

"You've convinced me," Tony said abruptly, brushing the lint off his hands. "We have no choice but to escort Mrs. Woodfin to Denver, confront her blighter of a husband, and get those Beasts off her trail once and for all."

Mal snapped his jaw shut. Only the hangover could have dulled him enough to be surprised. He'd seen the way Tony looked at Lissy the night before. Tony had a pronounced soft spot for women and a keen appreciation of feminine beauty, but Mal had not seen such yearning in his friend's eyes in a very long time.

A look that was proving as dangerous to Mal's peace of mind as to Tony's good sense.

"Oh, no you don't—" He fought his way into his shirt and stood. "No, you don't, Wayne. There is no way in hell I'm going anywhere with Lissy Woodfin, and neither are you."

"You don't have anything better to do for the next week."

"I certainly do." Mal finally got his buttons under control. He looked around for his boots, found them still laced to his feet. "There are trout to catch and stars to count. Elijah wants my help with that pack of rabid jackals you call geologists who want to freeze their nether parts off on Battlement Peak tomorrow. Who knows, maybe someone in that damnably peaceful town up the Park will even need a justice of the peace."

"She's in trouble."

For once, Tony's expression was serious. This was even worse than Mal had supposed.

"She's in trouble, and she's scared. She's asked us for help, and it's not much bother, not anything we can't do. Where's your sense of chivalry, Mal? You're not in the damn army anymore. Warm up that stone you call a heart."

That cheap shot struck much closer to home than the one about Elijah. Without warning, Mal remembered the stink of fear, the screams of dying horses, the foul breath of hell. He even remembered a prayer. That hell end. That he might have the chance to choose a different life, one that didn't bring death.

He didn't owe Elizabeth Woodfin anything. As he'd told Harry, she'd had another choice than the path she had taken. An unexpected thought pierced through the pain in his head. When he'd said that to Harry . . . She hadn't thought . . .

He stifled another agonized groan. If Harry had thought

he'd meant that ridiculous performance as some kind of drunken proposal, he would die of humiliation. Harry had much better options than Lissy Wilmer ever had. And Mal had learned the hard way that he could be just as heartless as Tony accused him of being. He would not have made any better of a husband than Charm Woodfin.

Though at least he would never have hired thugs to beat up his wife.

"I'm not a hired gun."

"Elijah thought you'd say that," Tony said, casually leaning back against the wall. "He said he respected you for it, and he shouldn't be asking you to do a job he should be doing."

"He didn't say that." Mal glared at his friend, but Tony just shrugged. "He won't leave his responsibilities here for Lissy's self-imposed problems. He won't go back on his word to Jordan."

If he did, it would be much too easy for him to slip back into that old, familiar life.

Mal jabbed the bottom of his shirt into his jeans. "I'm not a white knight." He shrugged into a black buckskin jacket. "I'm not going to Denver."

He scowled at Tony, trying to quell the pain in his head, the nausea in his stomach, the censure in his friend's eyes, and the qualms in his own heart. "Lissy won't be disappointed. You heard her last night. She doesn't expect me to help her."

"I think you may not be quite right on that account, old friend." Tony did not look at all discouraged as he pulled open the bedroom door. "I knew you'd see sense eventually."

Mal paused in his tossing of the bedclothes in a fruitless search for his socks. It occurred to him they were probably on his feet, under the boots. "What do you mean by that?"

Tony's genial smile hid nothing of the wickedness in his heart. "I've already told her we'll do it. We leave in an hour."

If Mal had held anything in his hand but a pillow, Tony's head would have been dented before he could escape into the hall. As it was, Mal stared impotently at the slammed door, watching a stray goose down feather drift through a bar of sunlight.

Chapter 6

The extravagantly tall windows at the rear of the entrance room of the Fox and Hound opened onto a view designed to take the spectator's breath away. A broad green meadow, threaded by a stream glinting with the gold of the low September sun, stretched up toward an ice-wrapped spire of a mountain that shouldered down to the crenellated ridge that gave Battlement Park its name.

The richness of the hunter green rug covering much of the gleaming wood floor, the plush armchairs, the huge central fireplace, the paintings of fox hunts and hounds on the walls, all were dimmed to quaint charm in the face of nature's grandeur.

That morning it seemed to Harry even grander than ever, the creeping gold of autumn gilding the aspens above the meadow, the clear morning light almost singing as it shimmered against fir and spruce.

So close to the windows and distanced from the crackling fire, the morning cool raised goose prickles on her arms, though her teacup settled warmly in her hand.

Ash had told her South Park had its own wild beauty, that the mountains surrounding the valley were stark and grand. The Mosquito Range. The Sangre de Cristos. They didn't sound particularly welcoming.

"Are you all right, Harry?" Jordan's voice brought her out of her reverie. In her soft, gray-blue morning dress, Jordan looked peaceful as a dove. And why shouldn't she, Harry thought. Jordan belonged here. An artist at home in a place of endless inspiration. A woman at home with the man she loved.

"Of course. I'm fine." Harry managed to keep the irony from her voice. Just fine. Fine with the realization that she herself did not belong here. Not anymore. Her new life had nothing to do with her childhood on her brother's ranch, with her friendship with a gunfighter and his wife, with hunting outlaws—or even rabbits. Nothing to do with helping damsels in distress.

"It's getting late." Harry settled her teacup in its saucer on the carved mahogany table beside her chair. It rattled. "I should be getting ready to leave. I don't want to spend another night in the hills."

Her skin itched under the collar of her plum-colored dress. She should have dressed in her blue jeans as soon as she awoke that morning. Idiotic vanity to wear the dress down to the lodge just because the lilac stripe brought out the hint of violet in her eyes.

Not that her eye color made any difference next to Lissy's fair perfection or Jordan's calm beauty. Harry felt like a crow between two swans. Though there was no one to notice, anyway. Elijah had already left for the marshal's office in town, to see about the horse thief he and Malachi had brought in the day before. Tony had disappeared abruptly after breakfast. And Malachi had not even put in an appearance to say good-bye.

She didn't care. She was happy that Elijah was happy with Jordan. She didn't care that Tony couldn't keep his eyes off Lissy; he couldn't help himself. And she certainly didn't care that impossible, irritating, socially irredeemable Malachi Kelly, who had just that summer asked her not to marry, had once been so besotted by young Lissy Wilmer that he had proposed to her.

"Harry, are you sure you're all right?" Jordan asked again.

"I'm fine. Honestly. I'm just tired of waiting." Tired of it not mattering if she waited or not.

"Could you keep me company for a few more minutes?" Jordan gestured at Lissy, pacing between their table and the fireplace. "I can't take much more of this."

Harry thought of the long ride ahead of her. She should be on her way. Alone. Then again, she'd never have this time to spend with these friends again. Considering Ash's disapproval of Elijah's former profession, he would never agree to her visiting the Kellys after their marriage.

Harry sat. "I'll just finish my tea."

"Where are they?" Lissy demanded, pacing over to the table. She looked as restless as Harry felt, impatience coloring her pale cheeks. "Major Wayne couldn't convince Malachi to help me. I knew it. The coach to Longmont leaves in less than an hour."

"The coach belongs to the Fox and Hound," Jordan pointed out. "I hardly think it will leave without Tony. I am more concerned with what you plan to do when you reach Denver. Let me send a letter with you for my cousin Nicky. You can stay with her."

Lissy shook her head, the silver curls behind her ears dancing. "You said your cousin and her husband have a newborn baby." She glanced at Harry. "I would not put a child in danger, whatever else you may think of me."

Jordan's skirts rustled as she stood and grasped Lissy's

arm. "I think you are a woman who has survived a great deal and who deserves to take some control of her life. Now, sit, before you wear out those boot heels Tony fixed for you."

Lissy's cheeks flushed as she complied. "Thank you." She picked restlessly at her gloves. "If Charm had taken only my money . . ."

She glanced up. "He took more than I can live without."

As Lissy's gaze caught hers, Harry almost understood what had driven Lissy headlong into their lives. Almost understood the aching regret of her marriage, the dogged determination not to despair of her life. Almost understood the deceit and the demands.

"I don't mean to cause you such trouble," Lissy continued, the words wrung out of her in a whisper. "I had nowhere else to go."

Harry's heart gave a silent prayer of thanks for the knowledge that whatever trouble she tumbled into, March and Maggie would never turn her out into the cold. Whether she deserved it or not.

"You haven't gotten anyone kidnapped or killed yet," she found herself saying, her antagonism melting just a little. "Jordan brought a whole gang of desperadoes down on our heads. Just being in the same room with her puts you in danger of being shot."

"Ha!" Jordan's eyes narrowed. "As I recall, it was one Miss Harriet Jackson who almost got me killed, missing a shot at a stationary target from ten feet."

Harry sniffed. "It was dark! And you were the one who got yourself hogtied to an outlaw's bed in the first place."

Lissy's guarded eyes widened, and her hands stopped their twisting. Jordan must have noticed their audience's interest. She smiled wickedly.

"And who was it who got herself expelled from finishing school for running the headmistress's drawers up the flag-pole?"

Lissy actually laughed. "I declare. Miss Harriet Jackson. Now, why doesn't that surprise me at all?"

Harry sat up straight, knees together, chin tilted just so. "Don't show your teeth when you smile, girl. You look like a horse."

Lissy managed a grin that showed every one of her pearly white teeth. "I would have cheered you on." The smile faltered. "No, I was too well-bred to cheer. Your headmistress would have adored me."

Harry arched an eyebrow. "Not anymore."

Lissy considered that a moment, glancing down at her travel-stained dress and hastily repaired boots. The hint of a smile returned. "No, perhaps not."

Jordan took a dainty sip of tea, pinky extended, and looked down her nose at them. "I think the two of you are not so very different, after all. You don't fool me in your gloves and lace. A pair of troublemakers, if I ever saw one."

"Suits me. I never had to go back to finishing school," Harry said, shrugging. Then, impulsively, "Don't worry. It will work out for you, Lissy."

Lissy's cheeks warmed again. "For you, too, Harry."

Jordan lifted her teacup in a salute. "To troublemakers."

Harry and Lissy reached for their own cups. Harry's heart lurched with the remembered camaraderie of the past summer. "To troublemakers."

"You callow, self-absorbed, arrogant limey bastard!"

"Speaking of which . . ." Jordan murmured, as Tony Wayne strode out of the guest wing of the hotel, Malachi Kelly hard on his heels.

Harry had heard Jordan comment once that Major Tony

Wayne did nothing to detract from the scenic splendor of Battlement Park. Noticing how his broad shoulders filled out his tailored blue coat, how his eyes gleamed with humor, Harry had to agree. She intercepted a surreptitious glance from Lissy that left her wondering if the other woman was as immune to Tony's charms as she pretended to be.

Ignoring the epithets following him across the room, Tony bowed smartly to the women seated by the windows.

"Good morning, ladies. I apologize for the delay. My erstwhile partner and I had a few last-minute details to discuss."

His erstwhile partner could not have contrasted more sharply with Tony's neat handsomeness if he had planned it. Malachi had neither shaved nor combed his hair, and Harry thought his old blue jeans and rumpled coat looked suspiciously as though he had slept in them.

Normally, she would not have hesitated to needle him about it. That morning, though, the tired lines radiating from his bloodshot eyes and the pained set of his beard-shadowed mouth twisted something sharp in her heart. He didn't so much as glance at her as he stalked up beside Tony.

"I'm not your damned partner," he growled. He turned his grim eyes on Lissy. "You don't want my help."

The amusement ebbed from Lissy's pale face, leaving behind the brittle edge of her desperation. She did not try to coat it with her accustomed praline sweetness.

"No." She met his gaze with steady gray eyes. "I'm not asking for your help because I want it. Or because I expect it. Or because I have any right to ask anything of you. I'm asking for your help because I need it."

For a long moment Malachi simply stared back at her.

Then Harry saw his mouth twitch, and she knew him well enough to know exactly what he would say.

"Hell and damnation." He blew out a long breath and turned on Tony. "This is your fault, Wayne. Whatever happens. And I'm not going unless I'm in charge. My campaign. Down the line."

"Of course, old man. Understood."

"And I'm not leaving without a cup of coffee. Black coffee. Coffee hot enough to burn your throat out."

Tony clapped him on the back. "Good show."

"Shut up and get me the coffee." Malachi grabbed a chair from a nearby table and swung himself across it backwards.

"The coach leaves in forty-five minutes," Tony reminded him as he headed toward the hall to the kitchen. "With a bit of luck we can catch a late train to Denver from Longmont."

Lissy's head snapped around. "We can't take the train!"

Malachi waved her objection off. "You won't be traveling alone this time, Lissy."

Her eyes narrowed at him. "You haven't seen these men. They're vicious, ugly brutes."

He leaned forward on the chair back, expression grim. "They've been hired to hunt down a lone woman. I expect they'll think twice before attacking a woman protected by two armed men."

"There are three of them."

"And three of us," Harry said. She blinked. She had to learn to think before opening her mouth, especially if such patently insane words were going to escape. Go to Denver on this fool's errand? Her heart pounded erratically, but she smiled sweetly as Lissy and Malachi turned to stare at her.

She might have imagined Jordan's muttered, "It's about time."

"I thought you were going home," Lissy said, a somewhat more encouraging response than Malachi's glare.

"She is."

"Of course I am," Harry agreed, steadying a shaky hand on her teacup. Her smile settled in. "After a little detour to Denver."

"Elizabeth can hardly be expected to travel in the company of two unmarried men without a chaperone," Jordan put in primly.

Harry decided that mentioning Jordan's own unchaperoned travels with a notorious gunfighter would be counterproductive.

"Harry has a wedding to plan," Malachi growled.

It was one thing not to be asked along on an adventure, quite another to have someone say they didn't want you. The fact that he had a valid point was neither here nor there.

"The wedding is planned," Harry said. "And this won't take long."

"Elizabeth will need female companionship," Jordan added.

"She's not going with us!"

"What's that?" Tony asked, returning to their group with a steaming cup in his hand. "Harry's coming with us? Capital!"

Tony's genial grin assured Harry that he did, indeed, think it was capital. She grinned back. This was starting to feel like old times.

"It's not capital," Malachi said. "Harry's not coming. Harry is getting married."

Even Malachi's objections had a nostalgic familiarity.

"The wedding's not for another month." Tony held out the coffee cup.

Malachi eyed it suspiciously. "If that's tea, you're going to be wearing it."

"It's not tea," Tony assured him with a shudder. "I can't swear it won't kill you, but I can promise you it's not tea. The chef calls it coffee, but no one will drink it but him."

Malachi took the cup and after a wary sniff took a deep swallow. Harry saw his eyes water. "Good," was all he could get out.

"We'd better get your things from the cabin, Harry," Jordan said, rising.

"She's not going with us," Malachi repeated, before taking another gulp of coffee.

"I am." Harry pushed back her chair to follow Jordan.

Malachi rose, too, taking a step closer to her. "You've got a wedding."

"Not for a month!" Harry repeated Tony's argument.

"Your brother and sister-in-law will be worried—"

"I'll send a telegram from Longmont."

"It's too dangerous!"

Heat rose in Harry's face. "How dare you!" She met his glare with one equally fierce. "After what you said last night."

His face turned a queasy shade of gray. "What about what I said?"

Harry suddenly realized she didn't want to discuss that in front of their attentive audience. She gritted her teeth. "About knowing who I am and what I want?"

"That." He looked almost relieved.

"You didn't mean it?"

For the first time that morning, humor flickered in his eyes, despite the frustration there. "I meant you should exercise your good sense. I forgot you didn't have any."

"Jolly good," Tony said, rubbing his hands together. "That's settled then. Is everyone ready to go?"

Harry glanced at Malachi. He raised an eyebrow, his eyes still not quite smiling. She didn't quite smile back. The prospects for the day had just become much more interesting.

"Harry, can I talk with you a minute?"

Harry tugged on the harness strap she'd just finished tightening on the wheel horse of the coach. Satisfied, she gestured to the stable boy that she was finished with her horse before turning to Jordan behind her.

"Sure. I think I'm just getting in Ben's way, anyway."

Jordan led her a short way from the bustle around the coach, to the shade of a Douglas fir that towered beside the Fox and Hound's entrance stairs. The shade felt good. Most of the heat she felt probably came from helping Ben harness the team, but the slanting fall sunshine had warmed the morning air considerably. She would be glad she wore muslin instead of wool by the time they reached Longmont.

"I wanted to thank you again for letting me borrow your valise," she said, watching Tony tossing the expedition's gear up to the coachman on the carriage roof.

"I didn't think a saddlebag was appropriate luggage for a young lady on a jaunt to Denver."

"Maybe not." Harry glanced at the other woman. "Thank you, too, for helping convince Malachi and Elijah to let me go."

Jordan smiled wryly. "How were they going to stop you?"

Harry started. Why hadn't she thought of it that way? A grim suspicion curled in her mind that she had been thinking much too much about Ash and the things he thought he would or would not allow. *Expecting a girl to muck out stalls and rope horses. My father wouldn't have stood for it.*

"I should thank you," Jordan said. "With you going, Malachi can't back out."

Her eyes lingered on her husband. Elijah had his brother cornered by the coach door, giving him obviously unlooked-for last-minute advice. For the first time, Harry saw Elijah's retirement from gunfighting through Jordan's eyes.

"I'm glad you'll be going with Elizabeth," Jordan continued. "She needs a friend."

"I'm not her friend."

"You will be." There was no irony in her sapphire eyes when she turned to Harry. "You have that ability. To befriend those who need it. Wolf. Nicky. Me. Malachi."

"You've all been friends to me."

"I don't think you even realize what difficult friends we can be." Jordan paused, choosing her words. "I'm especially glad of your friendship with Malachi, Harry. Not many people are willing to put up with his bluntness. But he needs friends. More than he thinks. He doesn't open himself up to people. But he does with you."

Harry shifted, unexpectedly uncomfortable under Jordan's scrutiny. "I'm not the easiest person in the world, myself."

"Maybe no one is. That's why it means so much to have friends who know you so well and like you anyway." Jordan paused again. "I hope that's how things are with your Ash."

Harry briefly shut her eyes. If one more person mentioned Ashton Brady . . . But of course they would. He was her fiancé. "We're getting to know each other."

"I'm glad. I think friendship is the most important element in a marriage." Her eyes glinted with a sudden shaft of humor. "And I've had enough marriages to know."

"Harry? There you are." Tony waved at her from the coach door. "We're ready to go in five minutes."

"I'm coming."

Impulsively, Harry turned to give Jordan a hug. "You're right about friends who know you. You've been a good friend to me, even when I haven't deserved it."

"Don't thank me, yet." Jordan's smile looked strained. "I think I've been spending too much time around you. It's making me unconscionably impulsive. But I did encourage your getting into this."

She reached deep into the pocket of her split skirt. "Elijah bought this for me. After what happened with Lucifer Jones's gang, he thought I should have it, but it's been a quiet summer."

She glanced at Harry, as if debating with herself. "I hope you never have to use it. For everyone's sake. But I don't think Lissy's Beasts are the sort to respond to reason."

She pulled an object from her pocket and thrust it into Harry's hand. Harry looked down at the little ivory-inlaid two-shot derringer sitting in her palm. It looked like a toy. But the weight of it assured her it was a deadly one.

"Good luck, Harry." Jordan hugged her again. "And for God's sake, don't point that at anyone."

The early morning sun warmed Lissy's shoulders as she waited at the edge of the Longmont train platform, though her fingers felt numb inside her gloves.

She had put on the old wool coat she had bartered from the prostitute in Cheyenne, but she wore her own blue hat, despite its conspicuousness. Apparently there were still some depths to which she wouldn't sink. One of them was wearing the soiled dove's bedraggled ostrich feather hat onto a first class train car.

Tony had made a joke of it: no English major, even a former one, would be caught dead in third class. His father would disown him. Again. It would blight his honor forever. And so forth.

Lissy looked toward the station. Dangerous how quickly she could pick him out of the small crowd, even through the reflections shifting across the building's windows. He stood at the counter inside, his wheat-colored hair bright above his blue coat, buying their tickets to Denver. One more debt she owed.

Though she was hesitantly coming to the conclusion that the Englishman would never consider asking her to repay the fare, even when he discovered she couldn't make good her offer to pay him and his friends a small fortune for their help. After growing up with Wilmer men, it was disconcerting to encounter a gentleman who acted like a gentleman.

Lissy caught herself chewing her lower lip as she watched Tony help an elderly woman count out her change. She couldn't pretend, at least not to herself, that his good-hearted act wasn't appealing. But would a gentleman serve as any protection from Spider Grant and his thugs?

From under her lashes, she turned a surreptitious glance on her two other companions. No one would mistake them for gentlemen, though that did not make her feel any better.

Missing the afternoon train on their arrival in Longmont the day before had given Malachi a chance to bathe and shave during their stay at the Longmont Arms. But he still looked rumpled in his jeans and battered black coat as he leaned against a pillar ten yards away, keeping one eye on their meager luggage and another out for trouble. His expression was fierce enough, but he didn't hold himself with the instinctive predator's grace of his brother.

Harriet Jackson stood to Lissy's side. She looked every inch the sweet young thing in her conservative plum dress, her unruly brown hair locked into place behind her head with an army of hairpins. No one would ever guess she carried Jordan Kelly's derringer in her stylish black velvet handbag.

Lissy sincerely hoped Harry knew which end of the gun to point at the villains. She glanced up and down the platform again, but saw no sign of the Beasts among the early rising travelers.

"This is a bad idea," she said. She'd repeated it so often that she was surprised when Harry answered her.

"They'll never even get close to you." Harry was also perusing the few other passengers waiting on the platform. The smart ones were all inside the station, keeping warm. "I know it must be hard to stop hiding, but Mal and Tony are right. They can't scare off the Beasts if the Beasts can't find you."

"They won't have to scare anyone off if I freeze to death."

Harry laughed. Lissy managed a smile in return. It felt good to smile again. It felt even better not to be alone. She had to remind herself not to get used to it. Had to remember what they would think of her when all of this was over.

"Excuse me, ma'am?"

The strange voice right beside her nearly brought Lissy out of her skin. The mild-faced businessman looked nothing like one of Spider Grant's associates in his snug felt hat and round glasses, his carefully-brushed suit hanging loosely on his thin frame.

Still, Lissy hoped Mal and Harry had noticed him approaching her. If not, they were going to be in real trouble in Denver.

The businessman clutched a flat leather case to his chest with one hand while he lifted his hat with the other. "Pardon me, ma'am, but do you know the time? I've lost my watch."

Lissy shook her head. "I haven't a watch, either, but I believe it's just on eight o'clock."

"Eight?" The man's voice squeaked in dismay. "Are you sure?"

"There's a clock inside the station," Harry offered, gesturing toward the building.

The man's free hand patted at his jacket front, searching for his pockets. "Is the seven forty-five to Cheyenne late, then? Isn't that the train you're waiting for?"

"This is the south-bound platform," Lissy said.

The man gaped at her. "That can't be right. I have all the information written down right here somewhere . . ."

He reached for his pockets with both hands, forgetting his case. It thudded to the platform, spilling unbound sheets of paper across the raw boards.

A female passenger walking by jumped to avoid them, brushing against Lissy and nearly bowling Harry over.

"My papers!" The poor man sounded on the edge of tears as he stared down at the mess.

Lissy just missed knocking heads with Harry as they both dropped to scramble for the papers before the morning breeze could snag them.

A high-pitched shriek brought them both to their feet with a start.

"Let go of me!" a woman's voice demanded fiercely, though not nearly so loudly as she had screamed a second before. "How dare you accost me! I will call for the guards!"

"I don't think so," a familiar male voice replied.

Lissy turned to see Malachi still leaning against his pillar with one hand tightly gripped around the wrist of the young woman who had just passed by them. Built much like the man who had dropped the papers, her large, lace-draped hat and voluminous coat overwhelmed her narrow frame. But there was nothing delicate in her sharp voice.

"Let me go, damn you!"

"What on earth are you doing, Mal?" Harry demanded, finding her tongue. "Have you lost your mind?"

"The question is," Malachi said, green eyes glittering, "what have you two ladies lost?"

Lissy understood what he meant a half-second before Harry clutched for her absent purse. "She stole our handbags!"

Lissy saw a flash of angry eyes as the woman's head turned briefly in her direction. Then, twisting her spine like a snake striking, the thief cracked the back of Malachi's knee with her sturdy boot.

Malachi fell heavily to the platform, cracking his head against the pillar. But he failed to let go of the thief's wrist, and she crashed to the floor along with him. She kicked at him savagely, landing several good blows to his hip and side before Harry reached her, dropping on her to pin the woman's legs.

The thief reached into her coat and pulled out Lissy's bag, which she swung with all her might at Harry's head. Harry ducked, but the bag connected with Malachi's stomach. He grunted, grabbing for the bag, but he let go of the woman's wrist. She pulled Harry's bag from her coat.

Harry rolled away before the woman could take aim with

the heavier bag. The thief leaped to her feet with a startling grace, considering the yards of skirt wrapped about her, but Lissy jumped forward to grab the back of her coat before she could escape.

With a grunt of rage and panic, the woman elbowed Lissy's ribs, giving herself room to swing Harry's bag again. Somehow Lissy managed to duck in time, and the bag banged heavily against the iron column holding up the platform awning.

The sharp crack that accompanied the blow didn't startle Lissy nearly as badly as the whistle of the bullet that flew past her ear.

Lissy guessed she shrieked as she dropped her hold on the woman's coat and tripped to the ground. Certainly Harry and Malachi and the thief cried out. Lissy heard booted feet pounding toward them as the thief sprinted in the opposite direction

"Bloody hell! What happened?"

"A thief." Malachi's voice, curt, in charge. "I think Harry's derringer went off. Harry?"

"I'm not hurt."

"Mrs. Woodfin?"

Lissy realized she'd been clenching her eyes closed. She opened them to see Tony Wayne's face inches from her own as he kneeled beside her on the platform. For the first time she noticed what a contrast his brown eyes, dark with concern, made with his fair hair and ruddy English complexion.

Not that they were a simple brown. Not so dark as chocolate or flat as coffee, not so pale as toffee, but a clear, deep color with hints of gold.

"Mrs. Woodfin?"

"Earl Grey tea."

"I'll find you some tea. Just tell me you're not hurt."

She shook her head. "The color of your eyes."

They blinked. "What?"

A smile tugged the corner of Lissy's mouth at the idiocy of her thoughts. "Your eyes are the color of Earl Grey tea."

For the first time, he seemed to realize how close his eyes were to hers. In the half-second that he stayed there, gaze locked with hers, Lissy felt a shock whisper along her nerves. Then he sat back on his heels, offering her his hand.

"Can you rise?"

"I think the gunshot rattled my wits, but the rest of me seems unharmed."

She took his hand, trying not to notice the easy strength with which he pulled her to her feet or the warmth of his fingers through both their gloves.

"No one's shot?" Malachi asked, giving her an excuse to turn from Tony's gaze.

"I think the bullet went into the platform floor," Harry said. She had retrieved both handbags and offered Lissy's to her.

Lissy pushed a hand into the bag, her fingers running over the tiny silver frame at the bottom. If the thief had gotten away with all she owned, it would barely have bought her dinner. But it was more than Lissy could bear to lose.

"You didn't recognize them?" Malachi asked, breaking into her thoughts. "The woman or her accomplice?"

"Accomplice?" Lissy glanced down the platform. A few stray papers drifted across the bare boards, most already swept by the breeze under the wrought iron benches along the building. The poor lost man with the case was nowhere to be seen, though a red-faced man in a railway cap was charging toward them from the station door.

Tony snorted out a long breath. "Prize bodyguards we make."

"Pretty damn useless," Malachi agreed, kneading a bruised rib with his thumb.

Harry's eyes flashed mutinously for a second, before she dropped her gaze to the ground, shoulders sagging in defeat.

"No one's hurt," Lissy reminded them. "And they didn't get away with our bags."

She looked down at the new rip in her dress hem, felt the ache in her rear end from her tumble to the ground, heard again in her memory the whistling of the gunshot. She studied her companions, considered their chaotically inept, but unabashedly wholehearted response to a pair of unarmed thieves.

"Denver had better watch out for us," she concluded. She had absolutely no idea why she felt so good.

Chapter 7

"Maybe you shouldn't carry that thing loaded," Malachi suggested dryly as Harry pulled her derringer from her bag.

They sat in an alcove off the red-carpeted second floor hallway of the Regency Hotel, overlooking the curving grand staircase leading down to the lobby. Tony had insisted on paying for rooms at the Regency. Harry suspected he couldn't resist the opportunity to inspect the professional competition, though the opulence set off the ragtag appearance of their group.

Harry thought Malachi looked like a raven in a nightingale's cage, slouched in his paisley-patterned overstuffed armchair. She straightened her spine, hoping she blended in a little more smoothly than he did.

Not that many of the female guests of one of Denver's premiere hotels would be checking the twin chambers of their tiny .22 pistols in the hotel's hallway. She glanced around to assure herself they weren't being observed.

"It would be a little more difficult to shoot the criminals without bullets," she told Malachi.

"And a little more difficult to shoot your friends, as well."

Harry gave him a look. "It's not my fault it went off. I

haven't shot anyone. Yet."

If he heard the threat in her voice, he chose to ignore it. "Let's try to keep it that way. Although if you'd managed to take out Lissy this morning, at least we could have gone home."

"We'll be home by tomorrow anyway," Harry said, irritated by his attitude. "Isn't that soon enough for you?"

"It may not be soon enough for Tony."

She glanced up from her gun to catch the troubled look on his face. "What do you mean?"

"I mean that soft southern charm hides sharp claws. I don't want to have to dig them out of Tony's hide."

Harry thought of the expression she had caught on Lissy's face that morning when Tony had helped her up after her tussle with the thief. She had looked younger suddenly, unsure. Almost frightened. But not of Tony. Of herself.

"You think Lissy's falling in love with Tony?"

"What?" Malachi's bark startled her. "Love? Lissy? His money, maybe. But she must have learned something from marrying Charm. You don't have to love someone to get what you want from them.

"I don't say she didn't love Charm," he admitted, his stubborn honesty showing through. "But even if he wasn't as handsome as Tony, he was just as popular with women. She's got to see that. She's not going to fall in love with Tony."

"Love doesn't work that way," Harry snapped, surprised at her own anger. "You can't control it. At least those of us with hearts can't."

"I'm not sure Lissy has any more of a heart than I do. She'd be a fool to make that mistake again. And Lissy's no fool."

"Why, I declare, thank you for your high opinion of my intelligence, Mal," Lissy's voice drawled, low and intense behind them.

Harry jumped in her seat, fumbling the derringer. The little gun slipped from her hand and clattered to the floor just off the carpet. It skidded across the gleaming hardwood, spinning toward the edge of the balcony above the lobby. Harry dove for it as Malachi did the same. Their heads cracked together just before the railing.

"Ouch!"

"Hell and damnation!"

"The gun!" Harry heard Lissy squeak.

With an unladylike oath, Harry grabbed at the derringer, snatching it back from a fall to the lobby. For a second all she could hear was her own rapid breathing and Malachi's and the ringing in her head.

"What, ho?" Tony's footsteps padded down the corridor toward them. "Everyone all right?"

Harry glanced guiltily up at Lissy, who shot a glare down at Malachi.

"Right," Tony said, after a long silence. "Shall we go frighten some malefactors, then?"

"We're certainly frightening enough," Malachi muttered. Harry ignored his offered hand and struggled to her feet.

If she had feared that she and Malachi looked out of place in the elegant hotel, Tony and Lissy had clearly found their element.

Lissy had managed to work the worst of the travel stains from her skirt, but no one would notice them anyway after being captivated by the soft, silver-blond ringlets caressing her slender neck and the one smoky eye not hidden by the drooping net of her hat.

Apparently Tony's pants and jacket were too well bred

to wrinkle, despite travels by coach and train and streetcar. His shoes gleamed. He'd even donned a crisp top hat for the occasion.

"You're the one in charge," he reminded Malachi. "Lead on, Captain Kelly."

"I think Harry should stay here with Lissy while you and I have a chat with Charm Woodfin."

"Going straight to inviting open insurrection," Tony said thoughtfully, eyeing Harry and Lissy. "Interesting command choice, that."

"Charm might be staying at this very hotel," Lissy pointed out, thought she did not seem as dismayed at the prospect as Harry would have expected. Ever since they'd reached Denver two hours ago, Harry had noticed Lissy's fear being edged aside by a tense energy. "We could run into him in the hall. What would Harry and I do then?"

"Shoot him?" Malachi suggested. "We can check for his name at the front desk."

"He might be using an alias."

"An *alias?*"

Lissy's hat didn't hide the spark of red in her cheeks. "He does that sometimes, when he goes away on business."

"Damnit, Elizabeth," Malachi said. "Just what is Charm mixed up in? I wondered why he'd come all the way to Denver to do business for an import-export firm out of Savannah. I should have guessed there was something shady about any business your brothers were involved in."

"I don't know much about it," Lissy said. Her voice faltered under his glare, but Harry was beginning to suspect Lissy's wilting southern belle act bore very little relation to her true personality. "Clay and Rafe financed the business with what they made running the blockade during the war. But Charm swore to me when he agreed to join the company that it was legitimate."

Malachi ran a hand through his hair as though he'd be happier tearing it out. "How are we going to find one man in a city of over thirty thousand if we don't even know what name he's using?"

"I know some of the names he's used," Lissy said, digging into her little blue handbag and pulling out a slip of paper. "It's always some kind of play on his real name." She peered at the list. "C. W. Luck. Woody Finch. Lucky Forest. Finlay Charming. If it's not one of those, it will be something like it. He can't resist being clever."

"So, all we have to do is ask to see the registration books of every hotel in Denver for the past three weeks and hunt down all the Woods and Finches and Spellbinders we come across."

Lissy's lips pinched in irritation. "All we have to do is describe him and ask if any of the clerks have seen him."

Harry could hear Malachi's teeth grinding.

"I haven't seen Charm Woodfin in over ten years," he said, slow and deliberate. "But I doubt he's gotten any taller or shorter or darker or lighter in that time." He glanced at Harry and Tony. "He's medium build, medium weight, medium blond. If there was ever a man more innocuous than Charm, I've forgotten what he looks like."

"How many people that average-looking are there, really?" Lissy asked, undiscouraged. "He's got green eyes, which aren't so usual, and he's put on a little weight around the middle. And he wears a pinky ring with a big emerald set in it. I told you he's got an eye for jewels. But that's not why people remember Charm.

"He truly is charming. He will have brought a flower to the maid or told a joke to the clerk. He has a sparkle in his eyes when he talks to people, even a hat clerk or the person selling tickets at the theater. He makes you feel special." Lissy's mouth twisted bitterly as she shook herself out of the memory. "People don't forget that."

Malachi snorted. "I don't know why I thought any part of this wild goose chase would be quick or easy. How many days until the wedding, Harry?"

"We should split up," Lissy said. "You and Harry, Major Wayne and myself. It will be faster."

"What if we find him?" Malachi asked. "Or, more to the point, what if *you* find him? As you said, you could run into him on the street. Two days ago you didn't seem to think only one bodyguard would—"

"No." Lissy was already shaking her head. "I'll be safe enough from Charm with Tony. He wouldn't dare try anything in public. Charm isn't dangerous alone."

She raised a hand to the fading bruises beneath the shade of her hat brim. "If the Beasts are still in Colorado, they are the ones to fear. We can make Charm see reason. I know we can. But we have to find him before the Beasts do. I mean, before they find us."

The urgency in her voice tugged Harry forward, to follow Lissy toward the stairs. Malachi's hand on her elbow stopped her.

"We need a plan," he said, the authority in his voice holding the rest of them in place. "Which hotels each group will hit. Where we'll meet. A message to leave here in case of an emergency."

He shook his head, as if realizing for the first time that he'd actually committed himself to such a far-fetched scheme.

"And what's our story?" Tony asked.

"Story?" Malachi repeated.

"The story we're planning to tell the clerks to convince

them to give us information."

Malachi frowned. Harry almost felt sorry for him. "There's been enough deception already. We'll tell the truth."

"Oh. Right," Tony agreed. "Right you are."

"Excuse me, my good man." Tony Wayne leaned an elbow on the gleaming bar of the Golden Apple Saloon and gestured to the bartender. He flashed his easiest, warmest, haven't-a-care-in-the-world-or-a-brain-in-my-head smile.

"I say, I'm looking for a chum of mine. He and I were partners in this god-forsaken claim, and the poor old blighter got sick with the pneumonia last winter. Had to pack it up. Wouldn't you know, I struck a vein just weeks later, sold the whole claim to one of those big British mining companies, and now my old partner is weighing on my conscience. If I can just find him and settle up . . ."

"Yes," Lissy said, dabbing a handkerchief to her nose. "My poor father's dying wish is to reconcile with my brother. They're both so stubborn. They haven't spoken these past five years, and now it's almost too late."

She turned damp eyes on the counter clerk. His heavy-lidded gaze shifted toward the grandfather clock across the lobby. Lissy pressed a little closer to the counter, letting it lift her bosom.

"I'd be ever so grateful if you could help me find my brother. And so would Papa. He doesn't care about the expense."

That opened the man's eyes.

"After all," Lissy continued, adding honey to her drawl, "what good is a vast fortune if you can't have your beloved son at your deathbed?"

★ ★ ★ ★ ★

"I don't know why he'd use an assumed name," Malachi growled, fixing the hapless young widow running the boarding house with his darkest scowl. "I expect it's because he's a rotten, no-good son-of-a—"

At Harry's elbow in his ribs, he paused and cleared his throat. "Pardon my language, ma'am." But he didn't intend to lie to the woman.

"Ma'am, this man hired thugs to beat up his wife, and we want to keep him from doing it again. But we need to find him first, and we're not having a damn bit of luck. We could sure use your cooperation."

Harry would not have thought a building in the clear, dry air of the high plains could ever be described as musty, at least not late in the afternoon of a golden autumn day, but the small, dark lobby of the Metropolitan Hotel somehow managed to exude a dank mustiness that she tried to pretend didn't smell like mouse droppings.

Squeezed between a warehouse and a huge three-story brick building that might once have held a bank, but now served as a German brewery, the narrow hotel building was one of the few clapboard structures in the city to have survived the fire of 'sixty-three. Denver itself was only thirty years old, but the worn, faded rug running from the door to the front desk of the Metropolitan Hotel looked at least a hundred.

"Charm wouldn't stay here," she told Malachi, reluctant to cross the threshold of the door he held open for her. "No self-respecting southern gentleman would stay in a dump like this."

"I would—" Malachi began.

"My point exactly."

"—If I wanted a room that was anonymous and cheap. If I were doing business that required an alias." He squinted into the dim lobby. "It's not like we've had any luck anywhere else."

Harry couldn't argue with that. After two days of fruitless searching, she had begun to doubt Charm Woodfin had ever arrived in Denver. She suspected Malachi would have called off the hunt already if not for Lissy's increasing desperation, and even that wouldn't keep him searching much longer.

Whether it was the thought of Lissy's urgency or a reluctance to contemplate returning home that pushed Harry forward, she didn't take time to consider.

"Let me do the talking," she murmured as she stepped gingerly onto the filthy rug. "I don't think your truth-at-all-costs policy will go over well here."

"Why? Because this isn't a fancy hotel? Because the people who stay here might be a little down on their luck?"

"Because it hasn't worked that well anywhere else."

A gray-haired man with a face as narrow and pinched as a ferret's sat on a stool behind the counter, watching them approach with an expression somewhere between world-weariness and disdain.

"Looking for a room for the night, sir?" The wispy mustache drooping beneath his nose twitched. "You and your . . . wife?"

"No," Malachi said bluntly, leaning one arm on the counter his other hand resting casually at his hip, where his jacket bulged over his Colt revolver. "I wouldn't let my wife set foot in one of your pest-ridden rooms, and if you say one word to her that I don't like, you'll find yourself missing part of your tongue."

Apparently Malachi's aversion to bending the truth went

only so far. Harry suspected her own eyes went as round as the hotel proprietor's. She also suspected the ferret-faced man had a weapon of his own somewhere nearby and that if he went for it, Malachi was irritable enough to make good his threat.

"Well, then," she said brightly, recapturing the hotel man's attention. "It's a good thing for you I ain't his wife. But I am here about my husband. The low-down snake's run off again, and I ain't about to let him get away with it."

The proprietor's mustache twitched, though he kept one wary eye on Malachi. "Drinker?"

"Drinking, gambling." When Harry was six, March had taught her how to spit properly. She put the knowledge to good use now, hitting the brass spittoon at the corner of the counter with greater accuracy than most of the hotel's clientele. "He's a louse."

"Maybe he's better off gone," the proprietor suggested, with a laconic shrug.

"Maybe if his name wasn't on the business lease, I wouldn't care if he never come back," Harry agreed. "But I don't aim to lose the saloon because he ain't there to sign the renewal." She gave the man a humorless grin. "I don't necessarily need him back alive. But I need him back."

"You think he's staying here?" the proprietor asked. "I have a lot of patrons coming and going."

Malachi snorted. "I can see that."

Harry dug into her purse and spun one of Tony's gold quarter-eagles on the counter. "You might remember my husband."

The ferret-black eyes gleamed, but Harry whisked the coin back before the man could grab it.

"The name's Charm Woodfin, but he might be going by a different one, on account of he'll know I'm looking to hunt him down. About my friend's height—" She gestured at Malachi. "Blond hair, pale green eyes. Silver tongue. Could charm the diamonds off a rattlesnake."

The hotel man held out his hand, palm up. "Might be I remember a fellow something like that."

Harry placed the coin in his hand. As his fingers curled around it, she grabbed hold of his fist. Years of roping horses had made her grip much stronger than most people expected. She held the man's hand in place.

She leaned a little closer to him. "Might be if you take that coin, you better have information worth the price."

He only smiled, a dry, ferret smile. "Fellow matching your description registered here under the name Lucky Bird a couple weeks ago. Dressed like a banker, except for that ridiculous gold and black checkered vest."

"That could be anyone."

"He wasn't real distinctive, so to speak. He said he was in town on business about his silver mines." The man's sneer expressed his thoughts about that. "Did like a drink, like you said, though I didn't see him drunk. Poured on the charm, but wasn't too free with a gratuity."

He twisted the coin in his fingers to illustrate his point.

Harry didn't doubt Ferret Face would make up a tale to earn a two-and-a-half dollar coin, but this story didn't sound interesting enough to be made up.

"Can't swear he was yours, though," he continued. "He was a southern boy."

Harry shot a look at Malachi, saw his eyes brighten, too.

"The louse hails from Georgia originally," she said. "Did you happen to notice . . . My husband wears a ring that you might remember."

The whiskers twitched. "I might at that."

Despite Malachi's grunt of protest, Harry gave him a

second quarter-eagle. With the other, it was enough for a week's rent of a room at the Metropolitan. But worth it if the man could lead them to Charm.

"With that ring and the smooth talk, I thought maybe he was a card sharp. Since he called himself Lucky and all. He wore a little ring on his pinky finger with a big green rock stuck to it. Worth a penny or two, I'd guess."

"That's him!" Harry could hardly believe it. Realizing she was bouncing like a schoolgirl, she dropped her heels to the floor and tried for an appropriate scowl. "The rat."

"Popular fellow, your husband," Ferret Face commented, a sly curl to his lips. "Had another wife in here looking for him, too."

Harry's elation wilted just a little. Lissy and Tony already knew. Though they were supposed to be hunting down jewelers that afternoon . . .

"Just about a week ago." The small, bright eyes watched her avidly. "Frenchy type. Dark hair, dark eyes. Not so fresh-faced as you." His pointy nose twitched. "Prettier, though."

Harry's face flamed. Good, she reminded herself. She had a part to play. "The low-down, no-good, rotten . . ." Her voice ground to a halt.

"She said she was having trouble with the boy."

"What boy?"

The proprietor shrugged. "Then there was those two men just yesterday. Short round one and a skinny redhead."

Harry's gaze met Malachi's.

"A spider and a fox," he murmured. It looked as though Lissy's Beasts had indeed come to Denver to meet up with their employer.

"They were looking for Charm? My husband?" Harry

asked. "Was he here? Did they find him?"

If they had, had they stayed in the hotel with him? Remembering Lissy's fear, she found her gaze dancing around the small, dark lobby.

"They were looking, all right. For him *and* his wife." Sharp teeth flashed in his grin. "Must have been a different one from you. This one was supposed to be a southern belle. Didn't find neither one of them here."

He slipped his gold coins into his vest pocket. "Your husband's gone. Been gone since Friday. I don't have any idea where, or I'd have been looking for him myself. He didn't pay his last night's bill. Those other fellows came by that afternoon, but I don't know as they've found him yet."

His grin narrowed. "Their story weren't near as sweet as yours." He patted his pocket.

"Ours could be sweeter," Malachi said, voice flat as his eyes. He passed the man a card. "We're staying at the Regency Hotel. If we get word he's come back—to pay his bill, or for any other reason—you'll see more of that gold."

Harry let him take her arm, only too happy to escape the weaselly proprietor and his dank grotto. In contrast, the afternoon sun nearly blinded her as they stepped out onto the broad, busy street.

"Three days," she groaned as they turned west, the Rocky Mountains rising in a magnificent backdrop beyond the city. "We missed him by three days."

"Could be worse."

Harry shrugged away from Malachi's arm to stare at him. "Worse? How? We've been looking all over Denver for him, and we just found out we've been wasting our time ever since we arrived."

She waved her hands in frustration. "Doesn't that bother you at all?"

"No." Malachi turned them down Blake Street toward their hotel.

Harry's breath hissed through her teeth. "But he's probably gone back to Savannah!"

"Good."

He grabbed Harry's elbow, pulling her out of the way of a stout man wrestling a large barrel of salted pork across the sidewalk.

Harry managed to smile apologetically at the sweating shopkeeper while unobtrusively stomping on Malachi's foot.

"What about Lissy?" she reminded him, in a fierce whisper.

"If Charm Woodfin and his thugs have returned to Georgia, they can't hurt Lissy here."

"What if the Beasts haven't left? What if they're still looking for her in Denver?"

Harry felt again the dread that had shivered through her when the proprietor of the Metropolitan Hotel had described Lissy's spider and fox. Walking Denver's wide, straight streets in the bright afternoon light, she suddenly felt she stood out like a hare who'd forgotten to turn white after the first snowfall. And the Beasts weren't even looking for her.

"Charm Woodfin is not going to waste his money paying three men to hunt for a runaway wife who might never have arrived in Colorado," Malachi said, too calmly.

"You were hoping we wouldn't find him."

His green eyes met hers with no attempt to duck the accusation. "Lissy wants us to get her money back from Charm. He's got wealth, the law, and Rafe and Clayton Wilmer on his side. I can't pretend I'm sorry we can keep her safe without having to take them on."

Harry paused under the striped awning of a tobacco shop, studying Malachi's face. "You've thought all this through." She should have known. He wouldn't take on a job without considering the ramifications. "What do you think Charm will do?"

"I think he'll assume Lissy will return to Savannah when she gets cold and hungry. Either she'll go to him or to her family."

"She won't," Harry said. She couldn't go back to Charm's Beasts and her family's indifference. Although, if she were cold enough and hungry enough . . . "She can't."

"If she's willing to get her hands dirty, she won't starve in Colorado. There's work in Denver."

"Taking in washing?" Harry asked, picturing Lissy up to her elbows in soapy water, her soft hands red and raw. "Working as a cook in a mining camp? She wouldn't last a week."

"You work on a ranch."

My father wouldn't have stood for it. The boy'll have the muscles for the work. He'll get twice as much done in half the time. Harry stretched her arms. Whatever Ash's opinion of her muscles, she had some. Lissy didn't.

"I work for my brother," she said. "Do you think anyone else would hire me? I have skill and experience, and I couldn't make a living on my own."

"It doesn't matter. I understand your future husband has plenty of money."

Harry's throat constricted, stopping her breath long enough for her not to say the first thing that came into her mind. Long enough for her to notice a flash of hostility in Malachi's eyes that she couldn't interpret. Long enough for her to put Mrs. Danforth's unwanted training to good use.

"*Mrs.* Woodfin doesn't have that option, now does she?"

she asked with icy calm.

Malachi stared back at her, his eyes blank with some internal argument of his own. To her surprise, he backed down, his gaze shifting as he stepped forward once more. The strong, sweet smell of pipe tobacco followed them from the shop front back into the slanted rays of the afternoon sun.

"We'll think of something," he muttered. His eyes flashed emerald at her. "Something better than Tony hiring her on as housekeeper at the Fox and Hound."

"What?" Harry knew Tony had not found a satisfactory housekeeper since the sudden departure of the last one that past summer. Philomena Jones had disappeared hours before her son's outlaw gang was apprehended by Malachi's posse for robbery, murder, and kidnapping. Harry tried to imagine southern belle Lissy Woodfin in the pale, bitter woman's place. "Tony's suggested that? Why?"

But she could answer her own question. Why would a canny businessman like Tony Wayne offer to hire an untrained, unsuitable, unskilled lady to run his hotel's housekeeping? For the same reason he would take time off from his work to play white knight on a ridiculous quest to Denver.

She remembered Malachi's dismissal of her suggestion that Lissy might be falling for Tony. He'd been worried it was the other way around.

"Tony's always gallant with the ladies," she objected as they crossed the street toward the Regency Hotel. "He could hardly refuse to help a damsel in distress."

"No, he couldn't," Malachi agreed. "But he could help her without leaving Battlement Park. Without spending every waking moment for three days squiring her around Denver."

"You and I've been together just as much the past three days." For some reason, the words brought an unexpected heat to her face.

Malachi moved ahead to open the hotel door for her.

"Such a perfect gentleman," she said, though she couldn't quite meet his gaze.

"For a perfect lady," he agreed. His voice dropped to reach only her. "Or a perfect actress. Are you sure you're not really a drunken saloon-keeper's wife?"

Harry gave him her coolest, haughtiest stare. "Why, sir, I have no idea what you're talking about."

Malachi's mouth twisted. "Maybe playing the lady is more practical than I thought."

Harry simply raised her eyebrows and preceded him across the lobby. He had no idea.

No idea how easy her performance at the Metropolitan Hotel that afternoon had been, how easy the past three days had been, once more part of Malachi Kelly's posse. Once more feeling as if she belonged. Would he understand that feeling? Of being able to accomplish anything as long as they worked together?

He had no idea how she'd come to dread returning to Oxtail, to the questions she had run from less than a week before. To the marriage that was so much closer now, and felt so strangely further away.

He had no idea that she hardly dared hold his gaze when his eyes searched hers with that unfathomable intensity. What was he looking for? Even she didn't know what she was afraid he would find.

One thing she was sure of, she didn't want to share any of that confusion with Malachi Kelly. She didn't want him digging any deeper into her desires and fears.

Playing the lady was practical indeed.

Chapter 8

"Gone? He can't be gone!" Lissy's knees weakened, and she sank onto the settee behind her in the alcove of the Regency's lobby. Harry and Malachi had met them looking so full of news when she and Tony had returned from yet another day of fruitless searching that a spark of hope had lit in her heart. But . . . "He left Friday?"

So close. She had to shut her eyes against a wave of dizzying disappointment.

"Perhaps Malachi's right," Tony said. The settee shifted as he sat beside her. "It could be for the best that he's returned to Savannah."

"He hasn't gone back to Savannah." He had been in Denver. She'd missed him, but he'd been here. She'd guessed correctly. She couldn't quite believe it. And if he'd been here, she could follow him. He must have left some kind of trail. If only she could have spoken to the hotel man, asked him if Charm had what she was looking for . . .

"Why wouldn't he go back to Savannah?" Malachi asked, his sharp tone snapping her back to reality.

"He's not due to return home for another two weeks." She was becoming more adept at the steps to this dance around the truth. "He never returns home early."

"Even to look for a runaway wife?" Malachi asked.

"Maybe the Beasts found him and told him they couldn't find you," Harry suggested. "The hotel proprietor said Fox and Spider were there the same afternoon he left."

"What?" A wave of cold terror slammed into Lissy's spine, knocking her breath away. If the Beasts had reached Charm before she did . . . "They found him? Did that man say they found him?"

A hand clasped her shoulder.

"Steady there," Tony said, his strong grip holding her back from the sharp edge of panic. "Are you all right?"

"Harry?" she pleaded.

"Ferret Face said Charm had already left before they came looking for him." Harry took the armchair across from Lissy, her brow creased in concern for Lissy's fear. "He didn't even tell the Beasts Charm had been there. He didn't find them very agreeable. I guess Charm didn't think to leave a forwarding address for them."

Lissy forced herself to breathe, to push the dread back down behind the necessity that had brought her this far. If Charm had taken the care to use an assumed name in an out-of-the-way hotel, he wouldn't leave a trail of bread crumbs after him. And she knew Charm's reason for coming to Denver, a secret that would give her an edge in the race with the Beasts. She hoped.

"Even if they did meet up with Charm," Harry continued, "they could only tell him they haven't found you. Maybe he completed his business early and headed home, hoping to find you back in Charleston or Savannah."

Lissy had hoped she wouldn't have to tell them, back when they were strangers she distrusted. Now that she knew them better, now that they had helped her, the shame burned even deeper.

"Charm didn't come to Denver solely for business," she said. The words were harder to force out than she expected, though the pain had long ago gone stale. "There is a person who lives here in Denver whom he wanted to see. A woman."

She took a deep breath, blew it out. "A certain kind of woman."

Tony's hand tightened on her shoulder. "The bloody bastard."

"A woman did come to see him at the hotel," Harry said.

"Why didn't you mention that before?" Lissy demanded, then stopped, her smile bitter. "Never mind. I know why not. Do you know what she looked like?"

"The proprietor said she was pretty. Dark hair, dark eyes. He thought she might be French."

"Angelique." She hadn't spoken the name aloud in years. It burned like vinegar on her tongue. "Angelique Dubray. She was his mistress in Savannah."

"The man's a bloody fool," Tony said. "The more I learn about him, the better I like the idea of having a little chat with him. No offense intended, but what were you thinking when you married this chap?"

Lissy risked meeting his gaze and found humor forcing out the pity in his warm brown eyes. She could have kissed him for it. A dangerously appealing idea. She hadn't noticed before what nice lips he had.

Fortunately, as Malachi had pointed out, she was no longer fool enough to fall for a handsome face and a warm smile. Marriage to Charm had cured her, although she apparently still showed some symptoms.

"She was thinking Charm had prospects."

Between Charm and Malachi, she should soon be well

rid of any temptation to kiss anyone.

"I was seventeen," she said. "I thought I deserved a white knight to sweep me away from all my troubles. Charm was the most gallant knight at the ball."

So there, *Malachi Kelly.*

"I considered him my white knight for almost three years. Even after he went to work for my brothers. Until I found out about Angelique."

Her left thumb strayed to her wedding band. Another few dollars in case of an emergency. "He told me he loved me, that he would never see her again, but he lied. He kept lying until I realized our whole marriage was a lie, one that I could not escape."

Maybe Charm had felt that way, too. The unexpected insight brought more sadness than anger. Maybe they had both been trapped by the youthful lack of judgment that had led to their marriage.

"I had my pride. I told him I would not live in the same town with his mistress. I don't know that he cared about my feelings, but I told him I would go to my father. That frightened him. I guess he didn't know about Daddy's mistresses."

"Angelique came to Denver?" Harry asked.

Lissy nodded. It was almost a relief finally to tell someone. Yet it nearly overwhelmed her to have them look at her without the condemnation she expected. "He wrote to her. He didn't know I knew. It wasn't worth making a scene by then."

Tony's hand stroked down her back, and Lissy felt an overpowering urge to lean against his shoulder, let the tears fall if they would.

Instead, she drew herself up with a shake. She couldn't let Charm's infidelity distract her from her goal. Angelique could be the only opportunity she would have to find him. And she had to find him before Spider Grant did.

"All we need to do is find Angelique Dubray," she said. "If we find Angelique, we'll find Charm."

Malachi pinched his nose wearily. "Another wild goose chase."

"Perhaps . . ." Tony hesitated. "Perhaps if Charm has met with this Dubray woman, it could be to your advantage. He may be less inclined to pursue you."

Hell and damnation, Lissy thought, in a distinctly unsouthern accent. Time to dance faster.

"He can't allow me to disappear," she said. "It would be too embarrassing. What would he tell my father and brothers? Besides, how will I pay you for your help if we don't find him? How will I live if he doesn't return what he took from me?"

"We don't care about the money," Tony said, with a decisiveness that almost convinced her he was sincere. Compounding her bafflement, neither Harry nor Malachi contradicted him. "And we can work out your living. You can write your family, let them know you are safe. Perhaps after some time has passed, you can obtain a legal separation from Charm."

Lissy had to control a sudden urge to cry, and to laugh. She had been forced to run away from home because she could not find safety with her own family, and these three, a man who had every reason to turn his back on her and two strangers, were threatening her only hope for the future in equal measure with their generosity and compassion.

Even Malachi dropped to his heels to look her in the eye. His voice was softer than his words. "Lissy, we're not going to tramp all over Denver for another three days looking for a woman of easy virtue, on the off chance she might lead us to a group of violent thugs. As much fun as that might sound."

"One more day?" Lissy asked, unable to hold back either the dampness in her eyes or the ironic smile on her lips. "I declare. A knight would humor a lady's quest with one more day."

"We'll never find her in one day," Tony said gently.

"We might," she said, digging into her blue silk handbag and pulling out the slip of paper on which she'd written Charm's aliases, among other things. "I have Angelique's address."

"This is insane," Mal ranted from his seat on his hotel bed, watching Tony shave in front of the mirror in the wash room. "I'm not taking Lissy and Harry to Market Street to look for a prostitute."

"This week has been quite a revelation," Tony said, stretching his neck to reach the stubble under his chin. "I never realized what a prude you are."

Mal glared at his friend in the mirror. "I don't think it's particularly unwarranted not to want to take a pair of ladies to a whorehouse."

"It's a saloon. The South Platte Saloon."

"You know as well as I do what trade any girl living above a saloon along that section of Market Street is plying."

Tony's eyes sparkled much too merrily above the lather on his cheeks. "You know this from experience, Mal?"

"Ha. I'm not worried about running into anyone I know, if that's what you're suggesting." His time in the army had precluded that. He'd seen too many camp followers—and army captives—used and abandoned. "How about you?"

Tony's voice sharpened. "No one should have to live like

that. I don't intend to contribute to it."

Mal grunted skeptically. "You're a regular choir boy. I don't even want to know how you managed to get my appointment to justice of the peace speeded through for me."

The gleam returned to Tony's eyes. "The Governor's secretary's dearest friend's widow, quite a lovely lady, just happened to have stayed at the Fox and Hound last—"

"I said I don't want to know."

"I didn't sully her honor, if that's what you're on about." Tony swished his razor in the wash basin. "I am capable of enjoying a woman's company without risking a scandal."

That was true, Mal knew. And the women enjoyed Tony's company. The women came and went from Battlement Park, a little innocent flirting, no one got hurt. He had thought Tony had found a way to protect himself from love's hurt. Until he'd seen the way Tony looked at Lissy Woodfin.

"We were talking about Angelique Dubray," he said.

"We were talking about Harriet Jackson and Elizabeth Woodfin," Tony corrected. "And how you don't want to expose them to Market Street. But Mrs. Woodfin is quite right. She's the only one of us who will recognize Mademoiselle Dubray, and you can't expect Harry to stay behind if the rest of us go."

He glanced over his shoulder at his friend. "It will be broad daylight, Mal. It shouldn't take more than a half hour to determine if Miss Dubray is at that address and whether or not she has any idea of where Charm Woodfin has gone."

"You and Harry think this is a game," Mal said, frustration tightening his voice.

Tony shook his head, turning back to the mirror. "Life is

a game, Mal. You don't always have to be so deadly serious about it."

"Death *is* serious. And I've seen quite enough of it." And enough misery, pettiness, hatred, violence, and selfishness to last a lifetime. The memories pressed closer with the press of bodies in the city, the press of human wants and greeds and unfulfilled desires.

He wanted to smell the damp grasses of the meadow behind the Fox and Hound, to hear the complaint of a blue jay, to taste the air expanding around him in clear, open space.

"You just want to get away," Tony said, once more striking uncomfortably close to Mal's thoughts.

"I won't mind leaving the city."

"Away from Denver, yes." Tony splashed fresh water from the pitcher over his face and dried it with the hotel's thick cotton towel. "And away from Harriet Jackson."

"Harry?"

"Bloody right, Harry." Tony turned, his expression suddenly serious. "It's obvious you don't like the idea of her marrying this Brady chap."

"I don't want her to end up regretting it," Mal said. "It doesn't sound like he knows Harry at all."

"Not like we do?" Tony suggested, shrugging into a clean white shirt.

"No. I just hope she's taken a good look at Lissy's situation."

"Maybe she should take a look at her," Tony retorted. "She'd see a woman with the strength to live gracefully in the face of adversity. What do you have against her, Mal, besides hating her brothers? You haven't given her a chance since she arrived here."

What did he have against her besides the fear of seeing

just such an expression on Tony's face? He had reacted to seeing Lissy again exactly as a twenty-one-year-old youth would react to seeing the girl who had spurned him. He was a thirty-two-year-old man now, and Lissy was not the girl he had known. If he had known her. For he had never guessed she had such strength and resiliency beneath that spun-sugar surface.

After spending time in her company these past few days, he realized that while he did not regret not marrying her, there was a humor and grit in her that he genuinely liked. He understood what Tony admired about her. Which only made it more imperative that he find a way to prevent their continued association. An attraction between Tony and Lissy could bring only heartache to both of them.

"I don't have anything against Lissy," he said, finally. "And you're right. She's survived a terrible situation with admirable grace. But I don't think Harry . . ." How had he gotten back to Harry? "I don't think Harry would survive a Charm Woodfin. I think it would break her spirit to be forced into being a lady."

"Harry plays a bloody fine lady," Tony reminded him. "Almost fools me from time to time."

"I didn't say she didn't like to play," Mal said. "But she couldn't even make it through finishing school. How long do you think she'd survive without being able to ride or wear blue jeans or go fishing? This Ash Brady doesn't even know she can shoot."

"Harry hasn't met a scrape yet she couldn't get herself out of."

"Marriage isn't a scrape!"

"I'm sure she knows that," Tony said mildly, adjusting his wide, striped necktie. "And maybe you're right. She's got a bit to prepare for. If she wants to marry this chap, she ought to be home getting ready."

Mal frowned. "Exactly. So what is she doing in Denver?"

Tony raised an eyebrow. "Perhaps she's not sure she wants to marry the bloke, after all."

"What do you mean? You don't think Harry wants to get married?"

"I didn't say that," Tony demurred, checking his reflection in the mirror. "I said perhaps she wasn't sure she wanted to marry this particular chap. There. What do you think? Do I look ready for a jaunt to Market Street?"

"You look like you can afford to pay, which is all they're looking for," Mal said coldly. Something hard had settled in his gut. Something he did not want to know. But he had to ask. "You think she's still in love with my brother."

Tony's smug smile disappeared. "No, I don't think that, Mal. I think she was getting over those feelings even before he and Jordan were married."

Mal forced himself to his feet. "Maybe. Maybe not. Are you ready?"

It was no business of his if Harry did still have feelings for his brother. Or if she married Ash Brady. He'd never had much luck saving his friends from their own mistakes. Which did not give him good odds on getting Tony away from Lissy Woodfin.

He rubbed the bridge of his nose, trying to force back a threatening headache, and made the mistake of glancing at Tony's mirror. He should have followed Tony's lead and shaved. Well, it could wait another day. A hat would have hidden his hair. If he'd thought to bring one.

Clean air and a cool mountain breeze. That was all he wanted. All he needed to hope for. Whatever harebrained scheme Tony concocted for Lissy's future, at least wrapping up this quest of hers would get Mal back to Battlement

Park. From there, he wouldn't be able to watch Harry's spirit being broken. Though he feared he would feel it, in that place where his heart had once been.

"Let's get this done," he said, grabbing his coat from the rack by the door. "I still say we should go without them."

"It won't take half an hour," Tony repeated, following him out into the hall. "How much trouble can Lissy and Harry get into in half an hour?"

Harry's boot caught on a warped board of the sidewalk, and she tumbled sideways, nearly knocking Malachi into the path of an oncoming wagon.

"The derringer's more reliable, if you're trying to kill me," he said, steadying her on her feet.

"That woman," Harry said, nearly stumbling again as her eyes were drawn inexorably back to the large Italianate brick building they had just passed. "In the window. She wasn't wearing . . . I could see . . ."

"Watch where you're walking," Malachi commanded, grabbing the back of her neck to turn her head. "You look greener than the greenest boy on the street."

Harry skipped a step to get her feet back under her and threw a hand to her head to make sure her broad-brimmed black hat was still firmly in place, hiding her hair.

It had been Lissy's idea that she would attract less comment by walking Market Street dressed as a boy, and Harry was glad of the disguise. Playing a wide-eyed country youth gave her every excuse to gawk at the cat houses, gambling halls, and opium dens that offered their wares to an impressive variety of cowboys, miners, and businessmen.

She would not have thought there would be much commerce occurring at such establishments so early on a Tuesday afternoon, but apparently she had been wrong.

Piano music spilled from saloon doors, women served drinks in scanty dresses and posed in windows in even less, and the smell of tobacco and more exotic smokes wafted in the still, afternoon air.

At times in Oxtail, she'd felt terribly worldly compared to the young women in town, having lived in the East, in Philadelphia. Some of her acquaintances had never been as far as Denver or Cheyenne. But at the moment, Harry felt every inch the country rustic, overawed by such an ostentatious display of debauchery.

"Here we are," Tony said, bringing them to a stop in front of a broad expanse of dark glass with "South Platte Saloon" etched across it. "Everyone ready?"

Lissy nodded. Determination sharpened her features beneath her powder and rouge, but Harry could see the strong grip she had on Tony's arm.

Lissy and Tony, posing as characters of questionable morals from Savannah, would ask about Angelique Dubray, an old acquaintance of theirs. Harry and Malachi were to wait in the bar, staying handy in case anyone matching Charm's or Angelique's description tried to slip out of the saloon.

"Let's get on with it," Malachi said. As he reached for the swinging door, it exploded outward, spitting out a tall, gangly cowboy who fell facedown on the sidewalk.

"And don't you come back until you can mind your manners," a voice bellowed after him, followed by a woman even taller than the cowboy wearing an elegant red silk dress trimmed in black lace.

"Why, Miss Lily, I didn't mean—" The towheaded young man's apology faltered under a firm application of Miss Lily's polished black high-heeled boot to his posterior. He stayed down, covering the back of his neck with his hands. "Honest, I didn't mean no harm."

"You'll keep your grubby hands off my girls until you can pay for the privilege," Miss Lily said.

"It was just the whiskey—"

"And you won't be getting drunk again at my place until you pay off your tab. Now get out of my sight."

The cowboy managed to stagger to his feet, though he wobbled. "Now, Miss Lily, there ain't no need—"

"I said, get the hell out of my sight," Miss Lily repeated. "Before I come back with my no-good-cowboy plugger."

At that, the young man scrambled away down the sidewalk, fear keeping him on his feet, at least around the nearest corner.

After watching him out of sight, Miss Lily turned her formidable presence on Harry's group. In her heels, she was as tall as Tony's six feet, but height didn't make her awkward. The red dress hugged ample curves that seemed to sway even when she stood still, and her face, while not beautiful, held an animation that caught the eye.

"What are you just standing there for?" she demanded. "That sun's only going to make you thirstier."

She stepped back into the cooler dimness of the saloon, leaning a shoulder against the door to hold it open for them. Harry dipped her hat as she passed her, to hide her face from Miss Lily's sharp appraisal.

"Why, thank you, Miz Lily," Tony said, forging a terrible Georgian accent that Harry thought could only reinforce his persona as a shady gentleman.

Harry and Malachi left him and Lissy to tell their tall tale and worked their way into the saloon.

At two o'clock in the afternoon, the establishment already held a number of patrons, but, to Harry's surprise after witnessing the ejection of the drunken cowboy, none appeared rowdy. Two more cowboys sat on far-separated stools at the bar, each drinking in silence. A table nearby held a serious-looking card game presided over by a gentleman whose long, silver hair brushed the collar of his elegant mallard green coat. Scattered at tables about the rest of the room sat several men in good suits, sipping brandy or coffee, smoking fine cigars, reading the *Rocky Mountain News*, for all the world as if the South Platte Saloon were nothing more than a respectable gentleman's club.

The diffuse light, the elegantly upholstered armchairs, the silence broken only by low murmurs and the rustle of newspapers, all contributed to an atmosphere of quiet gentility, though the grand piano in the corner, the unlit chandeliers reflected in the mirrored ceilings, and the faint scent of spilled whiskey and faded perfume hinted at the noise and revelry to come later in the evening. And Harry doubted that many of the city's legitimate business clubs featured either paintings of voluptuous nudes behind the bar or barmaids clad in dresses so short in each direction that they revealed both cleavage and garters.

Harry followed Malachi to a table by the window which gave them a clear view of the front door and of the staircase that led from the entrance hall to the upper two stories of the building. Among the tables along the window stood several three-quarter height statues of women, many of them appearing to represent Eve with the serpent.

Malachi took the chair facing the entrance way, leaving her to sit with her back to the action, but Harry's objection flew from her mind as she paused by the nude beside their table. This last statue broke the symmetry of the group by both its male gender and its artistic merit. The youth was more beautiful than all the Eves; Harry almost expected to see him breathe, despite the rough spots in the plaster. But it wasn't his beauty that caught her eye.

"A rough copy of Michelangelo's David," Malachi commented, then, following her gaze, "somewhat anatomically enhanced. Sit down, Harry. I told you this was a bad idea."

Harry sat, furiously trying to control the red in her cheeks. She had seen enough of birth and death and sex on the Jackson ranch to erase much of the embarrassment Mrs. Danforth had tried to instill in her charges toward those subjects, but she had never seen a naked man before.

She stared straight down at the table in front of her, fiercely *not* wondering if that was what Malachi looked like without clothes. Of course, it wasn't. When they'd ridden together that summer hunting outlaws, she'd seen him with his shirt unbuttoned. His chest was brushed with curls of bronzed brown hair, not smooth like the statue's.

Everything about him was rougher than the statue—his work-hardened hands, the creases in his face, the darkness that sometimes haunted his eyes. The statue might have been of an angel, cool and unconcerned with earthly matters. Much safer than human flesh and blood.

"You looking for your fortune in that table, hon?"

"Ma'am?" Harry squeaked, looking up into the thickly made-up face of one of the barmaids.

"This your first time at the South Platte Saloon?" The woman's broad red smile held a touch of sympathy under the amusement.

"The boy's not looking for female companionship," Malachi said bluntly.

"That right?" the barmaid asked, winking at Harry. "You just keeping this fellow company?"

"Yes, ma'am," Harry replied, remembering to drop her voice to a more masculine range. She could see the effort only increased the woman's amusement, and she could imagine the ribbing she would take from Malachi later. The thought steadied her nerves. She'd couldn't let him best her.

"Our girls don't bite," the barmaid said. "Not unless you ask them to, anyways. Sweet Sal will be happy to make a man of you."

"Oh, no, ma'am." Harry gave the barmaid her best pious look. "You see, I'm planning to study for the priesthood."

Malachi's cough sounded as though he were choking.

"I'm to catch the train to the seminary in Boston tomorrow. My uncle's brought me into Denver to make sure I get off safely. You can imagine how disappointed I am in his behavior."

"I sure can, hon," the barmaid said, shaking her head with a laugh. "I guess your escort won't be wanting Sweet Sal's charms tonight, neither. That right, Uncle?"

"Whiskey," Malachi said curtly. "A sarsaparilla for the boy."

"Coming right up." The barmaid winked at Harry. "I'll warn the girls to be on their best behavior. Wouldn't want them to tempt you into sin."

As the woman walked away, short skirt swishing, Harry met Malachi's exasperated gaze.

"Hell and damnation."

As one, they turned their faces to the window, choking back their laughter.

That was why neither one of them noticed when the Beasts walked into the saloon.

Chapter 9

Miss Lily didn't appear to find Tony's tale of an invitation to visit his old Savannah friend Angelique far-fetched. Lissy guessed the statuesque madam, who, upon closer inspection was probably ten years older than she appeared at first glance, had just about heard it all at one time or another.

She also didn't seem to find it strange that Tony had brought a new lady friend to visit the old one or to find it hard to believe that Lissy was a "bride of the multitude." Lissy might have found that unforgivably insulting a month or two ago. Standing in a brothel's entrance hall with no money, a vanished husband, and with three thugs on her trail, she wondered if a little makeup and some table etiquette was truly all that separated women of her class in Savannah from these soiled doves of the frontier.

Considering the young prostitute who had offered to return her diamond ring, Lissy suspected some of her Savannah acquaintances might end up on the losing end of the comparison.

". . . and I told her I'd hold her room for her for two weeks. I've seen it too many times, my girls running off with some man promising pie in the sky. Like as not, they're back in a week, sadder but wiser, and glad for a roof over their heads. Angelique's only been gone since Friday."

"And you don't know where she went?" Lissy asked, her hold on her courage beginning to crumble. Angelique was her last hope.

Miss Lily shook her head. "She said her man owned a silver mine, here in Colorado somewhere. He gave her jewelry, it's true. But I don't know why a man with a silver mine and an emerald the size of a butter bean on his pinky would need to borrow money from a prostitute to pay for his whiskey."

The madam's shrug suggested one could not expect much from such a man. Lissy had to agree.

"I warned her. My girls make a good living. They keep half of what they earn. And she's old enough to know better, not like some of these flighty young things. But she had diamonds dancing in her eyes and pearls in her ears.

"She wanted to make a better life for her sister's kid that had come to stay with her. And I warrant you, a place like mine ain't no place for a boy, though he wasn't no trouble. But it was the silver and jewels that got to Angelique."

"A silver mine?" Lissy prodded. Miss Lily's words set her heart pounding, but she had to stay focused. "Didn't she say where?"

Miss Lily raised arched brows. "Honey, it wouldn't matter where she said it was. Mine owners don't sit in a whorehouse with their backs to the wall, jumping every time somebody walks through the front door."

"Can you tell us this gentleman's name?" Tony asked, his steady calm keeping Lissy from screaming. She couldn't think about losing Charm's trail. She couldn't think about losing . . .

She forced herself to picture Angelique Dubray wearing

her grandmother's black pearl earrings instead. That steadied her nerves.

"I didn't care what his name was," the madam said bluntly. "If he hadn't taken one of my best girls, I would have been glad to see the back of him. I've seen my share of his type. Trouble is what they are."

"It was very kind of you to hold Angelique's room, Miss Lily," Lissy said, her mind grasping for the next step, anything to keep from admitting the trail was lost. "Would you object to our taking a peek inside? Maybe she left something that would tell us where she's gone."

"Just why are you so all-fired determined to find Angelique?" Miss Lily asked, suspicion abruptly narrowing her eyes. "The girls at the South Platte Saloon are my girls, and if you're looking for trouble with them, you're looking for trouble with me."

"Why," Tony began, his amiable smile broader than his phony southern drawl, "Why, Miz Lily, we're just—"

"The man Angelique ran off with is my husband," Lissy said. Her heart thumped coldly in her chest at the risk she was taking, but she thought Miss Lily's direct nature might respond to directness in kind. "I understand you want to protect Angelique. I don't care about her. He's the one I need to find."

She held her breath, prepared to find herself flying out the front door like the drunken cowboy, but Miss Lily simply raised one pencilled eyebrow. "Honey, if your husband's running around on you, promising to marry whores, maybe you're just as well off not finding him."

"I don't want him back." Lissy thought she caught a gleam of approval in the madam's eye at her vehemence. "Angelique can have him. But he took more from me than my pride. And I want it back."

Miss Lily's mouth twisted down. "Better to go forward than go back," she said. "I can tell you that from personal experience. But you can check Angelique's room if you want."

"Thank you," Lissy said, the words heartfelt.

"Second one on the left at the first landing." The madam waved them toward the stairs. "Just remember, I know every piece of furniture in that room. Every lamp, every mirror belongs to me."

"Understood," Tony assured her. "We'll leave it all as we find it."

As she preceded Tony up the stairs, Lissy shot a glance into the saloon where Harry and Malachi appeared to be ordering from one of the barmaids. She doubted they'd have time to finish their drinks before she and Tony were through searching Angelique's room.

She took a deep breath, as deep as she could in her corset, forcing air past the tendrils of despair twining up her lungs. When Angelique's room yielded no clues to Charm's whereabouts, Malachi would insist on giving up the search. She couldn't blame him.

All three of her companions had already done more than anyone in her life, besides her grandmother, had ever done for her before. Tramping across Colorado, prowling through cathouses, throwing Tony's good money after her bad judgment.

She could not give up the search, would never give up as long as she drew breath, but she could not ask them to continue it.

Second door on the left.

She breathed again, steeling herself. Lying, cheating, and stealing were one thing. She would never have believed she would stoop to ransacking a prostitute's bedroom.

"Let me," Tony said. He rapped on the door before swinging it open.

Lissy stepped into a larger room than she had expected. The afternoon sunlight, softened by the white lace curtains on the window, brightened a chamber as well-proportioned and elegant as the one she shared with Harry at the Regency Hotel. Though somewhat less subdued.

The wine-striped wallpaper, gleaming wood paneling, and heavy cherry wood furniture served only to showcase the risqué paintings, the bright, scanty dresses spilling out of the open wardrobe, and the huge, canopied bed with its crimson satin sheets.

"It looks as though she packed light," Tony commented, crossing to the wardrobe. "She must have been in a hurry." Without any apparent embarrassment, he pushed aside scraps of lace and satin that would not have dressed a squirrel decently.

However, the sight of his long, strong hands on ladies underthings brought a furious blush to Lissy's cheeks. Turning abruptly away, she yanked open the top drawer of the dresser. Angelique had been more thorough in her packing here. Only a few scraps of underclothes, some dried flower petals, and some half-empty bottles of perfume remained.

No papers, no envelopes, no maps proclaiming, "Charm Woodfin's nonexistent silver mine lies here."

She scattered the small pieces of cloth to make sure nothing hid underneath them. Not underdrawers, after all. Stockings? She pulled out a bit of black linen. Not unless Angelique had tiny feet. The sack was lined with velvet. Jewelry bags? They might be a clue to Charm's activities over the past few weeks.

"What do you think this is?" she asked, turning to hold up the little bag.

Tony was checking the space under the bed. He turned in his crouch to glance over at her. After a long stare at what she held, a flush began creeping up his neck and across his fair cheeks, though his eyes sparked with barely contained amusement.

"That, Mrs. Woodfin, is, how shall I . . ." He cleared his throat as he stood. "Those can be used to prevent various consequences of . . . an evening with a lady."

"Consequences?"

"Of one kind or another. In the case of an establishment like Miss Lily's, perhaps some patrons prefer to use them for reasons of hygiene."

"Hygiene." Lissy squinted at the item in her hand. It wouldn't serve as a washcloth. It was just a slim little bag of linen.

"The rubber variety are more efficacious, but perhaps not so elegant."

Rubber? As she examined the shape, long and tubular, she suddenly understood Tony's exaggerated circumspection.

"Oh, my God!" She crumpled the sheath in her hand and thrust it behind her back.

"Oh." She tried for nonchalance. "Those sorts of consequences."

She turned back to the dresser with cool calm. Holding up such a thing for a gentleman's inspection in a bordello bedroom could not possibly embarrass her after all she'd already been through.

Glancing in the dresser mirror, she grudgingly accepted that the fiery blush on her face and the imperfectly repressed amusement on Tony's suggested otherwise.

Much worse than the embarrassment was the sudden warmth that flowed down her spine and into the pit of her stomach at the thought of meeting Tony's gaze, of letting him see in her eyes where the linen contraption's purpose had taken her thoughts.

"Hey! You can't use this room."

Lissy stuffed the little sheath away and spun toward the doorway. A young blond woman with a narrow face and prominent front teeth stood in the hall, wrapped in an old dressing robe.

"This room's occupied," she said, the slightest of whistles hissing through her teeth. She glanced at Tony, then turned a fierce glare on Lissy. "And you ain't even one of Miss Lily's girls. You can just take your gentleman friend somewheres else, before I get Miss Lily up here with her gun."

Lissy pressed a hand over her eyes. The day just kept getting better.

"We're terribly sorry, miss," Tony said. "We didn't mean to trespass on your chamber. Miss Lily told us she was holding this room for Angelique Dubray's return."

"This is Angelique's room." The young prostitute crossed her arms under her ample bosom and regarded him with deep suspicion. "Miss Lily never said you could use it."

"She didn't," Lissy agreed. "She said we could look through the things Angelique left behind. We're trying to figure out where she's gone. We need to find her."

"Find her?" The girl uncrossed her arms. "Like bring her back here, you mean?" A faint light entered her dulled blue eyes. "Could you bring her back? I told Miss Lily not to let her go. That fella weren't no good for her. He said he'd marry her, but he was married already. I seen the mark of the wedding band on his finger."

"He's no good, that's for bloody sure," Tony agreed heartily.

"You know him?" the girl asked. "Mr. Prince?"

"Prince?" Tony asked. "We're looking for a Mr. Lucky Bird."

"Naw. Angelique's fella was Mr. Prince. I seen his card."

"That's the man we're looking for," Lissy said, her pulse beginning to quicken. A new name. But if he'd put money into having cards printed, he meant to stick with this one for a while.

"Prince doesn't fit the pattern of Charm's aliases," Tony said.

"Emerald pinky ring?" Lissy asked the prostitute.

She nodded.

"Haven't you ever read Monsieur Perrault's Cinderella?" Lissy asked Tony. "Charm has apparently transformed himself into Prince Charming."

And Lissy would have been happy to let Angelique play Cinderella, but Charm owed her more than a crystal slipper.

"I believe Mr. Prince could be involving Angelique in terrible trouble." Her voice rang with the truth of her words, and Angelique's young friend believed them. "Do you have any idea where he might have taken her?"

"Well, sure." The girl adjusted her robe, which threatened to slip off one bare shoulder. "To his silver mine. He said he called it the Lucky Lady after him and Angelique. Angelique said it was out near Central City or somewheres."

Lissy glanced at Tony, saw him as nonplussed as she. They couldn't be that lucky. More likely Charm had changed his name once again. The silver mine didn't exist. They'd left for California, not Central City. She couldn't afford to hope.

Yet hope was pounding in her chest.

"Thank you. Oh, thank you, Miss . . ." Impulsively, she strode to the door and grabbed the prostitute's hand. "What's your name?"

"Deirdre," the girl said, suddenly bashful. She brought a hand up to touch her mouth, tapping her buck teeth. "But the girls just call me Bunny."

"When we find Angelique, we'll tell her she has a true friend here at Miss Lily's," Lissy promised, and she meant it.

"Let's go find Harry and Mal," Tony said, touching her elbow to guide her out the door past Deirdre. "Central City's not far."

"If they're there." Lissy couldn't hold the doubt inside, any more than she could hold in the excitement as they reached the top of the stairs. "I can't believe it."

Tony touched her chin, turning her face to look into his suddenly serious brown eyes. For an instant, catching the swift spark of hunger in his gaze, Lissy thought he meant to kiss her. Long before the righteous indignation she knew she ought to feel at such a liberty flared came the knowledge that she very much wanted him to take it.

But he only brushed her cheek with his thumb. "Believe it. We'll find them. I promise you that."

She forced a smile. "But my luck—"

"Is changing."

Lissy turned to put her foot on the first step of the stairs. As she looked down the narrow staircase, she found her gaze suddenly locked on a face she knew. The Rat's faded denim eyes widened as he stared up at her. In the instant they stood frozen there, a gunshot popped in the saloon below.

Tony maintained an admirable calm as he yanked Lissy back from the stairs. Her only indication that his heart was racing as fast as hers was the tightness of his grip on her arm.

"What I said about your luck having changed?" he remarked. "I might have been wrong."

Malachi noticed them first. A thin-faced redhead, a scraggly-haired man with big teeth, a short, round man with pale skin and black eyes. He didn't realize until that moment that he'd half thought Lissy had invented these bugbears to gain their help in searching for her abusive husband.

"It can't be," he muttered, though, of course, it could. They were Charm's men, and Angelique was Charm's mistress. No surprise they should be found in the same place.

"What?" Harry asked.

"Don't turn ar—" He kicked her under the table, swinging her back to face him. "Don't turn around. I think Lissy's Beasts have finally made an appearance."

Harry froze, only her eyes straining to the side. Mal might have laughed at the picture she made, but the three men walking toward the bar gave him a bad feeling.

"That's all right," Harry whispered. "If they're here, they must have found Charm by now. They don't know us. We can make up some story to get them to tell us where he is."

It wasn't their size that bothered Mal. Only the fox neared Tony's height, and he probably gave up thirty pounds to the Englishman. The rat had a stronger build in the event of a brawl, but his faded blue eyes showed little sign of a rat's intelligence. The spider posed an almost ridiculous figure in his bowler, his smart, gold-striped waistcoat stretched taut across his rounded chest.

Yet as the three of them converged on the bartender, the

hair on the back of his neck rose. There was cold viciousness in Fox's narrow face, a casual violence in Rat's slouch, a gleam of cruel intelligence in Spider Grant's black eyes.

They reminded Mal of a pack of feral dogs he'd seen once. One had been wounded in a fight, and the rest of the pack had turned on it, tearing it to shreds. These Beasts had the look of men who would toy with their prey like a prowling tomcat with a baby bird. Whether they were hungry or not.

He'd known men like that. In the army. In the enemy camp and in his own. He'd seen men like that growing up in Charleston. His father had preached that slavery made animals of slave owners, and Mal had seen that, too.

He knew the smell of such men, like a healthy animal knows when another is mad with rabies. Lissy's Beasts stank.

These men were bestial in a way only the human beast had ever truly perfected.

"How are we going to approach them?" Harry asked, almost twitching in her effort not to turn and look at her quarry.

"We're not," Mal said. "We're leaving them alone."

"But they're our only lead to Charm! We can't let them get away."

The Beasts were not the ones he was worried about getting away from the South Platte Saloon unscathed. "We need to get upstairs. We have to get Lissy out of here before they see her. And we have to do it quietly, without arousing their suspicions."

Harry leaned forward, voice hissing. "Mal! We can con them. I know it. And if there's trouble, well, I've faced outlaws before, or don't you remember? With you, me, and Tony—"

"Tony's not armed," Mal reminded her, his voice low, but final. "You're armed with a toy gun and weigh less than half of what the Spider weighs. I can hit what I aim at, but I'm not fast enough to take all three of them. I don't see any guns on them from here, but that doesn't mean they're not carrying."

He expected her to point out that his brother would have known exactly how well armed each man was from how he carried himself. Harry probably believed Elijah could take all three men before a single one had time to draw.

Hell, even he believed it. But he wasn't his brother, and he wasn't going to get anyone killed pretending to be.

But Harry only frowned, considering his words. "If I had my rifle, and you had your shotgun . . ."

"I don't and you don't and I don't think Miss Lily would appreciate us taking out her decor with that kind of firepower."

"Probably not." She looked up at him. "You're right, we've got to get Lissy out of here. What's your plan?"

He had expected an argument, not her confidence. He took a moment to gauge the situation, evaluate possible actions and consequences. She'd actually asked for a plan instead of rushing in without one. He didn't intend to spoil it by telling her he didn't have one.

They didn't know where Tony and Lissy had gone after they'd disappeared up the stairs, didn't know whether or not they'd found Angelique. He certainly didn't intend to send Harry up and down the corridors banging on bedroom doors.

Perhaps she could corner Miss Lily, and—

"You son-of-a-bitch." The thin, sharp voice of the thin, sharp redheaded man sliced through the quiet saloon. His hand snaked out, grabbing the bartender by the front of his shirt. "If you're protecting that damned whore, I'll slit you from your gut to your chin. Now, where is she?"

"I told you. She's gone." The bartender, a white-haired man almost as round as the Spider, didn't try to break free, but he didn't look excessively frightened, either. He was obviously accustomed to unruly customers. "I don't know where she went. She didn't say."

"Then you won't mind if my friends take a look around." The Spider's voice was smooth as silk. "If we don't find her, we'll be on our way."

Back to Plan A.

"I'm going to distract them," Mal said, his pulse accelerating the way it did before a battle. "While you sneak up the stairs. You're going to have to knock on every door until you find them. Maybe one of the girls will point you in the right direction."

Harry nodded, her eyes dark and serious. Good. She'd heard the violence in the men's voices.

Before she could rise from the table, he grabbed her arm. The pulse at her wrist was fast, but steady. She had such a strong presence, he forgot how slender she was. How young. He squeezed a little tighter, suddenly not wanting to let her go.

"Be careful."

She nodded again. "You, too."

He rose from the table to saunter toward the bar, forcing himself not to watch Harry cross toward the stairs. He could only pray the Beasts were too wrapped up in their own concerns to notice two cowboys enjoying the South Platte Saloon's amenities.

But ten strides before he reached the bar, the Fox yanked the bartender forward, crushing his chest against the counter with more force than Mal would have guessed he held in those wiry arms.

"If you don't tell me which room belongs to that whore Angelique Dubray, I'll search every damn one, and when I get back, you'll wish I hadn't had to."

He thrust the portly man away, sending him stumbling back into the shelves behind him, and spun toward the stairs, the Rat close behind him. They would easily reach the staircase before Harry.

He opened his mouth to call out, to say anything to slow them down, but Miss Lily was ahead of him.

"Hold it right there!" The statuesque madam moved with the force of a freight train, knocking Harry unceremoniously aside as she plowed to the foot of the stairs ahead of the Beasts.

"Where the hell do you think you're going?" With her hands on her hips, she blocked the stairway. "This is my establishment, and I don't appreciate your manners, boys. When you get some, you can come on back."

Mal could almost feel the regulars in the saloon relax and sit back to enjoy the show. He had already begun to revise his hasty plan of distraction. If Miss Lily could buy him at least a couple of—

It happened so fast, he almost didn't see it. With the speed and violence of an alligator striking, Fox clenched his hands together and backhanded Miss Lily across the side of her head. Her temple struck the wall with a thud, and she staggered, slumping toward the floor.

Rat's boot caught her in the ribs, knocking her to the ground with only the shocked gasp of the air being forced from her lungs.

Even as Mal started toward her, shock numbing his legs, he saw the blade flash in Fox's hands. It slashed through the air, stopping just short of Miss Lily's throat. The madam stared at him with as much fury as fear, but she could not drag in enough air to speak.

"You get in my way again, I'll show you some manners, whore."

The blade flashed again, disappearing as fast as it had emerged. As the two Beasts turned toward the stairs, the Rat kicked the madam once more for good measure.

Mal still had a table to dodge to reach the pair, who had frozen suddenly at the bottom of the steps. He froze, too, when he heard the pop of a gun no self-respecting gutter thug would carry.

"Don't move, or I'll shoot you through the heart, you low-down coward." The voice of the slim cowboy squeaked even higher than normal, but Harry held her little parlor gun steady, pointed directly at the Fox's chest.

Not that Fox looked overly concerned.

The cocking of a shotgun hammer echoed louder than the shot of the .22. The clicking of revolvers being readied followed close behind.

In that instant, Mal saw he could never reach Harry in time. Her eyes unwavering on the Fox, a stray strand of hair stuck to her cheek, she looked as brave as any comrade he had ever failed to save.

With time slowed to a crawl, he plunged forward, striking his thigh against the table, rattling the dirty glasses, his only desperate thought to get into the line of sight between her and the third Beast at the bar, but the explosion of Spider's .44 came long before he made it there.

The shattering crash of falling glass from one of the ceiling mirrors echoed the shot. The sudden silence afterward left everyone frozen in place.

"Nobody move," the smooth voice from the bar commanded.

Mal had no intention of moving, not a muscle, not as long as Harry still stood with her derringer level, apparently unharmed. Still, his head turned almost against his will as his hand reached for the edge of the table to steady himself.

The Spider stood beside one of the barstools, a small pistol, much like Harry's, in his left hand pointed at the head of the bartender, whose shotgun pointed rather less steadily at Fox and Rat.

"Put it down."

The bartender complied.

The big Remington revolver in the Spider's right hand swung almost casually across the room, pausing at any patron who might be considering anything foolish.

The barrel's aim came to rest on Mal.

"This is none of your concern, cowboy. Go back to your table, and I won't shoot you."

"He's my concern." Without taking his eyes from Spider's black gaze, Mal nodded his head toward Harry. "He's my nephew."

"I'm sorry to tell you this, but your sister and brother-in-law are about to have a very bad day," Spider said, with no trace of regret in his voice. "Unless you can convince your young friend to drop that little toy."

"Ssspider!" Rat spat the name through his protruding incisors. His eyes twitched with excitement. "The sssslut! She up there!" His arm jerked as he pointed to the stairs.

"Miss Dubray is here, after all?" Spider asked speculatively, sparing a chilling glance for the bartender.

Elijah could have used that half-second to draw his Colt and drill the man through the heart. Mal's hand clenched, but he knew he'd never even reach the revolver hidden under his jacket before Spider killed him. And he did not plan to leave Harry to the Beasts' mercy.

"No!" Rat stomped in frustration. "The blond one. The Woodfin bitch."

"What?" Spider's shock quickly gave way to excitement. "What are you standing there for, you damn fool? Go get her."

"I'll shoot him," Harry said, voice thin as the lips she pressed together in grim determination.

"No you won't," Spider said, voice still smooth as silk. "You'll drop that toy now, little girl, or I'll drop it for you."

Chapter 10

Apparently Spider's black eyes didn't miss much, but they missed Mal's hand curling around the heavy whiskey glass on the table beside him.

They saw Miss Lily struggling to her feet, hands clutching the back of a straight wooden chair. But they missed Mal shifting his weight.

They saw Harry's hand shaking, though she never turned her eyes from Rat and Fox, never looked for help. But they missed Mal's sudden movement as he swept the glass off the table and hurled it at Spider's head.

Elijah liked to brag that Mal could throw harder than any boy in Charleston, but that he also had the worst aim. He didn't begrudge his brother the tale. Elijah still had a knot on his head from one of Mal's wilder throws. But Mal had not been a boy in a good many years.

Desperation focused him now.

Spider saw the flash of movement, tried to raise his arm in defense, but the glass struck his temple, knocking him off his feet so his head hit the bar counter.

Miss Lily struck at almost the same moment, swinging her chair with a strength barely dimmed by what must have been at least one broken rib. The chair legs struck Fox in the back, flinging him to the floor.

Rat, held in place by Harry's derringer, didn't see the man plunging down the staircase. Tony's rush caught Rat in the midsection, the Englishman carrying the thug fifteen feet before heaving him over a table.

"You move, I'll blow you full of holes!" the bartender shouted, wielding his shotgun once more.

Rat prudently kept still. Spider did not look as though he would be moving any time soon. Fox only twitched when Miss Lily's sharp black boot drove into his side.

"Vermin," she spat, clutching her own ribs with one arm.

"Are you all right, Miss Lily?" Lissy asked, running down the last of the stairs to take the madam's arm. Miss Lily allowed Lissy to help her into the chair she'd struck Fox with.

"Huh." Miss Lily choked out a laugh. "Better than that bastard by the bar. Nice throw."

Mal nodded. He had to take a deep breath before he could turn to look for Harry. Her little gun still pointed at Fox, both hands holding it steady.

"Harry?" The name croaked from his tight throat. He could see the pulse throbbing along her neck, but her pale face looked bloodless. Anger shook through him, almost as strong as his fear. "Harry, put that damn thing away."

Her gaze didn't waver. "It's not safe. He's still got that knife."

"It's a hell of a lot safer than you with that gun," Mal growled, trying not to picture all the myriad ways she could have died. "You could have gotten us all killed."

That brought blood back to her cheeks as she glanced his way. "What were you going to do? Let them beat up Miss Lily and go after Lissy?"

"I can tell you what I wasn't going to do, which was pull a ridiculous little derringer on three armed thugs."

"Jordan didn't give it to me for decoration," she pointed out.

"She gave it to you for protection!"

"That's what I was using it for!"

"For *your* protection, you little . . ." Frustration choked him. "If you can't show the sense God gave a goat, you shouldn't have it at all."

The gun moved from its lock on Fox's head. Harry's eyes flashed. "Try and take it."

What had been a terrifying, unbridgeable distance between them when Spider had her in his sights took Mal only three strides to cross. As he reached her, he easily blocked the fist she swung at his chest. He wasn't expecting the blow from her left hand.

The derringer smacked sharply against the side of his head, but it didn't hurt nearly as much as the explosion of its discharge blasting in his ear.

Harry screamed. He knew that only from seeing her mouth open. He couldn't hear anything but the ringing in his ear.

"Oh, God! I shot him! Mal!"

He heard that well enough; her voice shouting in his good ear was nearly as loud as the gunshot.

"Mal, where does it hurt? Sit down. Don't die, please don't die!"

"Hell and damnation, I'm not going to die," he managed, probably shouting himself. He couldn't tell. "You missed me. I think."

In the altercation, she'd lost her hat, her hair tumbling down her shoulders. Her surprisingly strong hands were grabbing his head, twisting it so she could see his ear.

"You're sure?" It sounded as though she were sobbing, though that might have been the pounding in his head. She ran her fingers through his hair, presumably looking for holes. "Oh, Mal, I'm so sorry. Please be all right."

"I'm all right," he promised, his own voice none too steady. "I'm all right, Harry."

Her arms went around his neck, and he found himself holding her tight as she cried, tight enough he could feel her heart thumping against his chest.

"I'm all right," he said again, murmuring into her thick, dark hair. Even after days in the city, it still somehow smelled of pines and sunshine. "It doesn't matter."

All that mattered was that she was all right.

"I'm sorry. I'm so sorry." She sniffled, and he thought about gallantly offering her a handkerchief, except he wasn't carrying one, and he had no intention of letting her go, anyway. "I wasn't trying to shoot you."

"I know." He smoothed a hand down her hair. "Just knock my head off."

Her next sniffle sounded suspiciously like laughter. He liked that. He liked her resilience. He liked her laughter. He even liked her bravery.

He liked holding her in his arms. That thought brought an acute awareness of just how good it felt to hold her. To have her pressed against his chest, to have her head tucked against his neck. How much better it would feel to wrap her even closer, bury his face in her hair.

The thought wrenched away his breath. He felt as if he might be drowning. He hoped she couldn't feel his heart pounding. Reaction. Just reaction to danger.

"Will your ear be all right?" She glanced up at him. He'd never seen her blue eyes so dark with worry. Hell and damnation. This was Harry.

"What?"

"Your ear. Can you hear anything out of it?"

"Huh?" He shook his head, furrowing his brow.

Her eyes narrowed. "I said—" She took a breath. Leaned forward. *"How is your ear?"*

"Ouch!" he shouted, as she expected. A good excuse to let her go, back away, though he could still feel where her hands had ruffled his hair. "I think it's only half deaf."

"It's not as though you ever listened to anything anyone else had to say, anyway," she grumbled.

"Who's the one who doesn't listen? What happened to letting me create a diversion? This isn't a game."

Her expression sobered. "I know." And he saw something in her eyes that said she did know. "You saved my life."

"And you stopped the Beasts from attacking anyone else. I've never seen anyone stand their ground more bravely." He bent down to pick up the derringer. "Or stupidly. But you can keep this."

She took it from him with reluctant fingers. "I'll be careful," she assured him.

"It's all right if you aren't. I didn't say I'd give you any more ammunition."

At her warning glare, he finally felt as though he'd recovered his equilibrium. This was Harry.

"It's a good thing it's only got two shots," she muttered, stowing the gun back in her pocket.

"Right, then." Tony's voice brought Mal solidly back to the South Platte Saloon. "Now what? All's well that ends well, and all that, but these chaps aren't going to be too happy with us when they wake up."

"I'll take care of them," Miss Lily said grimly, pushing

herself up out of her chair. "I want the rest of you out of my saloon. I don't want to seem ungrateful, and I like a barroom brawl as much as the next girl, but not in my bar. Mirrors and furniture ain't free. I can't afford any more of your trouble."

Tony cleared his throat. "Technically, it wasn't our trouble. They came here looking for Angelique."

"And so did you," Miss Lily pointed out. She gestured to the bartender. "Larry, get some rope and let's slow these sons-of-bitches down some."

She turned back to Mal. He saw that Fox's backhand had given her a bloody lip, but it didn't spoil her regal bearing. "I don't know what these scoundrels were after, anymore than I know what you're after. But you helped me out, so I owe you one."

She moved to lean on the bar.

"No one's going to care about a fight in a brothel, and ain't no one going to care if a madam gets a couple of broken ribs. I got a friend with the police who might be willing to throw these scum in jail overnight, but that's it."

The bartender handed her a shot glass before walking around the bar with a length of rope. Miss Lily slung back the whiskey in one gulp.

"I don't know what kind of trouble you're in," she said, thumping the glass down on the bar. "But I've got a feeling these men ain't going to take kindly to your interference today. If you've got someplace else to go, I'd go if I was you."

"She's got a point," Tony said, giving the bartender a hand as he trussed up Rat.

"Are you sure you don't want us to stay until the police arrive?" Mal asked Miss Lily. "These men are dangerous."

From Miss Lily's grim expression, he guessed she knew

what he meant. Not dangerous like a drunk cowboy whose favorite girl goes upstairs with another man. Dangerous. Even tied up and unconscious.

"We'll manage," she promised. "And we won't give them any particular reason to come back after us, neither. I don't know as you can say the same." She shot a glance at Lissy.

Lissy nodded, looking shaken. "We should go."

Harry tucked her hair back under her hat. Tony brushed off his sleeves. Together they headed for the door. Mal kept himself behind the others. He didn't want to turn his back on the Beasts.

As Tony opened the door for Lissy, a tall, fair young man, almost clinically handsome in his expensively tailored clothes, pushed through, blinking in the sudden dimness of the room.

"Pardon me, ma'am," he said to Lissy, strictly polite. But there was nothing polite about the way he took in the way she filled out her dress. He moved on before Tony could object, nearly running over Harry, who had frozen in place.

She jumped back, knocking against Mal. The young man sent her an annoyed glance before pushing past into the saloon.

"Hello girls!" he called out exuberantly. "Larry, I need a double shot of— Good Lord, Miss Lily, what on earth happened here?"

Mal nudged Harry forward, then grabbed her arm as she stumbled into the afternoon sunshine.

"Are you sure you're all right?" he asked, worried that he'd missed an injury back in the saloon.

"Fine," she croaked, jerking free of his hand. But as she started up the street toward the streetcar stop, she suddenly spun back around, her face nearly as pale as when Spider had threatened to shoot her.

"Hell and damnation," she squeaked, looking up at him with eyes wide in terror. "There's my brother!"

Harry had never been so certain she was going to die as when Spider said he planned to shoot her. Not when her pony had rolled over on her in the middle of the creek when she was eight. Not when Luke Deane and his gang attacked her brother's farm. Not when Lucifer Jones had caught her trying to rescue Jordan from his kidnapping plot.

Yet even with Spider's .44 pointed at her, she had not disgraced herself by throwing up. Not like that time Emily Culbert had accidentally locked her in the wardrobe during a game of hide and seek. Being shot had to be better than suffocating. That's how she felt now, hearing March's strides down the sidewalk. Unable to breathe. Her stomach turned dangerously wild.

She'd known March was supposed to be in Denver this week, arranging the sale of his colts and fillies, but she'd never expected to run into him. She'd sent a telegram to Maggie, of course, explaining her extended absence. But she hadn't exactly mentioned that she'd left Battlement Park. With Malachi Kelly.

It wasn't that March wasn't used to her escapades. But he might think this one had gone a little too far. Especially if he caught her dressed as a boy coming out of the South Platte Saloon with a man March didn't know. She hoped Tony in his elegant gambler's shirt and Lissy with her heavy makeup had the sense to keep their distance.

She glanced around, but the street offered nowhere to hide. Even with her chest wrapped and her hair tucked into her hat, March would have no trouble recognizing her in shirt and blue jeans. Not like another young man she could mention.

Her stomach flipped again. She would *not* throw up. Although her brother might not pay a second glance to a young cowboy vomiting against the wall of a brothel.

For a second she forgot to feel sick. Come to think of it, what was March doing heading for a brothel on Market Street? He was supposed to be selling horses, not visiting soiled doves.

If Maggie found out . . .

Malachi interrupted her thoughts by grabbing her by the back of the neck and turning her toward the wall. He bent her over far enough she had to prop her hands on her knees to keep from falling.

"It's all right, son," he said loudly. "Could happen to anyone the first time they drink that much whiskey. Breathe deep. You'll feel better in no time."

March's steps slowed anyway.

"Excuse me." Her brother's voice sounded more impatient than courteous. "I wonder if you could tell me which door a young friend of mine entered a minute or two ago. I'd like to catch up with him."

"A tall fellow?" Malachi asked.

"Blond," March said. "Strongly built— Wait a minute . . ." His voice trailed off, and Harry choked. But it wasn't she that he recognized. "This may seem like a strange question, but you resemble very strongly a friend of mine. I know he has a brother in Colorado—"

"Malachi Kelly," Malachi said, with a hint of resignation. "You know my brother, Elijah."

"March Jackson," March said, and Harry heard the rustle of a handshake. "I've heard a lot about you from my sister."

"Harriet?" Malachi asked, and Harry choked again. He *never* called her Harriet. He was as nervous as she was.

"I owe you a debt of gratitude for keeping her safe while you rounded up Lucifer Jones's gang."

"Elijah's the one who out-dueled Jones."

"Harry said it was your posse that rounded up the rest of the gang. She said you're an even better tracker than 'Lije."

"She did?"

Harry didn't know why Malachi sounded so surprised. Honestly. She knew enough about tracking to be a decent judge.

"Having tracked with 'Lije myself, I have to say that's quite an accomplishment."

"Thank you."

"I hope you're planning to come to the wedding next month," March continued. Harry groaned. Wouldn't he ever shut up and move on? "You can stay with us. Any family of Elijah's is family to the Jacksons."

"Elijah and Jordan will be there," Malachi said gruffly. "That's enough Kellys for any party. I'd only be in the way."

"We've got room. It would only be a cot in the hay loft, but I'll probably end up stuck out there for the duration, myself. Besides, it would mean a lot to Harry to have you there."

Harry slowly banged her head against the wall.

"Is your friend going to be all right?" March asked, as though noticing her for the first time. "He sounds bad off."

"The kid wanted to go to a saloon and 'drink like a man.' " Malachi snorted. "I let him. He'll live. Maybe he'll think twice next time."

"Alcohol's no test of manhood," March said.

Harry hoped he wasn't about to start into a well-meaning lecture. She'd knocked her hat loose against the wall. If her hair began spilling out, she was dead.

"Is that why you're looking for your friend?" Malachi asked, effectively diverting March's attention. "To keep him out of trouble?"

"That depends on where he's gone," March said, sounding grim once more. "I may be looking for him to kill him."

Harry's knees sagged a little in relief. She could stop worrying for Maggie. March wasn't looking for female companionship at all. He was simply being her overprotective big brother, as he had all her life. For once, she didn't mind. At the moment she didn't mind if he did kill the low-down, miserable, son-of—

"He went into the South Platte Saloon," Malachi said, amusement creeping into his voice. "He seemed to know the place pretty well. I don't think he was looking for a place to drink. Who is this fellow?"

Harry groaned wretchedly, but failed to distract either one of them.

"That *fellow*—" March spat the word in rare antagonism. "That fellow is my future brother-in-law."

"Your extra stockings are still hanging in the wash-room."

Harry closed her eyes against Lissy's impatience. She had no intention of getting up off the bed.

"Here, I've got them." Lissy's boots clattered on the floor as she retrieved the stockings and stuffed them in the valise Harry had borrowed from Jordan.

"I think we're just about ready."

Lissy's barely restrained energy had crackled around her like a localized thunderstorm ever since Tony had returned from the land office early that morning with the news that a Mr. C. W. Prince owned the title to a small mine in Silvercrest, Colorado, not far from Georgetown, which was not, as the crow flew, too far from Central City.

Harry could understand Lissy's urgency. After the previous afternoon, she had no doubt that Lissy's life would remain in danger until they could find Charm Woodfin and convince him to call off the Beasts. Even Malachi had quit comparing Lissy's elusive husband to a wild goose. And Tony had slept half the night in the corridor outside their hotel room door until Malachi had dragged him off to bed and taken his place until morning.

Harry had slept with the derringer under her pillow, despite Lissy's extreme misgivings. She had a slithering fear that the threat of the little .22 would not slow the Beasts down at their next encounter. But if one of them attacked Lissy, she was fully prepared to pull the trigger. Just as she was ready for the showdown with Charm Woodfin.

It was getting up off the bed that was the problem. Getting up off the bed would mean walking out into the hall. Which would mean facing Tony's solicitous cheer. Facing Malachi. Facing yesterday afternoon.

The bed was safe and peaceful. Except for Lissy's nagging.

"You're wrinkling your dress," Lissy warned, pushing Harry's feet out of the way to set their bags on the bed. "And you shouldn't put your boots on the furniture. Look at these bags. I declare, it's a pitiful state of affairs when the men have more luggage than the women."

"How could he?" Harry asked, because she could think of nothing else to say and because she needed to talk to someone and because Lissy was not going to go away.

"That's better."

Harry glanced down the bed to see Lissy watching her over the open bags. "It's not better," she assured her. "Talking about it is not going to change anything."

"Change what?"

"Change Ashton Brady visiting a Denver cathouse!" Harry threw her head back and glared up at the ceiling. Damn him. "I can't believe it."

If they hadn't run into March, if he hadn't recognized Ash, too, Harry might have been able to pretend to herself she'd made a mistake. She had known Ash might come to Denver on business for his father. Maybe she'd simply been thinking of him. Maybe it had been another tall, painfully handsome young man who had passed her in the saloon.

Except that it turned out that Lissy had recognized him, too. Thank God Ash hadn't recognized Lissy. He'd been too busy staring at her chest.

Harry's face burned, almost as painfully as her heart. "How could he?"

"He's a man," Lissy said. "There's nothing strange about a young man wanting to quench his desires. It doesn't mean he won't keep them at home once he's married."

Harry shook her head, not knowing what to say to that. She'd been struck dumb as a babe by a statue of a naked man, and Ash felt comfortable enough in the same brothel to call the madam by name and inquire about the mess.

She was an innocent, and he'd been doing . . . she didn't even want to imagine it.

"I've never even seen him with his shirt off!"

The noise of Lissy's packing paused. "You two haven't . . . ?"

"No." Her cheeks reddened again. "Of course not."

"It's not exactly unheard of, between people who are engaged."

No. She suspected March and Maggie had not waited for their quiet wedding at the ranch. Henna Culbert had met her husband Jed while working in a brothel.

But Ash had always been careful of her reputation. Even when his cousins had conspired to strand them together on a picnic at his uncle's farm, stealing their horses in a whirlwind of sly grins and giggles, Ash had been a gentleman, reading to her from a collection of poems by Dryden.

"He didn't want to sully my honor."

"Very commendable," Lissy drawled, checking the chest of drawers one last time to ensure they hadn't left behind any of their meager belongings. "He knows how to treat a lady."

"I'm not a lady," Harry objected. "Not a proper one, anyway. Look at me."

Lissy obliged, her voice amused. "I see your point. I doubt your fiancé would be pleased with your recent behavior or current companions. He obviously expects his wife to be above reproach."

"So why aren't *his* actions above reproach?" Harry demanded.

"You could confront him with that," Lissy said, finally closing the clasps on the bags. "Your brother saw him there, so you don't have to admit you did. You can tell him you expect respectable behavior once you're married."

"That didn't work with Charm," Harry said softly.

"True." Lissy pushed Harry's skirt aside to sit on the edge of the bed. "Though Charm's sense of right and wrong has never been terribly sound. Your young man appears to place more value on honor than he ever did."

"Then how could he?" Harry asked again. An easier

question than the next one. "What am I going to do?"

"Do you truly want my advice?"

Harry studied her problematic companion. Her tentative friend. The bruises around Lissy's eye had faded to a dim memory of shadow, the thin cut along her hairline almost invisible now, but sorrow and experience haunted the gray eyes as clearly as any physical mark.

"Yes."

Lissy nodded, lips pressed together as she gathered her thoughts. "I don't know Ash, Harry. I don't have much experience with what makes for a good marriage. Though I have plenty with what doesn't." She smiled with bitter humor. "So you don't need to take my words as the gospel truth."

"You may *look* like an angel, Elizabeth Woodfin, but you don't fool me any."

Lissy laughed. "Good. I'll just say my piece, then. I don't have an answer for you, but I do have a question. Have you ever been to a masquerade ball?"

"Oxtail is not exactly a whirl of social activity."

"All right," Lissy said, undeterred. "Imagine attending one. Let's say someone you love, like your brother, also goes, unexpectedly."

"It would certainly be unexpected," Harry agreed, trying to imagine practical, no-nonsense March at a ball of any kind.

"Imagine him in a costume that is completely out of character."

"Banker?" Harry said doubtfully.

"Pirate," Lissy suggested. "Arabian sheik. Ghengis Khan."

"Louis XIV!"

"Exactly. Powdered wig, white stockings, nose in the air.

Would you recognize him?"

"What sort of mask is he wearing?"

"No mask."

Harry frowned at her. "That's too easy."

"Say you were in London, England. You're at Queen Victoria's court. You're certain all your friends are here in Colorado. You catch a glimpse of Malachi Kelly dressed as a footman."

Harry pictured Malachi's watchful green eyes, the deep lines around his mouth when he couldn't bear polite society a moment longer, the humor that twitched his lips when she said something outrageous.

"Again, the wig, the stockings. Whatever they wear," Lissy said. "Would you recognize him?"

"That's too easy," Harry objected again. "Maybe I wouldn't recognize Tony. I might think I just expected to see someone like Tony because I was in England. Or—"

"Maggie?"

"Dressed like a footman?" Harry laughed. "She'd be easy to spot. She'd be the one with the red hair poking out from under the wig, telling the queen what to do."

"Miss Lily?"

Harry squinted, the picture harder to focus. "I'm not sure." She turned back to Lissy. "What does this have to do with anything?" Though she already knew.

"Ash didn't recognize you yesterday."

Harry pushed herself up to a sit. "The light was bad, and he only caught a glimpse of me."

"And didn't even take a second look."

"Lissy, that's not a fair test."

Lissy shrugged. "No, it's not. But I would have looked again. March would have. Malachi would. So, the real test is, do you love him?"

"Ash?" Of course she meant Ash. Harry swung her feet to the ground. "I thought so, before yesterday." Though, if she were honest, she had begun to dread returning home for the wedding long before the encounter at the South Platte Saloon.

"I think you'd better figure out how you feel now before you make any decisions."

Harry frowned at her. "Some help you are. You sound just like Malachi."

"I got you to sit up," Lissy pointed out, rising. "Now if I can just get you on your feet, maybe we won't miss our train."

"My feet are staying right where they are. Anyway, the train doesn't leave for another two hou—"

A sudden pounding at their door interrupted her. The door flew open before Lissy could reach it, spilling Malachi and Tony into the room.

"The Beasts," Malachi said tersely, grabbing Lissy's carpet bag and Harry's valise off the bed.

"What? Where?" Lissy paled, and Tony dropped his and Malachi's bags to grab her arm to steady her.

"They're in the lobby," the Englishman said, the undercurrent of urgency in his voice undermining his customary aplomb.

Harry saw Tony had unpacked his Smith and Wesson Schofield pistols. He wore them with more stylish flair than Malachi wore his Colt, but they looked no less deadly.

Tony snatched Harry's hat off the dresser and tossed it to her.

"Our good Captain Kelly had the military foresight to suss out a back exit to the hotel when we arrived. This seems a rather opportune time to try it out."

"What are the Beasts doing here?" Harry demanded,

scrambling from the bed.

"My fault," Malachi said grimly. "Tony was paying our bill when Spider came in waving that card I left at the Metropolitan Hotel. I guess the proprietor found him more congenial on further acquaintance."

"Or less," Harry muttered. Even a weasel deserved better than the Beasts.

"Fortunately, he didn't recognize me," Tony said, ducking his head out the door to make sure the hall was clear before gesturing them out. "Mal had knocked him cold before I entered the fray yesterday afternoon. But they are hot on our heels, and all that."

Harry grabbed her valise from Malachi as they hurried into the hall.

"You might need a free hand," she said.

His green eyes flashed acknowledgment, but all he said was, "I hope not. Let's go catch a train."

Chapter 11

Georgetown slept quietly beneath the infinite mountain night. Lights glowed in one or two rooms of the Hotel de Paris and bursts of merriment occasionally spilled from a saloon down Taos Street, but most of the town remained peaceful, its respectable family homes settled in for the night like ptarmigans in a nest. Almost a disappointment for a southern lady's first night in a mining camp.

Not, Lissy thought, that anyone would be likely to refer to a city of over five thousand residents as a camp. Inside the Hotel de Paris, a visitor could enjoy amenities that would put many a larger city's establishments to shame, from its hot and cold running water in every room to its first class cuisine to the live trout swimming in the fountain in the restaurant.

But standing at the corner of the front of the hotel, breathing in the sharp scents of ravaged earth, spruce and pine, it was impossible to pretend that flimsy human civilization could out-duel the mountains for supremacy here.

Here the stars glittered close enough to touch, here they spilled over Douglas Mountain like a river of silver flowing off the edge of the world. Only the solid resistance of the stucco wall against her hand kept Lissy from falling up into them.

Wildness licked like cold fire on the breath of the wind, chilling her ears and fingers, but burning her heart. A song sang in the wind, a song she couldn't quite hear, that made her want to run after it, dancing and golden as an aspen leaf.

And be dashed against the rocks and swept away under the forest litter like any fall leaf. Even the Beasts held no terrors against the eternal indifference of the mountains. Her own heartbeat felt as fleeting as the flash of a hummingbird's wing.

"Harry said you'd popped out for a stroll."

She doubted Harry had put it quite that way, though her smile never made it to her lips as Tony settled his coat over her shoulders. His warmth, trapped in the wool, stretched like a caress across her back.

"The temperature drops quickly after sunset."

She nodded, taking a deep breath of that cold, cold air, her eyes on the stars. His hand still rested on her shoulder.

"I thought you might want some company."

"You thought I might wander right into Spider Grant's web if you left me to my own devices," she corrected, turning her head just enough to give him a quick smile, not far enough to catch his eye.

"The truth?" he said, his own smile in his voice, and something else.

"Rarely a good idea." She took a half step forward, not quite far enough to dislodge his hand. Wildness laughed in the wind.

"I wanted a moment to speak with you."

"Did you?" Her voice was cool and clear as the stars' light.

"I wondered if you've thought about what you'll do after we find Charm. A destination, so to speak."

"San Francisco," she said, though she'd hardly dared think that far ahead. It was almost like saying the moon. Indeed, tonight the heavy swell of the half moon rising over the mountain ridge to the east seemed closer than California. "No one knows me there. With the money Charm owes me, I can open a boarding house, make a living somehow."

"Capital idea." He didn't sound as though he thought it was capital. He cleared his throat. "What if Charm won't cough up the money? Not that Mal and I aren't pretty tough characters, and we'll jolly well do our best to put the fear of God in him, but he sounds the sort of chap who might be more willing to part with a wife than a purse. And with the Beasts to help him—"

"The Beasts won't be with him," Lissy said, too sharply.

"I hope not."

A simple statement of fact. His mildness shamed her. His kindness shamed her. She wondered how she had grown up with her brothers and not learned how to lie, cheat, and steal without wracking her conscience.

The truth, he'd said. It tempted her. After all that he and the others had been through for her, they deserved it. But her goal was so close now. Her heart said her newfound friends wouldn't desert her, but she'd been wrong before. So wrong. She couldn't risk it.

"What I mean to say is," Tony continued. "You don't have to run to San Francisco or start a boarding house. You could stay here in Colorado."

"Colorado?" Lissy managed a laugh. "I'd have about as much chance as a camellia blossom in the snow. Can you imagine?"

"Georgetown doesn't compare to Savannah," Tony said, his smile forced.

"Look at those stars," Lissy said, clutching the stucco wall again. "Savannah stars are properly civilized. Any good hostess has stars to glitter for her soiree, discreetly softened, of course, by the damp air. Nothing to remind you that God created them."

That hadn't been what she meant to say at all. It was that accursed wind talking.

"Colorado isn't everyone's cup of tea," Tony said, an edge of regret in his voice. "I thought I'd go mad my first winter in Battlement Park. I planned in detail how I would murder my father if I ever escaped."

Lissy smiled, in spite of herself.

"But I can't imagine myself anywhere else now. Even though I don't know that I'll ever find a—" He paused, cleared his throat again. "Well, regardless, there's a place for you at the Fox and Hound, if you want it. You've run a household. I've lost a housekeeper. No soirees, I'm afraid. At least not until June. But you'd be safe."

She risked a glance at him. Starlight glinted in his eyes, that wild starlight. And she knew she would not be safe in Battlement Park. She would not be safe in Colorado.

"Charm was supposed to be my rescuer," she said, the twist of her mouth not hiding the bitterness. "He promised to slay my dragons and keep me safe forever. I don't think I need another white knight."

"I'm no knight, milady." Tony flashed that broad smile that hid so much. "Adeline is a sweet girl, and she does her best, but two weeks ago she starched the sheets, and I lost half my clientele."

He wasn't as perfectly handsome as she'd thought the first time she'd seen him, when his big shoulders and golden boy looks had loomed over her from Elijah Kelly's front porch. His nose was a little narrow, like hers, his ears a little large beneath the sweep of his wheat-colored hair, his fair eyebrows shaped like sparrow's wings over his Earl Grey eyes.

And she would recognize him anywhere.

"Go rescue some other damsel in distress, Major Wayne," she said softly. Yet it was her hand that lifted to touch his face, the sun-browned cheekbone warm against her cold fingers, his chin rough against her palm.

"Tony," he said, his low voice rumbling beneath her fingertips.

This close, she had to tilt her chin up to meet his eyes. "Don't waste your time on me."

As his face moved closer, her own eyes fluttered shut. In the high, dry air of the Colorado Rockies, she thought she felt a warm breeze touched with honeysuckle brush her skin. His mouth closed on hers, and she found she'd been right. He had wonderful lips.

His hand slid around her back, pressing between her shoulder blades as he drew her to him.

The wind's wild song burned across her skin, poured inside her like molten gold. Her lips parted in a silent sigh, and when his tongue brushed against them, she moaned. An answering noise rose from deep in his throat, and she felt him harden against her.

His mouth left hers as he wrapped her against him, brushing her temple with his kiss.

"Elizabeth," he whispered, his voice low. "You could never be a waste of time."

The fickle wind touched her again, frosted with glacier ice this time, shaking her deep, freezing whatever had melted inside. She wrenched herself from Tony's embrace, gulping the frigid air against the tears and the desire.

"I am," she said, cold as the wind. "You are wasting your time. I'm not one of your widowed countesses, Major Wayne. I've been charmed and used by the best."

"Elizabeth—"

She jerked away from his ragged voice as much as from his reaching hand.

He remained where he was. "I would never dishonor you."

She raised a hand to her flushed cheek. "I'm a married woman. Nothing between us could ever be honorable."

"I am your friend, if you will let me be," he said, keeping his hands clenched at his sides. "I will not kiss you again. On my honor. And that does still mean something to me."

She shook her head, mind numb with fear and want and despair. Hadn't she learned anything from the past eleven years? If it was not for what Charm had stolen from her, what would be keeping her from Tony's arms? From playing his widowed countess or his "housekeeper" as long as he found her entertaining? Not her own will, that seemed certain.

"I don't think I can be your friend, Tony," she said, the words strangled. "You see, I have no honor."

She turned and fled toward the front door of the Hotel de Paris. If she spent another minute in this wind, she would go mad.

If Georgetown had disappointed her expectations, Silvercrest looked exactly like Lissy thought a mining town ought to look. Where Georgetown had cozy white cottages with green trim, a half-dozen churches, and a fire house, Silvercrest had rough board shacks, rutted, tilting streets, and an air of dilapidation far exceeding its fifteen years of existence.

Five hundred feet higher in elevation than Georgetown and over three thousand feet above Denver's mile-high location on the plains, the town hunkered against a cold fall breeze even in the bright afternoon sunshine, and traces of a recent dusting of snow lingered in the shade of the buildings.

Yet there was not the mountain peace she had come to expect. The noise of ore-stamping mills rumbled up and down the narrow gulch, and heavy smoke rolled with it.

Though strings of laundry hung to dry in the cold, thin air, and the occasional shout of a child suggested the presence of women in Silvercrest, Lissy could feel hungry eyes following her and Harry as they walked up the main street—the only street—from where the supply wagon had dumped them in front of the general store to the sole hotel beside the largest saloon.

Lissy kept her hat tilted against those eyes, low over her face. If Charm chanced to be in town and caught sight of her . . .

The hotel had been painted once, which was more than could be said of most of Silvercrest, but Lissy feared the heels of her boots might plunge through the warped front porch before she reached the door.

Tony opened the door, and Lissy stepped through first, her gaze flashing around the entry room from beneath her hat brim.

"It's all right," Harry murmured, as Tony strode to the front desk to call for the manager. "Charm won't be expecting you to come here."

"I just don't want him to see me before I see him."

"We won't let him hurt you," Harry assured her. Her

solemn promise, hand clutching the gun in her purse, reminded Lissy of Harry's encounter with the Beasts, of how much danger she'd plunged her friends into, of how much she still hadn't told them. But she couldn't think of that now.

"I know you won't," Lissy said. "And I don't think Charm will try to hurt me here. Not without the Beasts."

At least some of it was the truth. She shook her head, looking around the bare lobby. "I can't believe he's here. Even after all his foolishness, all his indiscretions, I can't believe he would buy a silver mine in Colorado, set up house with his mistress in a hog wallow like this, and bring my . . ."

With a curse, she bit off the words and moved to the front window. She used her handkerchief to swipe a clear spot in the glass so she could see the street. Grim did not begin to describe this place.

"If I find him here, Harry," she said, jaw clenched tight, "you may have to protect him from me."

"Jolly good luck," Tony's voice interrupted, as he and Malachi strode over to them. Tony smiled a cat-and-cream smile, but Lissy noticed it didn't reach his eyes and that his eyes didn't meet hers. It was better that way. He would be glad she had pushed him away when he found out the truth, anyway.

"I think we've finally hit pay dirt with this mine, so to speak." Tony rubbed his hands together. "Our good host over there says the Lucky Lady is only a couple of miles from here, just over the next ridge to the north. Apparently Mr. Prince had a pretty little cottage built not far from the mine, and he and his family are in residence."

Tony paused, cleared his throat. "I suppose that means he and Angelique are in residence."

A succession of emotions roiled along Lissy's nerves. Fury, relief, desperate, agonizing hope. She fought back the undignified urge to collapse weeping to the floor.

"This is it, then," she said, tightly controlled, as she stepped toward the door.

"Where do you think you're going?" Malachi demanded.

Lissy paused to glance back. "Which way is north?"

"The way we're going after we get something to eat and arrange for transportation." Malachi bent to heft their bags. "Tomorrow morning."

"I am not waiting until tomorrow morning!" Lissy's control slipped. She lowered her voice to keep her words from reaching the hotel manager's curious ears. "We've wasted enough time. I'm going now. Give me one of those revolvers. You can stay here if you want."

"You can walk if you want," Malachi said with a stubbornness designed to infuriate her. "You can do it this afternoon and get stuck at the mine with Charm and Angelique overnight. I'm not going to stop you. But I'm not going out there until I have a decent meal and am riding a decent horse in decent light. And I'm sure as hell not going to give you a gun."

"Someone could tell them we're here," she hissed, the urgency raw in her voice. "We can't lose them now."

"I don't think we're too likely to scare them away," Malachi observed dryly. "I'm sure a silver mine will have some kind of security."

It was her fault he didn't understand her desperation, but she couldn't explain it now. They might miss their quarry; she might lose her objective forever. That thought spurred her to cruelty.

"Is that it?" she asked bitterly. "Are you frightened? Well, you're not your brother. I can't expect you to risk a gunfight. You've brought me far enough to salve your conscience about me. You can leave. Just give me a gun—"

"My *conscience?*" Malachi dropped the luggage with a thud, his neck reddening. "My conscience doesn't owe you a damn thing, Lissy Wilmer."

"No?" She met his gaze coolly. "You knew Charm was feckless and weak when you let me marry him."

Malachi's fists clenched. "That was your choice. Charm was your choice."

"And you didn't even fight for me." She hadn't known how much that had hurt her pride, until that moment. He'd almost seemed relieved to let her go.

"I came to that garden ready to take you away. To marry you."

"Marry you?" Tony echoed. She'd assumed Malachi had told him. Not that it mattered. Not compared to the need spurring her on.

"You told me you'd changed your mind," Malachi reminded her. "That you didn't want to leave Savannah. That you were going to marry Charm Woodfin."

"And you are punishing me for it now," Lissy accused, needling him, goading him into helping her or into leaving her the gun; she didn't care which. "Now when I need your help the most. All because I hurt your damned pride."

Tony stepped between them, though Lissy saw his own hands were clenched. "Bloody hell. If the two of you would be reasonable for one minute—"

"Nothing about this entire undertaking has ever been reasonable." Malachi took a deliberate step back, the look in his eyes telling her she'd lost. She couldn't hurt him into fury. "But maybe you're right about one thing, Lissy. I do have a conscience, of a sort. Maybe I thought I owed somebody something for all the violence I couldn't stop."

His fierce gaze never left her face, and she met it because she owed him that much.

"That's why I'm here. And that's the same reason I'm not going to rush out to a mine where I don't know the land, don't know the odds, don't know the numbers, and start shooting. I followed one damned yellow-haired devil into a massacre. I'm not doing it again."

The cold, hard ice of her will thawed all at once, though she struggled against the melting. It was the pain in his eyes that undid her. "Mal, I didn't—"

"I need a drink." He pushed past her to the door, banging through it into the dusty street.

For a second the silence hung heavy in the hotel lobby. Lissy forced herself not to shake. "Tony?"

"Mal's in charge." Tony didn't meet her gaze. "If he says we wait until morning, we wait until morning. He never made major, but he didn't have his commission bought for him, either. He's your knight, Mrs. Woodfin. Not much charm, but bloody good with a dragon."

He hefted all four bags at once and strode toward the stairs.

Harry sighed. "You didn't have to do that."

Lissy followed her gaze to the door. "I'd do anything, Harry. I'm desperate." It was a warning as much as an explanation, but she could tell Harry didn't hear that. Just as well. Harry held the only other card Lissy could think to play.

She didn't have a case full of papers, but there were more effective distractions. "Go bring him back, Harry. I don't want him too hung over to ride tomorrow morning."

Harry's eyes flashed protectively, as she'd known they would. "He'll be ready. Whether you deserve his help or not."

As Harry stalked toward the door, Lissy dodged the wrong direction, and Harry knocked against her shoulder. Lissy stumbled out of the way, catching herself on the window frame. She stood still for a long moment after Harry slammed out the door. Then she sagged against the wall, the dingy paint almost as dust-stained as her dress.

In her hand, she clutched Harry's black velvet handbag, the derringer a deadly weight in the bottom.

Chapter 12

The saloon next to the hotel undoubtedly catered to an assortment of miners, Cornish and Irishmen, transplants from the gold mines of Georgia and California, some Chinese if the proprietor was more interested in good coin than prejudice. There might be some freed slaves or even some Cherokees from Oklahoma. The saloon probably held one or two pretty girls, or at least, scantily dressed girls, and a selection of potent alcoholic drinks designed for maximum inebriation at a minimum cost.

It held no interest for Mal. He'd spent much too long in human company over the past week, crowded by human standards, hemmed in by iron and brick and the constant babbling of voices.

He ducked into the gap between the hotel and saloon, following the alley to where a track led up the hill behind them. Debris from the two businesses choked the narrow passage: broken chairs, a table split down the middle, a mattress spilling straw and mouse droppings.

Maybe it was the Panic of Seventy-three that had given this edge of despair to the heady rush of silver lust. Mal didn't much care; he simply wanted to escape it. If a silver strike brought you to a tumbledown shack in Silvercrest, he would just as soon be spared such luck.

The tightness around his chest that had driven him from the hotel eased as soon as he climbed above the level of the town. The path he followed led around the hill into a stand of sentinel trees that had somehow escaped logging for building materials or fire.

The firs closed around him like a haven, cool and damp, protecting his battered ears from the wind and the noise of the mills. A chickadee chirped somewhere briefly, but the trees preferred silence, whispering with circumspect voices high above him in the breeze.

Rounding the shoulder of the hill, he came upon a break in the trees where a small creek tumbled through a fall of rocks toward the gulch that led to Georgetown.

Malachi sat on a boulder beside the water. From there he could see out across an astonishing expanse of forest, mountain ridges, ice-capped peaks, and denim blue sky. Aspens blazed across broken slopes in their full, golden glory, a flash of fire against the somber Douglas fir, then flaring up into breaks in the spired forests of spruce and fir high above. It was almost enough to wash the ravages of human avarice from his brain.

He reached into his coat and pulled out his flask, dented from its flight of a week before. Turpentine. The memory almost made him smile. He was unscrewing the cap on the flask when the remembered voice intruded clearly into the present.

"You *are* planning to get drunk again!"

He turned to see her standing at the edge of the trees, hands on hips, the lilac stripes of her skirt no more vivid against the somber green trees than the flashing sparks in her eyes.

"I came out here for some peace," he said. "If I wanted

your company, I would have asked for it."

"If you're going to get snarly, I don't feel so bad about interrupting you." She picked her way across the boggy grass to his boulder, settling her skirts around her as she sat. "Don't you think you should keep your wits about you?"

"Are you implying I have wits to keep?" he asked. "I'm flattered."

He took a swallow from the flask before offering it to her. Once again, she met the challenge in his eyes and took it. This time she managed to swallow without choking.

"A nasty way to kill yourself," she said.

He took the flask back. "I brought it for medical emergencies," he said. "Knife cuts. Bullet holes. Cat claws. But it's not much good on festering old wounds."

He screwed on the cap and thrust it back in his coat pocket.

"She broke your heart."

Mal looked up, startled. "What? You mean Lissy?"

"Who the hell else would I mean, Malachi Kelly?" Her eyes met his only briefly. "Honestly. Do you have to be difficult?"

"Do you have to be here at all?" But he was afraid his scowl didn't hide the twitch at the corner of his mouth.

"Is it that hard? Seeing her again?" Her wide mouth pinched down to an indecipherable line.

It took him a moment to decide to answer. Or maybe he didn't decide. Maybe her implacable blue eyes dragged it out of him.

"No," he said finally. He picked a stone off the rock and turned it over in his fingers, watching a streak of quartz glitter in the cool, bright light. "Maybe I thought she'd broken my heart, back then. But that was before I knew what a broken heart looked like. You don't get a broken heart losing something you've never had."

It had taken him a long time to learn that, a long time watching others lose everything that mattered.

"She was lovely. She made everything around her seem special. I wanted that for my own. I wanted to rescue her from her brothers. Maybe I could have loved her if I'd had a chance to know her. If we had learned to become friends. But we didn't have time for that to happen. And when it came to a choice, she chose Charm.

"That hurt my pride, but it didn't break my heart." He tossed the rock into the creek below them.

"I see." Harry's mouth pursed. "Is that why you think I should get to know Ash better? So he can break my heart more effectively?"

"If someone doesn't have the power to break your heart, it means you haven't let them into your heart to begin with."

She blew out her breath in a heavy sigh. "Maybe you've got the right idea. You don't let anyone into your heart. You can't get hurt."

He only wished that were true. "Unfortunately, no matter how hard you try to keep certain people out, they force their way in, anyway." He shot her a look. "Friends are hazardous to one's peace of mind."

She wrinkled her nose at him. "They're downright dangerous."

They sat in friendly, dangerous silence for a long moment, listening to the splash of the creek, watching a red-tailed hawk circle high above the valley floor, far below them.

The boulder held the chill of coming winter, and Mal heard Harry wrap her coat more tightly around her.

"So," she said, her voice carefully neutral. "Lissy isn't the reason for your heartless, solitary existence. Who is? Who did break your heart, Malachi Kelly?"

"No one." Maybe everyone. "War."

She nodded slowly, not as though she understood, but as though she wanted to understand. Friends were dangerous, indeed.

"The yellow-haired devil," she said. In the thin air, her voice skipped over the words like the water over the rocks. "The one you followed into a massacre. You meant Custer."

"Would I say that about a martyred hero?"

"Was it his fault? The massacre at the Little Bighorn."

Mal snorted. "The Little Bighorn wasn't the only massacre he led us into."

She frowned at him. "I don't remember hearing about another defeat like that."

"Haven't you heard of the Battle of the Washita? It wasn't a defeat. It was the greatest victory the Seventh had against the Indians while I was with them. Just about the only victory. The only time we caught them sleeping where they couldn't melt away without a fight."

But he was not going to talk about the Washita.

Sitting on a solid, silent mountain with the sunlight slanting horizontal bronze bars across the solemn, achingly lovely face beside him, the memories hovered like ghosts, torn by the breeze. The regimental band played "Garryowen" as men shouted, guns roared and women screamed. Babies died. An old man with his arm severed at the shoulder stumbled past. Mal's nostrils caught the acrid smell of burning tepees, his ears the butchering of eight hundred ponies.

"They were sleeping," he said, the words coming despite

himself. "Black Kettle's Cheyenne. We thought they were alone. Custer didn't do proper reconnaissance there, either, but the other camps down the river didn't have time to come to their aid.

"We split into four sections, surrounded them, attacked at dawn. Captured fifty, killed twice that. Men, women, and children.

"The Battle of the Washita." He choked out a laugh. "It wasn't a battle. Most of the Cheyenne warriors didn't even have time to arm themselves. We were no better than butchers."

Her fingers touched his sleeve. "It was a war. They were the enemy."

"The enemy?" He shook his head. "Maybe. Or maybe they were just a peaceful camp of families trying to survive the winter. Since when do we wage war on mothers and babies?"

He breathed deep, trying to control the ragged emotion that gripped him. "Sometimes those memories are worse than the Little Bighorn," he admitted, voice quiet and hoarse. "Worse than Custer's recklessness, Reno's drunkenness, the whole damn unnecessary mess. Those ghosts haunt me, too. My men who died. I should have been able to do more to save them. But at least I was fighting for my life against armed men."

Not trying helplessly to stop the slaughter of innocents.

The ghosts shimmered, Cheyenne and Sioux, Irish and German immigrants, men in blue, women in buckskin, mutilated settlers, groaning soldiers, children with big, dark eyes. As faint as if they belonged to someone else, as if some other man's memories had grasped hold of him with pale, cold hands.

Here on a mountain, here beside Harry, her life so

strong and warm, he could almost forget the hell of his past. And then when he remembered, it was like falling off the mountain.

Her grip on his sleeve kept his imagination from slamming into the rocks below.

Her eyes searched his, held them. "You're not Custer," she said, with unnerving certainty. "And you're not a butcher. You were right to tell Lissy we have to wait until morning. You won't take us in there without knowing what we're facing."

"I won't do that," he managed to agree.

"Do you really think there will be guards? Do you think Charm would kill Lissy?"

"After the Beasts, I don't know what to think," he admitted. He remembered Charm Woodfin as a young man with an easy smile, quick to please those who could help him get what he wanted. He hadn't particularly liked him, even before Lissy. Maybe because Charm fit into the knife-edged magnolia society of Charleston and Savannah and Mal never had. But Mal would not have thought him capable of viciousness.

"I don't intend to underestimate the danger we could be facing if we confront him."

"Do you think the danger's too great? Are you thinking about giving up?"

"Do you mean am I frightened?" he demanded. *You're not your brother.* "Yes. I'm afraid Charm might have a half dozen hired guns just waiting to take turns shooting holes through us. I'm afraid the Beasts are on our trail and could cut off our retreat from Charm. I'm afraid you might pull that damn derringer out and end up shooting me or Tony by accident."

He couldn't tell her his greatest fear, that if they ran into danger like that they'd faced in the South Platte Saloon, he might fail this time, he might not be able to protect Harry. Even his army nightmares didn't compare to the agonizing dreams that had woken him, panicked and gasping, for the past two nights since he'd come so close to losing her to Spider's .44.

"Tony and I aren't gunfighters. I don't think Tony's ever had to kill a man." He touched the heavy gun on his right hip. "And I'm sick to death of killing."

The whiskey had soured in his mouth. "I've thought about turning back, but the Beasts are behind us, and Lissy won't be safe until we get them off her trail. Only Charm can call them off. So Tony and I talk to Charm. In the morning. After I've had a chance to scout the situation at the mine."

Harry jumped to her feet. "You're not leaving me behind."

He almost laughed. He'd known the exact expression she would wear saying those exact words. "It's too dangerous for Lissy to come with us, and we can't leave her behind alone." The cleverest part of the plan was that Harry's safety was only an added bonus. "Lissy will be safer in Silvercrest than at the Lucky Lady, but if anything goes wrong out there . . ." His gaze met hers steadily. "You'll be the only one who can take her to safety."

He didn't have to say safely back to Elijah in Battlement Park. That was understood.

Harry's eyes narrowed as she crossed her arms over her chest. "Nice try, Malachi Kelly, but I can see right through you. You just want to keep me out of the showdown. Don't tell me you've caught gallantry from Tony."

"Caught gallantry?"

"Treating me like a lady. It's contagious. Like the

mumps. It doesn't become you."

Damn, she'd almost made him smile again.

She plunked herself back onto the rock, leaning toward him, mouth thinned in intensity. "I have a better plan. Lissy will be even safer than she would be in Silvercrest, and we can help you if there's trouble."

"Like you did at the brothel?"

Predictably, she ignored that. "Get me a rifle. Lissy and I will find a place up above Charm's house. No one will even know we're there unless you need some cover fire to make your escape."

"That's a great idea." He laid on the sarcasm, in case she meant to ignore that, too. "Put our damsel in distress out unprotected on an isolated hillside somewhere and give you a gun just waiting for an excuse to start shooting in my general direction. A plan worthy of a five star general. I don't know why I didn't think of it myself."

"It's no worse than leaving us sitting in that hotel in Silvercrest waiting for the Beasts to find us."

He knew that she knew that he'd have to agree with her. And that she was damn good with a rifle.

"We'll stay out of trouble," she promised sweetly.

"I've heard that before," he growled. "The only way to keep you out of trouble would be to tie you up and dump you down the mine shaft. And even then I wouldn't feel safe."

She smiled. "Good. You wouldn't be."

"I'll decide on a plan of attack after I know what we're heading into," he said, hoping he sounded quelling.

"Don't forget the ammunition."

The bay gelding's teeth were yellow, his gums runny. The flea-bitten gray mare had saddle sores, and the two sway-backed sorrels were older than Harry. Not mounts designed for rapid escapes, but they were better than the other nags she had examined, and they would carry four people the few miles to the Lucky Lady mine and back.

Probably.

Harry leaned against the corral fence for a last regretful look at the stride of the big pinto she'd decided not to take. Definitely going lame. The fence rail creaked beneath her, and she straightened hastily.

"There's no one in town I can rent a sidesaddle from?" she asked the horses' owner again.

The short, potato-faced Texan who ran the Silver Dollar Saloon and the Silvercrest Stables and apparently half of the rest of the town, shook his head with aw-shucks regret. "I'm awful sorry, ma'am, but I don't know of none."

And he'd make less money if she rented the saddle from someone else. Harry decided not to press the issue. Lissy would just have to make do riding astride.

"We'll need them ready at dawn tomorrow morning," she said, reaching over to stroke the gray mare's muzzle.

"They'll be here," the Texan assured her. He took the cash she offered him, then stuck out his hand to shake hers. "Pleasure doing business with you, ma'am. I like a woman who knows how to drive a bargain."

She didn't comment. They both knew he'd gotten the better end of the deal, but desperate white knights couldn't be choosers.

She turned back to the horses, glad Maggie couldn't see them. They would break her heart. Harry doubted the Texan mistreated them. He probably collected the worn-out horses of miners desperate for a drink or the cash to get home and then sold them to the next hapless, footsore traveler who came along. They had water and food, at least, in this rickety corral, but they would end up as broken and bone-weary as their previous owners.

Though the owners weren't as likely to be shot for it.

"That man over there told me these are the horses you rented for us."

At the disbelieving tone by her side, Harry turned to see Malachi gesturing toward the Texan standing on the steps of his saloon. The man raised his hand in a cheerful salute before banging through the doors into his establishment, spilling piano music into the street.

"The bay, the gray, the two sorrels." Harry pointed them out.

Malachi squinted, as though that might improve what he saw. "I wouldn't eat those poor beasts, much less ride them."

"That might cost you a little more."

"What about that big white mare?" Malachi pointed. "Or that pinto. He might even be big enough so Tony's feet don't touch the ground."

"You're welcome to take the pinto, if you want to walk after the first mile," Harry said tartly. "And the mare's that big because she's going to foal any minute."

"Hell and damnation. Those are the best we can get?"

"You're welcome to see for yourself." She'd personally checked every beast in town.

He reached out a hand to brush the flies away from the face of one of the sorrels. The horse snorted softly in gratitude.

Malachi sighed in resignation. "You're the one with the eye for horses."

Harry rolled her eyes at the grudging acknowledgment. "That's right."

His mouth twitched. "At least the rifle I found for you is

in slightly better shape than these animals. We ought to be able to make do, even if we have to walk half the way back."

Harry raised an eyebrow. "You're the one with the eye for reconnaissance."

He nodded, obviously pleased with the information he'd gleaned from the locals. "It appears the Lucky Lady is not exactly a thriving money-maker, as yet. The previous owner had allowed it to fall into disrepair before Charm purchased it, and Charm hasn't yet hired the workers to start it up again. He may be easier to approach than I expected, though I won't know for sure until I take a look for myself."

"Good work, Captain Kelly." She gave him a little salute.

"Save the boot-licking, soldier. There must be some better prospect for supper in this town." He glanced toward the saloon. "Tony and I can bring something back to the hotel."

"Very good, sir."

He gave her a look that might been intended to chill her blood, but the humor glinting in those deep green eyes brought brightness back to the fading twilight. They could do this. They had their enemy cornered. They just had to finish the campaign.

Like old times. All of four months ago. Before Elijah's marriage. Before Ash. Before her life slipped out of her control. Back when she first learned to see past Malachi's blunt—well, if she were to put it bluntly, obnoxious—exterior to the heart beneath. When he taught her how to tell the difference between the track of a hunting cougar and a cat that was just covering ground. When she'd beaten him at five card draw and he'd threatened to challenge her to a duel for cheating.

"Do you remember the time I tried to teach you how to dance?" she asked.

"How could I forget?" The humor pulled at his mouth again. " 'The waltz is easy,' you said. 'You just count to three. You *can* count to three can't you, Mal?' "

His mimicry was terrible.

Harry shook her head, hands on hips. "Elijah played Mozart on his violin, and you started stomping all over my feet."

"It's what you obviously expected."

"You could have just told me you already knew how to dance."

"Perfectly."

"Not terribly."

"You can't be an officer if you don't know how to waltz." He cocked his head to the tune rattling out of the saloon. "One, two, three. One, two . . . three. One, two three. It's not exactly Wolfgang Amadeus, but . . ."

He held out his hands.

With a flourish of dusty skirts, she gave him an elaborate curtsy and stepped into his arms. He tucked his right hand above her hip beneath her coat and led with the other.

"One, two, three. One, two three," Harry sang. She didn't have to worry about her feet when Malachi led. She didn't have feet. She floated across the uneven ground. Even when the piano player missed the beat, Malachi incorporated it into the dance.

It felt good to move beneath the cold evening stars, spinning fast to the plinking of the piano, with the solid warmth of Malachi's hand holding her to the ground. It felt good to let her hat fly away, her hair falling loose on her shoulders. To breathe deeply of the thin mountain air, to laugh again. It felt very good to laugh, though the high altitude quickly robbed her of breath.

Malachi slowed them to a halt.

"I don't think I've danced so fast since 'Lije's Virginia Reel," he said, sucking in the scarce air.

"Jordan made him stop because she was afraid Nicky was going to go into early labor right there in the cabin."

"I think she was more afraid of Nicky falling on Wolf and crushing him to death."

Harry stomped on his foot. "Some gentleman you are."

"I'm every bit as much of a gentleman as you are a lady, Miss Harriet Jackson."

She laughed. "This is much more fun than being a lady."

"Ladies dance."

"Not in stable yards with unshaven men wearing guns on their hips."

"Unshaven men are more fun to dance with?" His eyes narrowed speculatively. "I'll have to remember that."

"Oh, honestly. It's not the stubble," she said.

"What is it, then?"

It was Malachi, she realized suddenly. It was the way he teased her. The way he listened to her. The way his smile drove the ghosts from his eyes.

But she wasn't going to tell him that.

Not when his hands still held her hand, her side. Not when she could feel the heat from his body across the short distance that separated them. Not when her breathing was as ragged as if they still danced. Not when the twilight had somehow slipped into dark, and all she could see of his eyes were the stars reflected in them.

Not when she suddenly wanted to reach up and touch that unshaven cheek, press her own cheek into his shoulder, lean into his warmth.

Too late, she realized she'd let silence fall between them,

no easy words to brush away the heat of her hand, the beating of her heart.

Slowly, deliberately, Malachi dropped his hands away from her and stepped back, cold night air swirling in to take his place.

"You'll be a wonderful dancer even when you are a lady," he said, his voice as solitary as the wind. For one moment, his hand lifted to brush the lock of hair falling across her cheek. "We'd better find your hat. Ladies don't have freckles."

She nodded and turned to search the ground. She was glad he'd let her go, before she had said anything foolish. Or done anything even more foolish than that. But the tightness in her chest had nothing to do with the altitude.

The knock on the hotel room door jolted Harry out of sleep. She'd sat on the bed to think, there being no chair in the tiny room to sit on, and she must have dozed off.

The ropes under the straw mattress creaked as she sat up. She hoped they hadn't been so gnawed by mice that they'd break during the night. She hoped there weren't too many mice currently living in the mattress.

Though mice were better than other things. She suppressed the urge to scratch all over.

The knock came again, louder.

Harry struggled to her feet, her mouth cottony with sleep.

"Harry? Are you in there? Lissy?" Malachi's fist struck the door with a little more force.

"Just a minute." Harry brushed her hair away from her face, surprised when her hands came away damp. She had been thinking of Ash before she slept, of the wedding now barely three weeks away. Thinking of his betrayal in Denver.

But she hadn't cried. That must have happened in her sleep. She couldn't remember what she had dreamed. Something about ghosts, a man with long, gold curls, the smell of buffalo hides. A man with dark hair and green eyes and blood on his hands.

"Harry!"

"Just a minute!" Annoyance snapped her out of the memory, and she grabbed her hairbrush to swipe it through the worst of her tangles. She was glad the room had no mirror; she didn't want to know.

She flung open the door to see Malachi and Tony standing in the drafty hall holding mugs of beer and what looked to be paper-wrapped sandwiches.

"Sorry supper took longer than I thought," Malachi said. "I had to drag Mad Anthony away from a duel."

"Mal's exaggerating," Tony said, glancing about the room for somewhere to place the beer. He finally squeezed his mug onto the tiny unfinished table that held the lantern.

"Mal always exaggerates," Harry said, almost managing to look Malachi in the eye as she took a sandwich from him.

"I only said that I thought the chap might want a bath before he sat at the bar, and he took it rather badly."

"The chap weighed three hundred pounds," Malachi said, unwrapping his own sandwich.

"Hardly." Tony tried to sit on the bed, misjudged, and only missed falling to the floor because there was not enough room between the bed and the wall.

"Tony's already drunk his beer," Malachi said, swiping Tony's mug off the little table before Tony could reach it. He handed it to Harry. She thought he was as careful not to touch her hand as she was to avoid his.

"I can't believe you didn't tell me you asked her to marry you," Tony said.

It took Harry a dizzying instant to realize he meant Lissy.

"I never intrude on the love affairs of friends. Bloody hell." Tony had finally hit the bed, but sprawled backward when it sagged beneath him.

"That proposal was more than a decade ago," Malachi said curtly. "I'm not having a love affair with Lissy Woodfin. And neither are you. She has a husband."

"Bounder," Tony muttered, struggling back up into a sitting position. "Doesn't deserve her."

"Where is she, anyway?" Malachi asked. "I'm about ready to eat her sandwich."

Harry looked up from her own supper, enough of a lady to swallow before answering. "What do you mean, where is she? I thought she was with Tony."

They both glanced at Tony, who shook his head. "I've been in the saloon. Not a half bad little pub, really. Haven't seen any of you all afternoon. Where the bloody hell have you been, anyway?"

Malachi turned to Harry. "She wasn't in the room when you got back?"

"I haven't seen her since I left the hotel to follow you."

Tony frowned. "No one's seen her since then? That was—" He pulled his watch from his pocket, squinted at it, gave up. "—hours ago."

The bed creaked and heaved as he struggled to stand. "Bloody hell. The Beasts." He unholstered one of his Smith and Wessons, and Harry swung out of his way in alarm as he struggled to corral his hand and spin open the cylinder. "They've gotten to her. Or Charm found her. If they've hurt her . . ."

Only part of the fire in his eyes came from the beer. "They'll beg to die."

"The little fool." Malachi's voice held more irritation than alarm. "She hasn't been kidnapped. She's gone looking for Charm."

"She's not a fool. She wouldn't do that." Tony paused, obviously remembering her desperate performance that afternoon. "At least not without a gun."

"Not without a gun," Malachi agreed reluctantly. "She didn't have the money to buy one. Yours are accounted for?" he asked Tony, checking his own holster.

Harry reached for her own little derringer, but she didn't have her purse. She glanced around the room. She couldn't have just left it somewhere . . .

"Hell and damnation," she muttered in admiration. "I've been robbed."

She was suddenly glad she'd caught a nap.

Chapter 13

"A couple of miles, my Aunt Matilda," Lissy muttered savagely, slamming a rock against the heel of her right boot with enough force to jar her shoulder. The left heel had snapped off easily enough. One wrong step in a hole in the road.

"Devil take it!" She adjusted the heel against the ground and brought the rock down again. If she couldn't get the heel off, she'd just have to go barefoot. She'd crawl on her knees if that's what it took, but walking was faster.

Another crack with the rock finally jarred the heel loose. She sat in the weeds by the side of the road and held the boot between her knees, wrenching at the heel until it came loose.

Her fist clenched to throw the cursed thing into the trees across the road, but pragmatism prevailed. She stuffed it into Harry's handbag with the other heel.

She sat Harry's purse next to her own and pushed her foot into the little kid boot. The lace snapped, of course. Fighting tears of frustration, she knotted it and finished lacing the boot. She stood, brushing leaves and dirt off her rear end. Charming.

The sound of her own laughter startled her. Sweet Miss

Lissy Wilmer lost in the middle of nowhere wearing a dusty dress with stains beneath her armpits.

"What will people say?"

It wouldn't matter much to her, one way or the other what they said, considering she was likely going to die of exposure or get eaten by a panther before morning. She glanced up at the sky, fading to a heartbreakingly clear blue-gray between the peaks to the west.

Already shadows had smoothed the road, if the deeply rutted track could be called a road, to a dim river of dusk that hid rocks and holes and other shoe-mangling pitfalls. Soon she would not be able to see her way at all in the places where the road ducked through the trees. If she didn't reach the Lucky Lady soon, walking off a mountain might be a more probable end than walking into a bear.

At least she could be sure no one else was likely to pass this way that evening. Charm would have no warning she was coming.

Lissy reached down to grab Harry's handbag. Perhaps her panic earlier had been premature. Perhaps this walk could have waited until morning. Her only reference had been Savannah where gossip traveled faster than an alligator's bite. And could draw more blood.

She stumbled over her first few steps. The smooth soles of the boots and the awkwardness of the missing heels would slow her even more than the aches in her feet and calves. But each step brought her closer to her goal.

Blood pounded in her ears, warming her more than her diamond-bought wool coat. Almost there. Soon she would confront Charm once and for all.

She touched the healed cut along her hairline. She wouldn't even mind the scar if the sight of it helped bring Charm to his senses.

If it didn't, she had Harry's gun.

The gray mare stumbled, but Harry barely flinched. She'd gotten used to it. It was the only thing keeping her awake.

The slow, steady plopping of horse hooves, the gentle rocking of the saddle, the warm scent of wool from her coat, all pulled at her weary mind, sucking her down toward sleep.

"Bloody hell," Tony burst out beside her. The clap of his hand against his thigh snapped through the quiet of the night. "We know she followed this road. Get out of the way, Mal. We have to move faster."

The light of the newly risen moon silhouetted the dark shape ahead of them. Malachi led the yellow-toothed bay, a closely shuttered lantern in his other hand illuminating a small circle of light before him.

"She came this way," Malachi agreed, not so much as glancing around. "But she wasn't moving fast in those ridiculous boots. She couldn't have reached the mine before dark. If we go any faster, we'll miss it if she lost the road or someone else found her out here or she got attacked by a bear and is lying unconscious behind a rock somewhere."

He sent a quick glance over his shoulder. "You're welcome to ride ahead and spoil the trail if you want to."

Harry reached across the space between horses to squeeze Tony's hand. "We'll find her," she said. "You know Mal's the best tracker in Colorado."

"I didn't know he was also the slowest," Tony muttered. Anxious energy radiated from him like heat.

"The horses can't move any faster on this road, either," she reminded him. "Not if we don't want broken legs."

As if in response, her mare stumbled again, this time

nearly spilling Harry to the ground. She pulled away from Tony and regained her balance.

"She broke a heel," Malachi said, pausing briefly ahead of them. "That will slow her down even more. We won't be far behind by the time we reach the mine."

Harry hoped he'd keep his mouth shut on that positive note. She had developed a grudging respect for Lissy's dogged determination, but she also knew the dangers of a cold Rocky Mountain night. And so did Tony.

Harry had tried to imagine how Ash might react if it were her lost on a mountainside in September in the middle of the night. Instead, her thoughts kept turning to what his reaction would be if he knew what she was doing that very night, riding through the dark in her blue jeans with two unmarried men, neither of whom had an impeccable reputation, chasing down another man's runaway wife.

He wouldn't just be furious. He would be humiliated that her actions might sully his good name. But, then, he would never believe she would be on this adventure in the first place. She wasn't "wild like Maggie."

Except she was. And maybe she didn't think her behavior was morally reprehensible, not like, say, frequenting cathouses. But Ash would think so, even though she was currently trying to help a friend in danger.

How well do you know yourself? Do you know what you want?

"Wait a minute." Malachi abruptly veered off the road ahead of them, examining the weeds along the edge.

"Snapped off the other heel, then kept going," he said. "And she left your bag behind, Harry."

He tossed the handbag to her. In the shifting moonlight, Harry misjudged the catch, and the bag hit her in the chest.

"Damn it, Kelly!"

"She left it?" Tony demanded, dismounting to stride over to Malachi. "She wouldn't do that. If she just forgot it there, she would have come back for the gun. Something's happened to—"

"The gun's not in here," Harry interrupted. "This isn't even my bag. It's Lissy's. Honestly."

She'd seen Malachi determine from a set of hoofprints in a muddy bank not only which horse from Tony's stables had passed that way, but who had been riding it, and he couldn't remember that her handbag was black velvet and Lissy's blue silk.

Harry reached into Lissy's purse. She'd have felt guilty, if Lissy weren't in so much danger. Not that they'd learn anything from her bag. There was very little in it. Harry's finger's identified a lacy handkerchief and one that felt like linen. A pitifully light coin purse. A pair of nail scissors. Some hair pins. A comb.

Harry thought of her own handbag, and grimaced. It still held a tiny piece of gold-flecked quartz March had given her for luck. The arrowheads she'd found by the swimming hole at the ranch. The half of a diaper she'd carried as an emergency vomit rag ever since Sarah was born. The pocket knife she'd won from Wolf in a spitting contest. The needle and thread for emergency falling-out-of-a-tree clothes repair. The fishhooks in a little wooden match box.

If Ash had ever gotten a look inside her handbag, he never would have proposed.

Her fingers ran over the object at the bottom of Lissy's purse.

"It's a picture frame." She pulled out the picture, the scrolled frame reflecting the moonlight. "Silver."

Tony and Malachi walked over to her horse. Malachi held up the lantern. The beam of light illuminated the photograph of a young boy, his face deadly serious beneath straight, fair brows. One lock stuck almost straight up out of his carefully slicked-back hair.

"She must have planned to sell the frame in an emergency." Malachi tilted the picture in Harry's hand for a better look. "I don't know why she hasn't destroyed the photograph. That's got to be Charm. He's still got that nose."

Tony pushed the frame back at Harry. "Right, then. It doesn't really matter who the bloody hell it is. We're looking for the lady it belongs to. Remember?"

He swung onto his horse with a flourish that nearly sent him all the way over the stout sorrel. "Let's find her before Christmas."

In the end, they were closer to their goal than they realized. Another half mile on, the road arched over a low rise. Ahead, the stars cascaded toward the earth, indicating a drop in elevation and possibly a decent view of what lay ahead.

Mal motioned his companions to a stop. "Wait here." He shuttered his lantern and handed the reins of his bay to Harry before following the road to the crest of the hill. Keeping to the trees, he crept forward until he could see down into the mountain saddle below.

Ragged tree stumps straggled down the hill, moonlight filling the cleared depression below. The Lucky Lady. Mal could just make out the cap of the mine shaft tucked against the far side of the saddle. In the center of the clearing, unprotected from the wind and coming snow, hunkered a small house, a thin breath of smoke rising from its chimney. Nearby, a haphazardly-erected stable leaned toward a broken-down corral.

After a long moment of scanning the scene, Mal's eyes picked out more buildings lined up against the hill below and to his left. Probably housing for the miners, equipment sheds, a manager's office. They showed no signs of life, consistent with the information he'd gleaned in Silvercrest. The "Princes" were reported to be the only current residents at the Lucky Lady while Mr. Prince arranged financing to pay the labor necessary to reopen the deserted mine.

Still, Mal intended to take a good look around the entire operation before he made a move on the house.

He edged back down the road to where Harry and Tony waited. Tony's breath puffed more impatiently than the horses'. Mal motioned them down from their mounts.

"We're there. The Lucky Lady is just over the rise."

"Then where is Elizabeth?" Tony demanded. "If that bastard has harmed one hair on her head—"

"There aren't any lights on in the house," Mal interrupted, holding Tony steady by force of will. "She can't have arrived long ahead of us, at the pace she was going. If there'd been any violence, I think we'd know. Right now, we need to scout out the situation."

"Scout?" Tony demanded. "We can't wait that long. We need to get Elizabeth out of there."

"The three of us are plenty to convince Charm to let her go," Harry put in.

"If he hasn't shot her," Tony growled.

Or she hadn't shot him, Mal thought. Lissy was not nearly as helpless as she would prefer others to think. Anyone who could walk five miles in those ridiculous kid boots was not going to give up without a fight.

"I'd like none of the rest of us to get shot," Mal said. "We do the reconnaissance first."

"There's no time!" Tony exploded. "She's in danger, and we're three against one."

"That's what we need to confirm," Mal replied, carefully calm.

"Oh, honestly," Harry said. "I understand what you're worried about, Mal, but Tony's right. Lissy's in danger. It's dark, and we have the element of surprise. This isn't the Little Bighorn."

"We didn't think the Little Bighorn was the Little Bighorn," Mal snarled back, sudden bitterness hitting the back of his throat. "Do you want to know how many times I've seen taking time for reconnaissance result in a massacre? Not one. That's how many."

Moonlight flashed in Tony's eyes. "This is bloody ridiculous. I'll go get her myself."

Tony flung himself into his saddle. Mal grabbed his reins.

"Damn it, Mal. Let me go, or so help me . . . If your brother was here, he'd be down at that house already. I'm not going to sit here while Elizabeth might be dying just because you're afraid there might be some unpleasantness."

Mal's voice hissed from his throat in sudden, blazing rage. "And I'm not going to let your asinine infatuation get anyone killed. My brother's not here, and I'm in charge. Get off that damn horse."

"It's my horse and my arse."

"I'm not worried about *your* arse, you damned fool," Mal growled, glaring up at the pale shape of his friend's face against the dark backdrop of the trees. "What do you think's going to happen to Lissy if you ride down there with guns blazing? Are you willing to get her killed because you can't wait half an hour? What if Charm isn't even there? Do you want to get us all hanged for blowing the head off an innocent bystander?"

Tony let out a blistering string of curses as he swung back to the ground. Mal dropped the reins, prepared to defend himself. Tony had four inches and twenty pounds on him, but the Englishman also had a definite weakness in physical combat: He refused to fight dirty.

But Tony slammed his fist into his horse's saddle instead of swinging it at Mal.

"Bloody hell, Mal. You are the most *difficult* person I've ever known."

"You're just mad because I'm right."

"That doesn't mean I won't jolly well knock you back on your bloody—"

"Shhh! Quiet!" Harry's urgent whisper broke into their exchange. "I heard something. Or I might have heard it, if you two could shut your mouths long enough for—"

"Hush," Mal reminded her. Sounds carried strangely in the thin mountain air. She'd probably heard a deer mouse or . . . In the sudden silence, they all heard the crack of a branch in the woods ahead of them. Maybe not a deer mouse. They didn't generally reach a hundred plus pounds.

He heard the click as Tony threw the safety on one of his Smith and Wessons, even as he readied his own Colt. Harry threw the bolt on her rifle.

"Why, I declare. Malachi Kelly, don't you listen to your own advice?" Lissy's hair glowed silver in the moonlight as she stepped out of the trees. "Whatever happened to scouting out the situation before you start shooting?"

"Elizabeth!" Tony thrust his revolver back into its holster, apparently remembering to reset the safety, since it didn't blow a hole through his foot.

"Lissy!" Harry grabbed her shoulders, and Mal wasn't sure whether she meant to shake Lissy or hug her. In the end, she just laughed. "I can't believe I fell for that purse-snatching routine again. Have you considered a career as a thief?"

"We thought Charm had you," Tony said.

"Why did you pull such a stupid stunt?" Mal asked. "You should have waited for us."

"I did," Lissy pointed out, quite calmly, Mal thought, for someone in imminent danger of being strangled. "What took you so long? You had horses."

"More or less," Harry said.

"You're not hurt?" Tony demanded.

"Of course not."

"Then we're going back." Mal swung into his saddle. The creaking leather, the horse's warmth beneath him, the sense of anticipation hanging in the night air, all took him back to times he did not want to remember.

"We came out here to do a favor for you," Mal reminded Lissy. "You have withheld information from us. You have stolen from us. You have endangered our lives needlessly. We agreed to protect you. You're safe for the moment. If you want to come back with us, we'll continue to keep you safe. If not, you're on your own."

"Mal, stop overreacting," Tony said, the humor restored to his voice now that Lissy had been found. "No harm done."

"No, Mal's right," Lissy said, sounding almost contrite. "I shouldn't have come out here on my own. It must seem terribly foolish to all of you. But I had to be sure that nobody warned Charm of our arrival. I didn't mean to place myself or anyone else in danger. I would have waited here for you until dawn."

It was Tony's turn to grab Mal's reins. "Come on, old man. You know you can't turn back now. We're too close."

"Besides," Harry added, "staying here isn't any more dangerous than riding back along that road in the dark."

Mal sighed heavily. He didn't like this quest now any better than he had the day they'd started out, but Tony and Harry were right. He couldn't turn back. After all, none of them, especially Tony, would ever be free of Lissy Woodfin and her magnolia-scented snares until they settled this once and for all.

"All right." He dismounted, taking his reins from Tony's hands. "Lissy, you're in charge of keeping the horses from bolting for home." He looked at his bay's sagging head. Bolting was probably not a problem. "Just a friendly warning, if you poke so much as a toe out into that clearing before I get back, I will shoot you and be done with it.

"Tony, I want you to circle the perimeter of the mine property. Make sure we won't have any unexpected company once we move in. Harry, you'll cover me and Tony from the trees. Understood?"

"Yes, sir," Tony said with a wry smile. "I beg forgiveness for my earlier insubordination."

"Just go," Mal said, waving him forward. He understood all too well what his friend had been going through, fearing the worst.

"Thank you, Mal," Lissy said, softly as a Savannah summer breeze as he handed her his reins. "I know I haven't made this any easier. There are some things I probably should have told you before. I—"

"Are they likely to get us killed down there at the mine?" Mal demanded.

"No. Absolutely not."

"Then save it until we get the hell out of here."

"Of course."

As he started off after Tony, Harry fell in beside him, her

rifle bumping against her shoulder.

"Mal, about what happened earlier. I didn't think we should wait to reconnoiter, but I wouldn't have gone in without you."

"Right." He grabbed her arm to stop her, meeting her eyes. "I believe that. God knows Harriet Jackson wouldn't rush into something without considering the consequences. When are you going to learn to think before you act? One of these times I'm not—no one's going to be there to bail you out, and you're going to get hurt."

He could see her mouth twist. "Sometimes you have to take a risk to help out a friend."

"I consider approaching a dangerous man to ask him to call off three even more dangerous thugs something of a risk," he said, voice low and curt. "That's why I want to be careful."

She blew out a sigh. "You're right. There, I said it. And I promise to stay right over there in the trees, silent as a mouse, until you get back."

"Fine."

He started forward, but she touched his sleeve, holding him back again.

"About what Tony said. If Elijah was here—"

"If my brother was here, he would agree with me. Despite what you all seem to think, he's not some kind of dime novel hero." The words had a savage force he couldn't control. "He's not still alive because of some supernatural power. He's still alive because he's smart. He'd never walk into a fight without knowing where every one of his opponents stood.

"Hell and damnation." He struggled for control, but an inexplicable rage shook him. "He couldn't have taken on Jesse James's gang single-handed and he doesn't walk on water. It's time you got over that damned hero-worship, Harry. He's happily married, remember?"

He heard the sharp intake of her breath, but she didn't give in to tears.

"Damn you, Malachi Kelly," she hissed. "Why do you have to be such an idiot? All I was going to say was that if Elijah was here he would have backed you up, just like he did when we were looking for Lucifer Jones last summer."

Her next breath was even more shaky. "Maybe I need to think before I act, but you need to learn to think before you open your mouth. I might get myself hurt, but you're going to hurt other people."

"Oh hell, Harry." He caught her sleeve, to keep her from running away. "Listen to me. I just—"

He just what? Just wanted to be judged for himself instead of always coming in second to his big brother? He couldn't say that. It wasn't the truth. The truth was, it was only Harry he couldn't bear coming in second to his brother with. And he couldn't say that either.

"I shouldn't have opened my mouth without letting you say your piece." He could say that with sincerity. "I'm sorry."

"Good." She breathed again, but the storm had passed from her voice. "So be quiet a minute so I can tell you to be careful down there. Mal . . . just be careful."

He could have reached out then and brushed the hair from her cheek. But he only nodded.

"As you said, this is not exactly the Little Bighorn."

"All right. Fine. Maybe I can learn to think before I speak, too."

Mal managed a smile, but as he turned back to the road, a ripple of dread crept up his back. Despite what he had just said, he had not felt this sense of foreboding since that wretched, hot day of Custer's Last Stand.

He shook his head, forcing himself to focus on the terrain before him, to listen to the night sounds, to begin to blend with the shadows. Despite his cautions to the others, he expected this to be a fairly straightforward matter. If his intelligence was correct, they would be facing only one man and his mistress. He and his companions had greater numbers, greater firepower, and the element of surprise.

Nothing like the Little Bighorn.

Except that since that day, he had never had as much to lose as he had now. On June 25th, 1876, he had lost friends and subordinates, lost his trust in his superior officers, his hope in human nature. He thought he had lost what was left of his heart, but he had been wrong. That was what he risked there at the Lucky Lady. The last remnant of his heart.

Clad in blue jeans and flannel.

Soft pink dawn warmed a wisp of cloud high above the mountaintops, but the light below was a thick, slow gray as Lissy picked her way up the dirt path to Charm's front door. Even in the ghostly light, the building's attempt at elegance drew the eye.

Milled lumber had been hauled for miles over the poor wagon road they'd traversed the night before to build a dainty cottage with scrolled eves, glass windows, and lace curtains. The whitewash was a hasty job; the door still bare. But with a coat of lemon yellow paint and some flowers on the sill, the little house would look quite at home in town, even in a modest neighborhood of Savannah.

In this remote setting, the faint smudge of smoke from the chimney turned the house into a haven of warmth and civilization.

Lissy didn't think she'd ever been as cold as she'd been the night before, with no fire, huddled against a tree in a blanket that smelled of dirt and horse. She had finally begun to appreciate Harry's warnings of freezing to death. Even now, she could see the breath of the horses puffing white about their faces where Malachi had hobbled them at the edge of the clearing.

But despite the thin, icy chill that sliced the morning air, Lissy felt her skin flush with heat as she neared the front door of the house.

With the strange gray light muting the landscape, the sky rapidly turning a clear, clean blue above them, the sun just beginning to strike gold sparks off the white mountaintops, she could not imagine the gates of heaven being in any more beautiful, frightening of a spot than this. She doubted she would feel any more trepidation facing St. Peter than she felt about knocking at Charm's door.

Though they were both equally likely to tell her to go to hell.

Malachi edged ahead of her to take his position beside the door, out of sight of the window. Harry had already slipped around to the back of the house with her rifle. Their calm efficiency working together helped keep her steady, but it was Tony's solid presence behind her that gave her the courage to take the last few steps to the door.

She took a deep breath, listening to the whisper of the sunrise, a silence that sang in the hushed air. The house sat in stillness. Charm had never liked to rise early, though he had always been the first to arrive at the office of her brothers' import-export company every morning.

Zealous, competent, mild-mannered Charm. How could you live with someone for eleven years and still be shocked by what you never knew about him? Even last night, she had not thought she would be afraid at this moment. Yet her hand shook as she lifted it.

She had spoon fed broth to this man when he caught the chicken pox, cleaned his socks, slept beside him. Yet she felt as though she were about to confront a stranger. A stranger who had taken all she held dear.

"Right, then," Tony said softly. "Go ahead. Don't worry. He can't hurt you now."

Lissy nodded. With desperate courage, she rapped sharply on the door.

The long silence afterward felt distinctly anticlimactic.

Lissy knocked again, harder this time, the sound echoing across the denuded clearing.

"There's still smoke coming from the chimney," Tony said, stepping back to check. "Someone has to be there to feed the fire. Not to mention those two horses in the stable."

"Charm always was hard to wake," Lissy said, the familiar frustration helping to calm her fluttering heart. She had just raised her fist to knock again when the door abruptly swung open.

Charm.

Thinner, she thought. In just a few weeks, his straight, fair hair was longer, mussed from sleep. His pale green eyes were smudged a darker green below, bruised with sleeplessness and strain.

It took a long moment for those eyes to believe what they saw. They focused in on her face for a heartbeat, two, before they widened in shock.

Charm's mouth dropped open, but no sound came from his throat beyond a ragged gasping as if he'd forgotten how to breathe. His face paled, and he swayed as if he might collapse.

"Oh, God, no. Help me," he blurted finally and slammed the door in Lissy's face.

Chapter 14

"That was not exactly the response I was expecting," Mal observed from his spot pressed against the side of the house. Through the door, he heard a bolt slamming into place.

"I didn't realize I was quite that terrifying," Tony admitted.

"Charm!" Lissy dodged past Mal to the window, where the white lace curtains obscured the house's dark interior. "We know you're in there, for heaven's sake!"

She came back to the door, her small fists pounding solidly on the unfinished planks. "Open this door, Charm Woodfin! You yellow-bellied coward!"

"What's going on?" Harry's confused voice sounded from the rear of the house.

Lissy stepped back to yell over the roof. "Stay where you are. Don't let them sneak out the back!"

An unlikely scenario, given that the house had no back door, but Mal would have preferred for the house's inhabitants not to know Harry was back there. Their quarry suddenly seemed more rabbit than wolf, but even rabbits fought viciously when cornered.

Lissy whirled on Mal. "Break down the door," she commanded. Her gray eyes flashed like an avenging angel's. "*Can* you break the door? Or should we smash a window?"

"I can take the door," Tony said, turning his shoulder toward it.

"Wait!" Mal commanded. "Wait just a damn minute. Just what the hell is going on here, Lissy? What is that man so afraid of?"

She looked at him, and he could see the play of desperate emotions across her face as she tried to decide what to tell him.

"My brothers," she said, finally. "He's afraid I've brought Clay and Rafe with me."

That would explain Charm's obvious terror. From his own childhood encounters with the Wilmer brothers, he had no doubt their proximity could turn a man pale and incoherent.

"He thinks they've come to avenge you?" Tony asked.

Lissy started to nod, then bit her lip, her face twisting in misery. "Probably not. I told you last night there were a few things I needed to explain, and I will, I promise. After we get inside."

"You'll explain it all right now," Mal said, with a discouraging sense of déjà vu. "Or I'm going home. I knew something felt wrong about this."

Tony hesitated in his door-battering stance. "Mal's got a point, much as I hate to admit it. What are we facing here, Elizabeth?"

"Please." Lissy shook her head, her agitation frustrating her speech. "Please get me in there. Charm's not dangerous. He couldn't kill a fly. Not like my brothers. You have to help me, before they find him."

She reached for both Tony and Mal, her deceptively delicate fingers digging deeply into Mal's arm.

"Rafe and Clay don't care who they hurt. He'll never be safe. You have to get me in there to help him."

"You're trying to *help* Charm?" Tony asked, rocking slightly from the shock.

"Damn strange way to go about it," Mal growled.

"Not Charm!" Lissy's fingers dug deeper. "Wesley. My son. Charm has my son."

The sound of wood breaking cracked like a gunshot across the clearing as two shoulders struck the plank door. Lissy thought the whole house seemed to rock under the assault, but the door was stronger than it looked.

Lissy stood aside as Mal and Tony rushed the door again. This time the hinges gave, tearing from the door frame, and the two men tumbled forward into the entryway.

Lissy rushed past them, her broken boots sliding treacherously on the remains of the door.

"Elizabeth! Wait!"

She ignored Tony's shout, plunging ahead into the dim interior. Despite what she'd said outside, she couldn't be sure Charm wasn't dangerous. He knew her brothers would be hunting him. He had to have a gun. But she couldn't wait for caution.

She dashed into the front parlor. A Turkish rug. A small pianoforte. Even in the poor light, the curved arms of the love seat gleamed with dark fire. Mahogany.

More than the richness of the wood warmed the room. The fireplace was empty, but Lissy guessed it shared a chimney with the next room.

Malachi and Tony pounded in behind her.

"The door!" She glanced behind them, half expecting to see Charm escaping into the sunrise. "We can't let him get away."

"I'll keep an eye on the door," Malachi promised, pulling open the curtains.

As light fell on the parlor's furnishings, Tony whistled. "The blighter didn't spare any expense, did he?"

"No reason he should," Lissy said, heading across the central hallway to the next room. "It's not his money."

The dining room was equally well-appointed and equally empty. The glass-fronted china cabinet held silver as well as china, including several pieces Lissy's grandmother had given her after her wedding. Charm had told her he'd sold them to pay off debts.

"Charm!" Lissy banged through the door into the small kitchen. "I haven't brought my brothers. I don't care about the money or Antoinette. I just want to see my son."

The kitchen was colder than the dining room, the cast iron stove squat and silent in the corner. Apparently Charm did not expect Antoinette to rise at dawn to prepare his coffee just the way he liked it.

Or, more likely, Lissy thought, Antoinette had the good sense to refuse to do it.

The door through the back of the kitchen let into a small, rectangular room at the rear of the house. Shelves along one wall held a haphazard array of canned goods, sacks of beans, flour, and coffee, and piles of linen tablecloths and sheets.

The room had obviously been intended as a pantry, but a small cot filled most of the floor space. Despite the chill of the house, the rumpled sheets felt warm to Lissy's touch.

"Wesley!" The cry tore from her throat as she ripped at the bedcovers, though she already knew she would not find her son huddled beneath them.

She spun around, searching the tiny room, knowing it

was empty. She pushed past Tony back into the kitchen, her breathing ragged.

"Charm, so help me God, if you don't let me see my son, I swear . . ." She had to grab the stovepipe to keep from falling.

Tony touched her arm. "Wait here. I'll find him."

"No." She struggled to catch her breath. "No. He's here, Tony. I was afraid he wouldn't be. I didn't know . . . But he's here. We have to find him!"

"We will."

Tony led the way across the central hall to the door to the master bedroom behind the parlor. Lissy reached for the knob, but Tony grabbed her hand.

"We've searched everywhere else," Lissy said. "They have to be in the bedroom."

"Precisely," Tony agreed, gently pushing her to the side of the door. "They're cornered. I'd rather not get shot this morning."

Lissy dug in Harry's purse for her little derringer. "You're starting to sound like Mal."

"It's about time someone did." Malachi already held his Colt ready in his hand as he came up beside her. "Get behind me, and put that parlor gun away. I'd rather not get shot this morning, myself."

Tony met Malachi's eyes and took a spot on the other side of the door frame. Malachi reached for the doorknob.

"Be careful," Lissy whispered, not relinquishing the derringer. "There's a little boy in there. I'd rather not have *him* shot, thank you."

Malachi turned the knob. In the sudden silence, the small click of the latch sounded nearly as loud as Lissy's pounding heart. Even holding her breath, she could hear nothing from inside the bedroom.

"One," Tony mouthed, holding up a finger. "Two. Three."

Malachi rammed the door with his shoulder, plunging into the bedroom. Tony swung around the door frame, revolver ready to cover him.

Lissy heard the loud thump of a body hitting the floor.

"Hell and damnation!"

Tony darted into the room. She heard another thump and another curse, and then a startled cry and a desperate scrabbling sound.

"Hold on!" Malachi shouted.

Glass shattered.

"What is going on in there?" Harry's voice demanded.

Lissy lifted the derringer, steadying her right hand with her left. "Bloody hell," she muttered, stepping through the door.

Harry ran the butt of her rifle across the window sill, clearing it of the last jagged shards of glass before she ripped aside the lacy curtains. Leading with the rifle's barrel, she leaned across the sill, peering into the dim bedroom.

Swinging the rifle sight across the room, Harry froze on a pale figure in the doorway, a figure pointing a gun directly at her head.

"Damn it, Harry," the figure said, her soft, southern voice tight with strain. "You didn't tell me how to take the safety off this thing."

"You tried to pull the *trigger?*" As Harry sagged against the window sill, her gaze caught on a darker figure lying across the bedroom floor. Malachi. He had hold of a pair of cavalry-booted ankles. Tony's front half disappeared into a dark space in the floor.

Otherwise the room appeared empty.

A muffled English accent rumbled from the hole in the floor.

"I'm *trying* to pull you up," Malachi grunted. "It's not my fault you actually like your Norwegian chef's food. Maybe if I had some help . . ."

Harry heaved her rifle through the window and followed it in, her boots crunching glass into a throw rug beside the bed. She grabbed one of Tony's legs, Lissy the other. Malachi heaved behind them.

As Tony's hips and chest rose from the hole, Harry saw it was actually a square shaft cut through the floor, with a trap door lying askew beside it.

"There's a ladder," Tony said, pushing himself up the last couple of feet, face red from his near headlong plunge. "They've flown the coop, or burrowed under it, at any rate."

"Who?" Harry demanded, frustrated that she'd missed out on the action. "You were supposed to scare Charm, but this might be a little excessive."

"We might have done this a little better, if we'd known all the facts." Malachi squatted on his heels to peer down into the shaft. "Lissy failed to mention one or two things."

"Like what?" Harry asked, eyeing the hole from a respectable distance behind Malachi.

"Like the fact that she has a son and Charm has stolen him away," Tony said.

"A son?" The picture in the silver frame. That explained why he looked like Charm.

"Like the fact that Charm is considerably more afraid of Lissy than she is of him," Malachi said darkly, pushing himself to his feet. "Not that I can say I blame him."

"He's running from her brothers," Tony explained,

though it didn't really explain anything.

Still, Harry had the salient facts. The chief valuable Charm had stolen from Lissy, the goal that had driven her to face down the Beasts and hunt through the wilds of Colorado for her wastrel spouse, was her son. And Charm had taken the boy down that hole.

"We don't have time for this!" Lissy exploded. "We have to follow them."

Harry had been rather afraid she would say that.

"Not without a light," Malachi said. "Lissy, see if you can find a lantern in the house. Harry, get the one from my horse. Tony, check the barn and make sure Charm's not riding away while we stand here talking."

Harry ran to get Malachi's lantern, meeting Tony at the front door as she returned.

"No trap doors," he said of the stable as they hurried back into the bedroom. "Horses still there."

"This tunnel probably connects with one of the mine shafts," Malachi said. "It could lead anywhere."

Lissy's hunt had dug up a box of matches, two candles in silver candlesticks, and the oil lamp that had hung outside the front door.

Malachi cut one of the candles in half, handed one half to Tony along with several matches and tucked the other half and the match box into his coat pocket. Then he lit his lantern.

"This could take a while," he said, lowering the lantern into the shaft to take a look. "Depending."

He straightened. "Harry, if we're not back two hours before sunset, take Lissy back to Silvercrest. Even on those nags, you ought to be able to reach town before dark."

"We're not waiting up here," Lissy said, gathering her skirt in one hand. "We're coming with you."

Malachi shook his head. "Somebody has to stay here—"

"Wesley is *my* son! I'm coming with you."

"—to make sure they don't circle back to the stable and escape while we're stumbling around in the dark. I don't think they plan to hide down there forever. You'll have to keep an eye on the house, the shaft here, and on the mine entrance shaft. Do you think you can do that?"

"Of course we can," Harry jumped in, trying to sound resolute rather than relieved. "They won't get past us."

Malachi blew out a breath and fixed her with a glance. "Just don't do anything stupid."

Harry put her hands on her hips and stared right back. "You either."

He snorted. "What could possibly go wrong?"

Then he started down the ladder, lantern in one hand, and Harry had to watch him descend into the darkness below, her heart rising in her throat as his head dropped beneath floor level. It looked dark. Dark and deep and narrow. She forced herself to breathe.

But it was only a moment before Malachi's voice called up, "I'm down. It's only about ten feet."

Harry dropped to her knees and leaned toward the edge of the hole. As he'd said, Malachi's head was only a few feet below hers. The tunnel from the shaft led north, toward the mountain and the mine, as Malachi had predicted. It looked cramped to Harry, but then, it hadn't been intended to accommodate ore carts.

She could hear Tony reassuring Lissy they'd find her son, but all she could think about was Malachi and Tony disappearing into that narrow, stifling tunnel, with dark earth heavy over their heads, like a grave.

"Let me go with you," she called down to the top of Malachi's head, only because she couldn't beg him not to go and she couldn't bear the waiting. "Let Tony stay with Lissy."

He glanced up, his face lit from beneath by the lantern. His eyes looked almost black in the contrast.

"A rifle's no good in a mine shaft," he said, instead of reminding her that he knew her fear of caves and other dark, closed spaces.

For a long moment he held her gaze, then he raised his hand toward her. Harry dropped to her chest. Reaching down, she grasped his hand. Rough. Strong. Solid.

Even in the South Platte Saloon, when Spider Grant had promised to shoot her, she'd known that as long as Malachi was nearby, they would find a way out of danger. She didn't know how she could let go of his hand and let him walk down that tunnel without knowing for sure he would be coming back.

"Be careful, Malachi Kelly. Or I'll make you sorry."

"Be safe, Harry," he said, his voice as rough as the calluses on his palm. "So much for reconnaissance."

Harry's heart lurched. "Whatever I said last night, I didn't mean it."

"Yes, you did." His smile was crooked. "Friends are hazardous to one's peace of mind."

"Downright dangerous."

Then Tony was climbing down the ladder, and she had to move out of his way.

"Right, then," Tony called out, "Onward!" And they disappeared down the tunnel, the weak light of the lantern winking out of sight almost immediately.

"Bloody hell," Lissy said.

"And then some," Harry agreed, crawling several feet back from the lip of the shaft before rising to her feet.

Lissy handed Harry her rifle. "I'll go crazy if we have to

stand around here for long. Let's go check the barn again."

Harry nodded. "Then we can see what kind of food Charm has stocked in the kitchen."

"I declare, Harriet Jackson. I don't know how you can be hungry. My stomach's tied in more knots than a cotton-mouth in a tornado."

Harry checked the rifle. "We'll be hungry when they get back. Cooking will pass the time."

She glanced at Lissy. "And then you can explain what's going on here. Why you lied to us. What other tiny bits of information you've forgotten to tell us. You're not being hunted by the Pinkertons or anything, are you?"

"Not that I know of."

Harry waited.

Lissy sighed. "Charm was embezzling from my brothers' import-export firm. When he disappeared last month, they discovered he'd stolen several hundred thousand dollars over the past decade."

Harry whistled. "That accounts for the feather bed in the middle of nowhere."

"I didn't know anything about it," Lissy said. "But my brothers thought I was protecting him. I would have helped them find him. Anything to get Wes back. I didn't care what they did to Charm, after he stole our son."

Her voice caught on the memory, and Harry could only imagine the pain Lissy had felt. If someone took Sarah from Maggie . . . Harry felt sick at the thought.

"But they wouldn't listen to me. They called me a liar and a whore. Their own sister." She sounded more disgusted than surprised. "They're the ones who sent Rat and Fox to find me, to 'persuade' me to give them all the information I had. They're the ones who threatened my grandmother and took what little she had left because they said I *owed* them."

Lissy looked at Harry, and her gray eyes were clear and sharp. "That's when I knew I had to find Wesley myself, that my brothers didn't care who they hurt, only that they got their money back and got a chance to punish Charm for besting them.

"That's what they're after. They don't need the money. They can't let their business associates see they can be cheated. I knew they wouldn't hesitate to hurt Wes if that's what it took to get Charm. Maybe that's why Charm decided to take Wesley with him."

"So your brothers hired the Beasts."

Lissy nodded as she led Harry out into the hall. "To frighten me and to find Charm. I thought they came to Colorado looking for me, but maybe they were following the same trail I was.

"I knew Charm had kept in touch with Angelique. I'd found the letters. When he disappeared, I guessed he might go to her. I burned the letters with her address, but Spider Grant obviously tracked her down somehow."

"But Charm never tried to hurt you."

Lissy paused at the broken front door. "Other than running away with his mistress and kidnapping my son?"

Harry grimaced. "Other than that."

"No."

"That makes me feel a little better about Mal and Tony in that hole."

Lissy's mouth curled. "Charm Woodfin may be a cheat, a thief and a liar, but he's not a violent man. He's used to talking himself out of trouble. Sometimes I think he could talk his way past the devil himself."

And maybe he'd think he was doing just that when Malachi caught up with him, Harry thought. But even if Malachi couldn't charm himself past a hole in the road, he had a way of making his point clearly enough.

"Why didn't you just tell us?" That was the real question. "Why make up such an elaborate story?"

"Why didn't I just ask complete strangers to risk their lives to help me find my son?" Lissy asked. "A little boy who meant nothing to you who was legally with his father? My own father shut his door in my face. My brothers don't care if they have to hurt my son to get to Charm. Why should I think you all would help me?"

The glint of tears marred her bitter laugh. "The only thing that would convince anyone in my family to help anyone else, including their own mother, is money. Lots of money. So that's what I thought I had to offer you."

She brushed impatiently at the tears, glaring at Harry. "How was I supposed to know I would end up with Galahad and Lancelot and Maid Marian?"

Harry's mouth twitched traitorously. "It's a good thing you did. You know Gal and Lance won't let any harm come to Wesley."

"I am praying," Lissy said, and Harry could see that she meant it literally. "Wes thinks he's so grown up, but he's only eight years old. He's probably terrified."

"Running around in an old mine shaft playing hide and seek?" Harry asked skeptically, thinking of seven-year-old Tucker Culbert.

Lissy actually smiled. "The best adventure he's had in his whole life."

"He'll be back here telling you all about it in no time," Harry assured her. "Let's check that barn. We can't let the boys have all the excitement."

She followed Lissy out onto the front step, shading her eyes against the bright morning sunshine.

"All the excitement?" Lissy echoed faintly as they both

froze abruptly in place. "I don't think we have to worry about that."

Three riders sat on three horses in a silent semicircle before the house. A faint morning breeze stirred the animals' tails. The black gelding in the middle tossed his head as his rider doffed a dapper black bowler.

"Good morning, Mrs. Woodfin," said Spider Grant in his silken, dangerous voice. "We would like a word with your husband."

Chapter 15

Since there was no front door left to shut, Harry simply yanked Lissy inside behind the door frame. She could hear her heart pounding against the wood behind her back. Unless that was Lissy's heart.

"Oh, God," Lissy squeaked, sagging against the wall. "What are we going to do?"

Harry's mind went blank. It wasn't that she hadn't been in tight situations before. She'd certainly come up with plans of action on her own. But no one had ever *wanted* her to.

"You would be wise not to make us come in after you," the spider's words carried eerily well in the thin, clear air. "This will be much less painful for all concerned if you and Mr. Woodfin simply acknowledge the inevitable."

Harry suspected that wasn't strictly true. Spider's voice held a relish for pain that no amount of soft southern manners could hide.

"It's not that I wouldn't throw Charm to the wolves right now," Lissy said, her voice fluttering from lack of breath. "But he isn't here to throw. I don't think Spider is going to like that."

"Mrs. Woodfin, you have exactly two minutes."

"I don't much care what Spider likes," Harry said, beginning to become annoyed. "In fact, the less he likes it, the better."

Hefting her rifle by the barrel, she smashed the stock through the nearest dining room windowpane. She already felt bad about the broken window in the bedroom, but the open front doorway didn't offer enough protection. Slipping the rifle barrel through the ragged glass, she hunched beside it.

"They haven't spent much time in the West," Harry observed, squinting down the sight. "Even with the sun behind them, they're just ducks sitting in a row."

Lissy crouched beside her. "How many of them could you hit before they reached the trees?"

"All of them. If I had my own rifle. With this one, I'm not sure." She wished she'd had a chance to practice with it. She hoped it fired at all.

Lissy rose from beside her and stepped to the doorway. "Mr. Grant," she called out, cool and calm in the bright sunlight. "You have exactly one minute to ride away from here and leave us alone."

"I'm sorry, Mrs. Woodfin. You know I can't do that."

"Very well." Lissy turned and stepped back to Harry's side. "Go ahead and kill as many as you can."

Something small and cold flipped sluggishly in Harry's stomach, and she was suddenly glad she had eaten nothing for breakfast.

"Kill them?"

The three men sat still as tombstones on their horses, black silhouettes against the glare of the rising sun.

"They would happily do worse to us," Lissy said, with a certainty that chilled Harry's spine.

Harry remembered the viciousness of Fox's unprovoked

attack on Miss Lily at the South Platte Saloon. She remembered the bruises on Lissy's face. She had heard death in Spider Grant's voice.

She had taken aim at men before, knowing that if she didn't, they would kill her and her family. Her bullets had hit at least two of the outlaws that had attacked the Jackson farm three years before. One had probably died from a wound she had inflicted.

But she had never shot at a man in cold blood.

Harry adjusted the rifle sight, pinning it on Spider Grant's heart. Or his throat. Or shoulder. Or left knee. She shook her head, trying to swallow the spinning worm in her throat.

"I can't," she said. At least her voice wasn't shaking. "If they start shooting at us, yes. But they haven't yet."

Lissy puffed out a breath. "I suppose that's better for our immortal souls, but it won't be much comfort to our mortal remains."

Harry shifted the rifle more tightly against her shoulder. "I didn't say I couldn't scare them."

The recoil kicked her shoulder back, but her gaze stayed steady, catching the almost casual lift of the spider's bowler as it spun into the sunrise.

"Ha!" The rifle was sighted well, in any event.

"Take that!" Lissy shouted exultantly as the three horses suddenly broke into a dance of spinning riders and surprised shouts.

A couple of bullets around the horses' ears should help convince them to stay out of range. Calmly, deliberately, Harry sighted down the barrel again, her finger testing the action of the trigger, squeezing with just the right pressure to get off a smooth shot.

Noise exploded in Harry's head. Stunned, she blinked,

trying to clear her eyes. All she could see was a pale haze across the world. No, that was Lissy's face.

"Harry? Are you all right?"

Harry was surprised she could hear Lissy's voice, with the roar continuing to rumble through her ears. She tried moving her arms and legs. They felt whole and unharmed, although they were apparently spread out on the floor.

Her chest hurt, as though she'd been kicked, but she managed to ask, "What happened?"

Lissy glanced toward the window. "I think your gun blew up."

Harry closed her eyes. That would account for the smell of fire and brimstone and the stinging in her hands. If the exploding powder had blown into her eyes, or one of the slugs had been kicked back at her head . . .

"No wonder Mal got such a good deal on it," she muttered, letting Lissy help her sit up. "I guess it jammed."

Harry scooted to where the wreckage lay under the window. The rifle had cracked in half, the stock blackened, the barrel twisted.

"Can you fix it?"

Harry poked at the rifle. "You've got to be kidding."

"I think it's time for a new plan," Lissy said.

Harry rose up on her knees to look out the window. The horses she'd bought in Silvercrest had scattered at the sound of gunfire, but hunger proved stronger than fear, and they had regrouped around a patch of blue grama grass.

The Beasts had disappeared. Not for good. Harry was certain of that. She hoped they'd retreated into the trees to plan their next move. If they'd merely circled around the house, she and Lissy had no chance at all.

Lissy pulled the derringer out of her coat pocket. "I don't think this is going to frighten them off. There's probably a carving knife in the kitchen, but we can't win a fight."

"We have to run," Harry said. "We can't wait for them to come get us."

"Run?" Lissy rested a hand on the wall as she peered out the window over Harry's head. "On those animals?"

The smaller of the two sorrels turned sideways at that moment, presenting a back nearly in the shape of a U.

"Charm and Antoinette have better mounts in the stable," Harry said. But that didn't matter much. The Beasts waited along the only road away from the Lucky Lady, and she had no intention of deserting Malachi and Tony, anyway.

She sat back on the floor and rested her head on her knees.

"Harry?" Lissy dropped beside her. "Are you sure you're all right? Are you dizzy?"

"The mine shaft." Harry didn't look up. "We have to go down the mine shaft after Mal and Tony."

And they had to do it fast, before the Beasts returned.

"Right," Lissy agreed. "Of course. Mal and Tony are still armed. Can you stand? We'll need light. There are more boxes of matches in the kitchen."

By the time Harry struggled to her feet, Lissy had returned with two large boxes of matches, one of which she tossed to Harry.

"Mal left the little lantern from the doorway," Lissy said, "and one of the candles. We can split it like he and Tony did, in case we get separated."

Harry stumbled against the wall in the hallway. Separated. Alone beneath the ground. Trapped.

"Harry!"

She took a breath and forced her feet to follow Lissy to

the bedroom. Lissy thrust a candle stump at her.

"Put this with the matches."

Lissy took only a second to get the lantern lit, then handed it to Harry.

"If I spend any more time in Colorado, I'm going to have to get myself a pair of those blue jeans," Lissy said, fighting with her skirts as she began backing down the ladder. "I declare. You'll have me roping horses and chewing tobacco if I don't watch myself. My mother would have a spell."

Lissy's fair head disappeared into the shaft. "All right, you can hand me down the lamp."

"I've got it." It had been a few years since she climbed up to the loft window at the ranch house with an apron full of kittens, but if she couldn't climb a ladder with one hand, she might as well let Spider Grant shoot her.

If she pretended she were escaping the ranch for a midnight ride with Wolf, she might even manage the descent without whimpering.

"There." Lissy grabbed the lamp from her as she reached the bottom of the hole. "Should we try to drag the cover back over us?"

She didn't wait for Harry to reply, for which Harry was grateful, since she had no coherent response to the idea of purposefully closing themselves inside a pitch black hole.

"Waste of time," Lissy decided, poking the lamp into the tunnel before turning back to Harry. "It would be obvious there's a trap door here, anyway. Maybe if we leave it open, one of them will fall in and break his neck."

She smiled tightly at that thought and then plunged into the tunnel.

Automatically, Harry stepped after her. As the tunnel walls closed in on her, sound changed, condensed, muffling all but their skidding footsteps and the sound of their breathing rustling the stale air. Harry tasted earth on her tongue, the scent clogging her nostrils.

It was worse than the root cellar at the ranch. Worse than being trapped in the wardrobe. She took a shuddering breath. She refused to throw up.

When the tunnel turned suddenly, jogging around a sharp thrust of granite, the lantern light thickened, too, a yellow ball of life projecting around Lissy's hand, with nothing but empty darkness pressing against Harry's back.

The thought of welcoming the Beasts into Charm's house for a nice cup of tea began to sound appealing.

"Bloody hell," Tony swore as Mal lifted the lantern to show a secondary passage breaking off from the tunnel they were following. "That's the third one. There must be dozens of passageways down here. It will take us forever to check all these dead ends."

"That leads down," Mal pointed out. "This one goes up. It has to connect with the main shaft eventually. Charm can't mean to hide down here forever. He'll be heading for the mine entrance."

"Unless there's more than one entrance."

"You didn't have to mention that," Mal growled. Despite the fact that they had their goal in sight—or would, if it weren't for about a half million tons of rock between it and them—grave apprehension clutched his heart. They were too late, too slow, too far behind.

They'd sprung the rabbit from cover, but he had reached his den, and now he had the advantage. But only for the moment. Because if they were the hounds, the Beasts were the wolves.

And the Wilmer brothers . . . They were the devil's own animals.

If he and Tony didn't find Charm, Clay and Rafe Wilmer would. Maybe not today or tomorrow, but eventually. And if Charm tried to use his son as a shield from their wrath, well, the Wilmer brothers Mal remembered would show no mercy for a little boy.

Hurry, his muscles urged him as he dropped to a crouch to examine the turnoff to the secondary passage. *Don't waste time.*

He forced himself to examine the hard rock for the recent scuff of boots, to check the dust, deposited by a fine, inconstant rain from the ceiling, for footprints.

Yet neither of those was what gave Charm's direction away.

He reached for the small object that sparkled in the dirt at the edge of the lantern's glow, just inside the smaller tunnel. A quartz pebble. There was nothing strange about quartz in a silver mine, but this pebble was smooth, worn to a white oval by the tumble of some mountain stream.

Another one lay not far beyond it.

"Markers?"

"Here's another," Tony said, lifting a pebble from behind them, back the direction they had come.

"Charm must have been afraid of getting lost," Mal said. "He must have hoped pursuers would miss them. Though I wouldn't think pebbles would make reliable markers."

"Not markers," Tony said, replacing his pebble. "Bread crumbs."

Mal looked at the rocks in his hand then back at his friend. "There may not be enough air in here."

"Lissy's fairy tales," Tony explained. "You heard her talking about Perrault. This is the Brothers Grimm. You know, Hansel and Gretel. The wicked witch. The bread crumbs."

"Wesley," Mal said, excitement building in his chest.

"Of course he's been forbidden from playing in the mine tunnels," Tony began.

"So of course that's exactly what he does, in secret," Mal continued. "And he keeps a supply of white rocks in his pocket to mark his way so he doesn't get lost."

"So these could be old markers."

Mal shook his head. "If he's a smart enough boy to leave markers, he's smart enough to pick them up on his way home so he doesn't get confused the next time out."

He took another step into the smaller passageway. And another. "There." He pointed to a small depression in the rock floor where silt from the ceiling had collected and then been flattened. "That's a lady's heel. Recent, too."

"Clever little blighter," Tony said. "I guess he doesn't trust his father not to get them lost."

"And they'll work just as well for us, on our way back," Mal agreed. "I think we can pick up our pace."

Tony grinned. "Jolly good."

They were going to suffocate, Harry thought, as the lamplight flickered off the sides of the narrow opening to their left. Die choking for air in the dark, never to see sunlight again.

A rock bounced down the wall beside her, followed by the hiss of sifting silt.

Or maybe they would simply be buried alive.

"This must be a new section," Lissy said, stepping into the smaller shaft. "Smell how fresh the supporting timbers are. Just like the tunnel beneath the house."

"Exploratory," Harry said, trying to sound dry and

knowledgeable. At least her throat was dry. "Seeing if the vein turns this way. There's no reason for Charm to go down there."

"That's the way they went, though." Lissy pointed to the little white stones inside the narrow entrance.

Harry was coming to hate those stones, hate the little boy who'd left them, hate Lissy for figuring out what they meant, hate . . .

The light ahead of her flickered again and then died. Sudden, absolute, palpable darkness collapsed on her, filling her eyes, her ears, her nostrils. She gasped, but the darkness clogged her lungs, suffocating her.

"Air," she choked out. "Not enough air."

"It's just run out of oil," Lissy said, her disembodied voice impossibly calm. "It's been guttering for a while. I should have thought to check it before we came down here, but I had other things on my mind. It's a good thing we have the candles."

Harry heard the rattle of matches as Lissy pulled the box out of her coat pocket. Her own breath rattled nearly as much, and she closed her eyes against the darkness. If she could make it to a count of ten, Lissy would have the candle lit.

One, two, three . . . The numbers clanged in her ears like the pounding of her heart. A rhythmic thudding like a hammer on wood. No, on stone. A hammer on stone, but with a quaver.

"Harry?" Lissy's whisper came startlingly close. "Do you hear that?"

"What?" Harry's eyes opened. Still no light. She'd light her own candle, except she knew her hands would shake too badly to strike a match.

"That banging noise."

"That's my heart trying to break out of my chest," Harry informed her. "Light that candle."

"It sounds like a shovel."

Hammer. Shovel. Harry wasn't going to quibble. Except that the distraction had quelled her ragged breathing, clearing up the other sound.

"A pick," she said, blinking her eyes as if that would help her hear it. "There's someone down there."

"I told you we were on their trail."

She didn't care how pleased Lissy was with herself. She only cared that if they were going to die a slow horrible death buried alive, at least they wouldn't do it alone.

"Light the candle, and let's go find them."

"If we light the candle, they'll see us coming," Lissy said.

Something touched Harry's shoulder, and she barely managed to muffle a scream as she realized it was Lissy's hand. Lissy's fingers ran down her arm to grab the cuff of her flannel shirt.

"Follow me." Lissy tugged her forward, giving her little choice. Harry certainly wasn't going to stand still and be left alone.

Lissy's boots scuffled along the uneven floor of the tunnel, and Harry heard her free hand grazing the left wall ahead of them. The tunnel had narrowed so far that Harry could feel the walls pressing in on both sides, just beyond the width of her shoulders.

A soft thunk ahead did not warn her in time to keep her from stumbling into Lissy's back.

"Low beam," Lissy whispered, just as Harry's forehead struck it.

"A little more warning," Harry suggested.

"Put your hand up," Lissy hissed back.

They continued on, the tunnel feeling as though it were angling up into the ceiling. Soon they had to duck their heads even where there were no beams.

Still, to her surprise, Harry found the journey somehow less terrifying without the lamp. She couldn't see the rock pressing on her, couldn't see the dust swirling. Without the light, it was almost as though she couldn't see the darkness. She might have been frightened of missing a turnoff, except she knew she would feel it if they passed an opening in the wall.

The strangest thing was, that without the lamp, she even thought her eyes were beginning to adjust to the dark. She could almost make out the surreal glow of Lissy's silvered blond hair ahead of her, almost see the wooden beam that leaned across the passage in front of them.

Lissy's hand hit the beam, and they dodged under it.

"Light." Harry barely breathed the word, but Lissy nodded, and they slowed to a stop.

The tunnel bent just ahead. Even at the bend, the light was dim, just a hint of luminescence.

"A lantern," Lissy said.

"No, it's too steady." Harry hardly dared say the words, much less believe. But even her tongue could taste the difference in the air.

The ringing of the pick grew louder as they approached the tunnel bend. Edging up to it, they peered around.

Before them, the tunnel gave way, spilling into a natural cavern that felt to Harry like the opening into a cathedral nave, though in reality it could not have been more than thirty feet across and perhaps fifteen wide, much of the floor made impassable by jagged slabs of rocks fallen from the walls.

Light drifted down from an opening across the cavern,

halfway up to the steepling roof. The rhythmic thud came from a man swinging the business end of a pick at the debris clogging the opening, which had apparently partially collapsed.

Sweat plastered a pinstriped silk shirt to the man's back, despite the steady cool temperature of the cavern. Harry knew him immediately, his thin, straight hair sweat-drenched as well, his breath huffing from the unaccustomed labor. Charm.

The dark-haired woman in the emerald green silk kneeling beside two large burlap sacks, shoving away the loosened rocks and dirt, must be Angelique Dubray. And the slender boy with the spiky fair hair who worked beside her must be—

"Wes!"

Lissy's shout rang off the cavern walls, splintering on the rocks into a thousand echoes as she ran out onto the cave floor, sliding crazily in her broken boots. Harry leaped after her.

"Wesley!" she called again as the boy jumped up, dirt-smudged face turning toward her.

"Mama?"

He bent as though to scramble down toward her, but Angelique reached out to snag him by the back of his shirt and haul him back against her.

"Do not come any closer," she ordered, her voice smoky from whiskey and cigarettes and the hint of a French accent. "Not if you value your son's life."

Chapter 16

Lissy skidded to a stop, Harry pulling up close beside her. Lissy didn't see a weapon in Angelique's hand. Her own fingers closed on the derringer in her coat pocket, the stock hard and cold against her palm.

Charm turned toward her, the pick clutched in his hand. The stark fear in his eyes muted to confusion as he took in the fact she was alone with Harry.

"How dare you?" Lissy's voice shook with her fury. "How dare you let your whore threaten my son?"

"Not in front of the boy. For God's sake, Elizabeth."

Lissy thought she could shoot him then, right through the head. "I promise to stop offending Miss Dubray, as soon as she takes her hands off my son."

She turned to Angelique. Even crouched in the dirt at the bottom of a hole in the ground, the woman had a sleek grace that slid the observer's eyes away from the slight hook at the end of her nose, the hard set to her obsidian eyes, the bitter lines dug into the corners of her mouth.

"Let him go."

Angelique shook her head, her thick, dark hair falling in waves across her shoulders. "You are the whore, with your arrogant pride and your monster brothers, thinking you can have whatever you want because you are better than anyone else. You won't take away from us what is ours."

"Where are Clay and Rafe?" Charm asked before Lissy could respond. His eyes flicked past her and Harry to the tunnel entrance as he shifted the pick to his left hand and pulled a revolver from the waist of his trousers. "Don't think I won't use this if I have to."

"As if it would do you any good." Familiar exasperation bubbled in Lissy's chest. "What made you think you could steal from them and just walk away? You know how ruthless they are."

"Then you understand why I had to get away from them." Charm looked at her, and she wondered how eyes she had met with love and anger and disgust and indifference over the past eleven years could belong to such a stranger. "I couldn't do it anymore. You have no idea what it was like, working my fingers to the bone, working extra hours for a pittance to make Wilmer Brothers Import-Export a success, knowing I'd never be appreciated, knowing Clay and Rafe despised me when I wouldn't help them 'encourage' a customer to pay his bill."

His eyes softened, the side of his mouth quirking in a self-deprecating smile she had once found heartbreaking. "I tried. You know I tried. For you and Wesley. But to come home every night to your disapproval was more—"

"Don't you dare blame this on me."

He backed up when she stepped forward, though he was the one with the gun.

Lissy shook her head, hot anger filling her mouth. "Don't you blame any of this on me, Charm Woodfin. I quit disapproving of your whoring and drinking and whining years ago. I warned you what my brothers were, before you ever went to work for them."

"They didn't respect me." Charm's cheeks puffed like a chipmunk's, appealing even in resentment. "They could have made twice the money they're making if they'd listened to my advice. I couldn't stay there, never getting ahead. I had a family to think of. Even if it meant risking their viciousness, I had to escape—"

"And if you'd just taken your family and left, they'd have let you go," Lissy said, taking another step toward Charm, toward Wesley. "But you didn't take your family. I saw that cupboard in the house back there. You didn't even plan to take Wes. Clay and Rafe wouldn't have cared, either way. All they cared about was that you stole from them."

"I *showed* them," Charm corrected, pointing the pick at her. At least it wasn't the gun. "Rafe said I didn't have the brains to become a partner in the business. He said I didn't have the guts to do what it took. I guess he's not saying that anymore."

"I guess not." Lissy didn't know whether to laugh or cry. "I guess he's just calling you a damned fool. You didn't really believe they wouldn't find you, did you? In *Colorado?* They would have hunted you to the ends of the earth, but at least it might have taken them a few years."

"Papa said if Uncle Clay and Uncle Rafe ever came, we had to hide," Wesley spoke up, glancing back at his father. "But I told him you wouldn't let them hurt us."

She could not allow tears to blur her vision. "Are you all right, baby?"

He grimaced. "I'm not a baby."

Certainly not. "Are you all right, young man?"

"Sure."

"They haven't hurt you?"

"Elizabeth!" Charm rolled his eyes. "He's my son."

"And if you were concerned about his health, you

wouldn't have brought him here," she snapped. One more step. "He doesn't even have a coat on. Let me check—"

"Do not move," Angelique hissed, yanking Wesley back. "You are not in control here, so you should be cautious, n'est-ce pas?"

But Wesley dropped suddenly in her grip. Even as she grabbed for his arm with her other hand, he wriggled out of his shirt, sliding down the slope of loose dirt to Lissy's feet.

He actually laughed as she grabbed him and pulled him close, his round face, so like Charm's, but so innocently sweet, breaking into a self-satisfied grin.

"You said I was slipperier than a buttered snake."

She hugged him tight, his bones so thin and light he hardly felt substantial. He smelled like sleep and dirt and smoke and hay, but mostly like boy.

Hot tears slipped down her cheeks, landing on top of his tousled hair.

"Thank you, God," she whispered. *Thank you for letting me hold him again.*

But then he started wiggling in her hold, snakelike again, and she had to let him free, though she kept a tight grip on his hand.

He turned his face up to Charm, his dusty cheeks streaked with Lissy's tears. "See, Papa. It's okay. Mama won't let them hurt us. We can go home now."

"Damn it, Wesley, I told you . . ." Charm's voice trailed off as he struggled to control it. "We can't go home, son. We can't ever go home. Your uncles are too dangerous. Even your mama can't protect you from them."

Her son scudded a foot in the dirt, and Lissy saw in his face that he wasn't as innocent as he had been just a few short weeks ago. As much as he wanted to believe his parents could protect him from anything, he knew his father was right. "That's all right. I like it here okay. I can't wait to show you the creek, Mama. I can play in it all I want. No snakes. Papa says I can have a dog. Angelique's not really mean, either. She's just scared. You'll like it here, Mama. I know you will."

He looked up at her, and for the first time she saw fear in his eyes. "You won't go home without us, will you? You'll stay, right?"

"Your mama doesn't understand," Charm said, picking his way down the slope toward them. "She wants us to go back to Savannah. She'll tell Clay and Rafe where we are. So, we can't stay here, either."

"She wouldn't do that. Mama can keep a secret." Wesley's hand squeezed Lissy's. "We have to take her with us. She could be in danger, too."

Charm snorted as he handed Angelique the pick. "Keep digging." He stepped down another step. "Don't worry son, your mother's not in any danger. That family protects its own, whatever the cost to anybody else."

"I'm glad you believe that," Lissy said, the words coming out despite the sudden weakness in her chest. "I really am. I knew you didn't love me. But I still hate to think that you deserted me to face my brothers' brutality alone."

"You seem to have survived it all right," Charm said, sliding to the bottom of the slope just a yard from her. He raised the revolver until Lissy could see straight down the barrel.

Still his voice held the ingratiating warmth that served him so well. "You shouldn't have come after me, Elizabeth. You must have known that. Let's not make this any harder than we have to. Let go of Wesley's hand."

"Why, Charm," Lissy said, surprised to find her hand steady as she lifted the derringer from her pocket to point it at Charm's heart. "Not in front of the boy."

"Mama?"

"Your mama and papa are fine," Harry said, her voice gentle and easy as if Wesley were a colt and not a boy. Lissy let her take his hand from hers and pull him away. "They're not going to shoot anyone."

"Put that toy down, Elizabeth," Charm ordered. "My gun is bigger than yours."

"Everyone's is," she agreed, keeping her aim steady. "But no one has stopped me yet. I don't want you, Charm. I don't want your money. But I'm not letting you take Wes. He deserves a home and a family. Not a life running from my brothers' thugs with you and your mistress."

"Charm." Angelique's accent turned the name to "Sharm." "Charm, maybe she is right. Don't ruin everything now. Let her have the boy—"

"Keep digging!" Charm ordered. His eyes never left Lissy's face. "He leaves with us, Elizabeth. You can let him go now or you can make him watch your brains get splattered across this cave."

"Papa!"

"If any brains are splattering anywhere, they're going to be yours, you bloody bastard."

Lissy turned her head, blinking in disbelief as Tony rose from behind a pile of boulders to her left, Smith and Wesson in hand. She could have cried in relief at the sight of him, his white shirt showing the effects of a night in the woods and a morning crawling around mine tunnels, but otherwise looking as dapper as ever. Though maybe a bit more dangerous than usual.

"Tony—"

With lashing speed, Charm's hand snared her wrist. The impact knocked the derringer free to clatter on the cave floor. Charm jerked her arm around, yanking her back against him. Pressed against her jaw, his revolver felt even bigger than it had looked.

"Don't move!" Charm's voice sounded steady, but Lissy could feel the tension shaking through his body. "I'm a desperate man. Nobody move or I'll pull this trigger."

"I don't think you will." Malachi stood beside Tony. His own gun remained holstered. "Because if you do, Major Wayne here will kill you. And you don't want to die."

"If I can't get out of here a free man, she's not getting out of here at all," Charm said.

Lissy couldn't swallow, hardly dared breathe. The gun jerked and jabbed against her jaw. If his trigger finger was shaking as badly as the rest of his hand . . .

She kept her gaze fixed on Tony. If these were her last seconds on earth, she wanted her last sight to be the promise to protect her that she saw in his eyes. Not the terror in her son's.

All her deceit, all her desperation, all her single-minded determination had brought her to this. Danger to her friends, pain to her son. Her eyes flickered closed as the revolver pressed into her cheek. Wesley would have been better off if she'd stayed in Savannah, if she'd simply taken the punishment her brothers dished out and let Charm disappear with her son.

She could not have borne losing Wes, but at least he would not have seen this, would not have seen his mother and father threatening each other with guns, not have seen his mother die before his eyes. He would have been safe.

Her eyes popped open. Safe? Had she lost her mind?

"The Beasts," she said, the words slurred by the gun's pressure on her jaw. "Tony, the Beasts are here. Harry's rifle jammed. We escaped down the tunnel, but they will follow us. You have to get Wesley to safety."

"What are you talking about?" Charm demanded, jabbing the gun so hard into her cheek she couldn't speak.

Harry answered for her. "Your bosses hired them," she said, still kneeling in the dirt with her hand tight on Wesley's wrist. "They beat up your wife and threatened to kill her if she didn't tell them where you'd gone. She came after you herself instead, to save her son and your worthless hide."

Maybe it was her simple directness or the honesty in her eyes, but Charm eased the gun back from Lissy's face. "She led them to me, you mean."

"They went to the South Platte Saloon looking for Angelique," Harry said. "They attacked Miss Lily when she wouldn't let them up to Angelique's empty room."

"Mon Dieu." The pick clattered to the stones as Angelique slid down beside Charm. Lissy could see the concern on her face out of the corner of her eye. "Madame, she is all right?"

"They broke some ribs," Malachi said, coming out from behind the rocks, hands still empty and loose by his side. "She'll be all right. But they would have killed her without a second thought. If Lissy says they're here at the mine, you've got bigger worries than us, Charm."

"Kelly?" Charm asked, the gun slipping to Lissy's shoulder. If she elbowed him in the ribs . . . he'd shoot her in hers. "I recognize you. You're Malcolm Kelly."

"Malachi." He looked pained.

"Your whole family were traitors for the Union."

Malachi was equally blunt. "Your whole family is about to get tortured and killed by Spider Grant and his boys if you don't let us help you out."

"Tell the Limey to put down his gun."

Tony's eyebrows rose as he thrust his revolver into its holster. Only the unaccustomed hardness in his eyes belied the mildness of his voice. "I don't mind if I do. I rather look forward to seeing what Fox and Rat will do to you."

"You're lying." Fear squeezed the beguiling affability from Charm's voice, leaving it high and sharp. "I don't believe there's anyone here at the mine but you four. And if Spider Grant really is here, then I bet he's working for you."

"You'd better make your decision fast, old chap," Tony said, hand once more reaching for his Smith and Wesson. "It looks like we've got company. Behind you."

"I'm not falling for that old—" Charm began, but the loud clang of a shovel on rock interrupted him.

Angelique screamed. "They come through!"

Charm spun Lissy around, giving her an unobstructed view of the collapsed wall of the cave. The small opening high above them had just become bigger. Outlined against the sunlit sky was a narrow face surrounded by a pelt of red hair.

His hand moved, and thunder burst in Lissy's head.

Sound exploded through the bubble-shaped cavern, knocking Harry to the ground. She yanked Wesley down with her and rolled them both toward the side of the chamber, ignoring the rocks digging into her flesh.

She heard shouts among the echoes, but not words. Dirt rained on her, making it hard to think, much less breathe. Only her experience with recalcitrant colts enabled her to keep her hold on the tow-headed boy scrambling away from her. He wasn't big, for eight, but he was wiry.

"Wesley!" She dug in with her heels and yanked him back. "Out through the tunnel." She pointed.

"We've got to help them."

Lissy and Charm had hit the ground hard, too. Harry couldn't tell if they'd been hit, but both appeared to be moving. Angelique crouched by Charm's side, yelling in French.

"Mal and Tony will get to them," she promised. "Our job is to keep you safe."

Scrambling to a crouch, she pulled him toward the tunnel. Another gunshot rocked the chamber. She saw wood splinter from the beam across the top of the tunnel opening. Rubble showered across the mouth of the entrance.

"Nobody move." Spider Grant's smooth voice poured across the chaos of sound like oil. "If you will all put down your weapons, no one will be shot. Otherwise, I will be happy to bring the whole cave down around your ears."

Though Spider gave the orders, it was Fox and Rat who were sent through the small opening first. They held their pistols with the look of two men more comfortable with knife and fist than firearms, but Harry had no doubt they knew how to pull the triggers.

Spider crawled through after them, his stout form blocking the sunlight for a moment before he appeared between his cohorts.

"Clever escape route, Mr. Woodfin," he said, as Charm and Lissy scrambled to their feet. "Or it would have been if you hadn't been making so much noise."

"The exit collapsed," Charm said, his face crumpled with defeat. "We had to dig it out."

"That was an unfortunate chance for you," Spider agreed. "But a fortunate one for us. We're tired of chasing you. I'm sure you're tired of running. All you need to do is tell us where the money is, and we can settle our accounts."

Harry suspected a good portion of the funds Spider was looking for were invested in the mine and the rest probably sat in the burlap sacks by Spider's feet, but she wasn't about to point out the obvious.

Spider gestured toward Charm. "Please kick that weapon away from you, Mr. Woodfin." He shook his head at Charm's hesitation. "I would hate to have to shoot your wife or Mademoiselle Dubray to convince you I'm serious."

Charm kicked at his gun with the toe of his dusty black shoe. At a nod from Spider, Rat scrambled down the slope to retrieve it.

"A pleasure to see you again, Mrs. Woodfin," Spider said to Lissy, touching his bowler as he crab-walked down to her level. "I'm afraid I told you this would be more difficult if you ran."

"You won't want to have to face my brothers if you hurt us."

"You think they'd rather do that themselves?" Amusement rounded Spider's pale cheeks. "Perhaps they'll get that chance. Sooner than you think. Where are the rest of your friends?"

Harry risked a glance around the chamber. Malachi and Tony had disappeared behind their boulders.

"They rode to Silvercrest for help."

Lissy hadn't even got the words out before Spider's hand lashed out, striking her across the mouth.

"That's why their horses are still hobbled out front?" he asked, his voice as calm as if he'd never moved. He looked across the chamber, black eyes glinting. "Hello, young Master Wesley. I think you've grown since I saw you last."

"If you hit my mother again, I'll kill you."

Harry felt the boy trembling in her grip, but she thought

it was from anger, not fear. He reminded her of her friend Wolf, Elijah's son. Innocent enough to believe in justice and courageous enough to fight for it.

Spider smiled at the threat, his eyes turning to pin Harry. The touch of his gaze chilled her blood, just as it had in Denver. She needed to protect Wesley from his malice, but she didn't know how.

"And there's our young lady friend, the one who likes to dress like a cowboy and frequent cathouses. Toss me that little parlor gun of yours, miss."

"I haven't got it."

"I'm sorry to hear that." Spider pulled his own silver-inlaid revolver from his belt. "If you can't produce it for me, I will have to shoot you."

Her heart jolted. He meant it. He was going to shoot her. She dropped Wesley's hand, so he wouldn't be hit accidentally, but the boy ran forward in front of her.

"You're a bully, Mr. Grant. Didn't your mother ever teach you not to hurt girls?"

"Stay where you are, young Wesley," Spider ordered, the barrel dipping just slightly. "I could hit you both with one shot. Now, where is that derringer?"

"Right here, Spider," Lissy said calmly. Harry hadn't seen her retrieve the gun from the ground, but even the derringer made a respectable noise in the acoustics of the cave as she fired.

A red stain blushed against the gray waistcoat that stretched across Spider's ribs. He blinked, more in surprise than pain. Lissy spun and fired the last round from the derringer at Fox.

Harry couldn't have hit the side of a mountain firing a snub-nosed .22 pistol from the hip, but Lissy must have struck something, because Fox's leg jerked as he fired back, sending his shot wildly across the cave, the ricochet pinging past Harry's head.

Harry leapt forward, knocking Wesley to the ground once more. She heard Tony shouting, heard Malachi barking orders as bullets roared overhead.

"Wesley! Come on!"

When she rolled off the boy, he started to crawl forward toward his parents, but then Lissy was there, and the three of them scrambled behind a rock fall.

"The tunnel," Harry shouted. Lissy and Wesley both nodded. Harry ducked around the rock nearest her. Fox was crouched in the dirt, firing wildly around the chamber. Rat had tossed aside his gun and thrown himself on Tony. The Englishman outweighed the other man, but Rat was using teeth and claws.

Angelique was scrambling for the cave opening, her dark green dress gray with silt, as Charm dragged a burlap sack after her.

She couldn't see Spider, but movement in the rocks halfway up the cavern wall caught her eye. Malachi leapt from a ledge, landing squarely on Fox's back, the two men tumbling to the cave floor.

She turned back to Lissy and Wesley. "Run. Run."

She pushed them past her toward the tunnel entrance, then followed, not having time to feel fear as she reached the shower of dirt that still fell from the tunnel roof.

She spun on her heel to look back at the cave. Rat had toppled Tony to the ground, but as she watched, Tony's knee found a target, and the scraggly blond thug convulsed in agony, rolling back toward the slope to the cave entrance.

Malachi had his knee in the middle of Fox's back, struggling to tie Fox's hands behind his back with Fox's own suspender strap.

The hem of Angelique's dress was disappearing through the small opening above their heads. Charm was thrusting a sack after her, his arms knotted against his shirtsleeves with the effort.

Lissy and Wesley waited behind her in the tunnel. Which left only one Beast unaccounted for.

A shadow flickered against the wall beyond Rat and Tony. Harry would not have thought a man as short and round as Spider Grant could have climbed the undercut wall or hung with such ease from his perch on a tiny ledge, especially not with a bullet wound to the chest. But maybe Spider was more than just a nickname, because he didn't even appear to be breathing hard as he leaned away from the wall, one hand grasping rock, one bringing his revolver to bear on the figures struggling below.

"Watch out!" Harry shouted.

As the others jumped, Spider fired, his shot digging a furrow in the wall inches to the left of Malachi's head. The Fox took advantage of the shift in his balance, bucking hard, throwing Malachi into a boulder.

As Fox rolled, Harry saw silver flash in his hand.

"Mal!"

She hurled herself forward, but the distance was too far.

Malachi's spin was hampered by the rock. The Fox's arm snapped like a whip. Blood flared from Malachi's side.

"Mal!"

Only three more strides. Only an eternity—

A revolver cracked, and the Fox's arm jerked back, the elbow shattered.

"Tony!" Lissy's voice carried across the snapping echoes. "Spider!"

Harry heard more shots, but saw nothing but the blood on Malachi's shirt as he struggled to his feet. A cacophony roared in her ears. She could see his mouth move, trying to yell at her. He stumbled forward, waving her back.

She grabbed for him, grabbed for his shirt, but he was pushing her, thrusting her back. She stumbled, and he fell with her, grabbing her to him and rolling, just as she had with Wesley, rocks gouging her ribs.

The roaring increased, not the blood in her ears after all, for it shook the earth beneath her, seemed to shake the mountain itself. A rock struck her temple. More pelted her side. Dirt poured down across her face, choking her.

She pressed her face against Malachi's neck as he rolled them again.

They were being buried alive. In darkness. The whole mountain was collapsing in on them. They were going to die.

A rock struck her shoulder, trying to knock her loose, but she clung to Malachi. His breathing gasped with hers. His heart beat against her chest.

She wanted to tell him she was sorry. For getting him into this mess. For her rifle jamming. For never listening to his advice. For letting him think she loved his brother. For getting him killed.

She wanted one last word with him. One chance to tell him she'd never met a braver man. That if she'd met him when she was a girl, she'd never have fallen for the wrong Kelly brother.

All she could do was grab his face in her hands, smearing the dirt across it with her tears, and press her lips to his, his warm, strong mouth, tasting past the dirt and salt to life itself.

Chapter 17

"Here. Come on."

Mal could hear the words, even through the roaring of the cave collapsing, the rushing of the blood through his veins, the bursting of his heart at Harry's kiss.

Tony's hands found Harry's shoulders, pulling her away from him.

"He's hurt," she yelled, her hands clutching his arms, dragging him with her. Mal felt Tony moving to his other side, the Englishman's shoulder heaving him to his feet as they struggled forward, the only way possible, away from the falling rocks, the flowing dirt.

"Tunnel's here," Tony shouted, as Malachi's head knocked against the entrance beam.

They spilled through the tunnel opening, choking and coughing. One of them tripped, and all three tumbled to the ground.

Mal thought the earth might have stopped shaking, although his head still spun. In the darkness, he had difficulty deciding which direction was up.

"Who's that?" Lissy's voice. "I'll shoot."

"I think you've run out of ammunition," Tony said. "Damn fine bit of gunplay back there, though, I must say."

"Tony?"

"I've got Mal and Harry."

"We're here," Harry said. "Mal's hurt."

He did hurt, now that he had a moment to think about it.

"How bad is it?" Tony asked.

"He's bleeding," Harry said, sounding as though she might be sobbing. "The Fox stabbed him in the chest."

Strong, slender hands grabbed him, yanking at his shirt. The movement jerked his wound. He ground his teeth, but a cry escaped him anyway.

Harry's fingers ran over his chest, a sensation that unsettled him despite the pain.

"Don't worry," she said, her own voice thick with worry. "You're going to be all right. We won't let you die."

"It'll take more than a little nick to the chest to kill Mal," Tony agreed, too heartily. "He's too mean to die. Let's get some light here. Where's the wound, old man?"

He grabbed Mal's arm and tugged on the shirt sleeve.

"Hey!" Mal sat up, jerking away from Tony's grip, knocking his forehead against Harry's.

"Hold still." Tony reached for him again as Harry pushed on his chest. "We'll get you fixed up right as—"

"Hell and damnation!" Mal pushed them away with his right arm. "If you fix me any more, I'll be giving your regards to the angels in a minute." He grabbed Harry's persistent hand.

"Lie down," she ordered fiercely. "If he hit a lung—"

"He didn't hit a damned lung!" Mal choked on dust and frustrated laughter. "Would you two quit yanking on my shirt? The knife slid off a rib or something. It's my damned arm that's sliced open. Would you quit pawing me so I can do something about it before I bleed to death?"

Of course, they didn't. Harry's hands found the blood on his sleeve as Tony thrust a handkerchief against his chest.

"We can cinch it on with a belt," Tony suggested.

"Only if you can see it." Mal sucked in a curse as the wound pulled under Harry's fingers. "Can we get some light here?"

"I'm trying," Lissy snapped. Mal heard the scrape of a match. "If I could just get my hands to stop shaking . . ."

"Here, Mama."

The sudden flare of the tiny flame dazzled like the rising of the morning sun. Wesley Woodfin's mouth tightened in concentration as the match flickered. Lissy's candle stump glowed to life.

"Jolly good show!" Tony put down the burlap sack he carried to dig in his pocket for his own half candle. "Light this one, too, if you would, old chap."

"What's that?" Mal demanded, pointing at the sack.

Tony glanced down. "It fell on me with the rockslide. I grabbed it."

A jolt of pain snapped Mal's attention back to his arm. Harry had managed to pull off his coat sleeve and was ripping open the slash in his shirt.

"It's bleeding heavily." Her face looked pale in the yellow candlelight, but her gaze was steady on the wound.

The sight of the blood only made him a little dizzy as he examined the cut. He didn't think the knife had gone to the bone. The wound looked clean. Fox kept his knife sharp. For a battle injury, he'd gotten off easy.

"I've had worse," he said.

"I've seen worse," Harry replied, unimpressed. "That doesn't mean you can't bleed to death. Where's your flask?"

She leaned into him, fumbling with his coat. He smelled

lavender in her hair. Dressed in an old blue flannel shirt at least two sizes too large for her, her hair a tangled mess down her back, her face streaked with tears and dirt, her hands smeared with blood, she took his breath away.

He swayed, suddenly lightheaded. Of course, he'd lost a lot of blood.

Harry pulled back, clutching the flask of Taos Lightning.

"That will help the pain," Mal agreed. "But don't you think you should stop the bleeding first?"

"Hold him."

When Tony grabbed his arm and shoulder, Mal understood what Harry meant to do. After all, he'd said he'd brought it for medicinal purposes. But Tony didn't need to hold him down. He could take—

"Aaaaah!" His vision dimmed, the candlelight shrinking to a pinpoint.

"Hold him still," Harry ordered. He heard his shirt tear again. Whiskey poured across the shallow cut along his ribs.

"Now drink."

The flask tipped against his lips. The alcohol seared his throat nearly as badly as it had his flesh, but it kept his mind occupied while Harry and Tony bandaged his cuts. They fashioned a sling from part of Lissy's petticoat and tied his arm against his chest.

"We need to stitch that wound," Harry said, apparently under the mistaken belief that she hadn't yet tortured him thoroughly enough.

"Jolly good," Tony agreed. "Just as soon we get out of this bloody mine."

Malachi felt a certain gratitude for the combination of whiskey and blood loss that dulled his alarm. Looking back toward the cavern, the flickering candlelight showed only a sloping wall of rock and rubble.

"I don't think we're going out that way," he said.

Harry's breath caught shallowly. "We could have been buried alive. We almost died."

He wanted to reach for her with his good arm, but touching her would remind him of her kiss. Being entombed in a cave collapse had its high points, but he retained enough of his good sense to know he should be forgetting it as quickly as possible if it turned out they were going to live—even if Harry weren't still in love with his brother and engaged to another man.

"The Beasts." Harry shuddered beside him, suddenly smaller, more fragile than the jeans-clad tomboy who had bound up his knife wounds as simply as she would care for a cut on a horse's flank. "They must be buried in there."

"Good." Lissy didn't hesitate.

But Harry shook her head, her breathing still shaky. "We can't leave them there. To suffocate. We should try to dig them out . . ."

Mal did touch her then. A hand on her shoulder, feeling her tremble as it sunk in how impossible a rescue would be.

"They were trying to kill us," Lissy said, impatient with the moment of pity. "They were animals."

"Papa and Angelique got out through the cave entrance. I saw them," Wesley spoke up, his round face serious, but not panicked. "Maybe those men did, too."

Mal did not find that a comforting thought. A rivulet of dirt ran down the wall beside him. "As much fun as this has been, I think it might be time to get out of this mine."

"While we can," Tony agreed. "No time like the present, and all that. I hate to think how the collapse must have destabilized the rest of these tunnels. They weren't in such good shape to begin with."

"I've lost my Colt," Mal said, taking inventory. Without

a word, Tony handed him one of his Smith and Wesson Schofield revolvers. "Lissy's out of ammunition. If the Beasts did get out, they might be waiting for us back at the house. We'd better—"

"We don't have to go back to the house," Wesley interrupted. "We can get out through the mine entrance."

"You can find the way?" Mal asked.

"Yes, sir. Once we get back to the main tunnel, it's easy."

"Then you lead on, son," he said.

"Yes, sir. It's not too far."

Mal might have argued that point as they worked their way back through a seemingly endless maze of narrow side tunnels. Wesley paused at each intersection to lower his flickering candle to find his stone markers. The ache in Mal's arm and ribs dragged at him with each step; the stale air refused to clear his head.

Harry insisted he rest his good arm on her shoulder for support. He found himself using it. At least his stumbling seemed to take her mind off the nearness of their escape and the closeness of the tunnel walls. When they reached the main tunnels, they no longer had to worry about ducking under the supporting beams, but they did have to pick their way along the tracks laid for ore carts.

When the hint of light from the entrance shaft finally brushed the tunnel walls ahead of them, Mal had to fight the urge to rush out into the sunshine and fill his lungs with clean, life-giving air. Since rushing anywhere seemed unlikely for the moment, he settled himself against the mine wall by the shaft with his borrowed revolver in his lap.

Tony was the one who crept out to size up the situation. The wait might have seemed interminable, if not for the combination of exhaustion, blood loss and alcohol. Mal kept dozing off against Harry's shoulder.

"Hullo! All clear."

Tony's cheerful voice snapped Mal's head up, clearing his brain of a muddled dream that had taken him much too far back in the past, to other battles and bloodier losses.

"No sign of the Beasts," Tony told them, leading them out of the mine into the dazzling late morning sunshine. "Their horses are gone, but it looks to me like Charm and Angelique took them, along with their own."

"They didn't take ours," Harry said.

"I can't imagine why not," Mal said, not hiding his amusement at her surprise.

Harry gave him a look as she slipped out from under his arm to walk over to the poor, spavined beasts. The gray mare nudged her shoulder and nibbled on the ends of her hair as Harry stroked her neck.

Wesley walked over beside her, and the mare lowered her head so he could scratch her ears. "She's kind of old, isn't she?"

"Smart though," Harry assured him.

"I suspect Charm and Angelique meant to scare them away," Tony told Mal and Lissy, his voice low to escape Wesley's ears. "They've been unhobbled and the bigger sorrel has a cut on his nose. I think Charm hit him with that piece of firewood over there. But they were all back to munching grass when I came out of the mine."

"We're lucky they didn't run all the way back to Silvercrest," Lissy said.

Tony raised an eyebrow. "Run?"

"We're lucky Charm didn't just shoot them," Mal said grimly. He didn't know if it was his injury, his memories, or his instincts, but he couldn't escape the nagging sense that they were not out of danger. "Let's go inside. I don't want everyone to be standing out in the open if he comes back."

"He's not coming back," Tony said. "The man is a craven. He's halfway to Canada by now."

"They're heading for Mexico," Wesley said, returning from the horses with Harry. "Papa says there's opportunities to be a big man there, and it's not so cold as Colorado."

"Wesley," Tony began in consternation, crouching down to the boy's level. "What I said about your father—"

"You meant he's a coward," Wesley said, meeting his gaze directly.

Tony grimaced. "I said that in anger. I was afraid, too, when those men started shooting."

"He didn't even come back to see if me and Mama were alive."

The matter-of-fact statement stabbed at Mal's heart, but it also nudged his practical caution.

"He may yet." He glanced around the clearing, the back of his neck itching at the exposure. "And so may the Beasts. We need to get as far away from here as we can before sunset."

"We need to eat first," Harry said, leading the way toward the house. "And put a proper dressing on your arm. We'll still have plenty of light left to reach Silvercrest."

"I don't want to stop in Silvercrest," Mal said, relieved to follow his companions into the comparative shelter of the house. The interior was nearly as cool as the mine tunnels had been, the afternoon breeze exploring through the empty front door frame.

Tony hefted the flattened door and leaned it against the opening. "The Silvercrest Hotel isn't quite up to the Fox and Hound's standards," he said. "But I'm so tired I could sleep on a bed of nails."

"I'm not worried about the accommodations," Mal said.

“It’s too close. We’d be too easy to find.”

“Come into the kitchen,” Harry ordered, digging a match out of her coat pocket. “We need to start a fire and boil some water. I don’t want that knife wound to fester, and it still needs to be stitched. Lissy, there ought to be a needle and thread in my purse.”

“I don’t think Spider and his crew are going to give us any more trouble, Mal,” Tony said, pushing him after Harry. “The odds are against it.”

“I haven’t seen their bodies,” Mal said, undeterred. “And Charm could well come back to see about his son. He risked a lot to bring Wesley to Colorado with him.”

“He only took me to hurt Mama,” Wesley said, still matter-of-fact, though his mouth pinched in at the corners to hold back the hurt.

“He did not.” To Mal’s surprise, it was Lissy who spoke up. She had returned from the bedroom with Harry’s purse and her own. She handed Harry the needle and thread.

“That’s what Angelique said.”

“Charm’s clever, but he doesn’t have that much imagination. He took you because he loves you, Wes. He wanted to have you with him and just forgot about what would be best for you, that’s all.”

“So he might come back,” Mal repeated, dredging the logic up from his weary mind. “And he might not stop to talk next time he sees us. Silvercrest will be the first place he looks. The Beasts—”

“Are dead,” Tony said. “Mal, we need rest. We’ll be safe in Silvercrest.”

“I have a bad feeling.”

“I agree with Malachi,” Lissy said. She touched her cheek where it still burned a dull red from Spider’s hand.

“That monster can’t hurt you anymore,” Tony said. Mal

saw his friend clench his fist to keep from reaching for her. He suddenly understood the impulse all too well. "Even if he's still alive, I won't let him near you."

Lissy shook her head. "It's not the Beasts, or Charm. It's what Spider said. About seeing my brothers sooner than I expected. Clay and Rafe wouldn't normally trust hirelings to recover the amount of money Charm embezzled from them. It wouldn't be as safe as taking possession of it themselves."

"Not as much fun, either." Mal had clear memories of the Wilmer brothers' amusements. "If there's any chance they're on their way to Colorado, we need to get back to Battlement Park as quickly as we can."

Tony blew out a breath. "I don't think we're in any shape to move quickly today."

Mal surveyed the group in the kitchen. Harry was washing her bloody hands at the pump while waiting for the water on the stove to boil, her face pinched with exhaustion. Lissy, pale and bruised, reached over to brush a hand over her son's fair hair. Wesley stood stoically, but strained with emotions. Tony looked almost as tired as Mal felt, though at least he had use of both his arms.

"I don't think we're in any shape to face Clay and Rafe," Mal said. "I can ride. How about the rest of you?"

"I can ride," Wesley said stoutly. "Papa says I'm half horse."

"I'm ready now." Lissy moved to glance out the kitchen window.

"I can ride, but you shouldn't," Harry said. She peeled back the dressing on Mal's arm, making him cringe. She frowned at the wound. "But if I get that stitched, I don't guess you'll die before we get to Georgetown."

"I'd feel better if we didn't have to go through

Georgetown," Mal said, even the pain in his arm unable to dampen the apprehension itching the back of his neck. "Or Silvercrest. I don't like the idea of being on the only road out of here."

"It's not the only road," Wesley said, face brightening at being able to help again. "Back at the cave, where the entrance collapsed? There's a trail there. That's the way Papa planned to take if Uncle Clay and Uncle Rafe ever came here. He said it was an old trapper's trail, maybe an Indian road before that."

"It's a trail horses can travel?" Mal asked.

"That's what Papa said. It goes all the way over the Continental Divide. He said we'd get to Mexico that way. But if you go east, it goes to Boulder. It's about two day's ride. He had it all worked out even before we came to Colorado."

Tony groaned. "Bloody hell. I was looking forward to that lumpy, bug-ridden straw mattress in Silvercrest."

"Better sleeping on the hard ground than sleeping under it," Lissy said tartly.

Even Tony couldn't argue with that.

Lissy didn't balk when she had to slit the front and back of her silk skirt to ride astride the sorrel mare. If she ever reached civilization, she planned to burn the dress anyway.

She held her tongue when Tony took Wesley up on his horse with him because her mare was too small for two riders. The bruise to Wesley's pride at having to share a horse was eased by riding with one of the heroes who'd fought the Beasts.

She didn't protest the long ride. She'd half expected to be walking within an hour, but though the horses they rode would never be fast, they proved to be strong enough and surefooted, even where the trail nearly disappeared across the steep mountainsides. Malachi said they'd made good time, and all the signs indicated Charm and Angelique had hightailed it west on their way to Mexico, leaving the trail east free of human hazards.

Without complaint, she'd eaten the salty bacon and doughy flapjacks Harry had cooked for supper from the supplies they'd taken from Charm's cabin. She'd gathered firewood and wiped her hands on her skirts like a hardened mountain man. Though what a hardened mountain man would be doing wearing skirts, she couldn't have said.

She'd groomed her horse, carried water, helped Harry change Malachi's dressings, without a care for the blisters on her hands and the pain in her seat from the long horseback ride.

She'd gone through Charm's burlap sack with Tony, pieces of her grandmother's silver wrapped beside bags of cut and uncut jewels, without giving in to anger or sadness or hysterical laughter. She could only think of all that Charm had thrown away for some spoons and coins and bags of rocks.

She'd watched her son earnestly answer Malachi's careful questions, emulate Tony's long-legged slouch, smile at Harry's ranch stories, without letting the mixed tears of relief and fear fall.

In the end, it was a deer mouse that undid her. She was rising from her seat on a rock by the fire when the tiny creature scampered up her skirt.

She jumped back, her shriek cut off by the hard thump to her bottom as she tripped over the rock and landed heavily in the thick, dry grasses at the edge of the meadow where they'd camped.

"Elizabeth?" Tony was at her side in an instant as Malachi drew his borrowed Smith and Wesson with his good hand. "What is it? Are you hurt?"

"Mouse!" Lissy flailed her petticoat as she scrambled to her feet, hoping to fling the little beast away. "There's a mouse on me!"

She looked to Tony for help, only to catch him desperately fighting a smile.

"A big mouse?" Wesley asked helpfully.

"Get it away from me!" Lissy panted, the air thin and light in her lungs. She saw movement in the grass barely a foot away. She jumped back again, pointing wildly. "Shoot it!"

The laughter broke from Tony's throat then, helpless, rolling laughter that spread like a wave through Malachi and Harry and even Wesley, his cheeks reddening as he tried to hold it in.

"It's okay, Mama," he said. "It won't hurt you. He's more afraid of you than you are of him."

"I'm not so sure of that," Malachi said, setting them all off again.

Lissy snorted, half laughter, half fury. "Oh, bloody hell."

That's when she felt the tears stinging her eyes and knew she couldn't hold them back any longer.

"I declare." She kept her voice light. "You all are enough to make Spider Grant look charitable. I'm going for a walk. If a panther eats me, I won't be calling on you for help."

"Do you mind if we feed the mouse the rest of your flapjacks?" Harry called after her.

"That will kill him fast enough," Lissy shot back, managing a smirk in return before escaping into the trees.

Aspens bordered the top edge of the sloping meadow, a park-like wood that could have been designed for strolling if it weren't so steep. As Lissy picked her way up the ridge, the evening breeze rustled the aspen leaves, a soft chorus of paper chimes burnished to the rich gold of ancient coins by the last kiss of the sinking sun.

It might have been a king's park, tamed for royal hunts and twilight dances, except the aspens, most delicate and graceful of trees, had never been tamed. When they laughed in the wind, there was nothing human in the sound, no hint of gardeners' shears or daisy chains.

Wildness seethed under Lissy's skin, fluttering at her heart, squeezing her lungs.

"Altitude," she huffed, forcing her feet the last few yards up and over the ridge.

Mountains. They marched north in ranks of white-capped companies, farther than she could see, fading into distance and snow mist.

The unexpected heat of the afternoon sun had slunk away faster than the light, the smoke-blue peaks promising a bitterly cold night. But the climb had warmed her. Lissy stood at the edge of a grove of gold-tipped saplings and let the tears fall if they would.

Staring into that expanse of soaring space, touched by eagles and angels and not much else, robbed Lissy of words. But her heart said a prayer. Of thanksgiving for her son's safe return. Of heartbreak for his ordeal, for the loss of his father. Of petition for courage to face the future. Of fear for what lay ahead of them and what lay behind.

Of fear for the way the wild sky pulled at her soul.

"Elizabeth?"

If any other voice had spoken her name, she might have run, the wildness in her heart pushing her to flee the ropes of civilization. But it was that very wildness that stilled her limbs as Tony walked up beside her.

"It's beautiful up here."

She didn't turn toward him. "It hurts too much to be beautiful."

She felt the wildness shimmer when his hand hesitated above her shoulder, pulled away.

"We put out a bedroll for Wesley and he's already sound asleep," Tony said, the words strange against the twilight. "Mal is, too, but he's too stubborn to admit it. That wound is troubling him more than he lets on. He lost a lot of blood. I hope his body can take it."

Lissy's lips twitched, concern and humor kindling the human in her wilding heart. "If Satan comes for Mal's black heart tonight, he'll be disappointed."

"Mal's a scrapper."

"Malachi? Just let the devil try to get to him past Harry."

Tony said nothing for a long moment. "He loves that girl."

"I know." Lissy shook her head, her heart twisting. "She's as stubborn as he is."

"Two peas in a pod, so to speak." Another silence. "We've got a long ride ahead of us tomorrow, but we'll have you back to civilization in no time."

"I don't want to go back." The statement was so ludicrous, she laughed, a dry laugh that reminded her of the aspens' song. "I just want to stand here forever. Just breathe. People make life too complicated."

"You'll have your independence. There's enough money in that burlap sack to keep you and Wes comfortably."

"It's stolen money," Lissy said. "I don't want it." Then, more quietly, "The important things that Charm stole I won't ever get back."

"Do you want them back?"

Her life. Her home in Savannah. Tea with her friends. Taking Wesley on boating trips up the river. Her marriage to Charm. Snakes and mosquitoes and hurricanes. Summer heat until Christmas. Christmas with her parents, her father cursing the end of slavery and Negro impertinence while silent black servants brought in trays of ham and sweet potato casserole.

Her brothers.

The wind shivered in her veins. "No, but he still had no right to take them."

From the corner of her eyes, she saw Tony's arm sweep across the vista before them. "He traded you this for them."

She had to laugh then, risking a sidelong glance at him. "Empty wilderness. Ragged clothes. Rocks for a bed. Half-cooked flapjacks for supper."

His gaze turned to hers, brown eyes flecked with gold in the dying light. Her heart jumped like a rabbit who's just stepped into a snare. He'd caught her. She couldn't look away.

"I'm glad you came to Colorado. I don't much care what Charm did to get you here."

She saw through his eyes to the fire behind them. The glacier-breathed wind wasn't nearly cold enough.

Chapter 18

"Don't say that."

"That I'm glad you're here? It's the truth."

Anger joined the heat flowing through her veins. "I'm not one of your widowed countesses, Major Anthony Wayne." The same reproach that had kept her from him two nights before sounded weak in the face of the wind.

"My husband left me and took up with his mistress. I ran away from my home. I've lied. I've pretended to be a prostitute. I've begged help from a man I didn't know. I've taken your money."

She tilted her chin defiantly. "Maybe I'm no better than I have to be. That does not make me a safe consort to take to your bed."

"I've never for a moment been misled into considering you safe."

No humor softened his eyes. The wind brushed his hair across his high brow. The fading light planed across the angles of his face, a dance of shadows. It was not only the mountains that hurt too much to be beautiful.

"I will pay you back," Lissy said, the wildness closing her throat on the meaningless words. "Every penny that you have spent helping me get my son back. Charm owes me that."

"I don't want Charm's money."

She realized she had tried to anger him, to push him back, but his eyes still held hers.

"I want you to come to Battlement Park with me. You and Wesley. You'll be safe there."

The sound she made sounded nothing like laughter. "Liar."

His eyes did spark then, color rising along his cheekbones. "I have never lied to you."

The mountains were tame and harmless compared to his eyes.

"Then you're lying to yourself." Wind licked her skin like fire. "I will never be safe with you."

She stepped toward him then, lifted her hands to his neck, her fingers running up into the cool caress of his hair. She pulled his head down to hers, feeling her heart break in the instant before his mouth found hers.

She had known how his lips would feel, firm, gentle, hungry. She had expected the desire that poured down her throat like smooth whiskey, pooling in a well of fire deep inside her.

She did not anticipate the tears that burned her cheeks.

"Elizabeth." He gathered her into his arms, his heart pounding against hers. He kissed her tears, licked them from the corner of her mouth. When her lips opened to him, he groaned, a sound that rumbled through her body.

His hands gripped her shoulders and he thrust her back half a step, his breathing heavy. "I promised I would never dishonor you."

"I told you I have no honor."

He shook his head, but she knew the wild thing in her

heart had its claws in him as well. She could feel it, electric, running between them where his fingers gripped her shoulders.

"Tony." She lifted her hand to his cheek, the fair stubble there. He hadn't been able to shave that morning, the first time in their travels that he'd missed a day. "As you said, tomorrow we return to civilization. Where we can't touch like this. Can't think like this. Tonight we're somewhere else. Where none of that matters."

"You're not a widowed countess." He almost smiled.

"No." She moved her hands to his shirt, the buttons falling slowly away. She ran her fingers up the muscles of his chest. "But I want you anyway."

"Bloody hell." His mouth found hers again, claiming it with a hot urgency that took her breath away. He pulled her against him, his hand running down her back to press her against his desire. "I want you, too."

His fingers found the front of her bodice. She didn't have time to be jealous at the dexterity with which he parted the buttons. His lips followed his fingers, and when his mouth closed around one breast, she could only lose herself in the burning of her need.

It felt so good to be touched. To be caressed. To be wanted. It felt so good to have Tony want her as much as she wanted him.

"Here." He shrugged her out of her old wool coat and laid it in the grass, pulling her down with him, cradling her beside him against the cold.

Slowly, gently, he pulled the combs from her hair, letting it fall across her shoulders. He buried his fingers in it, holding her still as he kissed her, softer kisses across her forehead, her eyelids, her chin.

"I want to taste you," he murmured, nipping at her earlobe. "I want to touch you. I want to drown in you."

He brushed aside the torn halves of her skirt to run his hand along her leg, up under her petticoat. She swallowed the cry that welled in her throat when his hand found her center. She knew he could feel the breathtaking heat coursing through her body. She could see his pleasure in it as he bent to catch her gasps with his mouth, could feel his own need aching against her lips.

But when she reached for his pants, he gently pulled her hand away.

"Let me pleasure you." His voice whispered low against her cheek. "Better safe than sorry, and all that."

She wondered if he could see her blush in the dusky twilight. "I think we can be safe."

She twisted on the coat until she could dig down into the pocket.

"Bloody hell, I've offended you. You mean to plug me with that derringer."

The humor in his voice warmed her deeper than even his touch. "That would certainly be safer."

"I hate to remind you, but you're out of ammunition."

She could see the laughter in his eyes as he bent over her, nose almost touching hers. Her heart nearly choked her. It shouldn't be this easy. To be with him. To feel so unself-conscious with him in such an intimate position. To feel as if she'd known forever the touch of his hand, the taste of his mouth, the sound of his voice.

She was a fool. Malachi had had it right. Only a fool would fall in love with Mad Anthony Wayne. Given her own particular circumstances, no doubt a damned fool.

Might as well be damned for a lioness as a lamb.

"I wasn't looking for my gun," she said in her softest, magnolia-sweet voice. "Just something for yours."

She shook the item in her hand, the black linen a dark shadow against her pale skin.

Tony's eyebrows rose. She thought he might choke. "Where in bloody hell did that come from?"

"Angelique's dresser in the South Platte Saloon. I stuffed it in my purse when Deirdre walked in on us and then I forgot to put it back. When Harry gave me back my purse last night, I moved it to my coat pocket. I didn't want her asking me what it was."

Tony's mouth twisted. "Can't ever tell what might come in handy," he finally managed. "I'm going to have to make a more thorough study of what ladies carry in their little handbags."

Making unflappable Tony Wayne blush emboldened her. Lissy reached for his pants again, his breathless reaction to her touch reigniting her own need. She had scarcely stroked the scrap of cloth into place when he pulled her over on top of him, her skirts bunching around them.

Ice-kissed air brushed her legs and bared shoulders, but the heat between them kept her warm. Lissy sucked in her cry as they joined, wildfire searing through her veins.

Sunlight had given way to the night and to the bright edge of the full moon rising over the ridge behind them. The icy light faded Tony's features, but his eyes still burned, holding hers, keeping her close as the wild stars danced in her sight and the wind called her home.

She came with sudden, wrenching release, and Tony cried out her name as he pulled her close, his body echoing hers. They lay still and quiet, Lissy not caring if her tears fell on his shoulder as she listened to him breathe.

"Thank you," she finally whispered, though words could never be adequate.

She had traded a lifetime of propriety, traded her right to

her life as a good woman in Savannah, for a single hour of stars and a man she could not have. And she would not regret it. Could not regret discovering how it felt to give herself freely to a man she loved, without debt or obligation or reservation.

"Elizabeth." His fingers brushed the hair back from her cheek.

"No one has ever touched me like that before."

"What do you mean?"

"So tenderly. As though I'm someone special." She gritted her teeth against the tears. This wasn't Lissy Woodfin. She never cried. Even her father liked that about her. Tough enough to be a Wilmer, despite her timid mother.

His fingers wrapped in her hair, holding her close. "You are special, Elizabeth. I've never met anyone like you."

She summoned up a laugh. "None of your lonely marchionesses or dowager duchesses has ever shot a man in front of you before?"

"Damned fine shooting, too," Tony said, his hand still tight in her hair. "But that's not what I meant."

"They've never stolen contraceptive devices from a brothel?"

His chest rumbled with a chuckle. "Not to my knowledge."

"Never absconded with a sackful of stolen jewels?"

"Not a one of them." He released her hair to brush her cheek again. "I know what you think of me, but there haven't been that many women. I pay attention to my guests. Jordan says I flirt. They like it. And so do I. And there's nothing to regret when they leave me to my solitude in the mountains. Very civilized."

"Not like this." Lissy forced a laugh as she brushed an

aspen leaf from his forehead.

"Not like this." Something in his voice made her shiver. He brushed her lips with his, pulled her face close so her cheek pressed to his. She almost thought his face was wet with tears, too. "Not like this."

Harry added more deadwood to the fire, the red flames lifting toward their cousins the stars. Light calling to light. She pulled her blanket closer about her shoulders. Her own soul called only darkness that night.

She could hear Wesley's soft breathing to her left, see his long, fair lashes resting against his cheeks, sleeping the gentle sleep of the innocent. To her other side, Mal's breathing sounded shallower, harsher. Whiskey had finally helped him sleep, but it did not make for easy dreams.

She'd boiled more water, cleaned and dressed his wounds with strips torn from Angelique's clean sheets. Her stitches had held for the long ride. The knife had cut clean.

Malachi had always seemed indestructible. Tough as leather and blunt as a rock. If he were at home in Battlement Park with a doctor to tend him and Jordan to feed him soup, she would worry, but she wouldn't be sitting here awake, listening to each breath just to make sure he kept breathing.

He'd lost so much blood, ridden so hard. He'd been nearly gray when they stopped.

She could still see the instant when Fox's knife had sliced into him, when the blood had followed the blade back out into the cave-dimmed light. She could still see the blood on her hands as she stripped away his shirt. Still see the pain in his eyes that hadn't dimmed until he slept.

Harry pushed her fingers into her brow, rubbing away

the images. They had all come close to death that day. She would never forget the taste of dirt and rock, the noise as the earth tried to swallow them alive. The deadly ricochet of bullets that had triggered the collapse seemed petty and foolish by comparison.

She looked up. Even blinded by the fire, even through the gauze of moonlight, she could see the blanket of stars overhead.

With her thoughts spinning, she couldn't listen for Malachi's breathing. She turned to where he slept, slumped against a rock, his revolver resting in his lap. She held her own breath until she could make out his chest rising and falling, just a faint shift under one of Charm's fine white shirts, spoiled by sweat and blood.

She wished someone else kept watch with her. Tony and Lissy had been gone . . . She glanced at the path of the moon. Hours.

She looked up at the ridge where Tony had followed Lissy. She'd been so worried about Malachi and about going home that she hadn't even thought to consider that they should have been back long ago.

They might have fallen down a cliff face or been mauled by a bear or, more likely, Lissy had gotten turned around in the unfamiliar wilderness and wandered off lost, and Tony had not been able to find her before it got dark.

Harry sat up straighter, peering up into the aspen groves. She couldn't abandon Malachi and Wesley to search for them. But she could go just to the top of the ridge. A second fire built there ought to be visible for miles. If Lissy and Tony were lost . . .

She started to rise.

"They'll be back."

The voice might have come from her imagination. That

would account for the shiver that ran up her spine. But when she glanced over at Malachi, firelight reflected in his eyes.

"Tony didn't take his overcoat."

"If they get cold, they'll come back."

"They've been gone for hours. How can they not be cold?"

His eyes glittered as he shifted his position against the rock, pulling the rough horse blanket up his chest. "You're not a child, Harry. I'm sure you can figure it out."

Sudden fire blazed up her cheeks, an equal mixture of mortification and anger. She wanted to point out that Lissy was married and Tony was a gentleman, but she had seen the hunger when they looked at each other.

"Are you in pain?" she asked instead.

"I'm fine."

Since he had to spit this through his teeth, she put her blanket down to move to his side.

"Let me check your dressing. If an infection has developed—"

"There's not a damn thing you can do about it." He pressed his good arm across his blanket, holding her back with his glare. "Just let me be. I'm fine. Or I would be if you'd let me get some sleep."

Harry sat back on her heels. "If you're feeling so great, maybe you could try some manners."

His nose wrinkled, but he couldn't stop the snort of laughter. For a second she could see the old Malachi, the one she'd met just a few short months ago. The one who wouldn't hesitate to confront a bully twice his size or tell a baron his hairpiece was crooked. Difficult. But she always knew where she stood with him.

She hadn't seen how much of himself he kept back, how

much was hidden behind the blunt honesty. She would bet her life he'd never lied to her, but that didn't mean she'd known him. Known the man whose memories of two very different wars haunted his eyes when he thought no one was looking. The man who would rather approach a potential opponent unarmed than shoot an innocent man.

The man she had kissed that morning.

She still didn't quite believe it had happened. Malachi had not referred to it at all. Perhaps he hadn't noticed, what with bullets flying by and rocks raining down on their heads. Although it had felt as though . . .

Maybe not. Maybe he hadn't kissed her back. Maybe if he'd noticed her kissing him at all, he had thought it was a momentary madness brought on by being nearly buried alive.

That was certainly a rational, reasonable explanation. Much more rational and reasonable than the madness that still pumped through her veins. A madness that made her want to kiss him again. That made her want to discover if he would return the kiss.

"We'll reach Boulder tomorrow," Malachi said, no echo of her own turbulent emotions in his voice. "You could be home the next day."

"I have to go back to Battlement Park."

"I think Lissy will be safe enough without you. Elijah will be there."

His very lack of intonation sparked a flare of fury in her chest. Did he think she wanted to go back to Battlement Park to moon over his brother?

"My mare is at the Fox and Hound." The thin words knifed through her teeth. "I'm not going to leave Portia behind. I'll be sure to be out of your way by . . ." It took her some time to work out the day. Friday? Had it really been only a little over a week since she'd left her brother's ranch? "By Monday."

Back home by Monday. Back to March and Maggie and little Sarah. Her heart suddenly ached as though she had not seen them in years. Back to Lemuel and Wolf and the Culberts. To the horses, the creek, the foothills she knew every inch of. Her own warm bed.

Back to her old life. Where she was a young lady about to be married to Ashton Brady, the handsomest bachelor in the state of Colorado. Where Henna Culbert was altering her wedding dress and March had hired Wolf Kelly to take her place at the ranch.

That old life must have belonged to some other Harriet Jackson, because she could hardly imagine it.

"You still have plenty of time to get ready for your wedding."

She couldn't bring herself to look at Malachi. She couldn't bear to see the same disinterest in his eyes that she heard in his voice. He was the one who'd told her to be careful, not to rush into marriage. Before she'd even met Ashton Brady.

Ash.

She had loved him. She had been sure she loved him when she agreed to marry him. Malachi was wrong. She couldn't have been such a child that she had agreed to marry Ash just because she couldn't have Elijah.

Yet it seemed like a much younger Harry who had dreamed of a little cottage by a creek in South Park, of lace curtains and fruit trees and fine horses. It had been a green girl who had returned Ash's chaste kisses with expectation and frustration.

No girl had shared that kiss in the mine tunnel with Malachi Kelly.

She wiped the back of her hand across her lips, but she couldn't wipe away the knowledge she had gained in that brief moment.

Despite his visit to the South Platte Saloon, if Ash died, it would break her heart. If anything happened to Malachi, a part of her soul would die.

The wind shifted, driving smoke into her eyes, and she had to wipe the moisture away. She was a fool. She might as well have been a Kelly herself, the way the Kelly men thought of her as their sister.

She grabbed her blanket and wrapped it around her shoulders, settling her head on the saddle she'd taken off the gray mare.

"I was wrong, Harry." There was something in his voice now, that even the low volume couldn't hide. "This isn't the life you should be leading. You'll be safe in South Park."

She shrugged the blanket higher, not even glancing over her shoulder. "I thought you needed to get some sleep."

She doubted she would sleep at all that night.

Mal did not think he had fallen asleep, yet the cry of an eagle woke him. Light spilled into the sky above him like liquid gold into a blue china bowl.

The throbbing in his left arm crescendoed to a burst of pain as he levered himself up to a sitting position, but the cut in his side, the bruises on his ribs, the wrenching ache in his back and neck from sleeping against a rock, all helped distract him.

He palpated the bandage with his right hand. He sucked in air against the pain, pressed again. He felt no heat, and his head felt mostly clear. He might have a low-grade fever, but he wasn't likely to collapse on the ride.

A ride they should have begun half an hour ago.

Oblivious to the dawn, his companions slept close around the fire. Tony and Lissy had returned, sleeping chastely on either side of Wesley's empty bedroll. Mal felt a rush of panic at the boy's absence until he caught sight of the small figure climbing through the aspen grove toward the ridge. It should be safe enough for Wesley to take a moment of morning privacy.

Harry still huddled against her saddle, but her body had finally relaxed in sleep. She looked so young it tore at his heart.

But she was old enough to choose her own life. She might have died in that mine yesterday, before her chance at marriage and a family, before her chance at love and heartbreak and growing old. He'd had no right to tell her that any of that was wrong for her.

He ran his good hand through his hair, then down over his face, a face hardened and scarred by memories and weather. He might not be old, but he felt that way. Ancient. Brittle.

His heart had cracked, sometime during the night. The pain surprised him. He hadn't thought he had that much of a heart left.

Harry had managed to dredge it up. The one positive result was that he'd found it had some good left in it. It had fought through the tangled net of his unacknowledged jealousy and the flare of desire that still raged through him when he thought of her kiss. What mattered was not what he wanted, but what would make Harry happy.

Harry hadn't said anything about the kiss. Either she had already forgotten it or she regretted it. Either way, she was right. He was bitter and broken, making just enough as a justice of the peace to live the quiet life he craved. He could hardly sleep through the night without visits from the worst of his memories.

Ash Brady was young, wealthy, and unencumbered by ghosts. And if he ever once hurt Harry, Mal would kill him.

Mal struggled to get his feet under him and push himself up onto the rock behind him. Wesley must have fed the fire before taking his morning constitutional. If Mal could work the kinks out of his back, he could start some flapjacks before the others woke. He certainly didn't want to eat Harry's cooking again.

He checked the cylinder of his borrowed Smith and Wesson, easier to do than with his lost Colt, then worked it into his holster. He had just pushed himself to his feet when he heard something crashing through the trees above them.

He looked up to see Wesley sprinting down the hill. Mal thought the boy was going to tumble right through the fire, but somehow he skidded to a windmill stop just a foot from Mal.

His gray eyes, so like his mother's, looked almost black against his pale skin.

"Are you all right, son?" Mal glanced back up the ridge to see if a bear had pursued him. "It's all right. You're safe now."

Wesley shook his head. "Uncles." He gulped air, tried again. "On the road. Behind us."

"Uncles?" Mal found his own breath coming faster. "Your uncles?"

Wesley nodded.

It couldn't be. Though he should have expected it. It was just the luck they'd had throughout this expedition. "You're sure?"

"Uncle Rafe and—" Wesley sucked in air. "Uncle Clayton. The man from the mine yesterday, the red-haired one. He's with them. They're coming up the mountain. They look madder than hell."

Chapter 19

Mal decided not to chide the boy on his language. He'd seen Clayton and Rafe Wilmer angry, and there wasn't any other way to describe it.

"What's going on?" Harry blinked up from her makeshift pillow, eyes still unfocused. Tony and Lissy shifted in their blankets, rolling over to glance across the fire.

"Company," Mal said, dragging over Tony's saddlebag. One-handed, it took him a minute to dig out what was left of his ammunition. Precious little. His own Colt cartridges were too long for the Schofields. "Lissy was right. Her brothers didn't trust the Beasts. They've come to finish the job. Wesley says the Fox is with them."

"Wes saw them?" Lissy stood up, managing even in a moment of crisis to accomplish it with poise.

"They're just over the ridge," Wesley said, pointing back down the trail they'd followed the evening before. "They've got shotguns."

Harry and Tony were up and out of their bedrolls, Tony strapping on his remaining Smith and Wesson.

"Get the horses saddled," Mal ordered, yanking off the sling Harry had made for his injured arm. Clay and Rafe could smell weakness. "Leave anything you can't pack immediately. Ride for Boulder, hard as you can."

He pulled on his coat, gritting his teeth against the searing pain as his stitches pulled. "Telegraph Elijah. Have him meet you. Get back to Battlement Park."

"You think you're going to face them down all by yourself?" Harry asked, looking not quite surprised. "Think again, Kelly. We're not going anywhere without you."

"Wesley said they have shotguns," Tony reminded him. "You're tough, Mal, but—"

"They've got shotguns. We've got two revolvers," Mal said. His heartbeat had settled, steady, as it always did when the battle finally arrived. "Two revolvers and six extra cartridges. What do you think they'll do to Lissy and Harry and Wesley after they get past us, Tony? Get to Boulder. I'll hold the bastards off as long as I can."

He thrust the box of bullets into his coat pocket and started back up the trail that wound around the mountain shoulder to the west.

"Mal!"

He didn't turn at Harry's cry. He didn't need a last look, if that's what it would be. He carried her image in his heart.

He heard scuffling. Tony would get her on that horse. She had a chance to escape, slim as it might be, if he could keep the wolves at bay. That was all that mattered.

He pushed up the incline, the altitude and his injuries robbing him of breath. The trail lay exposed across the mountain slope just around the curve ahead. He could have kept an entire army at bay from there if he had enough ammunition.

His mind flashed back to that terrible, endless day on the Little Bighorn. The disastrous charge with Reno, the "retreat" through the river, the rout, the slaughter. Trapped in a bowl with bullets buzzing around them like flies, the "savages" better armed with repeating rifles than the soldiers with their Springfield single-shot carbines. A third of them dead, missing, wounded.

He could still smell the blood, the fear. Feel the heat beating down, killing more slowly than the bullets. Reno drunk. The men terrified. He could hear the gunshots, far off in the late afternoon, remembered hoping that damned devil Custer was giving back what he and his men were taking.

The chill of a mountain breeze lifted his coat as the September sun touched his shoulders with warmth. He filled his lungs with the scents of pine pitch and snow melt, creeks and ancient rock.

This was a much better morning to die than that day in 'seventy-six, and the odds weren't any worse. This time he would make sure all his company got home safely.

He came to the crest in the trappers' road, where it curved around a granite knob and fell back into the next valley, back toward the Lucky Lady.

Not a hundred yards away, three horses pranced to a stop. Fox sat atop the pack horse, his red pelt dimmed by a crust of blood above one ear, his shattered elbow wrapped in dingy white cloth. His hazel eyes glittered with triumph and fear and fever.

Just behind him Clayton and Rafe Wilmer's sleek black geldings glowed ruddy with the morning sun, the two brothers sitting them with the casual grace of southern gentlemen. In the eleven years since Mal had seen them, Rafe, the younger brother, had expanded. From his boxy face to his gut, everything had swelled and rounded, as if he'd been kneaded with yeast. But it hadn't changed the glee in his eyes to be second in line when his brother went in for the kill.

The years had only hardened Clayton Wilmer's features. Beneath the white-blond hair he shared with his sister, there was nothing pale or soft, just cold eyes and firm muscle.

"I thought Dex here was pulling our leg," Clay said, his hard lips curving into a hard smile.

"I thought so, too," Rafe agreed, still his brother's faithful echo. "Dexter's such a trickster."

Mal almost looked for a fourth man before realizing Dexter was Lissy's fox.

"I said, that can't be our old friend Mal Kelly helping a womanizer and a thief," Clay continued. "He's got too much honor for that. Being a traitor and a Negro-lover and all."

His teeth showed in amusement at his own wit. "But by God, I'm going to have to apologize to you, Dex. That's Union Lieutenant Malachi Kelly and no mistake."

"Captain Malachi Kelly." Mal strolled over to lean against a lonely lodgepole pine. The boulder that sheltered its roots would offer him cover when the time came. "I confess the Union cavalry was a disappointment. I joined hoping I'd get the chance to whip a particular couple of Confederate jackasses, but they didn't have the courage to fight for their convictions."

Rafe's face reddened as he reached for the shotgun strapped to his saddle, but Clay laughed.

"Still the little banty cock I remember," he said, leaning over his horse's side to spit. "We had an old banty around when we were kids. No more brains than a grasshopper, but the most fearless little son-of-a-bitch you ever saw. Tomcat got him."

His teeth showed again. "There was feathers all over the yard for days."

Mal grinned back. *Just keep talking, you self-satisfied bastard. Take all the time you want.*

"Dexter here says you were rude to him back at that old silver mine," Clay said, the grin gone. "He's got a bullet wound in that elbow and one in his leg and a rock knocked him clean out, though I guess he's in better shape than his friends. He says when he came to he saw you riding off with my sister and nephew."

Mal shrugged. "They went their way and I went mine."

"Damn you." Rafe jerked the shotgun out of its holster. "Tell us where Charm Woodfin is or we'll fill you so full of buckshot your pallbearers won't be able to lift your coffin."

"Charm is dead."

The soft, honeysuckle voice startled Mal hard enough to jar his bad arm on the tree, but he had the presence of mind not to turn his gaze away from Clay and Rafe to look for Lissy.

Clay's eyebrows raised. "Hello, Lis. Still protecting that no-good son-of-a-bitch. You don't mind sharing him with that Frenchy whore?"

"She's telling the truth," Tony said mildly, coming up beside Mal's right shoulder. Mal risked shooting him a look that promised a slow, lingering death if they both somehow survived the Wilmers. Tony threw him a rueful grin and dropped a burlap sack at his feet.

"That little bitch wouldn't know the truth if it bit off her nose," Rafe said.

"Charm kidnapped my son," Lissy spat back. "He stole from my brothers, ran off with his mistress, and left me to take the consequences." Her voice sparked off the bare rocks. "If he were still alive, I'd be chasing him down right now to kill him myself."

Clay patted the neck of his horse, eyes narrowed

thoughtfully. "What do you say, boy? Where's your father."

Mal did turn then. There they were in a row. Tony, Lissy, Wesley and Harry. Harry's blue eyes flashed his glare right back at him.

You should have known better than to think we'd ride off and leave you. And maybe he should have.

"Papa's dead, Uncle Clay," Wesley said, clear and earnest. "The cave collapsed on him and Angelique. I saw it."

Clay's hooded eyes turned on Dexter the Fox, who cringed sideways on the pack horse, like a nervous dog about to bare its teeth.

"I never saw them after the cave-in," he said, obviously repeating something he'd said before. "Just these five."

Rafe's face reddened again, this time in frustration. "Damn the man. That's just like him. Never staying around to pay for his mistakes. How are we supposed to get our money back if he's dead?"

Clay spat again, disgusted. "The title on the mine will go to Lis, I guess."

"I'll sign it over to you," Lissy said.

Clay fixed her with a hard look. "Of course you will. And you'll tell us where the rest of the money is."

"And if I do, you'll ride back where you came from," Lissy said, her voice just as hard as his. "And you won't ever come looking for me or Wesley again."

Rafe gaped at her until Clay started to laugh, then he laughed, too.

They were going to enjoy this, Mal realized. The intimidation, the humiliation. They'd enjoy taking Lissy home to Savannah, to complete her disgrace, to watch her shunned by her family and friends, a woman deserted and paupered by her husband, dishonored by chasing after him. Their cruelty had grown more subtle. Though Clay had always had a keen eye for what would hurt his victims the most.

Mal had found an orphaned black and white puppy one morning when he was about seven, and the Reverend had actually said he could keep it . . .

He shook the memory away.

"Come with us, Lissy," Clay said, cool and reasonable. "There's no reason for your friends to get hurt."

"Bullshit." Mal pushed himself off the tree. "It wouldn't be any fun for you if you came all this way and didn't get to hurt anybody."

Clay's teeth glinted. "You always were a pain in the ass, Kelly. But I'll make you a deal. Lissy comes with us, we'll only hurt one of you. The word of one southerner to another. You choose which one."

Rafe was smiling now, too, lips slightly parted like a dog that sees a bone about to fly his way. "Pick Malachi, Clay. He came down to Savannah walking like a Yankee, acting like he was better than us because Lee surrendered. I've been wanting to hurt him a long time."

"He can't choose himself, you idiot," Clay said, with more exasperation than rancor. Yes, the subtlety was all Clayton's. "Who will it be, Kelly? The smart-mouthed Brit? The bitch in britches? The boy?"

At that moment, seeing the cruel pleasure sparkling in Clay's eyes, Mal would have sold his soul to the devil to rub the man's face in the dirt.

Unfortunately, the devil had already chosen sides and was firmly in Clayton Wilmer's camp.

"I think we should take the girl," Rafe said. He might start bouncing in his saddle soon in the sheer joy of anticipation. But Clay was watching Mal and must have seen the careful blandness in his eyes.

"The girl," he drawled, eyeing Harry speculatively. If he

wanted to see her flinch, he was going to be disappointed.

Even with the sick dread pooling in his gut, Mal felt the pride of knowing that given even odds, Harry had Clayton Wilmer beaten cold on courage and smarts.

"We wouldn't hurt her bad," Clay said, gaze flicking between Harry and Mal. "Maybe she'd even enjoy it. Then the rest of you can go on your way."

It would be sweet to shoot Clayton Wilmer. Mal wasn't Elijah, but he could fire a revolver faster than Rafe could lift that shotgun up. Of all the enemies he'd ever faced, none had ever held the terror of these bullies from his boyhood, the two boys next door and their gang.

General Lee, Lieutenant Colonel Custer, Crazy Horse. At least they had all been honorable men in their own way. He had felt no pleasure upon learning of their deaths. He could take pleasure in killing the Wilmer brothers. For the torments of his childhood. For Lissy's terror. For the smugness and wealth they had gained from a war that had devastated their neighbors.

And for the way Rafe looked at Harry now, as though she were nothing but a toy for his enjoyment.

Between the two of them, he and Tony might be able to kill the Wilmer brothers and the Fox, despite their low ammunition. He could almost taste the salty draft of revenge, the gratifying burn of it in his stomach.

But if he and Tony didn't kill them, if Clay and Rafe lived, even if he and his companions reached Battlement Park safely, none of them would ever be truly safe again. If he had a long memory, so did Clay Wilmer. And Clay would be willing to bide his time to strike until Lissy or Harry or young Wesley let down their guard. Maybe years from now.

So Mal swallowed his hatred, his memories, his revenge.

He wasn't a little boy anymore, to be goaded and teased into a mad rage. He'd learned something in the past twenty years or so himself.

He leaned over to heft the burlap sack Tony had dropped by his feet. With a contemptuous animal grace that would have done his brother proud, he slung the sack over his shoulder and crossed in front of his friends until he reached the edge of the trail.

Here on the shoulder of the mountain, the world dropped away. The cliff sheered downward two hundred feet before the first tree broke its face.

"Lissy told you she knew where Charm hid your money," he said, gazing down at a mountain creek rushing through the valley far below. "Half of it's buried back at that mine cave-in with your incompetent thugs."

"Not that I'm not grateful for the information—" Humor filled Clay's voice. "—But it's not going to keep us from enjoying your little hoyden. Lissy will tell us where the rest is."

Mal kicked a stone at the edge of the trail, watched it fall a long, long way before he heard the clatter of it striking loose scree.

"You don't have to go to the trouble of dragging it out of Lissy," he said, his voice as cool as the calm inside him. "I'll tell you where it is."

He dumped the sack off his shoulder to the dirt. He shook the mouth open, reached in and pulled out a small velvet sack. He dumped the contents into his hand. Small rubies. Nothing like some of the jewels Tony had dug out of the bag the night before. But they glittered like chips of fire in the sunlight.

"Damn," Rafe said, almost reverently.

"I don't know what was in the other sack, the one that

got buried," Mal said, extending his palm to catch the light. "But there's a lot of these little stones in this one."

"How much did that bastard steal?" Rafe asked.

"The question is how long," Clay said, voice cold. "And I'd say longer than we thought. What are you thinking, Kelly? That we'll bargain your pathetic little friends for our own money?"

"I'm thinking you'll take your pathetic little pile of rocks and ride back to Silvercrest." Mal tossed the rubies up an inch, heard Rafe's sucked-in breath as they pattered back into his palm. "I'm thinking you'll go back home to Savannah, to your pathetic little import-export business, and be glad that Charm stole a few pennies from you instead of turning you in to hang as smugglers and thieves.

"And I'm thinking you'll let me and my friends, including your sister, ride on our way, out of your lives and out of your business."

He looked up then, straight into Clayton Wilmer's eyes. He could make threats, too. The Wilmer brothers' business activities couldn't bear intensive scrutiny. Not if an accountant could steal this much money from them over a decade without them being aware of it.

"Your deaths would keep you out of our business," Clay said.

Rubies spun and flashed in the sunlight like a spray of blood before falling away into emptiness.

"No!" Rafe cried, as if it had been his blood wasted in the flash of a hand.

"Let's see what's in here," Mal said, digging out another little black bag. "Not so many in this one."

He lifted out a perfectly cut emerald the size of his thumbnail.

Faster than Rafe could wrench up his shotgun and throw

the hammer, Mal had the burlap sack in his fist, holding it out over the cliff.

"We could recover those, if we shot you," Clay said, icy calm.

"The ones that didn't crack on impact?" Mal asked, equally cool. "Or the ones that didn't scatter when the bags split open? You could try. There must be some way down there. You might even find it before the first heavy snowfall."

"What would you care?" Clay asked, his casual tone belied only by the pulse that beat in his neck. "You'd be dead. And so would all your friends. Every last one of them. After we had some fun with them."

Mal shrugged. "As you say, I'd be dead. What would I care? The real question is, what do you care? Would you rather have the pleasure of killing me or of taking home your stolen money?"

He shook the bag over the cliff, the pieces of silver jingling cheerfully.

"That's my money," Lissy said, her hard, proud voice as cool as any Wilmer's. "My grandmother's and mine. You can't give it to my *brothers*." She spat the word as if it were a curse.

"Bloody hell, Mal," Tony said, his accent thick as Yorkshire pudding. "You can't rob an angel to pay the devil, so to speak. That's more money than we'll ever see again in our lifetime. Let's just kill the bastards."

"I'd rather be shot than let those toads get their hands on our money," Harry agreed.

Maybe Mal's friends weren't subtle, but Clay and Rafe didn't appear to notice.

"That's *our* money!" Rafe howled. His horse snorted as he jiggled in the saddle. "You've got no right to it. None! If we let you go, that would be more than you deserve."

Clay's eyes narrowed. "What is your bargain, Kelly?"

"All I need is your word that you'll let us go. We'll stay away from Savannah. You stay away from Colorado."

"Their word?" Tony asked doubtfully. He lounged casually in Mal's place against the pine tree. No one had noticed him drawing his revolver. He was polishing the barrel on his sleeve. "I wouldn't trust those two to tell St. Peter the truth. I still say shoot them."

"Their word?" Lissy repeated. "For my whole livelihood? What good is their return to Savannah going to do me if I have nothing to live on?"

"Their word," Mal said firmly. He jingled the sack again for Rafe's benefit, though he kept his eyes on Clay.

"Do you think they'll keep their word to a traitor?" Lissy snapped.

"Do you think they'd be willing to let everyone know they have less honor than a traitor?" Mal asked.

For a long moment, no one moved. The horses' bridles jingled with restlessness, a hawk screamed far off. Mal's arm ached with the strain of holding the heavy sack steady. He never broke eye contact with Clay.

Clay bared his teeth, no smile this time. "Give Rafe the money," he spat finally. "We'll give you our word. You'll all be free to go."

"Even Lissy?" Rafe objected, though his gaze remained anxiously fixed on the burlap sack. "We can't let her walk away. She's family. And so is the boy. They can't get away with treating us like this."

"How long do you think our little sister is going to last with no money and no way to support herself?" Clay asked, his lip curling with anger and frustration.

"But I want to take her back to Father—"

"Your word," Mal said.

"Clay—"

"Say it, Rafe."

"All right." Rafe's pout shook his chin. "I give my word. Give me the bag, you bastard."

Knowing the brothers wanted that money more than the pleasure of revenge, it took all of Mal's willpower not to loosen his grip and let the burlap sack fall. Instead, he pulled it in toward his body. He heard Rafe's sigh of relief as it cleared the edge of the cliff.

Slowly, deliberately, he strode down the trail to where the brothers waited. The red-headed thug, Dexter, gave him a vicious look as Mal passed, but there was no reason to fear a fox when the wolves were near.

Rafe leaned over, nearly unbalancing his steed, to snatch at the sack as Mal approached. Mal thought he might be drooling.

"Check it," Clay ordered. Up close, his gunmetal gray eyes showed hard hatred and disgust. Mal's trust in his word was a gamble. Clayton Wilmer was no gentleman. But Clay liked to think of himself that way. Maybe that was enough.

If not, Mal knew Tony's Smith and Wesson was ready.

"Look at this," Rafe said, in almost childlike wonder. He held up a blue topaz the size of a peach pit.

"That's nothing," Clay snarled. "Are there real jewels in there or not?" He turned his glare on Mal. "If you've tried to cheat us, we'll spit and roast you right here."

"You'd make a good cannibal," Mal said mildly, "but I think Rafe's been eating your share."

"Silver," Rafe said, looking as though he might eat that, too. "Gold coins. Jewels. Diamonds. More rubies. Some are uncut, but they're good sized."

Rafe looked up from the sack, and for the first time in their lives, Mal saw raw honesty in Rafe Wilmer's eyes. "They're not cheating us."

"All right." Clay spat at Mal's feet. "That's what I think of you and your bargain. If you ever set foot in Georgia again, I'll kill you. That's a promise. Rafe, you go first."

Rafe turned his horse, an awkward procedure on the narrow space between his brother's mount and the cliff edge.

"Wait!" Lissy called out.

Mal turned to see her run a few paces down the trail toward them, jerky steps in her broken boots. "Clay, you can't leave me here with nothing. I've done nothing to you."

"You've made your choice." Clay spat again. "You go next, Dex."

Mal thought Clay didn't trust the red-haired man to ride behind him now that his brother carried so much wealth. He wondered if Fox would live to see Savannah again.

Fox's sly brandy-colored eyes sliced through him as the man rode past, glittering with a fever that had nothing to do with his wounds. On the other hand . . . Mal would have to lay odds on the Wilmer brothers, but he could hope.

"Clay, please." Lissy clasped her hands together, her pale face twisted in desperation. "Think of your nephew. Just a few coins, Clay."

Finally Clay smiled again. "Don't cry, Lis. It looked like they could use a washerwoman in Silvercrest. You might even be able to make a living on your back, if you can learn how to keep your mouth shut."

He whirled his horse about, the beast rolling its eyes at the proximity to the cliff. He looked back over his shoulder at Mal.

"You were wrong." Clay patted the butt of his shotgun. "I wouldn't have any hesitation about breaking an oath to a traitor." His canines gleamed in the morning sunlight. "But my sister will bring you more trouble than anything I could dream up for you. She is a Wilmer, after all."

He laughed with real humor. "I hope we meet again, Kelly. I surely do."

He dug his heels into the black gelding's flanks and trotted away after Fox and Rafe.

Chapter 20

"You did it." Lissy picked her way the few steps forward to stand beside Malachi. She recognized the expression on his face. Disbelief. "They're really leaving."

And then suddenly she was laughing, the tears running down her cheeks. She grabbed Mal's ear and pulled him toward her to kiss him on the cheek. She laughed harder when he blushed.

"Hey," Tony objected, as he and the others came up beside them. "I helped, too."

It was Lissy who blushed then, but she grabbed his ear and pulled, making him yelp before she brushed her lips against his cheek.

"What about me?" Harry asked, but she dodged when Lissy grabbed for her head.

Lissy wrapped her arms around Wesley instead, pulling him into her arms. He hugged her back for a long minute before pulling free, gathering up his dignity.

"You were very brave," she told him.

"It takes a great deal of courage to stand up to bullies like that," Tony agreed. He nodded at Harry. "Especially when they're threatening to hurt you."

Malachi grinned. "And when standing up didn't work,

whining and crying did. Your begging sealed the bargain, Lissy. Clay never suspected you were duping him."

"Who said I was faking?" Lissy asked. She clasped her hands tightly. "Oh, Clay. Please, please don't leave me here with people who don't want to hurt me and actually care whether I live or die."

"Some of that money *was* yours," Malachi said, eyes following Clay and Rafe's progress across the mountain. "It could have gotten you and Wesley settled in your new life."

"I rather thought of that." Tony's eyes sparkled as he held up a little black velvet bag.

He took Lissy's hand and lowered it into her open palm. She felt the shifting weight of coins. "Tony?"

"A few little trinkets Clay and Rafe will never miss. I purloined it before giving the sack to Malachi. He had that reckless, hell-and-damnation look about him. I was afraid he might do something rash."

"Good show." Harry laughed as she pulled another velvet bag from her coat pocket. "I guess you're not the only one who learned a little thievery this week, Lissy."

The contents of the bag felt like marbles in Lissy's hand. Wesley loosed the ribbon to look inside.

"Uncut," Harry explained. "I thought they'd be easier to sell without arousing your brothers' interest."

Lissy shook her head. She wasn't going to cry again. "Not only did you chase off my brothers, you cheated them, too." Her laugh sounded like a sob. "I'm so proud of you."

"We did it together," Harry said, giving Malachi a nudge with her boot. "You'd think our captain would have learned something about dividing his forces from Custer."

"Disobeying direct orders," Malachi said. "If I were Custer, I'd have you flogged, shave your heads, then dump you in a pit for a day or two. But since you pulled it off, I'll let it go this time." His eyes narrowed. "Though if you'd ridden off and left me like I told you to, I could have just shot the bastards."

Harry smiled sweetly. "Then you wouldn't have the pleasure of imagining them at the Lucky Lady digging for months for a bag of treasure that Charm has carted off to Mexico."

Lissy looked at the friends gathered around her, dirty, disheveled, desperately tired. And looking as if they'd just received Lee's surrender at Appomattox.

"Thank you," she said, though no words could express the depth of her gratitude. "Thank you for all you've done. For saving my life. For giving me a new one. Most of all, for returning my son to me."

Wesley took her hand in his. For her comfort, not his. She had to stop crying.

"After all the foolish things I did. All the lies I told." She wiped a hand across her face. "I've spent too much of my life with my father and Clay and Rafe and Charm. I thought only money would motivate anyone to help me. I didn't dare tell you Wes was the only treasure I hoped to find."

She met their eyes, one by one. Malachi. Harry. Tony. "I hope you can forgive me for not trusting your true character. For I gained an unexpected treasure. Your friendship. I hope I haven't lost that."

Tony took her free hand in his strong, warm one and squeezed. "That's all right, luv," he said in a terrible, broad accent. "It were the money I was after, right enough."

Malachi shook his head. "I don't associate with Wilmers. How about you, Harry?"

Harry straightened the front of her flannel shirt and lifted her chin. "I'm afraid Mrs. Woodfin is not a proper lady. If I befriended her, it might damage my reputation."

Lissy glared at them, through the blurring in her eyes. "Don't you dare make me laugh."

"Of course they're your friends, Mama," Wesley said. "Miss Jackson doesn't like mines. Major Wayne doesn't like sleeping on the ground. Mr. Kelly doesn't like Uncle Clay and Uncle Rafe. But they're all here anyway."

"I don't know," Malachi drawled, with a wink at Wesley. "Clay and Rafe sort of grow on you after awhile."

"I declare. Just wait until I have my salon in Denver." Lissy jingled her bag of coins at him. "When everyone who is anyone is a friend of mine. Then you'll come crawling back."

"You won't be in Denver," Tony said. "Let's saddle up our magnificent steeds while Mal keeps his eye on our friends' progress back toward the Lucky Lady."

He and Wesley started forward, but Lissy dug in her broken heels against the tug of their hands. "What do you mean I won't be in Denver? You don't think Clay and Rafe will come after me there?"

Or was Denver too close for Tony? Maybe he didn't want her in Colorado, didn't want to be reminded of her. Love 'em and leave 'em. So much easier that way.

She jerked on her hand, but he held it tight.

"You won't be in Denver because you'll be residing in Battlement Park."

Lissy's face reddened. On the other hand, Battlement Park was too close for her. She couldn't see Tony every day and pretend she felt nothing. The night before had been a mistake . . . She met Tony's steady eyes, and a taste of the night's wildness traveled through her veins, followed by the warmth of what she felt for him. No mistake. But she couldn't repeat it.

"I don't think so," she said with quiet, southern steel.

"Major Wayne was telling me all about Battlement Park on the ride yesterday," Wesley said, slanting a look up at her with bright gray eyes. "He's got a hotel where lots of famous people stay, even the governor of Colorado. And he's got horses we can ride. And he said he'd teach me how to fish for trout and we could go hunting. The elk are bigger than deer. And we might even see a mountain lion, but they don't look like lions, really, more like panthers. And—"

"And Major Wayne is very generous, Wes," Lissy said, shooting Tony a look that told him what she thought of his attempt to suborn her son. "But you'll like Denver, too. We'll have to make our living, and we can't do that in Battlement Park."

"You can," Tony said. He'd stopped trying to pull her along the path, but he still held tightly to her hand.

Lissy wondered why Harry and Malachi weren't rushing to her rescue. They had to know this was a bad idea.

"I have no intention of serving as your housekeeper, Major Wayne."

"I have no intention of asking you to be my housekeeper, Mrs. Woodfin," Tony said, but there was no mockery in his eyes, only resolve—and something warmer. "I'm asking you to be my wife."

Lissy slipped and might have fallen if Tony and Wesley hadn't been gripping her so firmly. And if she'd had a hand free, she might have struck Tony with it. She could feel her face flashing hot and cold.

"That is the most foolish, cruelest thing anyone has ever said to me."

It was Tony's turn to flush. "I say, that's not what I was aiming for."

She couldn't use the words she wanted in front of

Wesley, but her tone said them for her. "I am a married woman."

Tony shook his head. "You are a widow. Your husband was buried in a mine accident. Your brothers will ensure that he is declared dead so they can gain control of any remaining assets he may have in Savannah."

"You *are* mad, Anthony Wayne." She stared at him. "Charm's not dead; he's heading for Mexico right this minute. Wes saw him escape the cave-in, and Malachi saw the tracks."

"I saw tracks," Malachi said, his voice carefully neutral. "Anyone could have been riding those horses. Maybe Rat and Spider Grant."

"Papa was killed in the mine," Wesley said, turning her gaze to him. His chin hardened with stubbornness, the same way hers did. "That's what I told Uncle Clay. If he was still alive, Uncle Clay and Uncle Rafe would chase him forever. And then they'd kill him."

His eyes met hers defiantly, daring her to deny it.

Her own eyes, fierce as her son's, burned into Tony's. "How dare you put him up to this, you—" She cut herself off in time. "That's Wesley's father—"

"I didn't put Wesley up to anything," Tony said, his calm response infuriating her further. "He's a smart boy. He figured that out by himself."

She turned back to her son. "Wes, there's a difference between telling Uncle Clay your father's dead to protect him and knowing the difference ourselves."

Wesley dropped her hand and crossed his arms over his chest. "Will Papa ever come back for us?"

Lissy shook her head. "He can't, honey. He loves you, but . . ." Her voice broke on the words.

"Then there's no difference."

"It might be tricky to divorce a dead man, without arousing your brothers' suspicions," Tony said. "But I have some friends who owe me some favors. It might take a little time, but—"

Lissy snorted. "In seven years, Charm will be legally dead whether he survived that rock fall or not."

Tony caught her chin with his thumb and forefinger, holding her gaze with his. "I'll wait for you seven years, Lissy. If you say you'll have me then."

She wanted to mention all the widowed countesses he could have by then. She wanted to throw her agony at not being able to have him back in his face. But she could not do it, trapped by the simple sincerity in his eyes.

"Charm is Wesley's father," was all she could think to say.

"Papa's with Angelique," Wesley said, his voice small. But when she looked at him, his chin tilted in determination once more. "You need someone to protect you. Until I get older."

Lissy curled her free hand to keep from running it through his hair and spoiling his dignity. "I've learned a considerable amount about taking care of myself these past few weeks," she said instead.

No one responded. She turned to look back for Harry and Malachi.

Malachi shrugged. "And Tony says *I'm* difficult."

"Mal—"

"He's not Charm Woodfin, Lissy. But Battlement Park gets a lot of snow."

"I'll teach you how to shoot," Harry offered. "In case he gets out of hand."

Lissy turned back to Tony. He still gripped her hand as though he would never let her go, but now she could see the fear beneath his determination.

"Elizabeth, I've never asked anyone to marry me before. I seem to be making a bloody mess of it. But I've never cared for anyone the way I care for you. I love you."

Colorado was a long way from the social mores of Charleston or Savannah, but not far enough that she intended to respond to a statement like that in front of God and everyone on the side of a mountain before she'd even had breakfast.

Somehow, the thought of Harry's flapjacks brought back the tears.

"I declare, how can you say you love me when I look so frightful and haven't had a bath in days?"

The corner of Tony's mouth twitched, but there was no laughter in his eyes. "If I couldn't say it under those conditions, there wouldn't be much bloody point in saying it at all."

"Tony . . ." She met his eyes, but couldn't find the words to tell him what her heart felt. "I've made such terrible mistakes."

He nodded. "I've made one or two myself. I can't say this is right, just because I want it. I want you. Just tell me . . . Do you feel anything like that for me?"

She thought Tony might actually be holding his breath. Maybe Wesley and Harry and Malachi were, too, they were so silent. Maybe the mountain itself held its breath. All she could hear was her own heart pounding as she searched Tony's eyes.

Fear. She had only just been freed of the mundane misery of her life with Charm. Doubt. She'd known Tony barely a week and a half. Bewilderment. Her life had changed more in the past month than in the entire previous decade.

The only sure thing in all of the confusion seemed to be the steady flame in Tony's eyes. The way the sight of him, the strength of his hand in hers, calmed her soul and warmed her heart.

The Reverend Kelly had sent her west on her search for his sons with the words, " 'All things work together for good to them that love God.' "

She hadn't done much loving, of the Lord or anyone else in her life until Wesley came along. But maybe the Lord was looking out for her, anyway.

If she could only find a way to trust. The Reverend never tired of repeating that the right choice was always love. If it were only so easy to know what true love would have her do.

Yet the quiet of her heart knew enough to say, "I love you, Tony. I can't promise anything else right now. But I do love you."

"You love me?" He looked past her to Malachi and Harry, a smile blazing across his face. "She loves me."

He squeezed her hand so hard she thought her bones might crack, though she didn't care. "There's only one promise I want you to make right now. Just promise me you'll consider it. Marrying me. Tomorrow. Or seven years from now."

She shook her head, the tears streaming past her own smile. "Oh, all right. I'll consider it."

"Huzzah!"

Suddenly she was in Tony's arms, and he was spinning her with such enthusiasm, she felt certain her feet flew out over the cliff edge, though she closed her eyes so she couldn't see.

"I just said I'd think about it!" she reminded him when he finally set her down. But he just spun her once more until she laughed from dizziness.

Wesley's wiry arms wrapped around her waist, and then Harry was hugging her, laughing, too. And even Malachi put a hand on her shoulder and one on Tony's.

Lissy couldn't remember ever feeling as though she belonged anywhere as much as she did in their embrace at that very moment.

And if she hadn't worked through all the practical objections to marrying Tony, it was all right. She had plenty of time.

"He said seven years. I should at least get seven *days!*"

"Hold still," Harry ordered, ignoring Lissy's frequently repeated wail. "It's hard enough to get this collar to sit right without your histrionics."

She'd somehow managed to finish stitching the lace trim to Lissy's new collar while being jolted about on the bench of Tony's private coach, but it looked a little crooked now that she'd fastened it around Lissy's neck. Well, it was a miracle she hadn't sewn the edges together or pricked her finger and bled all over it. When they secured a fashionable black velvet ribbon around it, no one would notice the stitching.

"That will do," she decided. She still wanted to get the small veil attached to the tortoiseshell combs Tony had bought in Boulder before they reached Battlement Park that afternoon.

It had been Harry's idea that they spend Sunday in Boulder at church and resting. Tony had insisted on going shopping Monday to replace Lissy's and Harry's ruined clothes and the necessities they'd lost in Silvercrest. Between them, they'd managed to sneak in two days of rest and a doctor's care for Malachi.

Harry glanced up at the roof of the coach. Despite the continuing pain in his arm and a low-grade fever, Malachi had insisted on riding up front with the coach driver. Wesley rode between them, drinking in the scenery and Malachi's natural history lessons. Tony had ridden ahead from Longmont early that morning to prepare the Fox and Hound for their arrival and the wedding the next day.

Malachi had let Tony go, saying he doubted Clay and Rafe would follow them to Battlement Park, but his position riding shotgun on the coach was more than symbolic—he'd bought a Remington 10-gauge in Boulder. Harry wouldn't have admitted it to him, but she was glad.

She wasn't superstitious, but in the three days since their encounter with the Wilmer brothers, she'd lived with a curl of dread between her shoulder blades. Strangely enough, the sense of doom had only increased the closer they got to Battlement Park. And she wasn't even the one getting married the next day.

"I'm going to look like a German grandmother," Lissy said hopelessly, lifting a handful of the practical brown wool skirt she had bought in Boulder. It matched Harry's exactly, though Lissy's brushed the toes of her new boots, while Harry's came only to her ankles.

"The blouse is pretty," Harry offered. She had feared the wine-colored fabric might be too dark for Lissy's coloring, but the hue brought out Lissy's gray eyes and showed off the flame of silver-gold hair under her simple straw hat. But Harry didn't think her beauty had much to do with the color of her blouse, any more than the flush in her cheeks did.

Lissy's glow came from deep inside.

Though love hadn't altered her temperament. "Would you stop fussing with my collar? I declare, I feel like I'm being laid out for a viewing. I might as well be lying in a coffin. I'm already half afraid I've died and gone to heaven without noticing it."

"I don't think you've got to worry about heaven," Harry muttered, leaning across the center space between their benches to take back the collar.

"That's true enough."

Harry frowned at Lissy's pale smile. "Elizabeth Woodfin, if you go to hell, it's not going to be for marrying Tony. Even if you did decide not to wait seven years."

"I couldn't. Not after the past three nights."

"Tony's serenading convinced you to marry him?" Harry tried not to sound skeptical.

"Serenading?" Lissy asked. "I thought maybe he was having some kind of a fit. I realized that if he intended to do that every night for seven years, I had better marry him or I'd have to kill him. I've never heard anyone with less musical talent."

"I have," Harry assured her, thinking of her brother March's singing. "But I can see your point."

Lissy frowned down at her skirt, twisting the fabric with her fingers. "I had a talk with Malachi on the train yesterday afternoon. He said if God can forgive him for the men he has killed, God can forgive me for loving Tony. He said the Reverend said our duty to God is to love each other. But I've already failed at that with Charm."

Harry paused in knotting the last stitch in Lissy's collar. "Failed? I don't think you failed."

Lissy raised one pale eyebrow. "You're saying my eleven years with Charm were a hallucination? I didn't just fail to love him. I hated him." Lissy's cheeks reddened with feeling. "When I found out about Angelique, those years ago, I stopped loving him. When I found out he'd been stealing from Clay and Rafe, I despised him. And when I realized he'd taken Wes, I hated him."

"I hated my father." Harry hadn't meant to say that. She had not said those words in many years, but they burned her throat with harsh familiarity. "I did. I hated him. He loved his liquor more than he loved me and Jane and March. He didn't help when March got into trouble with outlaws. I knew he blamed me for my mother's death."

"Oh, Harry, you weren't to blame—"

"I told Elijah," Harry plunged on. "After Jane and Lucas took me and March away to Colorado, after March's brush with the law. 'Lije asked me if I missed my father, and I told him no. I hated him. I told 'Lije I was afraid I was going to hell because I didn't love my parents.

" 'Lije said love wasn't how you felt about somebody. It was how you treated them. He said I didn't have to want to live with my father again, I just had to forgive him and treat him with respect."

Harry could still feel how cold and hard her heart had been. "I couldn't do it. Jane wrote him letters, telling him how we were. She wanted me to add something, but I never would. When we heard that he'd died, I thought I'd be glad. But all I felt was horrible, that I'd never written him a letter."

"You were a child," Lissy said.

"I'm not a child now." Harry met her gaze steadily. "And if he hadn't died, I'd probably still be hating him. I couldn't have done what you did. Charm took your son and your life, left you to face the consequences of his actions, and ran off with his mistress. You let him go. You didn't shoot him. You didn't chase him down."

Lissy snorted. "That would have been too much trouble."

"And you protected him from your brothers." Harry let the comment hang for a moment. "It would have been easier to let them have him. Maybe even satisfying. But you risked their anger and your own safety to protect him, to give him a chance. He failed you. You didn't fail him."

"I promised to love him until death parted us."

"And death did part you," Harry pointed out. "No one else should have to die before you can be happy. You've been given a second chance."

Lissy took a deep breath. "There, that's it. That's why I told Tony I would go through with this. How many people get such a chance? It seemed . . . ungrateful . . . to throw it away."

"It takes courage to take that chance."

Harry's shoulder slammed the coach side as the wheels struck a particularly large rock. Lissy reached for the window, pushing up the glass and looking out to make sure her son hadn't been thrown to the bottom of the Little Fowler River canyon by the jolt.

Lissy slumped back against her seat. "I think I've used up any courage I ever had just reaching this point. I'm terrified. I don't know how Jordan went through it a third time."

Tony must have told her that Jordan had been widowed twice before her marriage to Elijah. Harry had never considered before what a risk Jordan had taken, falling in love with another man, much less a man like Elijah, a gunfighter who at one time had a price on his head.

And here was Lissy, brave enough to risk love again after eleven years of a disastrous marriage to Charm Woodfin.

"That takes a lot more courage than facing down Spider Grant." Harry didn't realize she'd spoken the thought aloud until Lissy laughed.

"Tony will be much more trouble than Spider ever was, I'm certain of that," she agreed. "But at least he's better looking."

"I'll tell him you said that."

"Don't you dare! He's vain enough as it is." But Lissy settled back with a curl of smile. "What about you? What about your wedding?"

It was a reasonable question. If only she had a reasonable answer to it. She leaned down to dig Lissy's combs and veil out of the bag at her feet. "What about it?"

"What about your feelings for Malachi?"

Harry jerked upright, dropping the combs.

"What are you talking about?" she squeaked, praying Malachi, Wesley, and the driver couldn't hear them. "That's not a reasonable question at all."

Lissy raised her pale brows. "It's not? Then pray tell me why you are turning such a charming shade of red."

"I am not." Clever response. Mrs. Danforth would be turning over in her grave, if she weren't an evil demon destined to live forever. Harry collected the combs, buying herself time. Not that all the time in the world would help her through this particular crisis. "Malachi doesn't want to marry me. Ash does."

"Are you sure about that?"

Harry felt as though she'd been kicked, although that might have been the coach hitting another bump in the road. "You mean after what he did in Denver? You're right. He wasn't much acting like someone's fiancé."

Which would solve one of her problems, but the other—

"No, I meant are you sure about *Malachi*." Lissy rolled her eyes in frustration. "Do you really care about what Ash thinks?"

"I'm sure. About Malachi." It hurt to think about him,

though she couldn't seem to stop. To think of what she had felt when she had kissed him in the mine, of how she would have regretted dying without having kissed him.

He had never mentioned the kiss. Not even alluded to it that night afterward. Pain and incipient fever hadn't brought forth anything sentimental from Malachi Kelly.

You still have plenty of time to get ready for your wedding.

"You're in love with him."

Harry met Lissy's eyes, and couldn't pretend she misunderstood whom Lissy meant. She couldn't say anything at all. Love. Had she really not understood before what a danger love was? How much it could hurt? *Friends are hazardous to one's peace of mind.*

"Harry?"

"Do you ever wish you'd married him?" she asked, the words breaking from her. "Instead of Charm?"

Lissy's gray eyes clouded as she thought. "Did I ever wish I'd taken the chance to escape Savannah, my family, all Charm put me through? A million times. But then I wouldn't have Wesley."

Her gaze sharpened on Harry. "Do I think I would have been happy married to Malachi? I didn't marry Charm just because he had prospects or because I wouldn't have to give up the comfort of my life in Savannah. I really was falling in love with him. And though I cared about Malachi, I think the idea of life with him frightened me a little.

"I need someone with softer edges. Someone who will tell me I'm beautiful, no matter how gray and wrinkled I become. And Mal . . ." She held Harry's gaze. "Mal needs someone who loves him for his honesty and won't let him get away with his rudeness. Someone like you."

Harry shook her head. "Mal thinks I'm a foolish girl, just like Elijah." She thrust a comb at Lissy. "Here, do something with this, so I can see what it's going to look like in your hair."

Lissy gave her a searching look as she took the comb. "Harry, if you want to talk . . ."

"We've got more pressing things to worry about than my wedding plans," Harry said. "You're the one who's going to the chopping block tomorrow."

Lissy let the matter drop. "I don't think I bear much resemblance to Ann Boleyn, but I do feel as if I've lost my head."

"Perfect love casteth out fear." Harry's grin was just a touch wicked. "As Elijah would say."

Lissy lifted off her hat and put in the comb. "I'm ready."

"No." Harry shook out the veil. "But you will be."

Harry set to work on Lissy's headpiece, the tedious, careful work taking on nearly heroic proportions against the brutal rocking and bumping of the coach.

She would rather have been plodding along on her ancient flea-bitten gray mare. But in Longmont they had put the horses on a train for Oxtail, with instructions for Colonel Treadwell to have them delivered to the Jackson Ranch. March would probably take their feed out of her wages, but she couldn't have borne the thought of the poor, gutsy animals being put down.

The one advantage to being thrown about in Tony's wretched luxury coach instead of riding was that the jolting kept her mind off what Lissy had said about Malachi. More or less.

By the time they rolled down the last stretch of the road into the Park, she'd even managed to put aside her nagging fear that something heavy and black was stalking them up the valley. Such concerns seemed foolish shadows in the face of the bright afternoon sun shining down on the rolling lawn of grass leading to the Fox and Hound's lodge.

The coach eased to a stop before the Fox and Hound's broad stairs. Harry threw open the coach door and breathed in the scent of pine and fresh water and maybe a hint of gingerbread from the lodge kitchens.

She hopped down and held the door for Lissy. "Safe at last," she said, turning to follow Lissy's glance up the stairs.

Tony strode through the double front doors, a peculiar expression on his face. "Harry, there you are. I wanted a chance to warn—"

Another man pushed past him, the younger man's fine features drawn together in a scowl. "Harriet! My God, where have you been?"

Harry sagged against the coach door. The black cloud hunting her hadn't been Clay and Rafe Wilmer at all.

"Ash," she said. "Hell and damnation."

Chapter 21

"Harriet, what are you doing here?"

Harry shook her head, trying to clear it. "What are *you* doing here?"

Ash stopped halfway down the steps to stare at her. "I'm looking for you. You were supposed to be waiting for me in Oxtail. Then March said you were here. Then I found out you'd gone to Denver . . . What is going on?"

Harry could hear the coach driver unloading their meager possessions and the boxes of tea and coffee and other necessities Tony had purchased for the hotel while the horses snuffled and shifted and shook their heads behind her.

If she just climbed back on the coach . . .

"Why, Mr. Brady," Lissy said in her most lilting drawl as she stepped forward to offer him her hand. "I do declare, it's a pleasure to see you again. How was your trip home to . . . Where is it? South Park? Such practical names you have out here in the West. How is your poor brother?"

Harry might have felt sorry for Ash if she hadn't wanted to murder him.

"Lionel? He's all right, I guess. He'll live. My father sent me to Denver on business, so I thought I'd run up to Oxtail to see my fiancée, but she—"

"I see you've met *my* fiancé," Lissy said, smiling up at Tony with a why-didn't-you-warn-us-you-bloody-Brit smile. "And I would like to introduce you to my son, Wesley. Wes, this is Mr. Ashton Brady."

Wesley dropped down from the coach to stand beside Harry.

"And this is Mr. Malachi Kelly," Lissy continued. "He's been a good friend of my family for many years."

"I thought he was your brother," Ash said, eyes narrowing.

"Oh, mercy no." Lissy laughed at the silly misunderstanding. Harry had to admire her iron nerve. "Although Malachi and Elijah have been better than brothers to me. Won't you come inside and join us for tea, Mr. Brady? That carriage ride has nearly done me in. I am in dire need of refreshment."

She offered him her arm, but apparently a western gentleman's roots didn't run quite so deep as she was used to, and he brushed past her down the stairs.

"Harriet, you've got some explaining to do. Come."

"Miss Jackson is not a dog, sir."

Harry glanced up to see Malachi sitting on the coach seat, his shotgun still lying across his lap. Wesley took a protective step in front of her.

"Oh, honestly." Harry squeezed Wesley's shoulder as she detoured around him. "It's all right. Let's go for a walk, Ash."

Confusion flashed in Ash's hazel eyes. For a moment he stood stiffly, scowling at Malachi and Wesley, but when Harry started out along the path around the lodge, he followed.

She could hear the anger in the tattoo of his steps as he

caught up with her. But he didn't speak as they circled the lodge and walked into the meadow beyond. Unlike the sweeps of grass and scrub around Oxtail, burned shades of bronze and gold by the late summer sun, this montane meadow still smelled wet and alive, though the cold nights had begun to bleach the stems of the sedges.

"It will be winter soon," Harry said, watching the shadow of a cloud pass across the crenellated ridge ahead of them.

"Harriet, what is going on?" Ash grabbed her arm to halt her. "Where the hell have you been?"

"Denver." She faced him, for the first time since she had seen him enter the South Platte Saloon. She had half expected him to look different, harder, perhaps, or slyer than she had thought him before. But he only looked flustered and out-of-place, and determined not to show it. "Lissy needed help."

"I told you not to go with that woman." Anger flared away the confusion. "I told you. What did you think you were doing?"

"Helping out a friend."

"You didn't even know her!" He glared at her.

She crossed her arms over her chest. Why had she ever been so afraid to be herself around him? "She is now."

"So you ignored a direct order from your husband to gallivant off into the countryside with a stranger? A stranger whose morals seem a little questionable, if you ask me."

Harry blinked, stunned. "Direct order? What do you mean by that? And you're not my husband yet."

"I will be, in just two weeks, or have you forgotten? Why aren't you home packing to move? I thought that's why you couldn't elope with me. You needed the time. What the hell were you doing in Denver?"

Righteous anger flushed his cheeks, and perhaps that was what finally ignited her outrage.

"As I said, I was helping a friend. What were *you* doing in Denver?"

He met her glare with his own for two or three heartbeats, until her tone registered. His gaze faltered, and he flushed deeper.

"What are you talking about? I was conducting business for my father."

She waited.

"Damn it." He sputtered in indignation. "March said he wouldn't say anything to you."

Knowing March, what he'd actually said was that he wouldn't say anything until Ash had a chance to talk with her first. That's what he'd said to Harry the time she'd gotten buried in a book and forgot to check Jane's peach cobbler and burned it to a crisp. And the time she tied Lemuel's suspenders together and tried to swing from the hay loft rafters on them. And the time . . .

"What do *you* have to say?" she asked.

"I'm a man," Ash said, blustering. "You wouldn't understand. You don't know how hard it has been waiting for our wedding. I've been a gentleman with you, haven't I?"

"So you couldn't control yourself?" She wondered how he thought that would improve her opinion of him. "Except around me."

"I treated you like a lady." His expression as he examined her indicated he was revising his estimation of her. "Maybe that was my mistake."

Before she guessed his intention, he grabbed her by the shoulders and pulled her to him. He took her hair in one hand to hold her steady while he crushed his mouth on hers. Harry's heart thudded in her chest, like the heart of a mouse that's been snatched by a weasel's jaws.

The last time they had talked, Ash had told her she didn't have the muscles for farm work, but she pushed him away with enough force to rock him back on his heels.

"Stop that!"

"See?" Ash was panting with his own anger. "You want to be treated like a lady. You just don't want to have to act like one."

He found his mark with that one. Harry struggled to breathe, to control herself.

"The hotel proprietor here said the passenger coach can return to Longmont tonight," Ash said, wiping the back of his arm across his mouth. "I'm taking you away from here. Away from these people. Back where you belong."

"I'm not going back to Longmont tonight." Where *did* she belong? "Lissy and Tony are getting married tomorrow."

"They hardly need you for that." His mouth twisted mockingly. "I think it's generally accepted that it's only the wedding night they'll remember."

Harry looked at his face, the perfect line of his jaw, the gold-flecked flash of his eyes behind thick lashes, the haughty set of his chin, and her heart wrenched at how empty she felt.

"I said I'd be here and I will."

Color stained his cheekbones again, running up the bridge of his nose. "You won't. You're coming with me. I won't have you consorting with these people."

Harry stepped back. She was not going to let him drag her back to the coach. But she could see the bewilderment beneath his anger, could see him wondering where his compliant, ladylike Harriet had gone.

And for a moment, she wanted to be that Harriet for

him. Take his hand and let him lead her into the life he had planned for her. A good life. Or at least a pleasant one. With enough money for leisure time. Pretty clothes and a feather bed. Their children would never go hungry. They could send their sons to Harvard or Yale. Their girls to Mrs. Danforth's Finishing School for Young Ladies.

Harry shuddered.

"If you don't want to consort with my friends, then I don't think you really want to consort with me."

Ash cocked his head, as though he hadn't heard her correctly. "Harriet, I don't know what has gotten into you, but I don't intend to put up with it."

Harry hugged herself against the cold, though her fingertips and cheeks felt hot. "I understand."

He nodded, slowly. "Good. Then you'll get your things and join me on the coach."

He turned to go.

"No, Ash. I won't."

He looked back at her, and there was no bewilderment left to soften his eyes. "You'll be on that coach in ten minutes, or you can take all the time you want to get back to Oxtail. You won't have anything there to get ready for."

"I understand," she repeated.

He stared at her for a long moment, long enough to see the tears and the certainty in her eyes. Then, abruptly, he strode away toward the hotel, his back rigid, his long strides stretched to their limit.

He wasn't Charm Woodfin. He would never steal from his father's business, would never run away from his responsibilities. Marriage to Ashton Brady would protect her from backbreaking work and poverty for the rest of her days. She would have a husband. Children.

And if she didn't marry? She would have the satisfaction

of knowing she had stood by her principles and not married a man she didn't love.

That ought to be a great comfort to her as a spinster living on her brother's charity.

She could still catch up with him, still apologize. It would take the driver some time to change the horses and prepare for the long, jolting ride back to Longmont. But she stood and watched as Ash's tall, achingly handsome figure disappeared around the corner of the lodge.

Involuntarily, her gaze flicked to the porch across the back of the building. She had known Malachi would be there, shotgun in hand. Damn him. At least he was far enough away he couldn't see her tears.

Malachi Kelly, Justice of the Peace for Battlement Park, Colorado, stood before the extravagantly tall windows at the far end of the Fox and Hound's entrance room, his back to the even more extravagant view beyond them.

A whispering snowfall had dusted the mountains the night before. Low clouds swathed the peaks to the west in ermine-trimmed cloaks of gray, but the ridge above the meadow behind the lodge flashed with diamond light in the late morning sun.

Major Anthony Wayne stood beside Malachi, his wheat-blond hair touched with gold, his royal blue jacket setting off the blinding white of his shirt, a bright contrast to Malachi's black shirt, black suit and dampened dark hair.

For once, Tony's face matched Malachi's for soberness. At least until he caught sight of Harry and Jordan leading Lissy down the side hallway toward him.

Harry's throat caught at the smile that turned Tony's lips, that lit his eyes. She thought he would have run over and swept Lissy into his arms to carry her the rest of the way into the entrance room if Elijah had not stood on his other side, the look in the gunfighter's eyes just enough of a deterrent.

Wesley Woodfin broke away from the group by the window and hurried over to escort his mother to her groom. The boy's green jacket and slacks, livery borrowed from one of the Fox and Hound's stable boys, hung large on him, but he wore them with smart dignity as he offered his mother his arm.

Tears clouded Lissy's eyes, but not her smile, as she touched her fingers to her son's elbow and followed him to Tony's side. Harry knew Lissy worried that the boy's distress at his father's abduction and then desertion of him went much deeper than he would let anyone see.

Yet Harry thought Wesley's innate good sense would serve him well, as would his mother's love and Tony's friendship. And he would have Malachi, too, if he needed someone impartial to talk with. Harry had seen Malachi draw out his nephew, Wolf, with nothing more than a quiet word and an understanding nod.

If only Malachi could relate to adults so well.

Jordan continued on to stand by Elijah's side, but Harry moved only to the edge of the well-wishers gathered around. The employees of the Fox and Hound, their families, and what looked to be most of the other residents of Battlement Park had come to celebrate Tony's wedding and meet his bride.

Harry's gaze strayed to Malachi, his sharp questions more suggestive of a criminal interrogation than a wedding. He had abandoned his sling for the ceremony. Dr. Gottfried said he might never regain full strength in his left arm, but he was lucky to have use of it at all.

Maybe that was true of his heart, as well. Harry was beginning to understand why someone would avoid loving another. Sometimes the pain was too much to bear. It hurt to look at him.

"By the power invested in me, as a Justice of the Peace for the State of Colorado, I now pronounce you man and wife. God help us all."

"Amen." Tony's grin lit the room. "Now I'm going to kiss my wife."

But it was Lissy who grabbed his collar and pulled his face down to hers.

The gathered crowd cheered.

"About time somebody put a halter on that mad Brit," one rancher shouted.

"Where's the food?" another demanded.

"Forget the food," the first one said. "Where's the beer?"

"Forget the bloody beer, Huell," Tony called back. "I need a shot of whiskey!"

Laughter followed him as he led Lissy down the hall toward the Fox and Hound's dining room.

Harry didn't have to turn her head to know who it was who fell in beside her as she trailed after the crowd.

"Almost enough to make you sick," she quoted, her self-deprecating smile as steady as Mrs. Danforth's Finishing School for Young Ladies could make it.

"Harriet Jackson, don't tell me this joyous occasion doesn't warm your heart."

"I wish Lissy and Tony all the happiness in the world." She risked a glance at Malachi. His eyes paused on hers for a long moment, as green as Charm's emeralds and as enigmatic. "I hope marriage only increases their happiness."

Malachi paused at the end of the windows, just before the hall to the dining room. He ran a hand through his hair.

"I damn well hope so, too. I'm starting to feel responsible. Marrying all these blasted fools."

"Brave fools," Harry retorted.

"There are many kinds of bravery," Malachi said, his expression darkening. "Not all of them involve charging into a situation without thinking about the consequences first."

Harry slanted him her best coquettish smile, though someone seemed to have run a knife through her heart. She tried on Lissy's drawl. "Mr. Kelly. I do declare. This is starting to sound awfully familiar. Are you about not to propose to me again?"

"Harry, you . . ." Something unreadable flickered in his eyes. "Hell and damnation. I—"

A hand settled on Harry's shoulder and another on Malachi's before he could reply.

"All right, what were you two talking about that was so bloody serious? This is my wedding day, and I won't stand for anything less than proper good cheer."

"I think if you pack any more cheer into this room, the roof is going to blow off," Malachi said. He scowled. "You're right, Harry. This whole day is too damned familiar."

She almost laughed. It certainly was. Hard to believe her heart could break so completely twice in one year.

Tony grinned. "You have a way with words, Mal. And it's time to put them to good use. I've come to drag you in to make a toast."

"You *are* mad."

"We can't start the drinking without a toast. And as my best friend, you must give it."

Malachi grimaced. "Even you can't be that hard up for friends."

"Buck up, old man. The briefer you are, the happier everyone will be."

Tony cuffed Malachi on the back of the head and pushed him toward the dining room. Malachi glanced back at Harry, though she couldn't tell from his expression if he regretted their conversation being interrupted or was simply begging her to rescue him. She had no intention of obliging. He deserved whatever ingenious torture Tony had planned.

When the two of them disappeared into the dining room, Harry slipped out the small side door onto the porch that ran along the back of the hotel.

The chill air shocked her lungs, bracing her against the other pain that filled her chest. The morning had dawned cold enough to rim standing pools with ice, but the early sun had warmed the air and the gathering clouds had stilled it, so Harry barely felt the breath of frost on her cheek.

"I gather you needed some fresh air, too."

Harry turned to see Elijah close the door behind him as he stepped out onto the porch beside her. He had shown the sense to bring a coat with him, but when he silently offered it to her, Harry suspected his appearance on the porch was not so coincidental as it seemed.

She shook her head to the coat, turning back to the view of the meadow and the mountains beyond.

"Malachi told me once I shouldn't let anyone stifle my freedom," she said. "As long as I can breathe this air I'll feel free."

"It can fill you with its clarity." Elijah folded his coat over the porch railing and leaned his forearms against it. "Help you look past the clutter to what matters."

Harry leaned against the rail beside him. "You always seem to understand what I meant to say."

He glanced at her, the oblique light slanting flat across

his eyes. "I didn't have a chance to talk with you after Jordan and I were married."

"We've known each other a long time, 'Lije. There was nothing you had to say." She flickered a smile at him. "Thank God you didn't try."

His own smile flashed back, relieved at the relief in her voice. " 'Let every man be swift to hear, slow to speak.' " His long hands worked the collar of the coat. "So, then, these are slowly considered words. If you ever need help, Jordan and I are here."

"I know that." She wrinkled her nose in mock irritation. "Honestly."

"We were talking . . . Your Mr. Brady didn't look very happy when he left yesterday."

Harry shook her head, watching the cloud shadows flow across the icy peaks. "Do you think . . . Do you think you can be happy settling for something else if you can't have what you want?"

"Harry?"

It took her a moment to recognize where the trepidation in his voice came from.

"I don't mean that, 'Lije." She had never told him how she felt about him, and he had been too kind ever to allude to her crush, but she had not fooled herself into thinking he hadn't noticed it. "I mean Ash. He wanted me to be someone I'm not. But maybe I could have been. It wouldn't be a bad life."

"I think God has given us a remarkable grace to find joy in even difficult circumstances." Elijah paused, choosing his words. "But when it comes to marriage, we can't consider only ourselves. I didn't know if I was the right person to make Jordan happy, but I did know I would spend my life trying to be."

"It makes me happy, to see how happy you are together. Truly, 'Lije, I'm so glad you've finally found some peace."

The words shook, but from conviction, not lack of it.

He reached over to squeeze her hand on the rail. "You're a good friend, Harriet. Don't forget that Jordan and I are your friends, too."

Harry nodded. "I know you all have my best interests at heart. But there are some mistakes you can't fix for me. But maybe I've learned enough from my friends that I can face them. 'Perfect love casteth out fear.' " She managed a smile. "It's time for me to go home."

Time to face the future. Time to quit dreaming about a life she couldn't have.

Elijah turned a glance upward. "Maybe not for a couple of days. It smells like snow. But we'll get you down to the train in Longmont as soon as we can."

Harry nodded. Snow. It was tempting. Stay snowed in at Battlement Park. A few more days to spend close to Malachi. They could take Wesley snowshoeing. Teach Lissy how to use a rifle.

She would give almost anything for those few days, a few more hours of their friendship. No matter the agony of knowing she'd have to leave. No matter that she might do or say something that could damage their friendship forever, that might hurt Malachi as badly as her broken heart hurt.

Tempting.

"Are you ready to face Tony's party?" Elijah asked.

"Almost. In a minute."

He squeezed her hand again. "All right."

The door closed softly behind him, and she was left alone on the porch. She stood still for a long moment afterward, giving him time to return to the crowded dining room where she would not be missed. Then she scrambled down the stairs that led to the meadow path below the lodge.

She hurried along the path, turning off onto the branch that led into the trees, heading for Jordan and Elijah's cabin.

It would not take her long to pack her few belongings. Portia would be eager for the ride. She could beat the storm home to the ranch.

She had told Elijah she was mature enough to make her own mistakes and face the consequences. She smiled a small, dry smile. Funny how sometimes the mature, thoughtful decision looked a lot like a typical Harry scrape. At least she was on familiar ground.

Once out of sight of the lodge, she broke into a decidedly unladylike run.

Chapter 22

Laughter and loud voices pounded against Mal's head, along with the smells of gravy and wool suits. The air tasted of tobacco smoke and alcohol fumes. He gripped his glass of whiskey so tightly his hand ached, but he couldn't drink it. The smell nauseated him.

Dr. Gottfried had pronounced him free of his fever that morning, but standing so long in such close quarters with this boisterous crowd left him feeling weak and dizzy.

He caught sight of Tony coming in from the kitchen and pushed his way over to the groom.

"I'm going out to get some air."

"Oh, no you don't!" Tony grabbed his arm. "You still have to give that toast."

"I think the drinking's well under way as it is."

"I couldn't interrupt everyone's eating," Tony said, gesturing to the remains of the feast scattered across the serving table.

It looked to Mal as though wolves had been at the deer. He wouldn't have wanted to interrupt those eaters, either.

"It's a party, Mal. You're supposed to look happy."

"It's a great party." Mal gestured to the guests. "They're

happy. You're happy. I'll be happy as soon as I can get the hell out of here."

"Mal wants to go?" Lissy had scooted through a break in the crowd to join her new husband. "Are you feeling all right? He's recuperating, Tony. Let him go lie down."

"He's all right," Tony insisted. "He's just mad because I got his girl."

Tony slipped an arm around her waist and pulled her to his side. Lissy's cheeks reddened. Mal had never seen so much color in her face before.

"She made a good choice," Mal assured him. "And the next time she gets into trouble, she's all yours."

Tony laughed. "Fair enough. All right, I'll get you out of here. Attention!" His martial bellow cut through the noise of conversation, turning heads toward them. "We're going to have a toast."

Scattered cheers and groans met his announcement.

"All right, all right. Give my friend Malachi a minute of your time and you can get back to the beer. Right? Capital. The floor is yours, old man."

Gritting his teeth against his instinctual reaction to bolt, Mal held up his whiskey glass. "I'm not big on weddings," he said. "But Anthony Wayne is a lucky man. He's found the love of his life, and she's mad enough to marry him. May their love endure."

The celebrants cheered, beer glasses tilted. Tony draped a companionable arm across Mal's shoulders. "Short and to the point. I knew you could dredge up some sentimental drivel from somewhere."

"I meant every word," Mal objected. And he had. It had occurred to him with brutal suddenness that Tony was indeed a lucky man. Whatever he might face in the future, for this moment, to have someone he loved love him back so deeply, he was one of the most blessed men Mal knew.

Lissy escaped from her husband's arm long enough to give Mal a kiss on the cheek.

"Thank you." Her soft, southern voice held all the joy of a honeysuckle-sweet spring breeze. "For everything."

Tony dropped his hand from Mal's shoulder to pull her back to him. "That's enough of that, wife."

Lissy laughed. "Just because I'm married doesn't mean I can't thank a friend."

"I'm grateful to him, too," Tony assured her. "But I don't plan to bloody kiss him."

"Just remember," Mal told Lissy. "If he gives you any trouble, you can always call on your brothers."

Lissy's eyes darkened. "If I get more luck than I deserve, I will never set eyes on Clay and Rafe again."

"I don't mean Clay and Rafe." Mal gestured toward Elijah, who was making his way across the room toward them, Jordan at his side. "I mean your real brothers. Between the two of us, we can take care of one mad Englishman."

Lissy smiled, patting the chest of her Englishman. "Why, thank you, brother. I'll keep that in mind."

"Elijah!" Tony grabbed Elijah's hand and pulled him in for an enthusiastic embrace, fully enjoying the gunfighter's annoyance. "I've just discovered you're to be my brother-in-law. A significant improvement over my own family, I must say."

"Wonderful," Elijah muttered as Tony turned to Jordan, embracing her, as well. "Look, Tony, I don't want to interrupt the celebration, but we've got a problem. Can we talk outside?"

At the expression on Elijah's and Jordan's faces, Tony sobered immediately. "Right. Through the kitchen. No one will notice if we disappear for a few minutes."

Mal followed his brother through the kitchen door, Tony, Lissy, and Jordan close on his heels. Another horse thief, he thought. Or maybe a rustled cow. Anything, as long as it got him away from the noise and the bodies and the overwhelming good cheer.

The kitchen offered no sanctuary. The Norwegian chef stood red-faced and shouting in the center of the room. Cooks and servers and dishwashers scurried around him with piles of dirty plates, trays of dense cakes and fluffy meringue pies, and a general look of orchestrated panic.

Mal dodged through the chaos, finally spilling out the back door into the yard behind the stables. As he breathed in the clear, cold air, he felt a sincere gratitude to the cattle rustlers for enabling his escape.

"Here we are, then," Tony said, unable to suppress his good humor. "Starting to feel like old times. The good old days. They feel like just yesterday. Now, if we—"

"What's the problem?" Mal broke in, deftly rescuing his friend from Elijah's simmering frustration. The more time they wasted, the farther away the rustlers would get.

"It's Harriet."

Mal's brain, sluggish from the food and the socializing, jerked to a halt. "Harry's been rustling cattle?"

Elijah stared at him. "What are you talking about?"

"What are *you* talking about?"

"Harry," Jordan said impatiently. "Wesley wanted to take one of the deer bones to Loki, so we walked up to the cabin together. All of Harry's things are gone."

A strange empty place expanded in Mal's gut. He'd never liked crowds of people. But it turned out that wasn't what had felt so wrong about the wedding feast.

"Gone?" Tony repeated. "She's probably just moved

them down to the lodge. She didn't want to be in your way, and I did offer her a room."

"Portia's gone, too," Elijah said. "Harriet said it was time for her to go home. I told her she might not be able to leave for a few days if we get a good snow."

Mal looked up at the swollen clouds crowding across the remaining patches of blue sky. He started for the stable, his stomach beginning to roll, slow and cold. The others followed.

"Hell and damnation, 'Lije," he growled. "Why didn't you just tell her, 'well, Harry, if you don't want to get stuck here for a week, you should ride off into the wilderness all by yourself into a blizzard'? Damn it. What's so all-fired important she couldn't wait a couple of days?"

"Oh, bother," Tony said heavily. "I'm afraid I might know. That bastard Brady told her if she didn't go back with him, the wedding was off. Perhaps she decided to go after him."

Elijah frowned. "She didn't tell me that."

"She told Lissy," Tony said. Beside him, Lissy nodded. "But she can't mean to go through with the wedding. That Brady's a bloody fool."

"She told Lissy that, too?" Elijah asked.

"She didn't need to," Lissy said acidly. "We saw him in Denver."

"Acting like an ass," Tony added. "Entering a brothel."

Mal didn't think he'd ever forget the look on Harry's face as they rode the streetcar back from the South Platte Saloon. Gray and fixed. Betrayed. Her eyes had turned older, colder, and there had been nothing he could do to reassure her. He had seen how people coped with betrayal. How so often the hurt was buried beneath politeness, the fire of life dimmed by pretense and making do.

"Why didn't any of you tell me about this?" Elijah demanded.

Mal met his brother's gaze with one just as fierce. "Because it was none of your damn business."

They'd reached the front of the stables, and Mal threw his shoulder into the door, pushing it aside, ignoring the pain that shot up his arm.

"Lissy and Jordan can put together some food and blankets," Elijah said, grabbing Mal's sleeve to hold him back. "You and I can split up the search."

"I'm in, too," Tony said, grabbing Lissy's hand. "I think my bride will understand."

"You can do whatever the hell you want," Mal said, shaking free of his brother's hold. "I'm going now."

"Wait." His brother's tone held him tighter than Elijah's grip. "If she wants to marry this boy, you can't stop her." Elijah's eyes softened only slightly. "I've seen the way you look at her, Mal."

Tony and Lissy and Jordan. He could see it in their faces. They all knew. Damn it, he didn't even know how he felt, how could they?

But he did know. Of course he loved her. Her courage. Her integrity. Her refusal to be cowed by his bluntness. Her optimism. Her loyalty. The way she set her jaw when she was about to fire her rifle and blow his marksmanship away.

The way her smile started at the corner of her mouth, a dainty, ladylike curl and then spread irresistibly across the rest of her face until her eyes danced with it.

"It doesn't matter if Harry marries Ashton Brady." He didn't have a heart. It didn't matter if it broke. "It doesn't matter who she loves." Even if it was his brother. "The only damn thing that matters is Harry wandering around lost in a snowstorm."

"You can't wander off after her, unprepared," Elijah said, his voice rough with feeling.

Mal met the eyes of his friends, letting them see the fear in his own. "She's already got at least an hour start on us. I might be able to move fast enough to catch her, but once that snow starts to fall—and it's going to start soon—I'll lose all chance of tracking her.

"If you want to help, get me out of here. Now."

Harry had been caught out in a snowstorm in the mountains once before. It had been spring. One of the pregnant mares had gone missing. She and March and the mare and her newborn foal had spent a night holed up in the lee of a rockfall out of the wind. A downed tree had provided firewood, and March had provided the storytelling. At twelve, it had all seemed a grand adventure.

Watching the fat, heavy flakes accumulate on Portia's forelock, Harry thought she'd had just about enough adventure for one year.

She glanced at the sky. Gray and looming, from what she could see through the drifting white. The snow had started with a few, bright flakes, as the forest became so quiet she could hear her own heartbeat. Despite her knowledge of the danger, she felt the touch of magic in a snowfall, and it seemed all of creation did, too, stilling to silence as if waiting for a miracle.

Harry had hoped the clouds would settle for a light dusting of brilliance, as it had the night before, but now the snow was falling thick enough to stick to her lashes and clog her nose if she tilted her face to the sky.

The narrow, ill-defined trail she and Portia followed dropped into a copse of Douglas fir, giving her a momentary respite from the suffocating flakes. The mare shook her head, scattering snow, giving her bridle a cheerful jingle.

From the protection of the trees, Harry looked out at what she could see of the foothills sloping down toward the plains. Not much. With the clouds low and thick, twilight was gathering quickly, regardless of the clock.

She couldn't have more than five or six miles to go, but they were five or six miles through rock-strewn gullies and over steep embankments. It would take much more daylight than she had left to reach the ranch.

She could see March's frown of disappointment that she would be so impulsive as to rush out into bad weather. She could hear Elijah's lecture and Malachi's exasperated sigh.

Or she wished she could. Even having to swallow her pride and admit that, just possibly, she should have shown a little more patience, despite its being overrated as a virtue, would be better than sitting here all alone in the growing dusk, listening to the whisper of cold, smothering peril.

Portia snorted, white clouds steaming from her nostrils. Harry patted the mare's neck, feeling the warmth on her chill fingers even through her gloves.

She knew she had to move. It had to be the right move, though. The wrong move at this moment would be as deadly as sitting still. There was no way she could reach home before dark.

She was going to be stuck out in the mountains overnight.

Mal ran.

The bright sunlight early that morning had melted the snow from the night before, softening the ground enough so even Portia's dainty hooves made distinct tracks in the damp earth. Mal's eyes flicked from one print to the next as he ran alongside her trail, his horse clopping steadily behind him.

Only once so far had he had to double back, at a rocky stream crossing. A broken pine branch had guided him forward again.

Even on foot, leading his horse—well, Elijah's horse, Rover—he was moving faster than Harry and Portia.

But it wasn't fast enough.

He paused, breath ragged in his lungs, at a bend in the trail where a rise gave him a long view down into the next gully.

Let me see her. Please, let her be there. But there was nothing but the burble of the autumn-slow creek.

Mal's lungs burned, his legs were weak from his bout of fever, his injured arm throbbed all the way up into his brain, but he plunged on down into the gully.

The first snowflakes had melted as they struck the warmer ground, but now they were beginning to stick, slowly filling in the only trace he had of Harry's path.

He moved too quickly, and his feet slid out from under him on the slick glaze of snow. Only his grip on Rover's reins kept him from a dangerous fall into the rocks and water below. As he regained his balance, he realized he was shaking with unaccustomed fear.

In this weather, a broken leg or a dunk in the creek could cost him a life. And it wasn't his life that he feared for.

Chapter 23

Harry wasn't sure what woke her. The cold, the damp, the tree roots stabbing into her rib cage were all familiar enough by now not to severely impinge on her unconsciousness.

She struggled to sit up. Despite the shelter of the embankment and the cover of the trees where she had set up camp, she had to shake a fine layer of white off her blanket.

Her fire still burned. She added some more wood. The damp outer wood smoked, but the inner wood was dry, and it flared up quickly. In the still air, the heat didn't dissipate too quickly for her to enjoy it.

Portia stood quietly nearby, her head to the rocky bank, her rump dusted with white. She snorted softly at Harry's attention, but seemed comfortable enough to weather the night.

The snowfall had stopped by the time Harry had gotten her fire started that evening. She had hoped that was the end of it. A couple of inches of snow wouldn't keep her from reaching the ranch in the morning. But now it had picked up again. She could hear it, whispering in the trees.

It was too early for this much snow. But here it was.

Still, there was no use panicking about it. If it didn't stop by morning, she would let herself panic. But not yet. She had an abundant water supply drifting down from the sky. She had two sandwiches left from the ones she'd made in Jordan's kitchen, as well as some jerked beef, two apples and a hunk of cheese. She had fire, plenty of wood from a ponderosa that had fallen and shattered on some rocks nearby. She had Portia for company and her own good rifle stuck in her saddle holster.

Compared to facing down the Wilmer brothers and their thugs, this was nothing. The only beasts she had to worry about were wolves and bears and mountain lions, and they were probably all holed up in their cozy dens just as she was.

She was settling back down onto her bedroll when she heard the muffled crunching of something moving through the trees uphill from her shelter.

Harry's heart jumped, and so did she, as she scrambled for the rifle stuck in her saddle.

Limbs creaked, and she heard the whoosh of snow dumping to the ground. Whatever was moving out there in the thick blackness beyond the firelight, it was big. And it was heading straight toward her camp.

For just a second, primitive instincts whispered to her brain that there could be worse things than bears and wolves lurking deep in the hills at midnight.

But then she heard the jingle of a bridle and the snort of a horse's breath. As far as she knew, ghosts and ghouls and hot-breathed demons didn't ride horses. And against all other beasts, her rifle gave her a fighting chance.

She slipped out of the firelight into the trees to wait, lifting the rifle butt to her shoulder.

Moments later, the shuffling horse entered the small open space along the bank. Though she'd dismissed the idea of ghosts, Harry's pulse still skipped a little at the strange beast that stumbled to a halt beside Portia.

Frosted with white from drooping head to sagging tail, with the slumped figure on its back smoothed into its frame like the hump of some arctic camel, it hardly looked like a horse at all. Until its ears twitched, and its head came up to whicker a greeting to Portia.

The camel's hump moved then, shedding its top layer of snow.

"Can't stop, Rover," it croaked. Green eyes, startled as a deer's, blinked against the firelight. "Hell and damnation. I've started hallucinating."

"Malachi Kelly." A familiar voice penetrated Mal's cold-fogged brain. "I could have blown your fool head off. What the hell are you doing riding around in the dark in a snowstorm."

"You'd think," he said, lifting his head just enough to see a rifle-toting vision step into the firelight, "that a hallucination would be more friendly."

"Get off that horse," Harry ordered, thrusting her rifle back into its holster. "He's just recovered from pneumonia from your brother getting him caught in a blizzard last winter. What was 'Lije thinking, letting you take him out in this?"

"Elijah was thinking Rover wouldn't get lost between Battlement Park and Oxtail. He was worried about you freezing to death." Malachi was thinking that both his fears for Harry's safety and his unacknowledged fantasy of some kind of heroic rescue had been badly exaggerated.

"Do I look like I'm freezing to death?" Harry asked.

No. And he was very glad. Though she could have pretended a little, to make him feel better.

"Does Rover look sick?" he countered.

In fact, the bright-eyed Rover had quit trying to nibble Portia's ear, and was snaking his nose toward where Harry's saddlebags lay next to her saddle.

"Those are *my* sandwiches," Harry told him firmly, nudging him back toward Portia. "Malachi, get off that horse so I can unsaddle him and rub him down. He was smart enough to save your life; he deserves a little attention."

Malachi shifted toward her, a movement that seemed to take more effort than it should. He stopped. "What if you are a hallucination? I could fall into a snowbank to freeze to death." He thought about that for a minute. It had to be better than the past God-only-knew-how-many hours bumping along on Rover's back. "Just promise not to disappear before I die."

"Ha, ha," Harry said. But as she glared at him, her expression began to change. Perhaps it was occurring to her that someone who had suffered a serious knife wound, significant blood loss and fever just days before and had been riding half the night through freezing cold and snow without so much as a decent meal might not be joking about hallucinations.

"Mal?" She grabbed the sleeve of his coat to hold him steady and reached for where his head rested on Rover's neck. Her hand felt reassuringly warm and human. "You're clammy."

"Possibly."

"Come on. Let's get you down."

She pulled, and he slid, shedding snow all over her as he swung heavily to the ground. He hung on to Rover's neck. He wasn't sure where his feet were.

"Are your fingers and toes cold?"

"I can't feel them."

"Hell and damnation." She grabbed his arm to throw it over her shoulder.

"Ahhh." His knees buckled, and he almost fell. "Other arm," he gasped.

She slipped under his right arm. He couldn't help liking having her so close. He thought he'd humor her concern for a little longer, but when he let go of Rover, he found himself sagging heavily against her. She wasn't much shorter than he was, but she was much more slenderly built. Still, she managed to maneuver him over to the fire without too much struggle.

"Here, sit against the saddle."

He fell as much as sat on her bedroll, pulling her down, too. He would have been happy to stay that way, but she wiggled out from under his arm. She wrapped her blanket around his middle and began tugging off his gloves.

"Ouch!"

"That hurts?"

He nodded. He'd nearly bit through his tongue.

"Good."

A hallucination would definitely show more compassion.

She got the gloves off and examined his hands. "They feel ice cold, but your skin is still pink. I wish I had some warm water to soak them in, but I don't think you're going to lose any fingers."

She started on his boots. The laces were stiff, and he could see that her own hands fumbled with cold, but she managed to work them off, and the socks, too. The relief on her face told him she hadn't found frostbite.

"I've been out in colder," he said, finally gathering himself to push her hands out of the way. "Much colder. This can't be much below freezing. At the Washita—"

"You're all right?"

He looked at his hands and felt for his feet. He took a deep breath. Everything seemed to be working. Even his brain was starting to clear. He could have done without that. He was afraid when he came to his senses, he was going to notice he looked like a damned fool.

"Those are going to hurt like hell when they warm up," she said, feeling his toes again.

"I think I'm going to live."

"Unless I'm just a snowbank hallucination," Harry reminded him tartly. She dug one of her sandwiches from her saddle bag and handed it to him. "Eat this. You'll feel better. There's water in this canteen."

"Thank you." He took an obedient bite of the sandwich. "Heavenly."

Harry's brows rose. "Maybe I'm not a hallucination. Maybe we've both frozen to death already and I'm an angel of mercy."

He managed a grin. "I think an angel could do better than a ham sandwich and some tinny water."

Her look was anything but angelic. "Eat. Before I decide I don't want to share."

She left him to it while she unsaddled Rover. Malachi took another bite of sandwich as he stared down his outstretched legs at his toes. He tried wiggling them. Stiff, but they moved.

He had been right. Now that he took in the situation, he did look like a fool. The knight errant stretched out like a war casualty being rescued by his damsel in distress.

At least he'd found the damsel. And she was safe. Safe enough for the moment, anyway. He could let go of the nightmares that had battered him through the long, dark hours on Rover's back.

Harry had been right about the sandwich making him

feel better. The fire helped, too, and the blanket. It even smelled like Harry. Or at least like Harry's horse. He might even be able to get some sleep before morning. Except she'd also been right about his toes. They hurt like hell.

Harry cut one of her apples in two and gave half each to Portia and Rover. Elijah's reliable, coffee-colored bay seemed none the worse for his late-night adventure. He hadn't gotten soaked or injured, so she thought he'd probably avoid another bout of pneumonia. He seemed content to escape the snow and share Portia's warmth.

Harry left them together and turned back to her more serious problem. He was lying in the same position she'd left him, propped against her saddle, feet toward the fire. His toes were curled like claws, and his face twisted in a grimace of pain.

"Serves you right," she said, sitting down beside him. He gasped when she touched his feet, but they felt better to her. "Where's your bedroll?"

He glanced at her through slitted eyes, a flash of green. "You don't want to know."

"You didn't bring one?"

"Of course I brought one." He jerked his feet away from her hands. "And I wrapped the blankets around me when I started to get really cold. Rover appreciated it, too. I must have lost them when I hit my bad arm against that tree. I think I passed out for a while."

"How about the food?"

"What food?"

"The food you were going to revive me with when you found me freezing to death in the wilderness."

"No need to get sarcastic," he growled. "There wasn't

time to collect food. I had to find you before the snow obscured your tracks."

His expression dared her to comment, but she passed on to more important things.

"You rode out into a threatening snowstorm without proper provisions, weak and possibly feverish, toward a destination you've never visited before in your life." She shook her head. "That's not Captain Malachi Kelly. I don't believe it for a minute."

He leaned forward to pull his socks back on, ignoring her.

"What happened to 'not charging into a situation without considering the consequences'."

He glanced at her. "I did consider the consequences. 'Sometimes you have to take a risk to help out a friend.' "

Something in his eyes forced her to look away, her heart fluttering erratically in her chest. It was the fire that burned her cheeks. It had to be. She was not going to make a fool of herself over another Kelly brother.

"What consequences?" she demanded tartly. "You thought I'd get lost in the snow and die of exposure? Honestly. You'd think you'd have a little more faith in me than that."

"Faith in what?" He leaned toward her, eyes boring into hers, and she had to steel herself not to back away. "Faith that you won't run off without telling anyone where you're going? That you won't ride off alone into the wilderness after being warned snow was coming? That you won't act like a damned little fool?"

"No." She glared right back at him. "Faith that if I act like a little fool and get myself into a situation like this that I am also capable of getting myself out of it."

"Like you did this summer when you and Wolf tried to

rescue Jordan from her kidnappers and nearly got us all shot instead? Like you did at the South Platte Saloon when Spider was planning to shoot you through the head?"

"I kept Tony and Lissy from getting shot, didn't I?" she demanded. "Or at least from being beaten within an inch of their lives like Miss Lily. And I saved your worthless hide back at the Lucky Lady mine, or have you forgotten that already?"

"Damn it, Harry." He sat back, his mouth set in a grim line. "I haven't forgotten a damn thing that happened in that mine."

Harry heard Portia shifting her weight, heard a tree sigh under its blanket of snow, heard embers sifting through the campfire's flames. She thought she could probably have heard the mountain breathe if she listened hard enough, the sudden silence was so deep.

Malachi broke it first. "We'd better get some sleep. Tomorrow is not going to be an easy ride, but I know you want to get home as soon as possible."

His eyes glowed dark with the firelight. Maybe they weren't unreadable. Maybe she'd just never known the key to deciphering them. They met hers steadily, though she thought she could see the effort it cost him.

"Lissy told Tony about your fiancé," he said, his voice gruff. "He was just angry when he made that threat. He'll still be in Oxtail, Harry. He'd be the biggest fool in the world if he weren't."

"Is that why you think I'm going home?" Harry crossed her arms over her chest to hold down the confusion. "To beg Ash to take me back?"

Malachi shrugged, looked away. "It's your life, Harry. Your choice. If you love him . . ." He glanced back. "Maybe I think he doesn't deserve you, but maybe that doesn't matter if you love him. Maybe I'm beginning to understand doing foolish things for love."

She was not going to make a fool of herself over another Kelly brother. She was not. But sitting there alone with Malachi on a wild mountainside, in a cocoon of firelight, while the world slowly transformed itself into a magical landscape of silent white, she found herself shaking with the fear that turning away from those dangerous green eyes would be committing another kind of foolishness, a foolishness without the redemption of courage.

"Malachi Kelly—" Her voice sounded distant to her ears, or maybe too close. If this was courage, why did she feel as though her heart was going to stop? "— you've been a damned fool for as long as I've known you. What makes you think I'm suddenly going to buy love as an excuse?"

"Hell and damnation, Harry!" For a second, she saw the old, blunt Malachi without the sense to hold back his true feelings on a subject. "I'm not a white knight. I didn't come out after you because someone has to be there to help poor fools who get themselves into trouble. I came because the thought of you dying cold and afraid and alone was more than I could bear. Because I would rather die myself than have that happen. Because I love you."

Red seeped up his cheeks. "Damn it, Harry. Of course I love you. And if that means I have to help you get back to your brother's ranch so you can marry that feckless son-of-a—"

"Oh, honestly! I'm not going home to marry Ashton Brady!" Harry could hardly get the words out around the emotion clogging her throat, but the words were safer than laughter or tears. "I don't want to marry him. I don't love him. If he's still in Oxtail, I'm going to have to explain that to him. I have to explain it to March and to Maggie, who's making all the wedding arrangements, and to Henna, who's fixing my dress . . ."

The enormity of it all washed over her again, though she felt like a drowning victim who has suddenly grabbed hold of what might either be a life rope or a lead weight.

"I've made such a horrible mess of this," she said, wiping a sleeve across her eyes. "There's Wolf. March hired him to take my place. And Ash's uncle has already bought us a wedding gift, though he won't tell us what it is. I have to go back and try to make things right."

Malachi blinked. "That's what couldn't wait? That's why you rode off into a snowstorm?"

"Yes. No." She couldn't lie. What good were all Mrs. Danforth's lessons in social deception if they deserted you when you really needed them? "No." Hell, she couldn't let him be braver than her. "I had to get away from you."

He sat back, almost as if she'd struck him, and it took her a second to realize why.

"Mal, I couldn't bear to be there for another wedding with two people who were so happy when I knew there wasn't a chance for me to be with the man I loved."

He nodded, though she wasn't sure he'd even heard her. He looked like a man who had been deafened by a dynamite blast. "I understand."

She could read his eyes plainly this time. They nearly broke her heart.

He tried to smile. "I'm not my brother. But I will always be a friend if you need—"

"Damn it, Mal, I'm not in love with your brother!"

So much for not making a fool of herself. He wouldn't even give her the chance.

"Oh, honestly!" Harry reached forward on her knees, grabbing the lapels of Malachi's overcoat and pushing him backwards onto the frosted pine duff. She landed heavily on his chest, feeling his solidity, feeling his heartbeat, feeling his aching fears and doubts as if they were her own. And, maybe if they were, he could feel her response.

She found his mouth with hers by instinct, suddenly, desperately gentle, as if only that touch of their lips together could make him understand.

His hands found her shoulders as if to push her away, but instead they clutched her, pulled her close. She could taste his tears on his lips, or maybe they were hers, salty against the warm sweetness of his mouth. She touched his cheek, held him steady, pouring all her heart into her kiss.

Chapter 24

For a breathless moment, Mal was back in the Lucky Lady mine, the world roaring and collapsing around him, and he didn't care, didn't care if it all came crashing down on him, as long as he had Harry in his arms for these precious seconds.

But she pulled back from the kiss, pushing herself up on his shoulders to look down at him. Her eyes were almost black in the faint light, but he could see the heat that burned behind them.

"I'm well aware that you're not your brother, you difficult, impossible, bullheaded man," she said, fierce as any avenging angel. "What I feel for you is nothing like what I feel for Elijah."

She glared at him, daring him to say something foolish, but as long as she was going to kiss him like that, he could wait to see what she meant.

"Your brother was a hero to me when I was growing up. Bigger than life. Clever, mysterious, dangerous. Free. Like having a mountain lion for a friend. You know no one is going to bother you as long as he's around."

"Clayton Wilmer killed my dog." Mal hadn't ever even told his father that. "Threw him in a cistern with a copperhead. He was just a puppy."

"Oh, Mal."

He shook his head. "Elijah caught Clay alone one afternoon after school, without his gang. Clay was older and bigger, but Elijah was madder. Beat the living hell out of him. I worshipped my big brother."

"I guess I did, too," Harry said. "I wanted to be free like he was. I guess I wanted to be dangerous like he was. I wanted his attention, and approval. I thought that was love."

Suddenly, her fierce confidence ebbed, and he caught the distress in her eyes. "That must be why I thought I was in love with Ash. It was a similar feeling. He was the handsomest, smartest, wealthiest man to come through Oxtail in . . . well, ever, and he wanted me. I never would have agreed to marry him if I had known what love was."

"You know now?"

She stared into his eyes as though she might be able to see into his heart and pull the answer out from there. Then again, maybe she had already. He had not thought his heart could feel love until she had cracked it open.

"You're my friend, Mal." Her voice shook, and he could feel her body shaking, too. He pulled her back close, holding her tight. "You know *me,* not who you think I should be. If I stripped off all my clothes in downtown Denver and started squawking like a crow, you'd still be my friend."

He tried not to laugh, and failed.

She punched his shoulder. "You know what I mean. Don't you?"

"Yes." He kissed her forehead, smelling the sweetness of her hair. "Not too many people are willing to put up with me. I didn't really care. Until I met you, and you did."

She pulled back again, smiling at him through her tears. "Don't tell me we're two of a kind. I'm a perfect lady."

"Is this something they taught you in finishing school?" He sprawled his arms out. "Pin a man down and hold him helpless until he declares his love for you?"

"If you want to escape . . ."

He grabbed her before she could roll away, kissing her as she'd kissed him, their laughter mingling a sudden, aching joy with remembered pain and loneliness. Mal wrapped his hands in her hair, felt it brush across his cheeks, veiling them in their own soft night.

He didn't deserve this. Didn't deserve to hold her. Didn't deserve to love her. But he had been right when he'd said it about Ash, and it was right now. It didn't matter if he deserved her, if she loved him.

She loved him.

He thought his heart might expand right through his rib cage, yet he'd never felt such a sense of rightness in his life. There was terror. Certainly. How on earth could she ever be happy with a bitter, irritable ex-cavalryman like him?

But there was hope, too. Because as long as he drew breath, he would never stop trying to bring her happiness.

Malachi's hands cupped Harry's face, pushing her back just far enough to touch her nose with his. "I don't think I ever told you this." His breath tickled her lips, slipping heat down her throat. "But the first time I saw you, when you and Wolf came to stay with Elijah and Jordan and Nicky this summer, you took my breath away."

"Ha." Harry breathed it against his mouth, amazed by the way his eyes widened at the brush of her lips. "As I recall, I was wearing jeans and one of March's old shirts."

"Just like now," Malachi agreed, his hands leaving her

face to brush over her shoulders and down her back. "And you're doing it again."

"You can't breathe because I'm lying on your chest." But she couldn't breathe so well, either, as his hands worked under her coat to run up the flannel of her shirt along her ribs.

"That's part of it," he acknowledged, a wicked glint flashing through his eyes.

The heels of his hands brushed the sides of her breasts, and Harry gasped at the flood of feeling that flowed through her body. She heard Malachi's breath catch too, at her response.

Slowly, eyes still locked on his, she lowered her mouth back to his. This time, it felt like striking a match, a sudden flare of heat almost too hot and bright to bear. Her mouth parted in wonder, and his tongue slid between her lips, flicking the tip of hers.

Her body felt like it might be melting, the heat pooling between them, as though they could meld together. He ran his hand down her lower back, and she shifted against the pressure, suddenly recognizing the hardness of his desire against her thigh.

Maggie had given her a detailed account of the facts of life, in an attempt to prevent Harry from making the same mistakes Maggie had in her own wild youth. But Maggie had not told her how right it felt to move against the man she loved, how natural to touch and be touched.

She wanted to touch more. She shifted to one side and reached for Malachi's shirt buttons. His chest felt hot to her burning fingers.

"Harry," he caught her hand, his voice hardly more than a gasping whisper.

"Sh." She moved again, and his head fell back, the muscles in his neck cording. She loved being able to make him feel the same loss of control she was experiencing. She kissed the hand that held her hand still, daring a dart of her tongue between his fingers.

"Harry!" He was gasping again, and laughing as he pulled her tight across his chest. "We have to stop this."

"I don't want to stop." She shifted against his desire.

"Oh, God, I don't want to, either, but—" Suddenly his whole body jerked, his legs flailing beneath her. "Ouch! Hell and damnation!"

He wrenched himself up into a sit, pulling her, too, so she sat beside him.

"Mal? What's wrong?" Maggie hadn't warned her about them being so sensitive. "Did I hurt you?"

"What? No. My damned feet are on fire!"

Harry couldn't see any flames, but with Malachi flailing the end of her blanket at his feet, sending pine needles and ashes flying everywhere, it was hard to tell. Choking back her laughter, she grabbed his arm and held him still long enough to look at his feet.

"They're not even smoking."

He wiggled them for her. "Just hot."

"It's a good thing you were wearing wool socks."

Malachi stood and shook out the bedroll, then laid it out carefully at a slightly greater distance from the fire.

"We've only got one," he said. "We've got to share." Then he took her hand and pulled her down beside him. She thought she ought to feel embarrassed or awkward. She had never been so physically intimate with anyone.

But it was Malachi. Just looking into his eyes, she could not feel awkward. But he turned her away from him and settled behind her, wrapping her in his arms.

"Mal?" She tried to turn toward him, but he held her still.

"This is good."

Harry managed to wiggle onto her back, far enough to turn her head toward him. Any fear that he'd suddenly realized he'd made a horrible mistake and had never loved her for an instant and couldn't wait to escape her was allayed by the look in his eyes. "Malachi Kelly, don't you dare pretend to be a gentleman with me."

He shook his head. "I'm not, Harry. I've made plenty of mistakes in my life. This is one thing I want to do right. It should be special for you. On your wedding night."

She narrowed her eyes at him, though her heart began to flutter. "That's great. Except I'm never going to have a wedding night. I'm not going to marry anyone else, and you've said you're not going to get married at all. As I recall, you asked me not to marry you."

"And as I recall, you never accepted." He brushed a thumb across her eyebrow with great tenderness, but his voice remained maddeningly matter-of-fact. "Besides I'm resigned to it."

"Resigned to what?"

"Marrying you."

"Oh, that's romantic!" She might have punched him, but she was too tangled in his arms and the blanket. Still, she couldn't help the laughter that bubbled in her chest. "Typical. You don't have to marry me."

He raised his eyebrows. "I disagree. When I take you home tomorrow after having spent the night alone with you, sharing a bedroll, and you tell everyone you've decided not to marry Ashton Brady, I suspect your brother will be coming after me with a shotgun if I refuse to do the right thing."

"March?" Harry asked skeptically.

"I saw the expression on his face, going into that brothel after Ash." Malachi shuddered dramatically. "I don't want him angry at me."

Harry managed to struggle up onto her elbow, to look down into Malachi's face. She touched the rough growth on his jaw. "You don't have to marry me, Mal."

His hand covered hers. "I'm not going to lose you, Harry. Even marriage is better than that." But his eyes held no laughter. "I love you, Harriet Jackson."

The words took her breath away.

"I love you." He brushed the hair back from her cheek. "Marry me. Please."

She was crying again, but she didn't care. "Oh, honestly. Of course I will."

"How romantic."

She laughed through the pounding of her heart, through the tears on her face. "I love you, Malachi Kelly, you son-of-a—"

Then she kissed him. Thoroughly.

"When?" she asked, touching his nose with hers.

"There's Wolf," Malachi said. "March and Maggie have hired him to take your place. And Maggie's done all those preparations. The preacher is ready. You said Henna's fixing your dress. Tomorrow might be too soon, but maybe the next day. Unless you want to wait . . ."

He brushed his knuckles up the side of her rib cage, his thumb sweeping the edge of her breast. Harry dropped her head to nip his lower lip with her teeth. He gasped.

"Do you?" she asked sweetly.

"No."

"Good." She settled back in beside him, her head on his shoulder, arm across his chest. Physical desire burned deep inside her, but the peace of being in his arms would see her through the night.

"Of course, it was safe to ask me," she murmured into his ribs. "We're probably going to freeze to death out here in this blizzard. But I suppose that's romantic."

"I think we'll make it back to your brother's all right. It's stopped snowing."

Indeed, Harry could no longer hear the soft whisper of the snowfall. "It could start again."

"I don't think so."

"How can you tell."

"The moon."

She followed his hand pointing up into the pines beyond the fire. Clear white light shone through the branches, touching her cheeks with the promise of a fair morning, of sunlight on snow almost as bright as her newfound hope for the future.

"I asked you to marry me knowing I'd live long enough to have to see it through."

Harry nodded, hugging him closer. "I'm glad to hear it. But you should know that if you change your mind, I'm just as good with a shotgun as my brother."

His laughter rumbled against her cheek. "That doesn't surprise me at all."

About the Author

Tess Pendergrass is a native of California whose love of writing developed early, and who published her first book (*Hearts of Gold* by Martha Longshore) in graduate school. She currently works as a middle school librarian and continues to write.

CWMARS